Acclaim for Neta Jackson

"In Jackson's superlative novel in the new SouledOut Sisters, the plot and characters remain fresh and vibrant, shining spiritual truth from each page."
—*Romantic Times* TOP PICK! review of *Stand by Me*

"Readers will enjoy the antics of Kat and her open-mouth-insert-foot ways, and watching God orchestrate His will in the lives of the people of the SouledOut Community Church."
—*CBA Retailers + Resources* review of *Stand by Me*

"This book is an absolute delight. The depth of the faith element, coupled with a well-plotted story, makes for an absolutely winning combination."
—*Romantic Times* TOP PICK! review of *Who Is My Shelter?*

"This well-written tale is captivating and at times heartbreaking; an essential read for women's fiction fans and readers who enjoy Jackson's 'Yada Yada Prayer Group' series."
—*Library Journal* starred review of *Who Do I Talk To?*

"Laced with humor, fine description, and interesting and realistically flawed characters . . . this well-paced story is certain to keep fans turning the pages."
—*Publishers Weekly* review of *The Yada Yada Prayer Group Gets Down*

"The author's faith-affirming fiction will encourage readers to plumb new depths in their own faith . . . [a] well-written and emotionally meaningful story."
—*Romantic Times* 4.5-star TOP PICK review of
The Yada Yada Prayer Group Gets Rolling

"God's love and mercy are uniquely and boldly displayed throughout this exquisite novel."
—*Romantic Times* 4.5-star TOP PICK review of
The Yada Yada Prayer Group Gets Caught

come to the table

Also by Neta Jackson

come to the table

Book 2

A SouledOut Sisters Novel

neta jackson

THOMAS NELSON

Since 1798

NASHVILLE   DALLAS   MEXICO CITY   RIO DE JANEIRO

Published in Nashville, Tennessee, by Thomas Nelson. Thomas Nelson is a registered trademark of Thomas Nelson, Inc.

The author is represented by the literary agency of Alive Communications, Inc., 7680 Goddard Street, Suite 200, Colorado Springs, CO 80920. www.alivecommunications.com.

Thomas Nelson, Inc., titles may be purchased in bulk for educational, business, fund-raising, or sales promotional use. For information, e-mail SpecialMarkets@ ThomasNelson.com.

Scripture quotations are taken from the following: THE HOLY BIBLE, NEW INTERNATIONAL VERSION®. © 1973, 1978, 1984 by International Bible Society. Used by permission of Zondervan Bible Publishers.

Holy Bible, New Living Translation, © 1996, 2004, 2007. Used by permission of Tyndale House Publishers, Inc., Wheaton, Illinois 60189. All rights reserved.

THE NEW KING JAMES VERSION. © 1982 by Thomas Nelson, Inc. Used by permission. All rights reserved.

Publisher's Note: This novel is a work of fiction. Any references to real events, businesses, organizations, and locales are intended only to give the fiction a sense of reality and authenticity. Any resemblance to actual persons, living or dead, is entirely coincidental.

Library of Congress Cataloging-in-Publication Data

Jackson, Neta.
  Come to the table / Neta Jackson.
      p. cm. — (A SouledOut sisters novel ; bk. 2)
  ISBN-13: 978-1-59554-865-8 (trade paper)
  ISBN-10: 1-59554-865-3 (trade paper)
  1. Christian women—Fiction. 2. Women in church work—Illinois—Chicago—Fiction. 3. Shared housing—Illinois—Chicago—Fiction. 4. Triangles (Interpersonal relations)—Fiction. I. Title.
  PS3560.A2415C66 2012
  813'.54—dc23   2012033497

Printed in the United States of America

12 13 14 15 16 QG 5 4 3 2 1

To our agent,
Lee Hough,
because God is faithful—and so are you

Chapter 1

The dark, curly head at the other end of the table busily slurped each long, limp noodle with obvious joy. Nick Taylor, pretending to ignore him, watched sideways as the boy selected another noodle between thumb and forefinger, lofted it high above his open mouth, then sucked it down his gullet like a baby bird devouring a juicy worm.

"Conny!" snapped the boy's mother, coming back to the table from the kitchen holding a steaming pot of spaghetti sauce between two pot holders. "Those noodles gonna be gone before you get any sauce on 'em. And quit slurping."

"Don't want any sauce." The boy sucked in another noodle, leaving half of it hanging out of his grinning mouth. "Like 'em bald."

Nick hid a smile. Life in the apartment he and a few other CCU students had sublet for the summer had sure turned topsy-turvy in the past week. Olivia, the youngest of their group of four, still an undergrad at Chicago Crista University, had found urban living too intense. Having her purse snatched and falling

1

down the stairs at the El station had been the last straw, and she'd gone home for the rest of the summer. And Kathryn—dear Kat, in her own impetuous way—had brought home a homeless mom and her kid to take Olivia's place.

Who just happened to be the missing daughter and grandson of the middle-aged African American couple upstairs.

Huh. Nick wanted to laugh. He oughta write a novel.

Rochelle Johnson pointed at the steaming pot. "Sauce?"

"Please." The seminary student held out his plate as Rochelle, her honey-brown skin glistening from the steam, scooped hot spaghetti sauce over his pasta, then served her own plate and sat down. Tiny tendrils of black hair stuck to her damp face. She was a pretty young woman—like her mom, he decided. Avis Douglass, on the third floor of the three-flat, was one of those classy black women who turned heads even in her fifties.

"When are Kat and Bree getting home?" Rochelle nodded at the two empty plates at the table. "There's lots of pasta, but we gotta make sure we save enough sauce."

"Uh, well, Kat oughta be back anytime now. But Bree's got the evening shift at the coffee shop." The other two young women sharing the apartment each had part-time jobs at The Common Cup, a local hangout, their shifts often running back-to-back. Nick wound another forkful of spaghetti and shoved it into his mouth, avoiding the "save the sauce" issue. Knowing Kat, she'd probably opt to stir-fry some zucchini, onions, and red pepper to top off her pasta rather than sauce from a jar.

A key rattled in the front door of the apartment. *Speaking of Kat . . .*

"Hey!" The door flew open and Kat Davies practically fell into the room, her thick brunette hair frizzing from the humidity and falling out of the clip on the back of her head. "That darn door's starting to stick something awful— Oh, yum! Something smells good, and I'm starving." The young woman tossed her backpack toward the couch in the living room and pulled out a chair in the dining nook between the living room and kitchen. "So, Mister Conny, did you save me any food? Is that mine?" And she pretended to steal the little boy's plate, which he grabbed back with a squeal.

"Hello to you too." Nick tossed out his greeting, half amused and half annoyed at the way Kat bounced into a room already running on five cylinders.

Kat blew a damp curl off her forehead. "Hi, Nick. Sorry I'm late . . . Oh, thanks, Rochelle." She took the bowl of hot noodles Rochelle handed her. "What goes on top?" She peeked under the lid of the pot. "Is this that jar stuff? Hmm . . . do you mind if I add some veggies?" Kat got up and headed for the kitchen. "I'll just be a minute."

Rochelle frowned at Nick. "What's wrong with spaghetti sauce?"

"Don't mind Kat," he murmured. "She's got her own ideas about food. Vegetables, lots of vegetables."

"Yeah, but on *spaghetti*?"

Nick shrugged. He should have warned Rochelle about Kat's "food issues" when she offered to cook her first meal for them tonight. But with four unrelated adults sharing an apartment, they all had to get used to each other's cooking, didn't they? And frankly, he'd been grateful their newest apartment-mate had offered to cook supper, because he was a little nervous about the meeting at SouledOut Community Church tonight. He glanced at his watch. In just a little more than an hour.

This was the meeting where his name was going to be proposed to the congregation as a paid pastoral intern, a requirement to complete his seminary studies at CCU. And he wasn't even a member! Not yet, anyway, though he'd do it in a heartbeat. But everything had happened so fast after the death of SouledOut's beloved copastor, Pastor Clark—

"Veggies coming up!" Kat breezed back into the dining nook holding a sizzling frying pan. She spooned out a generous helping on her spaghetti noodles and then looked around the table. "There's more. Anyone else?"

Conny turned up his nose. "Yuk. I like my noodles *bald*."

But between the three adults, the stir-fry vegetables disappeared, and Kat and Nick cleared off the table—the general agreement being that the non-cooks on any given night did the dishes. "Can we let the dishes air dry?" Nick asked, sticking the last of the leftover pasta in the fridge as Kat ran hot soapy water in the sink. "I'd like to get to the church early. Uh . . ." He looked at Kat hopefully. "You going to the meeting?"

"Who, me?" She whacked him playfully with a dish towel. "Would I miss my first opportunity to call you *Pastor Nicky*?"

Nick groaned. Knowing Kat, she just might. In public!

But as the two friends turned out the kitchen light—dishes in the drainer with a clean dish towel over them—and got ready to leave, Nick was tackled by forty-two inches of boy, nearly making him lose his balance. "I want Nick to put me to bed!" Sprawled on the floor, Conny hung on to Nick's legs as his mother tapped her foot.

Nick reached down and pried the little boy's arms off his ankles. "Hey, buddy, I can't tonight. Miss Kat and I gotta go to church."

Conny scrambled to his feet, crossed his arms, and screwed up his face into a pout. "Church! It ain't Sunday."

Rochelle rolled her eyes and wrestled Conny toward the bathroom. "Sorry, Nick. You guys just go. He'll be fine."

"Noooo-o-o-o-o!" Conny yelled as the bathroom door slammed behind them.

Kat laughed. "We're outta here." She grabbed Nick by the hand and the two scurried down the stairs of the three-flat and out onto the street. "Whew. I think you've got a new append-age, my friend."

Nick grunted. *My friend.* He'd like to be more than that, though he'd never told her so. He wished Kat would keep hold-ing his hand, but she let go as soon as they got outside and walked two steps ahead of him, chatting away about . . . what? He wasn't listening. This was the first time he'd been alone with Kat in days. Maybe weeks. Ever since they'd moved into the Chicago neighborhood of Rogers Park, it'd always been the four of them from CCU—Kat, Brygitta, Olivia, and Nick—or some combination. But Olivia had moved back home, Bree was at work, and Rochelle was back at the apartment putting Conny to bed.

Now. They'd be at the church in twenty minutes. Maybe he should talk to Kat about "taking their friendship to another level." Weren't those the buzzwords these days? Take your career to another level? Take your goals to another level? Why not—

"Are you nervous? You shouldn't be. It was the Douglasses' idea, after all, to put your name out there as an intern on the interim pastoral team. And Pastor Cobbs agrees, right?"

It took several seconds—felt like a whole minute—for Nick to shift mental gears. "Uh . . . well, sure, a little nervous. But it's not a slam dunk. Some people might want to keep the original proposal for both Avis and Peter Douglass to assist Pastor Cobbs until they find a new copastor. I mean, they're mature folks, been at the church since the beginning. I'm just a greenhorn, don't even have my seminary degree yet."

"Silly." Kat stuck her hand through his arm and playfully pulled him along. "Mr. D said he doesn't really need to be on the interim team, since he's already an elder. And you have to do your internship *somewhere*. Why not SouledOut? *I*, for one, think it's a cool team. Pastor Cobbs, Mrs. D, you . . . old and young, black and white, two men and a woman, new blood and fresh ideas alongside age and wisdom—"

"Hey! Are you saying I don't have any wisdom?"

Kat pulled her hand away and ran ahead, laughing over her shoulder. "Did I say that? Who, me?"

The moment was gone. Nick sighed and picked up his pace to keep up with Kat. Well, maybe they could "talk about us" on the way home. Right now they were both distracted by the upcoming meeting anyway—a meeting with a multicultural congregation in a retail space tucked into the Howard Street Mall along Chicago's northern city limits that might determine his whole future.

❋

"Congratulations, son." Pastor Joe Cobbs pumped Nick's hand as the congregational meeting broke up a couple hours later. "I'm excited to see how God is going to use you in the life of this church. I think you and Sister Avis will make a good team."

Nick swallowed. At six feet, he had to look down at the five-foot-eight, stocky black man. "Thanks, Pastor Cobbs. I know I have a lot to learn, but I'm excited to work with you and Mrs. Douglass and the elders. It's a dream come true for me."

The vote to confirm the new proposal had been nearly unanimous, especially after Peter and Avis Douglass—who had both been proposed as interim leaders at the last congregational meeting—had themselves proposed that Nick replace Peter, since he was already an elder. They gave all the good reasons: Nick needed an internship to complete his seminary studies, he was studying to be a pastor, it made sense to do his internship in the church he was currently attending, *and*, they said, they had seen his character, his integrity, and his pastor's heart even in the short time the CCU students had been living in the apartment below them.

He hoped he could live up to their expectations. Right now he had butterflies.

Many other members shook his hand, wished him the best, said they'd be praying for him, told him that working with Avis Douglass and Pastor Cobbs would be a privilege. He nodded, said thank you, said he agreed. But he didn't know what to say to the woman—one of the elders' wives, he thought—who pulled him aside and whispered, "Sure glad to see a white face on the interim pastoral team. No offense meant. Just got to be careful we don't slide into . . . well, you know."

No, he didn't know.

But he was glad when the well-wishers thinned out. The Douglasses offered him and Kat a ride home, but Nick thanked them and said no, he'd rather walk, he needed to unwind. Well, it was the truth, even if not the main reason. He caught Kat's eye—those blue eyes, so striking with her dark-brown mop of hair. "Ready to go?" He grinned, relishing the walk back to the apartment, just the two of them.

Kat looked at her watch. "Almost nine . . . perfect! I told Bree we'd stop by the coffee shop and walk her home after the meeting. She gets off at nine."

Bree?! Nick felt his happy expectations deflate faster than a balloon stuck by a pin. A few nasty words rose like bile to his mouth, but he pressed his lips together. Right. How would *that* go over for the newly appointed pastoral intern at SouledOut Community Church?

❊

Brygitta Walczak—a brown-eyed brunette with a short, pixie haircut—and Kat chatted nonstop from the time they met her at the door of The Common Cup to the time the trio let themselves into the foyer of the three-flat on the narrow residential street. Bree wanted to hear all about the meeting—What happened? Did they confirm Nick? What about the whole interim team? What did the pastor say? Did anybody protest that Nick wasn't a member yet?

Nick let Kat do most of the talking.

Climbing the stairs to the second-floor apartment, Nick let them in with his key, motioning to the girls behind him to be quiet. "Conny's probably asleep."

He needn't have bothered.

"Nick!" Swathed in summer-weight Superman pajamas, the little boy launched himself off the couch and jumped into Nick's arms. "*Now* you can put me to bed!"

"What are you doing up, young man?" Nick loosened the stranglehold around his neck.

Rochelle appeared from the hallway that led to the two bedrooms and single bathroom. "I'm sorry, Nick. It's been one big fight ever since you left. I finally gave in. He . . . I think he misses his daddy. Conny stayed with him a couple months, you know, when I . . . well, you know what it's been like for us lately."

"Don't miss Daddy," the little boy pouted. "He didn't read me stories. Just had to go to bed." Conny wiggled out of Nick's arms and ran to the coffee table, grabbing a couple of books "Grammy Avis" had gotten for him at the library. "Read me a story and then I'll go to bed. I promise!"

Nick chuckled. "Okay. *This* time. Come on, buddy. We'll read in the study." Nick led Conny into the study that served as his bedroom ever since he'd surrendered the larger bedroom to Rochelle and Conny. Kat and Bree had claimed the twin beds in the second bedroom of the apartment they'd sublet from the owners of the condo, who were currently traveling in South America on business.

Conny cuddled under Nick's arm as they settled on the futon in the study and opened *The Saggy Baggy Elephant*. Nick pulled him closer, conscious of the little boy's sweet, soapy smell. Maybe someday he'd have a little boy like Conny . . .

Halfway through the second book he realized the boy's breathing had slowed and his head had fallen forward. Carefully picking him up, he tiptoed through the living room, passed Kat on the couch doing the newspaper crossword, and headed down the hall to the far bedroom. He knocked. Rochelle opened the door. Her long black hair, which she usually wore wavy and full—looser than what he expected from "black hair"—had been braided and wound around her head for the night.

"He's asleep."

"Okay." The young mother stood aside. "Just lay him on the bed."

Nick laid the little boy on the large queen-size bed, drew the sheet up over him, and turned to go. Rochelle was still standing in the doorway as he squeezed past. "Thanks," she said. Quickly standing on her toes, she kissed him lightly on the cheek. "Thanks for being there for Conny." And then she closed the door behind her.

Nick was so startled he just stood in the hallway a moment. What was *that* about? . . . *Nothing*, he decided. Just a thank-you from a grateful single mom.

He turned to head back to the living room . . . and saw Kat at the opening, framed in the light from the front room. "Sweet," she said. But there was an edge to her voice. Before he could say anything, she took several quick strides to the doorway of the bedroom she shared with Bree, disappeared inside, and quickly shut the door.

Chapter 2

K at Davies flopped down on the twin bed in the "perfectly appointed" guest room of the sublet and punched her pillow.

Her roommate peered over the top of the book she was reading on the other bed. "What?"

"Nothing."

Brygitta rolled her eyes and tossed the paperback onto the bedside table between the two beds. "Right." Yawning, she kicked off the lightweight bedspread and pulled the sheet up to her chin. "You're going to tell me, you know."

Kat said nothing. She felt confused by her feelings. So she'd seen Rochelle Johnson give Nick a peck on the cheek after he read her little boy to sleep. What was *that* about? Probably nothing. At least Nick would say that. But what did she know about Rochelle, after all? The girl was a mystery. *Girl* . . . not really. Might even be a few years older than she was. She'd been married, after all, and had a six-year-old kid.

And it was her own fault Rochelle and Conny were staying

in the condo she and the other CCU students had sublet for the summer. It was her big idea to invite them when their fourth housemate moved back home. Seemed to make sense at the time. Skinny thing like Rochelle digging in Dumpsters for food, living from hand to mouth, with a kid to support—all because she'd had a falling-out with her parents who lived one floor up.

Well, okay, it was more complicated than that. But still.

Kat slid off the bed, shed the skirt and top she'd worn to SouledOut that evening, wiggled into the sleep tee wadded up under her pillow, and turned the fan in the window on low. She hadn't brushed her teeth, but no way was she going to the bathroom now and risk running into Nick. She didn't want to deal with him right now. Or Rochelle. That was the problem with these older apartments—only one bathroom per unit.

Kat turned out the bed lamp and slid between the cool sheets. She lay staring into the darkness for several long minutes.

"Bree?"

"Told ya."

Kat ignored the snicker from the other bed. "Do you think we were too hasty inviting Rochelle and Conny to live with us?"

"Why? What's wrong?"

"Nothing. It's just . . . when we got this apartment, the four of us knew each other pretty well, knew we'd basically get along and be able to work out any little problems."

"Well, yeah. Except it didn't work out for Olivia, did it?"

"But that's different! It wasn't *us* not getting along. Livie was already edgy about living in the city. I might freak too, if I got robbed at the El station. Can't really blame her."

In the dim light coming through the blinds from the street, Kat saw Bree lean up on one elbow. "Kat. What's this about? Did you and Rochelle have a fight or something? I thought you two were tight."

"No! It's just . . . I'm realizing we don't know Rochelle very well. And cute as Conny is, there's a thin line between cute and annoying. I mean, he's all over Nick! Not going to bed until Nick came home tonight? Get real! What kind of mother lets her kid do that?"

Bree punched her pillow and lay back down. "Oh, he'll settle down. He's just excited. I wouldn't worry about it."

"Easy for you to say. He's not clinging to you like some barnacle on a ship."

Bree giggled. "Well, ask Nick if it bothers *him*. He's the one who has to work it out with Rochelle and Conny."

Kat sank into silence. Nick didn't seem bothered. Maybe that was the problem . . .

Oh, give it up, Kat, she scolded herself, flopping over onto her side. *Am I jealous of the time Nick's spending with Conny? How petty is that!* Even if Nick was one of the best friends she'd ever had. Nick and Bree, that is.

But then . . . there was that kiss.

Should she tell Bree about it? No . . . that *would* sound jealous. They were all just friends, right? Or were, until Rochelle and Conny came along.

Kat rolled back. "Bree?"

A muffled, "What?"

"Do you think other people think it's kinda weird, a single guy like Nick living with three women?"

A snort in the darkness. "You're worried about that now? We've been here a month already! Far as I know, nobody's said anything. Why should they?"

"I know. Still, I'm kinda surprised somebody at SouledOut didn't bring it up at the meeting tonight when Nick was proposed as a pastoral intern. You know, that whole 'avoid any appearance of evil' thing."

Bree sat up again. "Kathryn Davies. You of all people, worried about that? It's not like just one guy and one girl sharing an apartment. There're three women to one man—*and* a nosy kid. And we've practically got chaperones upstairs. I mean, Mr. D is one of the elders at SouledOut and Mrs. D happens to be one of the interim pastors . . . Oh, darn. Now I've got to go to the bathroom." Bree's dark shape loomed up between the two beds, marched toward the bedroom door, and disappeared into the hall.

Kat sighed and closed her eyes. She should have told Bree about Rochelle giving Nick a kiss—okay, a peck on the cheek. Maybe it was nothing. Still, it seemed weird. As close as the four students had been for the past three years at CCU, she'd never kissed Nick, not even in a sisterly way. Hugs, sure. Wrestling and goofing around, fine.

Maybe Rochelle was more of a kisser. What did Kat know about her culture anyway? Still, shouldn't she be careful about stuff like that? After all, Rochelle was HIV positive, even if it wasn't her fault.

Kat's eyes flew open. *That's it.* Of course. She was worried about Rochelle being HIV. They had all acted so liberal and tolerant when they found out—but now they were living together like a family. Shouldn't they be taking some precautions? And kissing of any kind had to be out, didn't it?

Cradling her pillow, Kat somehow felt relieved. Her eyelids closed. She could talk to Nick about that, tell him she's concerned. That would make sense.

❋

Kat had set her alarm for six thirty, giving her plenty of time to get ready for her morning volunteer job at the Summer Tutoring and Enrichment Program—known as STEP—at Mary McLeod Bethune Elementary School. But who needed an alarm? Childish feet thudded down the hall past her bedroom door and she heard Conny yell, "No! Wanna play!"

Kat squinted at the digital alarm. Six fifteen. *Good grief.* What was he doing up this early? He'd still been awake at ten!

In the next bed Bree groaned and jammed the pillow over her head. She didn't start her shift at the coffee shop until one o'clock today and had said she wanted to sleep in.

Good luck with that.

Well, it was almost time to get up anyway. Kat groggily swung her feet out of bed and peeked out the bedroom door. Coast was clear. She zipped into the hallway and then into the bathroom and locked the door.

Standing in the shower, Kat let the hot water run over her head, trying to clear her mind. *Thursday* . . . STEP ran from nine till one, and she had to relieve Bree at the coffee shop at five. Which meant she had four hours free that afternoon. It felt like a gift! So much had happened in the past couple weeks, she needed some time to herself just to get her feet back on the ground.

Except . . . when could she talk to Nick? About that HIV thing. Alone.

But by the time she'd washed her thick hair, given it a blow-dry, which seemed to take forever, and dressed in a pair of denim capris and a denim top—trying not to wake up Bree—she was having second thoughts. The whole thing felt awkward. Maybe she should just forget it. Wait a few days and talk about what kind of precautions they should take living with someone with HIV in some other context.

Except . . . Nick knew she'd seen Rochelle give him that kiss. Saw her flounce into her bedroom. *Dumb, dumb, dumb.*

Sucking up her courage, she walked into the living room. The double doors into the study were open, the futon folded away, and the room was empty. Wandering into the kitchen, she found Conny bent studiously over a kids' activity book, following a maze with a pencil. Rochelle was stirring a pot on the stove, wearing a kimono-type short robe, her hair still braided and wound around her head.

She looked up, dark eyes bright. "Hi. I'm making oatmeal. Want some?"

Kat had been thinking granola, but, oh well, they were both oats. "Sure. Uh, where's Nick? The study's empty."

"Went for a run, I think. Conny woke him up . . ." The young mother grimaced. "Bet he woke you up too. I'm sorry. I thought he'd sleep in after getting to bed so late, but somehow it doesn't seem to matter when he gets to sleep. He's up at six or six thirty."

Her apology softened Kat's annoyance at the early waking. "It's all right. He'll settle down. He's just excited being some-place new." She grinned, hearing herself quoting Bree.

Rochelle dished up three bowls of oatmeal and set them on the table. "Couldn't find raisins. You got any here?"

"Uh, think so." Kat had used most of them when she made up the batch of granola, but she found some in a box in the baking cupboard, along with a bag of walnuts, and set them out with the brown sugar and milk on the table.

"Um, wanted to let you know . . ." Rochelle suddenly seemed shy. "I'm going to call that family about the nanny job you told me about. The one Olivia had before she left. See if they still need someone."

"That's great, Rochelle! Good for you. Just, you know, be honest about your situation. That's all you can do."

"I know." Rochelle's voice fell to a whisper.

"I did it! I did it!" Conny crowed, holding up the page he'd been working on. "See, Mama? See, Miss Kat? I found the treasure!"

Rochelle seemed glad for the interruption. "You sure did." She sprinkled brown sugar on his cereal. "Put it away now. Do you want raisins in your oatmeal?"

Conny seemed to notice the steaming bowl at his elbow for the first time. "Don't want oatmeal! I want Froot Loops!"

Rochelle rolled her eyes. "There aren't any Froot Loops and we aren't going to buy any either. You like oatmeal. Now eat."

Conny stuck out his lip. "Daddy let me eat Froot Loops."

His mother rolled her eyes. "Grr. If I hear 'Daddy let me' one more time," she muttered to Kat, "I may do something I'll regret."

"Did I hear somebody doesn't want his oatmeal?" boomed a male voice coming in the back door. Nick appeared, wearing a sweat-stained T-shirt and athletic shorts, his sandy hair plastered against his forehead. "Guess that means I can have it!" He plopped down on a chair and reached for Conny's bowl.

"No-o-o! That's mine!" Conny pulled it back, giggling.

Rochelle jumped up. "I made enough for everybody. You can have your own bowl."

Conny watched wide-eyed as Nick enthusiastically doctored

his oatmeal with raisins, walnuts, brown sugar, and milk. Then the little boy did the same and lifted a heaping spoonful to his mouth.

"So, is it good enough to thank God for?" Nick asked the little boy. "You want to say a blessing on the food?"

Conny shook his head, his mouth full, milk running down his chin. He pointed at Kat. "You do it," he garbled.

Well, at least somebody notices I'm in the room. But seeing Nick and being ignored and Conny getting all the attention left Kat in no mood to say a blessing for the food. She folded her arms across her chest. "I think Pastor Nicky ought to pray over the food. He's the one who brought it up."

She'd tried to keep it light, but Nick gave her a strange look. Kat looked away—and didn't close her eyes when she heard him say, "Fine, I'll do it . . . Jesus, thank You for oatmeal and a new day. Amen."

"That was short!" Conny giggled.

"Yeah, well, short is good when you're hungry, right, buddy?"

Kat had about had it with all this "buddy buddy" and "perfect parenting" stuff Nick was into. She was tempted to pick up her bowl and take it into the next room, but just then Bree wandered into the kitchen, holding a cell phone and looking anything but pleased. She held out the phone to Kat. "Next time I'm trying to sleep in, take your cell phone with you."

Kat jumped up and took the phone. "Sorry, Bree." She was too. But putting the phone to her ear, she headed for the living room. "Hello? Kat here."

"Kathryn? Hi, it's Edesa! Hope I didn't get you up."

Edesa? "No, no, I'm up. Especially now that we've got a six-year-old in the house. Rochelle Johnson and her little boy." Why in the world was Edesa Baxter calling her at seven thirty in the morning?

Edesa's laugh sounded like a tinkling glass wind chime. Kat could just picture the pretty black woman with her bright smile and dancing eyes. "Ah! That's right. *Sí*, I know what you mean. I have my own *gallito* waking me up each morning."

"*Gallito?*"

The laugh again. "Little rooster. Back home in Honduras, we always kept chickens, and oh! That *gallo* started crowing *before* the sun was up! Just like my Gracie. But now I just put books in her bed and go back to sleep. Often she does too."

Hmm. Good idea. I should tell Rochelle to try that.

"Anyway, I wanted to catch you before you left for the day. You volunteer mornings with Sister Avis's STEP program, don't you?"

"Yes." Had she mentioned it to Edesa? Maybe Mrs. D told her . . . or probably Jodi Baxter, Edesa's mother-in-law, who also volunteered at the summer program. That Baxter family had been hard to figure out at first: white middle-aged couple, young married son, black daughter-in-law—who spoke Spanish, no less—and Hispanic grandchild, who turned out to be adopted. Kat could just see her own mother raise an eyebrow if she ever met the Baxters.

"And you work at The Common Cup . . . when?"

"It varies. Brygitta and I split an eight-hour shift, so sometimes I work afternoons and sometimes evenings." What was this about?

"Ah. Well, I've been remiss getting back to you—you know, your idea about teaching a nutrition class together."

Kat perked up. Well, it was about time! Edesa Baxter had a

master's degree in public health, and she'd thought the woman would jump all over her idea. Instead, Edesa kept putting her off . . . in fact, had once basically told her she had no idea what she was talking about when it came to poor people and food issues. Miffed, Kat had let it drop. But if she'd changed her mind . . .

"I'd love to! When?"

"Well, that's why I'm calling. I teach a Bible study at the Manna House Women's Shelter on Friday mornings, and then I'm helping do lunch with Estelle Bentley—you know Estelle, don't you? Harry and Estelle at SouledOut?"

"Sure, sure. Well, I know who they are. She works at Manna House?"

"Yes. Chief cook and bottle washer—and a dozen other things. Anyway, I wondered if you'd be free tomorrow afternoon to come to the shelter, and maybe the three of us could talk."

"Drat! I work at the coffee shop tomorrow afternoon—but I don't go in today till five. Any chance we could do it today?"

"Well . . . sure, why not. I'll call Estelle and see if she has time after lunch. Do you mind taking the El? It's very near the Sheridan El Station—north of Wrigley Field."

"I'll find it! Thanks, Edesa. I'll come as soon as I'm done at STEP. Be there about two, okay?"

Kat flipped her cell phone closed. Awesome! Edesa was finally taking her seriously. She'd go straight from STEP, catch the El—maybe even have time to take a pass by the Dumpsters at that Dominick's store along Sheridan Road where she'd found so much good food thrown out *and* found Rochelle—

"Kat?"

Kat spun around. Nick had come out of the kitchen and was

standing between the dining nook and the open living room, still in his haphazard running clothes.

"Could we talk a minute?" he said.

Yes! . . . *No.* She wanted to talk, but not now. At least he was acknowledging her existence, which she'd doubted back there at the breakfast table. But her mind was spinning in another direction. And she had to pack her backpack to be gone from the apartment most of the day.

Besides, she knew what he was going to say. Protest that the kiss last night was nothing, just a thank-you for reading to Conny. Well, she had things that needed to be said about that, and right now she didn't have time.

"I'm sorry, Nick. I've got to run—and I might not be back until after work tonight. Maybe tomorrow?" She held up her hand, palm out. "Tomorrow. Scout's honor. Okay?" And she fled to her bedroom.

But not before she saw the disappointment on his face.

Chapter 3

~~~~~~~~~~~~~~~~

"Who was that?" Lanky Josh Baxter came into the kitchen of their third-floor apartment, a tousled and jammie-clad Gracie riding on his hip, as Edesa stuck the cordless back into its cradle.

"Kathryn Davies."

"The Kat girl? What's up?"

"Miss *Gato!*" Gracie giggled.

"Miss *Kathryn*," Edesa corrected, taking Gracie and setting the two-year-old in the booster seat at the kitchen table. "Here's your juice, sweetie."

Josh poured himself a cup of coffee from the Mr. Coffee sitting on the counter. "She calls herself Kat, and so do her friends. I think it's okay."

Edesa wrinkled up her nose at him. "It just sounds . . . disrespectful when you-know-who says it like that."

Gracie banged her sippy cup. "Miss *Gato!* Miss *Gato!* I wanna play ina sand with Miss *Gato!*"

"We're not going to the lake today, *niña*. Drink your juice.

You want some banana?" Edesa took a banana from the fruit basket on the counter and started to peel it. *"See what I mean?"* she mouthed at her husband.

"Whatever." Josh chuckled as he sipped his coffee. "So what's up?"

"Kathryn's been bugging me about the two of us teaching a class on nutrition for 'poor families,' and I've been, uh, putting her off. She's . . . how do you say it? So eager beaver! But we're going to meet at Manna House this afternoon. Might try to catch a ride with Gabby. I thought any discussion about food ought to include Estelle."

Josh laughed. "Good idea. She'll tell it like it is. Anything else? Everything all right at the apartment the students are renting?"

Edesa shrugged, cutting the banana into little wheels. "As far as I know. Kathryn did say Avis's grandson is waking them all up early. I can imagine it'll take some getting used to, having Rochelle and Conny living there. Can you start the toast?"

Josh took a loaf of wheat bread from the refrigerator and stuck a couple of slices in the toaster. "That whole scenario is really something. Sister Avis's daughter and grandson go missing for a couple of months, and then Kat runs into them Dumpster diving behind that Dominick's store. What a coincidence."

"Gracias, Jesús! I don't believe in coincidences . . . No, Gracie! Not on the floor!" Edesa rescued several pieces of banana from the floor, rinsed them off, and put them back in front of the little girl.

The toast popped up. Josh buttered both slices, stuck in two more, and brought the early birds to the table. "Well, guess they'll work it out. That Nick Taylor seems like a responsible guy. Not sure I'd want to be in his shoes, though, living in an apartment with three females and a six-year-old—*and* interning on the pastoral team at SouledOut to boot. Does he have any idea what he's getting into?"

Edesa shot her husband an amused glance. Nick and Josh were probably around the same age—just shy of twenty-four in Josh's case, who was younger than she was by three years. "Hmm. How different is that from you living here at the House of Hope, with four apartments full of single moms and kids— not to mention your *own* two females. Right, *niña?*" Edesa was enjoying the tease.

"Hey. At least Philip Fairbanks is here half the time with Gabby and the boys. And I'm thinking they may be retying the knot one of these days. It's been a year and a half since . . . Oh, shoot. Speaking of Gabby's boys, I promised her I'd let them work with me painting the back porches and stairwells today while the weather's good. She doesn't want them frittering away their whole summer. Wonder if they'll stick it out. It's going to be a big job."

Being property manager for the House of Hope was a big job, period, Edesa mused—bigger than either of them realized at first. Gabby Fairbanks, the program director at Manna House, had bought the six-flat with the dream of housing homeless single moms so they could be with their kids. Second-stage housing, they called it. She'd offered Josh the position of property manager in exchange for one of the three-bedroom apartments and a modest salary—a definite upgrade for the struggling newlyweds who'd been marooned in a studio apartment with an infant. At the same time, helping the House of Hope become a reality for homeless women with children was deeply rewarding. More like one big extended family than isolated apartments.

Josh had stuck his head back in the refrigerator. "We got any eggs?"

Edesa jumped up. "Let me make some *huevos rancheros* for breakfast." She pulled out a frying pan. "You're going to need a lot of energy trying to paint the back porches with two squirrelly teenagers."

Come to think of it, she could use some extra energy herself trying to talk with Kathryn Davies, whose well-meaning but off-the-wall ideas needed a *lot* more reality and practical experience. But someone needed to come alongside the girl. And Edesa hadn't been able to ignore the nudge she'd been getting in her spirit that she was that someone.

❄

Edesa strapped Gracie and her car seat in the back of Gabby Fairbanks's red Subaru and then jumped into the front. "Thanks for giving us a ride, Gabby."

The curly topped redhead, mother of two teens and housemother for a flock of single moms and their kids at the House of Hope, pulled away from the curb. "No problem. I needed to come back to have lunch with the boys anyway. For Josh's sake! Can't expect the man to supervise them all morning and cover lunch too."

Edesa laughed. "I'm sure he appreciated the break. Though they seemed to be doing all right so far. Heard no screams or death threats this morning. Just a lot of loud music on a boom box."

"Yeah, well, hope he can stand them through Saturday. They're earning money to help pay for sailing camp next week."

"Good for you, *mi amiga*! It's not good for children to have everything handed to them."

"Didn't have a choice. Neither Philip nor I can afford the whole tuition. It isn't like it used to be when Philip was top dog in his commercial design business."

Edesa studied her friend as she navigated the stop signs and one-way streets on the way back to her staff job at Manna House. The fact that Gabby could say that so casually was a miracle in itself. If Josh ever treated her like Philip had treated Gabby—kicking her out of their penthouse, leaving her homeless and virtually penniless—she didn't know if she'd have the grace to give him another chance. A moot point, because she couldn't imagine Josh *ever* doing something like that. But Philip Fairbanks had certainly been going through a transformation—giving up his business, teaching commercial design at Roosevelt University downtown, coming to SouledOut regularly, and "courting" Gabby again. Josh said the man even showed up from time to time at the "brothers" Bible study that met a couple of Tuesday nights each month.

Should she ask? "Um, speaking of Philip, how are things going with you two?"

Gabby snorted. "Huh. What you really mean is, are we going to get remarried, right?"

"Remarried?" Edesa felt confused. "But aren't you still—"

"Married? Technically. Never got divorced. But, Edesa"—Gabby suddenly sounded teary—"our marriage was in pieces! You know that." She was silent a long moment, frowning at the traffic. Then she took a long, shuddering breath. "I know he's really trying. And our counseling is going pretty well. But . . . it's taking me a long time to trust him again. When I think about him moving in with the boys and me and sharing my bed, I . . ." Her voice trailed off.

Edesa reached out a hand and gently touched Gabby's knee. "I'm sorry. I didn't mean to pry. I'll just continue to pray, okay?"

Gabby nodded, wiped her eyes with the back of her hand, and pulled into a parking space half a block from Manna House. "Thanks. Don't worry. I'm fine." She waited as Edesa unstrapped Gracie from the car seat. "Need a ride home? I'm leaving around five."

"Thanks. I'll let you know." Edesa had no idea how the afternoon with "Miss *Gato*" was going to go. *Oh, good grief, now Gracie's got me calling her that.*

After signing in at the front desk, Gabby gave Edesa and Gracie a quick hug before disappearing into the office of Mabel Turner, the director of the emergency shelter. Hefting Gracie to her hip, Edesa passed through the large multipurpose room they called Shepherd's Fold and navigated the stairs to the lower level of Manna House, which housed the kitchen, dining room, rec room, and laundry.

Lunch was over and the cleanup crew looked as if they were almost done. "Well, look what the cat drug in. Hey, baby, how's my sweetie pie?" Estelle Bentley, swathed in her big white apron and adorned with the unflattering white net cap required of all kitchen workers, came around the counter and held out her arms to Gracie.

But Gracie turned her head. "No! Wanna play ina sand with Miss *Gato!*"

Estelle looked taken aback. "What'd I say?"

Edesa rolled her eyes and held up a finger. "Be right back." Making her way past the tables in the dining area, she took the little girl into the rec room where two of the shelter residents were playing Ping-Pong. "Can I leave Gracie in here a few minutes?" Edesa asked. "She likes to look at books."

"Oh sure. We'll look after her," one of the women said. "Hey, Gracie, you remember me? Want me to read you a story?" The thin young woman, hair tied up in a bandanna, put down her paddle and plopped into a beanbag chair. "Bring me a book. I'll read to ya."

Edesa grinned. "Thanks, B.B. I just need to talk to Miss Estelle a minute."

The shelter's chief cook had poured two cups of fresh coffee and commandeered a corner of one of the tables, one foot stretched out on the seat of another chair. "Feet were killin' me anyway. What's this about 'Miss *Gato*'? Whoever she is, got my feelin's hurt." The large black woman sniffed dramatically.

Edesa laughed. "That's what Gracie calls Kathryn Davies— you know, one of the students from CCU—because she calls herself Kat. And you said 'cat'—"

"Humph. So I did. Remind me to say 'what the *dog* drug in' next time. But what's this about playin' in the sand?"

"Oh, Josh invited the CCU students to tag along when the SouledOut youth went to Lighthouse Beach on Memorial Day, and Kathryn built sand castles with Gracie. Made a big impression on Miss Muffet. And this morning she heard me telling Josh I was going to talk to Kat today, and now she's like a broken record."

"Talk to her? What's up?" Estelle doctored her coffee with two heaping teaspoons of sugar from the table dispenser.

"Well, that's actually what I wanted to talk to you about. I tried to call you this morning, but only got your voice mail. She's been bugging—*perdón*—*asking* me about teaching a class on nutrition at SouledOut. I think she's appalled at seeing kids in the neighborhood walking to school drinking sodas and eating potato chips. I've told her that food issues for poor folks aren't as simple as teaching them the basic food groups—but I've been feeling I should have a more serious discussion with her."

"Uh-huh." Estelle looked at Edesa skeptically over the rim of her coffee cup. "And where exactly do I come in? You the one with a fancy degree in public health."

Edesa felt the top of her ears grow hot. "*Sí.* Which is why Kathryn's been after me. But the fact is, I'm only a few years older than she is. I think we could use your age and wisdom when it comes to food. You've been cooking here at Manna House for—"

"You sayin' I'm old?"

"Estelle! You know good and well what I mean."

Estelle chuckled. "All right, all right. I'm just playin' with you." The fifty-something woman pursed her lips a moment. "You say you're talkin' to her today? Here?"

Edesa nodded. "She said she could get here around two. Would you have some time to—Uh-oh. What?"

Estelle was shaking her head. "I got my cookin' class this afternoon. Plannin' to do a grocery shoppin' trip with my girls, ain't gonna be here but two shakes of a saltshaker 'fore we leave."

"Oh, right!" Edesa should've remembered the cooking class. Estelle occasionally asked her to do a session on nutrition with every new set of residents who signed up. "Wait . . . you're going shopping for food? That's perfect! Can Kathryn and I tag along? That would be a good experience for her."

Estelle shrugged. "If she got the time. You know there ain't anything but a couple mom 'n' pop convenience stores in this neighborhood. We gonna have to take the El someplace to find a decent grocery store."

A smile widened on Edesa's face. "Exactly."

Chapter 4

L ittle Red Riding Hood?!" Nine-year-old Kevin Green screwed up his face beneath the blond thatch. "That's a baby story."
"Yeah," echoed Latoya Sims, sticking out her lip. In spite of their obvious dissimilarities—boy/girl . . . braces/perfect teeth . . . towheaded/tiny black braids . . . leader/follower—these two usually presented a united front on any idea Kat suggested as a morning volunteer at Avis Douglass's Summer Tutoring and Enrichment Program. Kevin usually reacted first, with Latoya providing backup. Might be "yay." Might be "nay." Either way, it was usually two against one.

"One" being her third tutoring student, Yusufu Balozi, whose family had arrived from Uganda only a year ago. Usually eager to please, today he looked blank. "Red Hooding? What it is?"

The boy's charming accent always made Kat smile. The three students she tutored were doing drama that week for their last activity of the morning. The drama option alternated with computer skills a week at a time. But the volunteer who was supposed to work with all the children on a play came down with mono, so until another drama coach could be found, Kat had to come up with something roughly resembling acting for her three charges.

Theater games. That was as close as Kat had come to anything remotely like acting in high school. Her speech teacher had them do theater games—spontaneous, unrehearsed improvs—to loosen them up and get them comfortable speaking in front of people. She'd had to go online to refresh her memory about actual games—her clearest memory of that high school speech class was of laughing so hard she'd ripped a seam in her best blouse—but she'd come back to STEP the next day armed and ready.

They'd already done "The Bench" and "Freeze and Switch" the previous two mornings, and today she was trying "Movie Genres."

"We take a familiar story like Little Red Riding Hood," she explained, "and act it out in different movie styles—like a Western, or a Three Stooges movie, or sci-fi. I'll give you a movie style to start, then I'll call out a different one and you have to change the story to fit—"

"Can we call it 'Little Red in the Hood'?" Kevin wanted to know. "The wolf could do a break dance or a rap or something."

Kat wanted to laugh. A strange comment coming from a yellow-haired, blue-eyed, white kid. But . . . "Why not? 'Little Red in the Hood' it is. Latoya, we need a girl to be Little Red, and, Kevin, you can be the wolf. Yusufu, would you like to be the hero woodsman?"

The boy's dark eyes widened in panic. "But, Miss Kat, I don't know what hero woodsman does. What is this story?"

So she sat them down and told the story of Little Red Riding Hood—which seemed a bit grim, now that she thought about it. Eating Granny? The hero killing the wolf with his ax? She ad-libbed a few changes—Granny in the closet, the woodsman chasing off the wolf.

By that time, Avis Douglass, Bethune Elementary's principal during the school year and the creative force behind the STEP program, was ringing a bell to close out the morning session. Those who stayed for sports activities in the afternoon—or field trips on Friday—got sack lunches.

"Miss Kat! Miss Kat! Stay! Stay!" Latoya hung on her arm so hard Kat thought her shoulder was going to pop from its socket. "Can we do Little Red if we eat fast?"

At least they'd gotten excited about the theater games. Kat hoped Mrs. D had noticed. "Sorry, kids. I can't stay today. Gotta go." Which was true and not true. She didn't have to be at Manna House until two. But she'd already decided not to go back to the apartment for lunch and risk running into Nick, though she supposed he was either at Software Symphony working in the mail room at Mr. D's business, or at the church, getting the lowdown on his other job as a pastoral intern. Still, she didn't want to risk it.

Begging a sack lunch "to go," Kat shouldered her backpack and headed for the Morse Avenue El station. She'd been to the shelter once before—one of the places they'd visited as part of the Urban Experience program at Crista U—but she'd made a Google map just in case.

A surge of anticipation sent her running up the stairs of the station just as a train pulled in. As the doors slid shut, Kat hung on to a pole and studied the map above the window. The Sheridan El station was barely halfway to the Loop. Shouldn't take too long. Looked like an easy walk from the El station.

The car was almost empty at this time of day. Kat swung into a seat and stared out the window as the elevated train rattled past the back sides of brick apartment buildings, past a park full of lush trees and jogging paths, and over busy intersections, scenes that were starting to feel familiar.

The train picked up a few more passengers at each stop. Munching on an apple from the sack lunch, Kat paid little attention until the recorded voice announced, "Berwyn. The next stop is Berwyn." A smile tipped the edges of her mouth. This was where she and the other CCU students had transferred to the Foster Avenue bus that took them back and forth to the campus this past spring and early summer.

But no more. Not her anyway. Bree had one more semester to finish up her master's degree and would go back to campus in the fall, and Nick had to complete his internship before getting his M-Div. But Kat had graduated in June. Well . . . officially, anyway. She hadn't attended her own graduation. What was the point? Her parents hadn't come. Off on some cruise. The school would mail her diploma. She'd spent graduation day checking out the apartment in the Rogers Park neighborhood the four friends were going to sublet for their "summer in the city."

So much had happened already—and it was only the last week in June. At first it seemed like everything was going wrong. Pastor Clark, one of SouledOut's pastors, had had a heart attack in the pulpit when they'd been attending the church only a few weeks. Then Olivia got banged up when her purse got snatched at the El station, causing her to fall. She'd decided to go home, leaving them one short to pony up on the rent. And to Kat's disappointment, the Douglass couple upstairs had seemed a bit distant, even though they held leadership roles at SouledOut. Hard to put a finger on, until Kat discovered one of the street people she'd met Dumpster diving turned out to be Mrs. D's missing daughter. *That* explained a few things.

But she had to admit God was working things out. Give credit to God, wasn't that what Nick always said? They'd all found summer jobs, enough to get by for a few months. With Olivia gone, they had a room to offer to Rochelle and her little boy, for the summer anyway. And Nick had landed the internship at SouledOut, thanks to the Douglasses' support.

Not to mention that Edesa Baxter had called that morning, offering to talk about teaching nutrition to— *Wait. Did the intercom just announce Sheridan is next?*

Sure enough, the station sign said Sheridan as the train slowed and stopped beside the wooden platform. Grabbing her backpack, Kat scurried out the door and made her way down the stairs and out onto the sidewalk. Pulling out her computer map, she tried to get her bearings—but her eye caught the sign of a tiny shop tucked underneath the El tracks.

Emerald City Coffee.

Whoa. Just what she needed. And it was only one o'clock. She had plenty of time.

Kat went into the coffee shop and ordered an iced raspberry tea and a cup of homemade minestrone soup. But as she sat down at a rickety table with her soup, her cell phone rang. "Hello? Kat here."

"Kathryn? It's Edesa. Um, any chance you can get here sooner than two? Estelle Bentley needs to—"

"I'm already here! I mean, I just got off the El. I can be there in five minutes." That was a guess, but it'd be close.

"That's great!" Kat heard Edesa turn away and speak to someone. "She just got off the El . . ." And then she was back. "See you in a few minutes."

Kat hastily put her phone away and took her food back to the counter. "Can I have these to go, please?" A minute later she was out the door with a coffee cup of soup in one hand and iced tea with a straw in the other. She walked fast, chugging the soup at corners when she had to wait for cars to pass.

Turning the corner by a Laundromat . . . there it was. The church-like building she remembered from her first visit that housed the Manna House Women's Shelter. Tossing the soup cup in a trash basket, she saw several women sitting on the cement steps that led up to the double oak doors. Two were playing cards on the step between them, but a few more just sat, not talking, having a smoke.

"Hello." Kat smiled as she threaded her way between them.

"If ya came for lunch, it's come an' gone," one of the card players growled, not looking up.

"That's all right. I'm here to see someone." Kat pressed the doorbell, waited, then pulled open the door when the buzzer went off.

Edesa met her in the foyer, holding her sleepy two-year-old. The foyer was cool and welcoming after the muggy heat outside, lit only by sunlight streaming in through the two stained-glass windows on either side of the doors and the round stained-glass window above the doors. Two wooden struts dissected the high round window, one vertical and one horizontal, throwing the shadow of a cross on the floor.

Edesa stopped by the reception cubby. "Angela, would you sign Kathryn Davies in? Check 'Volunteer.' But we'll be leaving in a few minutes, so go ahead and sign her out too." She beckoned to Kat. "Come on downstairs and meet the others."

"Leaving?" Kat felt confused. *Others?*

They crossed a large room with various couches and chairs, coffee tables with magazines, a slightly leaning bookcase with table games and books. An assortment of females of varying ages dotted the seating areas, one woman zonked out, lightly snoring.

"I didn't have time to explain on the phone," Edesa said, leading her down a flight of stairs. "I wanted to include Estelle in our conversation, but it turns out her cooking class meets today and they're doing a grocery shopping trip, so we're going along."

Kat tried not to show it, but she was irked. She came all the way down here to the shelter just to go *grocery shopping* with some cooking class? This was *not* what she had in mind at all.

Chapter 5

A h! There they are." Estelle Bentley peeled off the ugly net cap covering her long silver and black hair, which had been straightened and piled up on her head in a loose knot, untied the big white apron she was wearing, and tossed both into a laundry cart. "Ladies, this here is Kathryn Davies—some folks call her Kat. Kat, this is Penny, LaDonna, Beverly, and Shawanda."

The four women—all black except Penny—nodded curtly at Kat.

Edesa signaled Estelle. "Give me a moment. I'm going to change Gracie. Maybe she'll fall asleep in the stroller on the way."

Kat didn't know what to do. But the other women were still sitting around one of the tables, so she sat down too.

"Soon as Miss Gabby gets here with some CTA passes, we can go." Estelle squirted some hand cream into her palm and passed around the tube. "As I was sayin', good cookin' means havin' the right ingredients on hand when your kids come in actin' like you haven't fed 'em since the day they was born. That means plannin' ahead, knowin' how to shop, how to stretch those food stamps if that's what you got, an' gettin' the best bang for your buck."

"Ain't that easy down where I live," the woman named Beverly groused. Kat guessed she was somewhere in her forties. Thin mouth. Hard eyes. Hair cut so close to her head it looked military. "Ain't nothin' but liquor stores, hamburger joints, and a 7-Eleven. Ain't no fresh vegetables or fresh fruit, nothin'. They don't call it a food desert for nothin'."

"Now you talkin'," LaDonna butted in. She was a big-breasted woman with yellowish skin and packing extra weight, but younger than Beverly—maybe in her thirties? Her hair had been pulled into a tight knot on top of her head, and she wore large gold hoops in her ears. "Them white neighborhoods got two, three big grocery stores within a couple blocks of each other. An' some neighborhoods got *nothin'*."

Heads nodded. But Kat was still stuck back on Beverly's comment, "*down where I live*." Weren't these women homeless?

"Well, until this city gets serious about those food deserts or Jesus comes again, whichever come first, that's somethin' we can't solve in a day," Estelle said. "So you gonna have to travel to another neighborhood a couple times a month to stock up. That's what we're doin' today. But it's worth it. Otherwise—"

"—we be givin' the kids five dollars to run down to the White Castle." The girl named Shawanda—she looked all of twenty—snickered and high-fived LaDonna.

A woman with a head full of curly red hair clattered down the stairs. "Okay, got your passes," she said, waving a handful of cards. She passed them around but stopped at Kat. "Oh. Hi. You're Kat, right? Uh, do you need a CTA pass?"

Kat shook her head. She'd seen this woman regularly at SouledOut—hard to miss, all that curly red hair—but had never actually talked to her. "You work here?"

Estelle broke in. "Sorry. Didn't know you two didn't know each other. This here's Gabby Fairbanks. Gabby is the program director at Manna House. Watch out, she'll have you signed up as a volunteer faster than you can say *da Bears.*" Estelle clapped her hands as Edesa returned, lugging Gracie and a folded-up umbrella stroller. "Okay! We're all here. Let's move, ladies."

Everyone stood and trailed Estelle up the stairs. Kat carried the umbrella stroller and unfolded it once they got outside. "I'll push her," she told Edesa after Gracie was strapped into the stroller. At least it gave her something to do. What was she doing here? She didn't need a shopping lesson. Good grief, she'd been doing the grocery shopping for their summer household for the past six weeks and had managed to put healthy meals on the table most days, thank you very much.

"She's asleep," Edesa murmured after the first block. "Now if we can just keep her that way!"

"Uh-huh." Kat didn't trust herself to talk, afraid the disappointment she was feeling would leak out. But when the group ended up right back at the Sheridan El station, she couldn't help it. "Edesa! I was just here! Why didn't you just tell me to wait for the rest of you since you planned to come this way?" She could've at least enjoyed her iced tea and soup in peace.

Edesa shrugged. "I thought you'd like to meet the ladies in the cooking class and hear Estelle's explanation of what they're going to be doing today, rather than just 'Hi' and 'Good-bye' on the street. No?"

Thought *she'd* like . . . ? Not much. This whole afternoon

was turning out differently than she'd expected. But for the next few minutes she just concentrated on helping Edesa get the stroller over the turnstile and up the stairs to the platform without waking the sleeping two-year-old.

Once the Red Line pulled in and she and Edesa found seats together at the back of a car with a space for the stroller, Edesa laid her hand on Kat's arm. "I know I said we'd talk, but it will be good to tag along with these women. Just be patient, *mi amiga*. Listen. Try to understand their situations. These are the kinds of families who might benefit from learning more about nutrition, right?"

Well . . . Edesa had a point. And it would only be an hour or two, and then she'd need to excuse herself to get to work on time. But Kat hid a smile when Estelle and her crew got off at the Berwyn Avenue stop and headed for the big Dominick's store. At least she could check out the Dumpsters, see what "pickin's" she could salvage today.

But so much for keeping Gracie asleep. When they got to the store, jackhammers and a backhoe were digging up the parking lot next to the store behind a temporary fence with a Danger—Keep Out sign posted on it. Big signs in the store windows said Open During Construction. *Uh-oh.* Might not be so easy to check out the Dumpsters.

Kat followed the others as they trooped in. Penny—a pale woman who wouldn't look half bad if she had a good hair styling and some makeup—gave a long, low whistle as she gawked at the front displays piled high with flowers, fruit, and gift packages of chocolates and candles. "Looks like a whole mall in here."

Estelle herded them all into a corner near the front door. "What we're goin' to do is this: Each of you take a cart and select food for three meals to feed you and your kids—break-fast, lunch, and dinner. Then we'll meet . . . let's see, back by the fish counter in half an hour, and take a look-see how we're doin'." Estelle winked at Edesa. "All right, you're on your own."

"Money don't count?" Shawanda asked suspiciously. "I don't get any more food stamps till first of the month an' I'm out."

"We're just window shopping." Estelle chuckled. "Gonna have to put it back."

"Wait." LaDonna glanced around uneasily. "I been here once before, an' some white dude in a tie followed me around like I was gonna steal somethin'. Made me so nervous I left my cart without gettin' nothin'."

Some of the other women nodded their heads and made faces.

Estelle frowned. "All right. Hold tight. We'll take care of that." She marched off, leaving the rest of them looking at one another. Gracie, short on sleep, fussed about nothing in particu-lar. Kat was wondering if she had time to excuse herself and check out the Dumpsters when Estelle came back with a fleshy man in a white dress shirt, dark patterned tie, and metal name tag that said Seth Young, Manager.

"These are members of my cooking class, Mr. Young, and I'd like your permission to conduct a shopping lesson today, how to read prices, make use of sales, things like that. We'd be glad to check back in with you before we leave." Estelle's chin was up, her tone courteous. But Kat caught a hint of daring him to disagree.

"Well . . ." The manager seemed to count heads. "Six, uh, students—plus yourself, Mrs. Bentley." He allowed a toothy smile. "We're happy to host your cooking class, Mrs. Bentley.

Be our guest. But, yes, why don't you just let me know when you're done." He smiled as he backed off. "Enjoy."

"Don't nobody laugh," Estelle muttered under her breath. "If you can't lick 'em, join 'em, I always say. Now go. Remember, food for three meals. Meet up in thirty minutes by the fish counter."

Kat watched as the four women grabbed carts and took off in different directions. So what was she supposed to do for—

"You too." Estelle pushed a cart at her. "This is a one-size-fits-all exercise."

All right. They didn't usually shop for groceries till the weekend, but maybe she could pick up some things. Gave her something to do anyway. She waved at Gracie, buckled in the child seat of Edesa's cart, and headed for the produce section.

She really did want to check out the Dumpsters, though. Today was Thursday, the day of the changeover from last week's advertised items to this week's. A lot of food got tossed out that was past its shelf date. Then she'd know better what to buy. But Estelle said to meet up in half an hour . . .

Breakfast. Kat picked up bananas, Greek yogurt, and a package of Swiss Müesli granola. Added fresh-squeezed OJ in a half-gallon carton. *Lunch.* Pita bread, sprouts, can of black beans, fresh peaches. *Supper.* Whole wheat pasta, extra-virgin olive oil, garlic, organic tomatoes—though not really in sea-son—white English cheddar cheese, and fresh basil leaves. A salad would go good with pasta. She picked up a bag of baby spinach, a red onion, sunflower seeds, and dried cranberries for a great salad. Might as well get the large bag of cranberries. Made a good snack.

Done. She headed for the fish counter, avoiding LaDonna,

who was frowning at a display in the bakery section. She was tempted to get some fresh catfish—great sale—but getting it safely home and in the refrigerator was iffy if she had to go straight to work.

The six carts met in the back of the store. Gracie was digging a chubby finger into a snack-size box of raisins. "She was fussing, had to get something to keep her busy," Edesa hastily explained. "Don't worry, I'm buying the six-pack."

"All right," Estelle said. "Let's see what we've got."

As each woman ticked off the items in her cart, Estelle made comments. "Check out the ingredient list on those boxes of cereal. If sugar's in the top three, forget it . . . Those cinnamon rolls are okay as an occasional treat, but whole wheat toast sprinkled with cinnamon sugar will keep most kids happy . . . This can of stew would be easy but has lots of preservatives. Not hard to make your own stew, tastes a whole lot better too . . . Anything that comes in individual packs is convenient, sure, but costs a lot more than buying the same thing in bulk . . ."

Kat couldn't believe the stuff in Shawanda's cart. Grape *drink*. A frozen package of buffalo wings. A frozen pizza. ("Cheaper'n orderin' from Pizza Hut," she protested.) A large box of Kraft macaroni and cheese in SpongeBob shapes. ("Dessa an' Bam Bam won't eat nothin' else.")

Estelle chuckled. "They will if they get hungry enough. Depends on what you keep on hand. Most of you got brand names. Look for generics and store brands. They're cheaper and usually just as good, *unless* the brand names are on sale. All right, let's put this stuff back. Next time we'll bring calculators, see how far we can stretch twenty dollars—"

"What about *her* cart?" Shawanda crossed her arms and

glared at Kat, who had hung back. Part of her wanted Estelle and Edesa to note the healthy choices she'd made—a good example for the other women—but mostly she just wanted to buy her groceries and get out of there.

"Miss Kat! Almost forgot you!" Estelle seemed to think it was funny. "All right, let's see what you have here . . ." She pawed through the stuff in Kat's cart. "Mm-hmm . . . hmm . . ." Kat fidgeted. Was that good?

Finally Estelle looked up. "Kat has chosen some healthy foods here. Wouldn't mind going to dinner at her house!" The large woman laughed, and Kat thought she was actually very attractive, nicely proportioned for her size.

"Unfortunately," Estelle went on, "most of these items are pricey and probably out of reach for anyone on food stamps. But there are alternatives." She pointed. "Spinach is good, but anything already bagged costs more. Ditto with organic—nice if you can do it, but always more expensive. Choose fruits and vegetables in season and look for sales. You can make your own granola . . ."

Kat felt her face growing red. Of course she could make her own granola! But the woman had told them to shop for three meals. What was she supposed to do?

"What we *need*," Beverly said, "is more of them food pantries like the Salvation Army does. They *give* food away. I read about it once. Don't know where it is, though."

Estelle nodded. "Good point. A list of food pantries around the city would be very useful. I'll tell Gabby, she's good at making lists. Just remember, most food pantries can only stock nonperishable food, so fresh fruits and vegetables aren't usually available, and that's—"

"I find lots of still-good veggies and fruit in the Dumpsters." Kat was startled by her own voice. But what did Estelle know about how she shopped? Sure, good food cost a bit more, but she also *saved* money by Dumpster diving.

Four pairs of eyes stared at her. Then LaDonna snorted. "You ain't gonna find *me* digging around in no Dumpster to feed my babies. Not less'n it be the last place on earth got any food."

"Well, I done it before"—Penny sniffed—"when things was really bad. But I'm lookin' to get *off* the street an' *stay* off."

"All right, that's a conversation for another time," Estelle interrupted. "Right now we need to get this food back on the shelves. Go on now." She shooed them away with a flap of her hands.

"Why can't we just leave it in our carts?" Shawanda fussed. "They hire people to put stuff back you don't want, don't they?" But a glare from Estelle shut her up.

Kat stalked off with her cart. She'd intended to buy her groceries and take them home, but she felt too embarrassed now. After replacing her items, she looked at her watch. Almost four. Relieved, she found Edesa as Estelle checked out with the manager. "I've really got to head back. Got to be at work in an hour."

"Oh. Okay." Edesa looked at her closely. "Are you all right? Shall we talk about our experience today—maybe after worship on Sunday?"

Talk? Kat wasn't sure she wanted to now—not if Estelle Bentley was going to be included. The woman was so bossy, and so . . . so know-it-all. "Maybe." She shrugged and scurried out the door.

Wait. She still had time to check out the Dumpsters. So

what if those women were too proud. Wasting good food was a crime. She could carry quite a bit in her backpack. Maybe her afternoon wouldn't be a total loss after all.

Quickening her steps, Kat hurried toward the alley on the other side of the store from where all the construction was going on. A large truck was backed up to the loading dock, and she could hear voices and the *bump, bump, bump* of hand trucks going in and out. *Just walk natural,* she told herself. *Nobody's paying any attention to you.* A few more feet around the front of the big truck cab and she'd—

Kat stopped short.

The Dumpsters were gone.

In their place were two huge compactors built into the brick wall.

※

All the way home on the El, Kat felt on the verge of tears. The whole afternoon had been a total bust. Her feelings jerked around with every bump and sway of the train. That Estelle! Made her feel about two inches high. No way could she work with that woman. Were all the big stores getting rid of their Dumpsters? Where would that leave people like Rochelle, who'd survived partly by Dumpster diving those few months when she had nowhere to go and no money? . . . And those women in the cooking class! You'd think they'd be glad to get free food. How different was rescuing food from a Dumpster than getting free food at those food pantries they mentioned?

Kat was pulled from her thoughts by the intercom. "Morse Avenue is next!" Her stop. She joined the throng pushing out the doors and headed down the stairs. Her stomach growled. Did she have time to go home to the apartment before work?

The apartment. Nick.

Nick and Rochelle last night . . .

Nope. Couldn't deal with that right now. Kat headed down Morse Avenue toward The Common Cup.

Chapter 6

The mail room was growing warm as the temperature outside hiked up to the mideighties. Nick's short-sleeve dress shirt started to feel wet under his arms as he read the next order and pulled the appropriate software from its bin. Box it, add the invoice, tape it, peel the address, and stick it . . .

"Here." He slid the package to the guy who worked the postage meter, glancing enviously at Juan's pullover sport shirt and cargo shorts. "Casual Friday" wear and it wasn't even Friday. But he'd noticed that Peter Douglass, the owner of Software Symphony, and Carl Hickman, the general manager, both wore dress shirts and ties, and Nick had figured he'd start out somewhere in the middle dress-wise. Short-sleeve shirt, no tie, khaki slacks.

But he hadn't counted on the air-conditioning going out.

Another order. And another. The mail room fulfilled orders, packaged, printed postage, and shipped them out. Not exactly a demanding job, except needing to get it right. But he had no complaints. He was grateful to have a job for the summer, and working for Mr. D was a bonus.

"Taylor! Message for you."

Nick looked up. Carl Hickman was leaning in the doorway waving a slip of paper. The Hickman family had been one of the first African American families Nick and the other CCU students had met when they first visited SouledOut in the spring, but then Carl was out for most of a month with a work-related accident. Hard to imagine in a software business that had a relatively small staff: a few computer programmers, a tech support guru, a small sales and advertising staff, a couple of secretaries, and three guys in the mail room. But Carl had tripped and cracked his head on the sharp edge of a counter in the mail room, causing a neck injury. According to office gossip, the father of three had started in the mail room and worked his way up to general manager, making himself indispensable. So much so that at the height of the economic crisis, Mr. D seriously considered selling the business when he thought Carl might not be able to come back.

Nick left his stool and took the note. "Thanks." He unfolded the paper. *Pastor Cobbs called. Can you meet tonight at the church at 7:00?*

Huh. Kind of last minute. But the pastor had said he wanted to meet with Nick and Mrs. Douglass in the next few days to talk about roles and responsibilities of the team during this interim time. Well, better sooner than later. At least he'd have time to go home, change out of his rumpled shirt, and gather up the necessary papers from the seminary that detailed expectations for his internship—he'd already given Pastor Cobbs a set when he and the elders were deciding whether to recommend him to the congregation—before heading back over to the church.

Except . . . was he supposed to cook tonight? Rochelle cooked last night. No, he was pretty sure Bree and Kat had tonight and Friday, and he had Saturday.

When five o'clock rolled around, Nick punched out and quickly headed out the door. Mr. Douglass had given him a ride a few times since they lived in the same building, but Nick didn't want "the boss" to think he was expecting that kind of favor regularly. And even though the humidity was fairly high, it felt good to walk.

Gave him time to think.

About Kat.

What in the world was going on with her?

If only she hadn't seen that kiss! Didn't she know he hadn't initiated it? And Rochelle didn't mean anything by it. The young mom was just so grateful to have a roof over her head and friends to support her caring for Conny, it just happened! And good grief, it was just a peck on the cheek at that.

Though he had to admit it had rattled him. The soft lips brushing his cheek. The sweet floral smell of her hair. The young woman was attractive, no denying that.

He should be so lucky, sharing an apartment with three beautiful women! Because, to tell the truth, both Kat and Bree were also stunning in their own ways. He'd been kind of proud of himself, able to be "just friends" with the two of them on campus the past couple of years. And they'd gotten tighter taking the Urban Experience class together, which is where they'd added Olivia to their circle, even though she was still an undergrad. Taking on Chicago with all its magnificence and melded cultures and seething underside had bonded the four of them in a way that was hard to explain.

But that was before he'd started to have deeper feelings for Kat . . . even though some of the very things he loved about her—her zest for life, her passion about things she cared about, the way she threw caution to the wind once her mind was made up, even her innocent naiveté about the new faith she'd found four summers ago at the Midwest Music Fest—could be maddening sometimes. But just looking into those mesmerizing blue eyes surrounded by all that dark, wavy hair, especially when she wore it down instead of clipped up in back in a careless tangle, had a way of turning his insides to jelly.

He was so deep in thought he almost passed their street, but caught himself and turned the corner, picking up speed the last half block to the three-flat. It was already five thirty. He needed to get some supper, change clothes, and walk up to the church—

"Mister Nick! Mister Nick!" A childish voice from above his head caused him to look up. Conny was leaning out of the second-floor window waving at him. "Come see what Grammy got me today."

Alarmed, Nick shouted, "Conny! Don't lean out the window!" Why in the world wasn't the screen in place? "Hold on! I'm coming up."

In the background he heard Rochelle yell, "Conny! Get back in here!"

Good. His mother would pull him back in. Pushing into the foyer, Nick fished out his keys, let himself into the stairwell, and raced up the stairs. Conny met him at the door to the second-floor apartment. "See what Grammy got me?" He held up two large plastic dinosaurs. "Grrrrr! Gonna eat you up!"

"Not before I eat *you* up!" Nick grabbed the little boy and pretended to nosh on his arm as he carried him inside and kicked the door closed behind him. He was going to have to do something about that window.

Then he saw Bree sitting with her arm around Rochelle on the couch. Rochelle looked as if she'd been crying. He set Conny down. "Hey, buddy, why don't you go find something for those dinosaurs to eat? I think they like lettuce."

"No! They're *meat* eaters!" But Conny ran into the kitchen.

Nick looked at the two women on the couch. "What's up? Is something wrong?"

Rochelle sniveled again and blew her nose. Bree shook her head. "She didn't get the nanny job. Because of . . . you know."

Nick sank down into the overstuffed chair catty-corner to the couch. "You told them you have HIV?"

Rochelle nodded. "Kat said I should. To be up front about it." Her wet eyes flashed. "It's not like I'm dangerous. Don't they think I know how to be careful around kids?" She sagged against the cushions. "Should've taken Conny with me so they could see I'm a mom too, but my mother thought she was helping me out by taking care of him while I went." Her voice got tight. "*Knew* I shouldn't have gone," she spit out. "Say *HIV* and people treat you like a leper."

Nick didn't know what to say. It did feel like a catch-22. They might need some help with this. He sure didn't have any experience. "I'm sorry, Rochelle. Really sorry. I'm sure you'll find something. We'll all keep our eyes open."

He got up, walked over to the open window, and shut it. "But, uh, speaking of safety, we gotta keep this window locked. It doesn't have a screen. And I hate to run, but I've got a seven o'clock meeting at the church. Is there something I can grab to eat?"

Bree jumped up. "Sorry, Nick. I know it's my turn to cook, but I just got home and Rochelle was upset. Uh . . . scrambled eggs okay?"

❅

Nick was halfway to the shopping center where SouledOut was located when a black car pulled up alongside and a window rolled down. "Going my way? Hop in."

He peered into the window. "Mrs. Douglass? Sure. Thanks." Nick opened the front passenger door of the Toyota sedan and settled into the leather seat.

"Seat belt." She smiled.

"Oh, right." He buckled the belt.

"I stopped at your apartment before I left, but you'd already gone."

"Yeah. Had to give myself time to walk. Which is fine. I like to walk. But thanks for the ride. The AC feels good." Silence settled into the interior of the car for several long moments. "Conny showed me the dinosaurs you got him today. He was wired!" Nick chuckled. "Don't blame him. I collected a whole set of dinosaurs when I was a kid—but I was about ten. He's starting early."

Pleasure warmed her voice. "It's wonderful having Conny so close by, being able to spend time with him in little, everyday ways. I'm grateful that you folks took them in. Can't thank you enough." Another long silence. Then . . . "I suppose you heard that Rochelle didn't get the nanny job."

He nodded. "It must be tough. The HIV thing, I mean.

Never really thought about all the implications—about getting a job and stuff like that. Guess I have a lot to learn."

"Mm. Our whole church has a lot to learn. We haven't really faced what it means to welcome all who come into the kingdom, but if we look at what Jesus did, He ministered to the sick, the lame, the blind, the hungry, the poor, the outcasts— and that has a lot of implications for average church folks."

Nick laughed nervously. "Makes me wonder if I know what I'm doing, wanting to be a pastor."

Avis Douglass turned into the Howard Street shopping center and pulled into a parking space. "That makes two of us."

Pastor Cobbs was waiting for them in his office. "Come in, come in, Sister Avis and Brother Nick! I apologize for the short notice, but I'm glad you could both make it." He waited as they settled into their chairs, then leaned forward with clasped hands and his elbows on his desk. "I think starting out with a time of prayer would be appropriate."

Nick tried to push other things out of his mind—Kat, Conny, Rochelle, HIV—and simply soak in the passionate prayer. Pastor Cobbs thanked God for the life of Pastor Clark, acknowledging that the "homegoing" of the elderly pastor had left a big hole in the life of the congregation. But he also thanked God "for faithful stalwarts like our sister Avis here, and an up-and-coming generation of young people called to preach the gospel, like our young brother Nick here . . ." Then he went on to name the challenges they faced right there on Howard Street. Too many kids without fathers in the home. Too many jobless men hanging out on the street. Too many young girls having babies and dropping out of school. Too many drug pushers taking advantage of the bored, the restless, the hopeless . . .

The back of Nick's neck prickled. This wasn't seminary. This wasn't theory. This wasn't even life neatly packaged inside the church. This was life teeming outside the doors.

He suddenly felt like a Kiddie Car at the Indy 500.

"Amen." Pastor Cobbs looked up sheepishly. "Sorry. Sometimes I get so caught up in all the situations so desperately in need of prayer, I forget what I started out to pray for. But God knows." Picking up a couple sheets of paper, he handed one to each of them. "Let's talk about some practical schedules first. We can meet together once a week to start, to work out preaching schedules, who's handling which pastoral duties, situations that come up . . ."

They agreed on Monday night, if the elders would be willing to move to Tuesday so they could deal with anything coming out of the pastoral team meeting. Then Pastor Cobbs went down the list of basic responsibilities:

Choosing the worship and teaching themes for each month.

Preparing the sermon. They decided Pastor Cobbs would preach twice a month, Avis and Nick each once a month.

Pastoral oversight of the various ministries, which basically meant mentoring the various persons in charge. Pastor Cobbs would oversee the elder board, missions, discipleship, and men's ministry. Avis Douglass agreed to oversee the worship teams, Wednesday night Bible study, and women's ministry. That left Nick to oversee youth ministry and outreach—"which," Pastor Cobbs admitted, "is woefully underdeveloped."

"Oh, one last thing, Nick," the pastor said as they prepared to close. "How do you feel about becoming a member of SouledOut? I know your internship is time limited, but I think it would be meaningful to both you and the congregation if you became a member of this church. Committed yourself one hundred percent while you're here."

"Absolutely. When?"

The pastor handed him a packet in a folder. "Look through these papers—our statement of faith, our covenant with one another. We normally go over all of this in a membership class when several are interested in becoming members. But if it all looks good to you, maybe . . . a week from Sunday?"

Nick nodded, but his brain was churning—not to mention his gut—as they walked out into the long twilight of late June. "I . . . think I'll walk home, Mrs. Douglass. I need some time to unwind before I hit the apartment, if you know what I mean."

She smiled sympathetically. "If you're sure. And please, Nick, call me Avis—or Sister Avis, if you like. If we're going to be part of this pastoral team together, we need to be on a less formal footing."

He allowed a grin. "All right. I like Sister Avis. Good night." He gave a wave as he walked toward Howard Street. Maybe he'd get something to eat. Bree's scrambled eggs had slid off his ribs long ago.

Tucking the membership folder under his arm, Nick headed east on the lively drag between Chicago and Evanston. He felt excited—excited and scared at the same time. This had been his dream ever since he'd been accepted at Crista University. Now it was no longer a dream, but the nitty-gritty reality of real life.

A train thundered overhead as he passed under the El tracks and walked past the small shops and tiny ethnic restaurants lining the border street between Chicago and Evanston, most of them still open. What time was it, anyway? *Almost quarter to nine.* Suddenly his pace picked up, food forgotten. He turned south on Greenleaf and walked quickly, block after block, until he came to Morse Avenue.

Kat got off work at nine o'clock.

Nick showed up at The Common Cup just as Kat barreled out the door, intent on slipping her arms into the straps of her backpack. "Whoa! Not so fast," he said and laughed as she crashed right into him.

"Nick!" Kat's blue eyes widened. "What are you doing here?"

He couldn't help the broad grin that creased his face. "Just coming from SouledOut. Had my first meeting with Pastor Cobbs and Mrs. Doug—uh, Sister Avis." He felt his face flush. "She asked me to call her that."

Kat giggled. "Do they know we usually call them Mrs. D and Mr. D? Probably not. Don't think we've done it to their face."

"Yeah. Afraid I'm going to slip. Anyway, thought I'd come by, walk you home. I needed to unwind. The meeting gave me a *lot* to think about."

"So tell me."

He wanted so badly to take her hand, but he just held on to the membership packet as he reviewed everything they'd talked about. "I think I'm in over my head, Kat."

She stopped in the middle of the sidewalk. "Now listen here, Nick Taylor. Of course you're in over your head. It's called swimming. You can't swim if you're still wading in the shallow end. This is what you've been preparing for, for years! You've told me yourself that God put a call on your life. Right? So now it's time to jump in."

Standing there, he watched the animation in her face. This

was the Kat he liked so much. Upbeat. Positive. Plunging ahead. Sure of herself. Sure of *him*.

Maybe now was the time to talk about how he felt about her.

"Anyway . . ." She started walking again. "Don't mean to change the subject, but this morning you said you wanted to talk to me. Guess now's as good a time as any."

What—? For a few precious minutes he'd totally forgotten he had to clear up whatever misimpression she'd gotten last night. Guessed he better do that first. "Oh. That. Yeah, well, just wanted to say something about what happened in the hallway last night—"

"Uh-huh. I knew that was it. Sorry about the way I acted. Just took me by surprise, you know?"

He snorted. "Took *you* by surprise. Me too. But I just wanted to say—"

"I know, I know. Don't get your tail in a knot about it, Nick. She was just thanking you for reading to Conny, for being such a good buddy to him. Didn't mean anything. Right?"

He felt flustered. "Yeah. That's what I was going to say. Didn't want you to get the wrong impression."

"Don't worry about it. I get it. But—" She stopped again and faced him. "There is one thing I need to say. And it's a serious problem."

Nick's heart felt like it skipped a beat or two. She got it? But there was a serious problem?

"Don't forget, Rochelle is HIV positive. We don't want to freak out about it, but we can't ignore it either. It's passed by body fluids—blood, saliva, what have you."

"Saliva! That's not what I've—"

"Nick." Kat laid her hand on his arm. "I know she was just being friendly, but to be on the safe side, don't let her kiss you again, even on the cheek. What if you'd nicked yourself shaving or something! We should talk about how to protect the rest of us too."

Nick shook his head. "You're wrong, Kat. I mean, you're right, we should educate ourselves about living with HIV and take any necessary precautions, but I've never heard it can be passed by saliva or kissing."

Kat gave him a strange look. "Fine."

But she walked the rest of the way back to the apartment in silence.

Chapter 7

Gracie whined and rubbed her eyes as Edesa lugged her up the stairs to their third-floor apartment at the House of Hope. She found her husband sprawled on the couch in the living room, dabs of dark-green paint in odd places on his face and clothes. Josh sat up and yawned. "You're back. How'd it go?"

Edesa grimaced. "Could ask you the same thing. But Gracie's falling apart. She only napped twenty minutes. I need to get her in the tub and ready for bed. Any chance you could heat up these leftovers Estelle sent home with me?" She held out a plastic grocery bag.

"Uhhh, I guess." Josh reluctantly pushed himself off the couch, took the bag, and trudged down the hallway to the kitchen. Edesa bit back a frustrated comment. All he had to do was heat it up, for goodness' sake!

Peeling off Gracie's sweaty shirt, shorts, and diaper, Edesa squirted bubble bath into the tepid water filling the tub. Gracie used to be able to take a nap just about anywhere, but those days were over. "In you go, *niña.*"

Gracie's tears turned to giggles as the bubbles clung like gossamer fairy frocks to her tawny legs and torso. Edesa sat on the closed toilet lid, letting the child splash herself clean for the most part. In spite of her weariness, her heart swelled with amazement that God had brought them this far since that cold November day . . .

The day she and Josh, newly engaged, had discovered the Hispanic woman shivering in a doorway, clutching her tiny, three-month-old baby. They'd quickly brought the mother and child into the warm arms of the shelter where they volunteered. Who could've known that simple act of kindness would cause the woman to leave a note at the shelter saying if anything happened to her, she wanted Edesa to raise her baby—a note found after the woman, gone missing, was discovered in a crack house, dead of a drug overdose.

"Look, Mommy!" Gracie was piling handfuls of airy suds onto the top of her head. "See my hat?"

Edesa smiled wearily. What she wouldn't give to soak in a bubble bath and go to bed herself. Except she still had the Friday morning Bible study at Manna House to prepare—and so far no ideas.

Finally gathering her slippery daughter into a large towel, Edesa dressed her in a clean diaper and lightweight pajamas and headed for the kitchen. Josh had the small table set and was dishing up Spanish rice, green beans, and fried chicken warmed up in the microwave. "You, my darling," he said with a grin, "can bring home Estelle's leftovers anytime. Do those women at Manna House realize what a gem they've got cooking for them?"

Edesa's previous irritation melted. Josh was like the son

in one of Jesus' parables, who at first balked at doing what his father asked but did it anyway—which Jesus commended over the other son who said, "Sure!" but never followed through.

But supper turned out to be a wrestling match, with Gracie deciding she didn't *like* green beans and throwing them on the floor. But when the rice followed, Edesa unbuckled her from the booster seat and took off her bib. "That's enough, young lady. Time for night-night. Come on, you can choose one story and—"

"No! Want Daddy to read me a story!"

Josh held out his arms. "It's all right. I'll put her down."

Edesa watched as Josh sauntered down the hallway with Gracie snuggled on his shoulder, disappearing into her bedroom. *Daddy* . . .

Sighing, she started cleaning up the remains of Gracie's supper from the floor. Did that little girl have any idea how blessed she was? One day they'd tell her the story about how Josh had dropped out of college and moved up their wedding date, just so baby Gracie could have both a mom *and* a dad right off the bat. They'd had a Christmas wedding at Manna House—and to Edesa, the story of Joseph the carpenter being told by God's angel, "Don't be afraid! Go ahead, marry this young virgin and raise baby Jesus as your own," felt very close to home.

Amazing grace. Amazing Gracie.

Floor cleaned and dishes done, Edesa finally curled up in the living room with her Bible, trying to prepare for tomorrow. Her eyes drooped . . . Why was she so tired? But a few minutes later Josh joined her, flopping on the other end of the couch. "She's out. And I'm done in."

"Looks like you could use a bath too," she smirked. "Have you looked in the mirror lately? You've got paint—"

"Ha. You think this is bad? P.J. and Paul looked like little green men from Mars by the time we got done. Gabby sent them in old T-shirts and shorts, but that outdoor paint is weather-resistant. Might be resistant to coming off their hair, legs, hands, and faces too."

Edesa laughed. "So how'd it go?"

Josh shrugged. "Gabby's paying the boys, so I think they'll show up tomorrow. We got more done with three of us than just me, though I had to ride herd on them pretty hard to keep them on task. We'll probably have to work Saturday too." He looked at her curiously. "How'd it work out doing the shopping trip with 'Miss *Gato*'?"

Edesa didn't know whether to laugh at the green spot on his nose or groan at his question. "I don't know. I think she and Estelle got off on the wrong foot."

"What happened?"

She held up her Bible. "Uh . . . maybe we can talk later. I still don't know what I'm doing tomorrow for the Bible study at Manna House."

"Oh. Okay." Josh pushed himself off the couch. "Do the women in Estelle's cooking class come to the Bible study? You could always talk about Jesus feeding the five thousand with just a few loaves of bread and a couple of fish. Talk about making food stretch!" He chuckled at his little joke and disappeared into the bathroom.

Jesus feeding the five thousand? That was in all four gospels, wasn't it? Edesa turned to the concordance in the back of her study Bible. *Jesus feeding the people.* Not a bad idea. Not a bad idea at all . . .

✻

Gabby Fairbanks helped Edesa arrange several of the couches and chairs into a circle the next morning. Gracie was being doted on by two of the Manna House residents waiting for the Friday morning Bible study to start.

"Hope more women show up for the Bible study." Gabby shoved one last chair into place. "A lot of the residents have gone out. The rain last night cooled things off and it's a pretty nice day, not too hot."

Edesa shrugged. "Can't worry about that. Jesus said if even two or three gather in His name, He'll be present with us."

The curly headed program director wagged her head. "See, Edesa? Nothing gets you down. How do you do it?"

Edesa looked up at the mural overlooking Shepherd's Fold. A life-size Jesus had been painted on the wall, surrounded by a ragtag flock of sheep in all different colors: black, tan, brown, white. Most of the sheep looked a bit worse for wear. Some had dirty, patchy wool, a few looked worried or sad, several had bandaged wounds, one had a torn ear. Edesa pointed to the small brown lamb tucked in the arm of the Good Shepherd. "That's me. Not very strong. Not very brave. But as long as I remember who's got me in His arms, I know I'm okay . . . Oh, Gabby!" She gasped. "I didn't mean to make you cry."

Gabby had fished out a tissue and was blotting her face. "I'm fine, I'm fine. Just thinking about my mom and how she'd love to hear what you just said."

Edesa gave her a warm hug. "Naming this room after Martha Shepherd is a fitting memorial—and you, dear friend, are more like her than you realize."

"What's with all this lovey-dovey stuff?" A familiar voice broke into the hug. "We gonna have a Bible study this morning or not?"

Edesa grinned at the wiry woman who'd flopped onto one of the couches holding a squirming one-year-old. "Precious! What are you and Timmy doing here?" Precious McGill was one of the single women living at the House of Hope with her daughter, Sabrina, now seventeen, and grandson, Timmy.

"Came for the Bible study, whatchu think? Well, that, an' the fact that Sabrina is off lookin' for a summer job an' I'm stuck watchin' Lil' Turkey here. Had an idea Gracie would be here too. I got some toys from the playroom, thought they could play together durin' the study. I'll keep an eye on 'em while you teach."

"Precious," Gabby murmured, "if you keep calling that boy Lil' Turkey, it's going to stick . . . Oh, here come a few others." The program director raised her voice. "Ladies? If you're here for the Bible study, Edesa's ready to get started."

Edesa was glad to see Penny, LaDonna, and Beverly among the several women who wandered into the circle and took a seat. After yesterday's shopping trip, the Bible study today might be particularly relevant. No Shawanda, though. Like Precious, Shawanda and her two children lived at the House of Hope and came back to Manna House for her case management meetings and some of the activities. But the Bible study hadn't been high on the young woman's priority list.

After passing out the stack of hardcover Bibles some church had donated to the shelter, Edesa began with a prayer. "*Señor*, we want to thank You for sending Your Son, *Jesús Cristo*, to live among us here on earth, showing us by His words and deeds the truths You want to teach us. Help us to have open ears, open minds, and open hearts today as we study Your Word. Amen."

A few amens peppered the circle, along with childish voices in the far corner playing with a shape sorter under Precious's supervision.

"The story we're going to read today is found in all four gospels. Penny, would you read Matthew, chapter 14, verses 13 through—"

"What page number?" Penny interrupted.

Good thing they were all using the same Bible. Page numbers worked as Edesa also assigned the same story in the gospels of Mark, Luke, and John to different women. It took awhile to read, even though the story was short, as some were better readers than others. But finally the story of Jesus feeding the five thousand had been read four times.

"Tell me what stands out for you in this story."

"You the teacher," LaDonna complained. "Ain't you s'posed to tell us?"

But at Edesa's prompting, several of the women ventured comments.

"Don't know why people didn't bring they own food."

"How did Jesus talk to so many people with no microphone?"

"Why's it say five thousand *mens*? Musta been a buncha women an' younguns too, 'cause it was a boy who gave Jesus his lunch."

"Yeah. Now *that* was a smart mama who sent *him* off that day"—a comment greeted with general laughter.

Precious had wandered closer to the circle, still keeping an eye on Timmy and Gracie. "I'm thinkin' the disciples wanted to send all them folks away because they own stomachs was growlin' an' *they* forgot to bring anything to eat. Just like a man. My two cents." More laughter.

LaDonna snickered. "Yeah, but says here Jesus put the brakes on that. Told 'em, no, *we* gonna feed 'em. Bring Me what little you got."

Edesa beamed. They were getting it. "Think about that, *mi amigas*. Even though Jesus had just been teaching these people 'many things' and healing their sick, at the end of the day He was concerned about a more immediate need: these people were hungry. They needed food. Not just spiritual food. Something to put in their stomachs."

"Humph. Somebody oughta tell some o' the preachers in this town 'bout that," LaDonna muttered. "They talk a fine talk, but ask 'em for some money to feed your kids? Like as not, they gonna send you someplace else."

Out of the corner of her eye, Edesa saw Estelle Bentley leaning against the open doorway, arms crossed across her big white apron. How long had she been standing there? "Estelle," she called, "you work with food all the time. Do you have anything you'd like to add?"

"Uh-huh, I do." Estelle moved closer to the group and leaned her hands on the back of one of the couches. "Jesus called Himself the Bread of Life. Used to wonder why He did that. But the way I see it, our souls *need* Jesus the way our bodies *need* food to survive."

"Didn't Jesus cook breakfast on the beach for His disciples after He rose from the dead?" Precious added. "I mean, that Man could *eat*."

"Uh-huh," Beverly said. "My mama useta read Bible stories to us kids, an' seemed like Jesus was always eatin' with folks—rich folks, poor folks, sinner folks, sick folks, women folks, ha-ha, even *short* folks like that Zacchaeus fellow."

Loud guffaws this time.

Edesa felt goose bumps prickling the back of her neck. In reading the story of Jesus feeding the five thousand, she'd wanted the women to see that Jesus was concerned about their physical needs as well as their spiritual needs. But they were recalling other Bible stories and making connections. If only Kathryn Davies had been here for this discussion! It might have been a good launching pad to talk about—

A wail broke into her thoughts and Precious darted back to the corner. "No, no, Timmy. No hittin'! Gracie, sweetie, are you okay, baby?"

Edesa realized she should wind this up. "Ladies, let's come back to this topic next week. In the meantime, read those Bibles! Just choose one of the Gospels—Matthew, Mark, Luke, or John—and read it through this week. Those are the Jesus stories. Come back next Friday with more thoughts and questions about Jesus, the Bread of Life." She looked around the circle. Could she squeeze out five more minutes? "Before we leave, *mis hermanas*, let's pray for each other . . ."

❋

Edesa sat Gracie on the counter between the kitchen and dining room on the lower level and handed Estelle a sippy cup. "Can you spare a little milk, Estelle?"

"For you? No. For Miss Sugar here? Anything." Estelle chuckled as she got out a jug of two percent and filled the sippy cup. "Here . . . you two stayin' for lunch?"

Edesa shook her head. "No. Just waiting for Miss Gabby. She's giving me and Precious and the babies a ride back to the House of Hope. Her boys are helping Josh paint the back porches and she wants to check in. And *I* want to be sure Gracie gets a good nap today. Going food shopping with your cooking class was fun, but . . . you-know-who kind of fell apart later."

"Who? Miss *Gato*?" Estelle winked.

"Ha-ha. Very funny. Though . . ." Edesa frowned. "Kathryn did act kind of funny before she left the store yesterday. I don't know, Estelle, what do you think? She wants us to teach some kind of nutrition class together. I think she means well, wants people to 'eat right' both for their own health and for 'the environment,' whatever that means. I thought going along on the shopping trip with some of the ladies here would be an eye-opener. But she seemed . . . how do you say? *Perturbado*."

"Uh-huh. Rattled. Uncomfortable." Estelle yelled a few instructions at her kitchen helpers chopping vegetables for a lentil stew, then turned back. "Here's what I think. I think that young lady's got a heart in there somewhere, just hasn't got connected to her brain yet, and it's her brain that's in overdrive. She's concerned about people eating healthy. She wants to talk at 'em. Or dive into some Dumpster and hand out some food now and then . . . when what she *really* wants—needs—to do is feed the hungry. Even if she don't know it yet."

Chapter 8

The apartment seemed awfully quiet when Kat let herself in after her Friday afternoon shift at The Common Cup. "Hellooo?" No answer. Where was everybody? Brygitta was doing the evening shift at the coffee shop, but Kat had been hoping *somebody* would want to go to a movie or out for pizza or something. TGIF and all that.

But she'd been gone since eight thirty that morning, hadn't really had a chance to talk plans with anyone before heading over to Bethune Elementary for her morning stint at STEP, and after that it'd been straight to the coffee shop.

Kat dumped her backpack and wandered toward the kitchen. It was her turn to cook supper, but how was she supposed to know how many to cook for? She headed for the refrigerator to check what was on hand—which was when she saw the note taped to the door.

Kat, gone clothes shopping for Conny with Mom, then meeting Peter for supper. See you later!—R

So much for Rochelle and Conny. A smile tipped her mouth.

That left her and Nick. Good. He got off work at five, same as she did. Probably just wasn't home yet. They could use doing something fun and mindless together. The past two days had been rather weird and, frankly, she wanted to get her relationship with Nick back on track. They just needed some time, that was all.

She pulled open the refrigerator door and studied the contents. Not much. They needed to grocery shop tomorrow. Should she cook? Or wait to see if Nick wanted to try one of the ethnic cafés dotting the Rogers Park neighborhood? That'd be fun. She shut the door. Maybe she'd have time to do some research online while she waited for Nick.

Kat got her laptop from the bedroom and settled down on the couch, waiting for it to boot up. Her conversation with Nick last night had been niggling at the back of her brain all day. Seemed like he'd pooh-poohed her concern about Rochelle's HIV and needing to take precautions. What was *that* about? But she better do her research before bringing it up again.

She found a website with "Guidelines for Household Contacts of People Living with AIDS." Well, Rochelle didn't have AIDS, she'd only been infected with the immune-deficiency virus by that scum husband of hers. But they still had to be careful.

Kat skimmed the article. *Hmm.* So Nick was right. The only body fluids posing a risk were blood, semen, vaginal fluids, and breast milk. Not tears, sweat, saliva . . .

She tapped the Print key, sending the document to the inkjet printer in the study Nick was using as a bedroom. Okay, so HIV wasn't spread by casual contact or even kissing. At home, the article said, normal precautions included hand washing before and after preparing food or using the bathroom—*duh, people ought to do that anyway*—not sharing personal items like toothbrushes or razors, and, of course, using disposable gloves to treat a wound if the infected person got a cut or had an open sore.

Well, whatever. They should talk about this openly with Rochelle anyway. Be matter-of-fact about it so she wouldn't be offended if they reminded her to wash her hands before fixing food, stuff like that.

Still. Nick had been awfully quick to defend kissing when she'd brought it up. Maybe he'd enjoyed that kiss from Rochelle more than he was letting on. Not that it was any of her business. Why should she care? Except . . . she did. He was her best buddy, wasn't he? After Bree, anyway. Friends cared about friends—and he'd made a big deal that the kiss from Rochelle didn't mean anything more than a thank-you from a grateful single mom.

Really?

Humph. Where was he, anyway? Kat glanced at her watch. Almost six! It didn't take him *that* long to walk home from Software Symphony. He hadn't left a note, or called, or anything. Unless . . .

Retrieving her backpack, Kat dug out her cell phone and checked her messages. Oops. Nick *did* leave a message while she was at work. She punched Voicemail on her options and listened.

"Hi, Kat! Hey, I won't be home for supper—the guys here in the mail room asked me to hang out with them tonight. We're going to get some pizza, then catch a movie. Thought it'd be a good chance to get to know them. Hope you get this before you prepare your usual banquet. Take care."

Kat tossed the phone so hard it skittered across the floor and landed under the dining room table in the nook. Nothing was turning out like it was supposed to!

❊

Rochelle and Conny got home around eight, but Kat just poked her head out of her bedroom long enough to say hi and went back to writing in her journal. The journal was a mix of random thoughts and even prayers. She wasn't very consistent writing in it—mostly when she was upset or frustrated or confused. Anyone reading it would think she was always in a funk, since she didn't usually bother to write when life was clicking along happily.

Well, no one was going to read it. She'd burn it first.

Kat was in bed with the light off when Bree got home, and she never did hear Nick. How late had he stayed out anyway? She saw no sign of him when she got up the next morning either, eating a quick breakfast of granola and yogurt before heading out the door for her morning shift at the coffee shop, which started at seven.

The early morning walk did her good. So had writing out her thoughts and feelings last night about everything that had happened the past few days—including the weird fake shopping trip with Estelle Bentley and her cooking class. Somehow it had helped clear the cobwebs from her head and given her some perspective. She'd go ahead and talk with Edesa on Sunday, as she'd suggested, and see if they shared a similar vision for educating poor families about healthy eating habits. Then she'd ask for a house meeting to talk about sensible precautions living together with HIV, maybe print out the guidelines from that Web site she'd found. And she should take Nick's assurances at face value—why wouldn't she? He'd always been a straight-up guy. As for last night, he had every right to hang out with the guys, especially when they hadn't made any plans ahead of time.

As for Rochelle, there were bound to be some bumps along the way as they adjusted to living together. To be honest, it was Kat's first experience having a "woman of color" for a friend, much less sharing an apartment. There had to be some cultural differences. Maybe it was weird for Rochelle too.

Besides, reading a previous entry in her journal had reminded her that God had used *her* to find Rochelle, get her off the street, and reunited with her parents. That counted for something, didn't it? She couldn't back out now. She needed to give things time. Time and trust.

"Good morning!" Kat called out as a coworker let her in the door of the coffee shop at ten to seven. "Whoa! That coffee smells sooo good. Need a guinea pig to test the first batch before we open up? I'm your girl!"

The coffee guy grinned and filled a fat mug with the House Blend. Stashing her backpack and tying the short apron around her waist, Kat made a mental note to call Bree when she got a chance, offer to do some grocery shopping on her way home, and ask if anyone had something to add to the list.

*

"Spare a dollar, lady?" The panhandler seemed to appear out of nowhere as Kat walked up Clark toward Howard Street after her morning shift.

"Uh, sure." Kat dug into one of the pockets of her backpack and pulled out her little zippered money purse. A dollar wouldn't buy much. She handed the man a five. That would buy him a meal.

"Thanks, lady. 'Preciate it." The rather scruffy man with at least two days of unshaven whiskers took off ahead of her, no doubt heading for the same destination—the large Dominick's grocery store in the shopping center with SouledOut Community Church. She almost called out to tell him to come back and she'd buy him some fruit or vegetables at the Rogers Park Fruit Market she'd just passed. But too late.

Turning into the parking lot of the shopping center, Kat slowed. She'd never checked out the Dumpster situation at this particular Dominick's—which made no sense, since it was only fifty yards or so from the large storefront that housed the church. Well, now was as good a time as any.

Walking the long way around to the back of the store, Kat passed the busy loading dock, which was receiving deliveries from a Pepsi truck and another from Lay's Potato Chips. Passing the last truck, she looked in vain for Dumpsters. Maybe she was on the wrong side of the building . . . but no. There they were. Not Dumpsters, but those evil compactors! Arrrgh! Just like that other store on Sheridan.

Stalking back to the parking lot, Kat briefly debated not giving the store her business—but frankly, she didn't know where else to go. She could go back to the fruit market on Clark, but it didn't have everything they needed.

Except, maybe the fruit market had Dumpsters! She'd check it out on her way home. And maybe she'd scout out the little mom-and-pop grocery stores in the area. She was sure they wouldn't have those new-fangled compactors.

But for now she had no choice but to go ahead and do some of their shopping here. First thing she'd do was buy one of those collapsible wheeled shopping carts—Bree had said it was fine by her to take it out of their food budget. Good thing, 'cause there was no way she could lug home more than a couple of bags by herself, even if she carried some of the groceries in her backpack.

Just as she got to the revolving door at the front of the store, the panhandler she'd met earlier came out, a pack of cigarettes in one hand and a can of Coke and a candy bar in the other. "Hey!" she said. But the man took one furtive look at her and hustled away. The nerve! Kat had half a mind to yell at him for wasting her money.

Okay, so she was stupid to give the man money. From now on she'd stock up on some granola bars and carry them in her backpack. Next time a panhandler wanted money, he was going to get something to eat instead.

Chapter 9

The knocking drummed into Nick's sleep-drugged consciousness like a woodpecker using his head for a tree. And then . . . "Nick? Hey, Nick. You awake?" Untangling himself from the sheet, he rolled over and squinted at the digital alarm clock: 10:22 . . .

10:22?! Man, he hadn't slept in that long since moving into the apartment with the girls. He tried to find his voice. "Yeah?"

Brygitta opened the door of the study and stuck her head in. "Sorry to bother you. But Mrs. D stopped by a few minutes ago, wants you to call her. Thought you'd want to know."

Oh, great. Now Mrs. Douglass was going to think he was a lazy slob. "Uh, did she say what for?"

Bree shrugged. "Nope . . . Oh, and Kat called awhile ago, wants to know if it's okay to use our food money to buy a shopping cart—one of those collapsible things. She's going to pick up groceries after her shift. I already told her I think it's a good idea. All three of us can't always go together to lug stuff back."

Nick swung his feet off the futon and rubbed a hand over

his short hair. "Sure. Whatever." Then he cocked his head. "Hey, how come the apartment's so quiet? Conny's usually the first one I hear in the morning. And not after ten either."

Bree laughed. "You must've been really dead to the world then, because *I* heard him. About seven thirty, I think. Not too bad. But when I got up at eight, Rochelle had left a note saying they'd gone to the park." The pixie-haired brunette started to leave, then ducked her head back in. "She's really trying to fit in, you know."

True enough. Still, Nick didn't like Rochelle thinking she had to take her kid to the park on the weekend just so the rest of them could sleep in . . . though he had to admit, after getting in after midnight last night, sleeping in felt mighty good.

But he'd better get moving and see what Mrs. D wanted.

Nick trudged out of the study and down the hall to the bathroom . . . then back again to fold up the futon and get dressed in jeans and a T-shirt. But as he straightened the little room, he noticed several pages sticking out of the ink-jet printer. *What's this?*

He lifted out the sheets—about three of them. "Hmm," he murmured, reading the heading. "Guidelines for Household Contacts of People Living with AIDS." Where'd this come from?

Stupid question. *Kat.* She'd been all worried about it the other night.

He stood there skimming through the article. Well, he hoped she'd read it. Should put a lot of her worries to rest. But what was Kat planning to do with this? They shouldn't make Rochelle feel the same way as when she'd applied for that nanny job: *"People treat you like a leper . . ."*

Folding up the pages, he stuck them in the back pocket of

his jeans. Hopefully he could talk to Kat before she unloaded her anxiety on Rochelle. Now, where was his cell phone? He'd forgotten to plug it in when he came in last night . . . Oh, right. Still in the pocket of the cargo pants he'd worn yesterday. On his way to the kitchen, he called Avis Douglass. "Hi, Mrs.—uh, Sister Avis. It's Nick Taylor. You wanted to see me?"

"Oh, hello, Nick. Pastor Cobbs would like us to help plan the worship service for tomorrow. Do you have some time this morning?"

"Sure. I can come now if you'd like."

Grabbing the last banana from the fruit bowl—a rather overripe one—he took the stairs to the third floor two at a time. This would be the first time he stood in front of the SouledOut congregation—or any congregation, for that matter—as a pastoral intern. He felt like letting out a loud *Wahoo!* But at the Douglasses' door he turned around and ran back to the apartment to get his Bible and the folder Pastor Cobbs had given him the other night. Better show up with more than just a banana!

❈

Avis Douglass closed her Bible and notebook and smiled at Nick. "That should do it. I like your suggestions." She got up from the table and brought back the coffeepot. "Warm up your coffee?"

"Sure." Nick held out his mug. "I can hardly believe this is happening. Have to admit I'm nervous."

"Don't be. It's not about you, anyway." She gave him a teasing smile. "If it makes you feel any better, I'm always nervous too when I'm scheduled to lead worship. I have to remind myself that the whole point of *worship* is focusing on God—who

He is, what He's done. Once I put my focus on the right person, I forget about myself."

Nick couldn't imagine this woman being nervous. She always seemed so composed, so completely at home in front of the church. Even today, dressed casually in white capris, sandals, and a bright-yellow summer blouse, her hair done in those stylish "twists" unique to black women's hair, Avis Douglass personified calm and poise.

"Thanks, that helps," he admitted. "But you'll need to remind me again when I actually have to get up there and preach." He laughed self-consciously. "At least that's a few weeks away."

"And you have permission to remind *me*. I'm supposed to preach next Sunday—my first time as an interim pastor." She rolled her eyes. "I don't think of myself as a preacher, but I can get excited about teaching the Word. It's communion Sunday too—and isn't that when you're becoming a member? Oh, I think I hear Conny."

They both heard stomping feet and a childish voice coming up the stairwell and then fading into the apartment below.

Nick grinned. "Yeah. Rochelle took him out to the park so the rest of us could sleep in. Except Kat. She had to leave early to work at the coffee shop." *Kat . . . and Rochelle.* Nick remembered the papers he'd stuck in his rear pocket. Rochelle was Mrs. Douglass's daughter. Surely she and Mr. D had had to deal with the subject of precautions before. Maybe she'd have some wisdom about how to approach—

"How's that going, Nick?" Mrs. Douglass lifted an eyebrow at him. "I've been trying to stay out of it, but I know it can't be easy adding a six-year-old to your living space—even a six-year-old as charming as my grandson."

Can't believe it! She asked. A perfect segue. "Going great for the most part. Conny's a great kid—and I really admire Rochelle. She's a good mom. But . . ." Nick leaned forward. "There's something I'd like to ask. It's kind of awkward, but maybe you can give us some advice. It's about, uh, about Rochelle's HIV status."

There. It was on the table. He'd try to leave Kat out of it, though. "We don't know very much about HIV, and I'm wondering how to talk about it—how it affects her, but also what kind of precautions we should take. I"—he reached for the article in his hip pocket—"uh, this article came off the web. Seems like pretty commonsense stuff. But I'm not sure how to bring it up. I don't want to embarrass Rochelle."

Avis Douglass wagged her head. "Nick, I am so sorry. We—Rochelle and I—should have brought this up when you three were making the decision to invite her and Conny to share the apartment. I was just so overwhelmed with finding my daughter and grandson again, I didn't even think about it."

"No problem, it's really okay. I just—"

She held up her hand. "Rochelle should bring it up. She needs to take responsibility for letting the rest of you know what commonsense precautions to take. I'll speak to her about it. The sooner the better."

"Wow. That's great." Nick felt enormously relieved. "It'd be much better coming from Rochelle than for us to bring it up. Thanks a lot."

"Can I see the article? Maybe I could give it to her—wouldn't have to tell her it came from you. That would give her something to use."

Nick hesitated. What would Kat think about him going behind her back like this, giving away the article she'd found . . .

but Mrs. D's idea made all kinds of sense. "Sure." He handed over the article. He'd just print out another copy for Kat. And find a way to hold her off before *she* brought the whole thing up.

But lately, he thought glumly, heading back downstairs a few minutes later, all his conversations with Kat were like putting out brush fires. When was he going to get a chance to talk with her about how he felt about her?

The girl confused him. That wild hair of hers seemed like an extension of her personality and her spirit—beautiful, exciting, but not very tame. Soft to the touch, but frenzied.

Nick hesitated on the second-floor landing before entering their apartment. How, exactly, *did* he feel about Kat Davies?

Chapter 10

K at heard childish laughter and squeals coming from the apartment even before she finished bumping the new cart full of groceries up the carpeted stairwell to the second floor. Whew. Somebody was home.

"I come bearing gifts!" she announced, pulling the cart inside. "Who's going to help me put these groceries away?"

"I will! I will!" Conny leaped up from the living room floor, where it looked as if he and Nick had been wrestling.

She eyed Nick. "And . . . ?"

He hefted himself to his feet and grinned. "At your service, ma'am." Then he murmured, "You saved my skin, Kitty Kat. I'd just been attacked by a talking alligator who was determined to eat me."

Kat pinched his arm. "I dunno. Feels pretty tough to me. He'd probably spit you out." She smiled inside. This was her Nick, teasing, easy . . .

Taking the cart from her, he wheeled it into the kitchen. "This was a good idea, getting a cart. But what's all this stuff on top? You go Dumpster diving up at that *designer* Dominick's?"

Conny was busy grabbing things from the cart and piling them on the kitchen table. "Yuk. What's this?" He held up a purple eggplant with brown spots. "Did you buy any Lucky Charms?"

"No-o, I didn't get any Lucky Charms, Mr. Sweet Tooth, and no, I didn't go Dumpster diving at Designer Dominick's. They've got those new-fangled compactors designed to keep out all comers. *Arrgh*. Makes me so mad. But . . . ta-da!" Kat held up two yellow-red mangoes. "I *did* get a whole bunch of stuff behind the fruit market on Clark. We better eat these today 'cause they won't last. But I'm going to take all this other stuff to church tomorrow and give it to Edesa Baxter for Manna House—or for that House of Hope where she lives."

Nick lifted out a sad-looking cabbage and several heads of discolored broccoli and stacked them on the table. "And our regular groceries are—?"

"At the bottom. In the paper bags, ninny."

Conny stuck out his lip. "Did you buy somethin' for *me*?"

"Sure. Got some yummy granola bars in here somewhere." Kat dug around in the first paper bag Nick lifted out. "You can have one if your mommy says it's okay." She looked at him quizzically. "Where is your mommy, by the way?"

"She an' Miss Breezy ina basement, doin' laundry. Can't I have one now? Mister Nick! Can I? Please?"

Kat found the box of granola bars and absently handed it to Nick. If Rochelle and Bree were both here, maybe they should talk about those precautions she'd printed out. Except . . . where had she put them? Wait. She'd never picked them up from the printer in the study. Slipping out of the kitchen, she headed for Nick's study-bedroom.

The glass-paneled double doors with the gauzy curtains on the inside—giving some modicum of privacy when the doors were closed—stood open. The printer was on the desk . . . but no papers in the tray. She glanced at the various stacks of books and papers on the desk. Nick's stuff. No article on precautions—

"Looking for this?"

Kat whirled. Nick leaned against the doorway, waving a set of papers. She snatched them and read the title. "This is mine. What are you doing with it?"

"Hey, calm down. It was sitting in the printer, which is in my bedroom, by the way. I picked it up to see what it was and read it. Good stuff."

"Well . . . okay. I thought we could use it to talk to Rochelle—"

Sudden voices in the kitchen alerted them that the laundry duo had come up the back stairs.

"—like *now*, when we're all together. With our crazy schedules, it's not very often we're all here at the same time."

Nick shook his head. "Not now. I want to—"

"Want to what? What's up with you, Nick! We need to do this!"

He put a finger to his lips. "Quiet, will you? I just want to tell you something Mrs. D said this morning about this."

Kat felt her back stiffen. "You told *Mrs. D* what I said?"

"No, no, I didn't! If you'll give me half a chance—"

"Hey, you two!" Brygitta's voice calling from the kitchen door broke into their whispered scuffle. "Can you come in here? We've got a favor to ask."

"Okay! In a minute," Kat called back. She shook the pages at Nick, again lowering her voice. "This would be a good time,

Nick Taylor. We can't keep putting it off, even if you're right that the whole, uh . . ." She stopped, suddenly embarrassed to say "kissing thing" or "saliva thing." She rolled her eyes. "You know, even if what I said isn't an issue."

"I agree! And it's gonna happen. Just don't bring it up right now. I'll explain why—"

"Guys! We need you!" Bree appeared at the study door. "Rochelle's mom is coming down in two minutes to take her shopping for some decent job interview clothes, and it'd be a lot easier on them if we can keep Conny. But I've got evening shift at the coffeehouse, and it's already three thirty. Gotta leave in an hour. Can one of you—?"

"Sure," Nick spoke up. "Kat and I'll take him to the beach. Right, Kat?"

Kat opened her mouth to protest. Where did Nick get off volunteering her like that? But something in his eyes stopped her. He was pleading. "Uh . . . sure. No problem. As soon as we finish putting the groceries away."

❀

Kat had to admit taking Conny to the beach was fun. It felt good to have Nick all to herself for a change—well, "all to herself" as could be with Conny yelling, "Watch me swim, Mister Nick!" and "Lookit the pretty stone I found!"

"He sure has got a thing for you, *Mister Nick*," she teased.

"Huh. You think?"

They'd finally spread out their towels after splashing in the shallow water with Conny, who was now busily digging in the wet sand with a plastic bucket and shovel Grammy Avis had bought him. Kat had worn her bathing suit under a pair of shorts and tank top, but that water was *cold*. "Like the Pacific Ocean," Nick said when they came out, teeth chattering just from wading in up to their knees.

Now, parked on the beach towels they'd borrowed from the Candys' towel cupboard, he said, "We used to go to Cannon Beach when I was a kid—you've probably seen pictures of it. Big rock formations sticking up out of the water like monolithic shark fins. There's one called Haystack Rock that's a couple stories high. But the sandy beach is one of the prettiest stretches along the Oregon coast. We'd jump the waves as kids and think nothing of staying in the water for an hour. But last summer when I went back there with my family? The water was so cold it turned all my fingers and toes blue! Don't know how I did it when I was younger."

Kat grinned. She liked hearing about Nick's previous life in Oregon. "So while you froze in the Pacific Ocean, I chased lizards in the Arizona desert. Talk about different childhoods." Not the only difference either. Nick had grown up in a Christian home and came to Crista University wanting to be a pastor. She'd grown up in a home that didn't need God, and the only time she heard the name of Jesus—except for the occasional pilgrimage to the Episcopal church at Easter and Christmas—was when her schoolmates needed a convenient expletive.

Finding Jesus—and Nick and Bree—at the Midwest Music Fest a few years back had changed everything.

For several minutes they watched Conny running back and forth to the water's edge, scooping wet sand into his bucket as seagulls swooped overhead. A bank of billowy clouds was building up south of the city. "So," she said abruptly, "why didn't you want me to bring up the need to talk about precautions back there? Besides the fact that Rochelle had a date with her mom to go shopping, which we didn't know about till last minute."

Hugging her knees, Kat listened as he told her about his meeting with Mrs. D that morning, how she'd asked how things were going with Rochelle and Conny, and he'd blurted out their concern about needing to talk about precautions.

"*Our* concern?" Kat was going to kill him if he'd even hinted to Mrs. D that she'd gotten all bent out of shape over that stupid kissing thing.

"Yes, *our* concern, Kat. I agree with you that it's important. I just wanted us to get our facts straight before we did anything. And she agreed it's important too. Said they should have done it when we first talked about her sharing the apartment with us. But here's the thing—she said Rochelle should be the one to bring it up, not us. And she promised to talk to her about it. Maybe she'll do it while they're together this afternoon."

"Because . . ."

"Think about it, Kat! If Rochelle brings it up, then she's owning it, it's her initiative. If we bring it up, it's like we don't trust her or something. Makes sense to me."

Kat chewed on her lip. He had a point. It was just . . . it seemed like Nick was always defending Rochelle, bending over backward to protect her feelings.

What about my feelings? I was his friend first.

A low rumble of thunder in the distance made them look up. The thunderheads had turned gray and menacing, even though the sky to the north was still blue. Jumping up, she called out, "Conny! We gotta go. Thunderstorm's coming!" Nick rolled up their towels while she gathered up Conny and his sand toys, and they ran across the grassy park heading for the tree-shaded side streets.

Conny hung on to both their hands and yelled, "One, two, three . . . wheeee!" every few yards, picking up both feet so he'd be carried along like a monkey swinging from a tree.

"Okay. I'll wait," Kat said, huffing from the exertion.

"Wait?—oh, you mean wait for Rochelle to bring it up. Thanks, Kat . . . Uh-oh! Here it comes. C'mon, Conny, we gotta run for it!"

They still had half a block to go when the rain began to fall in huge *splats* on the sidewalk. Laughing, they ran up the steps into the foyer, already soaking wet. "Just as well the rain chased us in," Nick wheezed when they finally made it into the apartment. "I'm on supper tonight. Better get started."

The apartment was silent. "Guess they're not back yet," Kat said. "Okay, little buddy, how about if I run a tub of water and you can play like it's still the beach. Gotta get that sand off of you anyway."

But when the tub was full, Conny wouldn't let her undress him. "Want my *privacy*!" he yelled and slammed the bathroom door.

Okaay. Kat wandered into the kitchen. "Sir Conny wants his *privacy.*" She rolled her eyes. "So might as well put me to work. Just go check on him now and then, okay?"

"Okay." Nick handed her a knife. "Peel those mangoes you brought home. I'm making a mango-chicken salad. Sound good?" He grinned at her, his gray eyes soft. "Besides, there's something else I wanted to tell you. Here . . ." He shoved a sheet of paper at her. "That's the covenant people make when they become members at SouledOut Community . . . and, uh, I'm going to become a member next week." He shrugged. "You know, especially because I'm doing my internship there. Might as well jump in all the way."

Kat pulled the sheet toward her, reading the title: "Membership Covenant of SouledOut Community Church."

"And, uh, I was kinda wondering if you and Bree wanted to become members too. At the same time, I mean."

She looked up at him. "Become a member?" She hadn't really thought about it. Actually, she'd assumed that if you went to a church all the time and got involved, you were a member. But it felt good that Nick wanted her to. And Bree too, of course. The Three Musketeers, all for one and one for all, and all that. "Well, sure. I mean, why not? As far as I'm concerned, SouledOut's my church. Might as well be a member."

Nick grinned. "Great. Go ahead, read over the membership covenant, and if you can affirm those things, then . . . guess we could tell Pastor Cobbs tomorrow. But"—he pointed at the mangoes—"chop up those first, 'cause I need 'em for the salad. And don't get any mango juice on the paper."

Loud splashing noises radiated from the direction of the bathroom. "Uh-oh," he said, "I better check on Conny."

As Nick disappeared, Kat peeled the juicy mangoes, only slightly overripe. She popped a tidbit in her month. *Mm.* Still good. As she chopped, her eyes strayed to the piece of paper. "*. . . and having been baptized as an expression of my faith, I gladly join in covenant with—*"

She stopped chopping. *You had to be baptized?*

Chapter 11

Edesa stood on the sidewalk in front of the House of Hope, holding a squirming Gracie in her arms as Josh carefully positioned the toddler car seat into Gabby Fairbanks's secondhand Subaru. "Are you sure, *mi amiga*?" she murmured. "We can always take the El. You don't have to drive us around everywhere."

"Goose." Gabby tossed her head, the early morning sunlight turning her red-gold curls into a headful of fire. "It's no problem. The boys are with their dad and will be coming to church with him, so why not? Plenty of room. But"—she rubbed her bare arms—"think I'll run back in and get a sweater. Kind of cool for late June, don't you think?"

It was cool that morning, barely sixty degrees, though Edesa knew hotter days lay ahead. But her mind wasn't on the weather. All weekend she'd been praying and trying to think how best to come alongside Kathryn Davies as an "older sister in the Lord," even though there was only a few years' difference in their ages. She'd done some research on various food pantries in the Chicago area, hoping she could suggest one close enough where Kat could volunteer. But would she even be willing to talk after church?

"Okay, sweetheart, in you go." Josh took Gracie from Edesa's arms and buckled her into the car seat.

"Hey!" called a shrill voice. "Wait for us!" Edesa turned to see Precious McGill hustling down the front steps of the six-flat with her grandson, Timmy, in her arms. She was dressed in a sleeveless yellow dress, heels with a backstrap, and a yellow hat with a wide brim—a stunning contrast to her dark-brown skin. "It's just Timmy an' me. Sabrina layin' up in the bed, got her monthly. You got enough room?"

"Uh, I don't know, Precious. We're hitching a ride with Gabby. Her boys are gone, so I guess there'd be room for one more in the backseat, but—"

"No problem! I can hold the baby on my lap, ain't that right, Lil' Turkey?" The thirty-something grandmother nuzzled the little boy in her arms.

"Hold who in whose arms?" Gabby showed up, wearing a lightweight white sweater over her shoulders. "We've got more passengers for church?"

Precious beamed. "Thought we'd catch a ride." She'd recently traded in her all-over-the-head tiny braids for a short, straightened 'do that looked like a little cap, now lost under the big yellow hat. Edesa thought the new hairdo was cute, but hard to get used to after the succession of braids and twists Precious usually wore.

Gabby shook her head. "I'm sorry, Precious. It's not safe for Timmy to ride on your lap. He needs to be in a car seat."

"Well, I got one of them. But . . . oh, forget it. Guess you don't got room for two."

Edesa felt helpless. Maybe she and Josh and Gracie ought to take the El after all.

"Look, it's fine. I'll just call Philip and ask him to swing by and pick me up. You guys take the car." Gabby dug in her purse, pulled out her cell phone and car keys, and handed the keys to Josh. "Precious, go get Timmy's car seat." She flipped open her phone and punched a few keys. "Go on, go on. I'll be fine . . . Philip? It's Gabby . . ." She turned away as she spoke into the phone.

Josh stood on the sidewalk, shaking his head and holding the keys like a hot potato. "This is ridiculous," he muttered. "We need to get a car, Edesa. It's like this every Sunday morning, like Russian roulette. Who goes? Who gets left? I know we said we don't need a car for just the three of us, but—"

Edesa heaved a sigh. "*Sí*. It's time."

❁

People were still going in the double glass doors of SouledOut Community Church as Josh swung the red Subaru SUV into a parking space. At first glance, the church didn't look much different than the other stores anchoring the Howard Street shopping center, but soon the lively praise band and singing would differentiate it from the open-for-business neighboring shops.

Once inside, Edesa, Josh, Precious, and the two little ones quickly found seats, as it looked as if the service was about to start. A quick glance around the large room found Kathryn and Brygitta sitting in their usual places near the back. Edesa caught Kat's eye and gave her a smile and wave, and to her relief the young woman smiled back. *Bueno*. She wasn't still pouting about the shopping trip.

"Good morning, church!" Hearing Avis Douglass giving the welcome and call to worship, Edesa turned her attention to the front. Nick Taylor was standing beside Avis—he must be leading worship with her today. Edesa smiled to herself. Did the young seminarian realize how fortunate he was to be doing his pastoral internship alongside a woman of the Word like Avis? *Bless young Nick, Jesús,* she prayed in her spirit. *Train him up to be a mighty man of the Word too.*

As Avis stepped aside, Nick announced the morning's Scripture reading from John 17. "Jesus is praying for His disciples," he said. "Not only for the Twelve, but for everyone who would become one of His disciples down through the ages until today. So this prayer is also for you and for me . . ."

Nick began to read, but Edesa was distracted by a glimpse of Philip Fairbanks's blue Nissan pulling into the parking lot—the secondhand car he'd bought after getting rid of his fancy Lexus, one of many efforts Gabby's estranged husband had made to help him pay back his gambling debts.

She poked Josh and nodded in that direction. "We definitely need to get a car," she whispered. "We made them late."

She saw him cut his eyes at Precious sitting a few seats down the row in her bright-yellow hat. Well, all right, it was Precious wanting a ride at the last minute who'd made the Fairbanks late, but it was the same thing. The House of Hope needed more than one car among the various families who lived there!

"'. . . Father, protect them by the power of your name," Nick was reading at the mike, "'the name you gave me, so that they may be one as we are one . . .'"

Edesa turned quickly in her Spanish Bible so she could read along. The verse he'd just read was already underlined: ". . . *para que sean uno como nosotros somos uno."* She sighed. *That they may be one . . .* That was one prayer she hoped *Jesús* was still praying for His church. Christians had done a poor job over the years "being one," fighting and dividing over everything from modes of baptism to worship styles to racial issues to which Bible translation to use.

After the Scripture reading, the praise team filled the room with lusty singing—even that overused favorite "They'll Know We Are Christians by Our Love." Edesa shook her head. *So easy to sing, so hard to do. Help us, Senór!*

When it was time for the children to go to their Sunday school classes, Edesa took Gracie and Timmy McGill to the nursery. When she returned, Pastor Cobbs was already preaching on Jesus' prayer for unity, reminding the congregation that even SouledOut Community Church needed to be vigilant and not let the evil one use the current transition after the death of Pastor Clark as an occasion to spark division in the church. "We may have differing opinions about how to move forward," he said, mopping his glistening forehead with a large handkerchief, "but let's remember that Scripture says love covers a multitude of sins." Half the congregation laughed, and Pastor Cobbs chuckled. "At least some of you got my joke. But kidding aside, our differing opinions *can* become sins if we let them cause quarrels and create divisions among us."

Edesa shot a questioning look at her husband, wondering if Pastor Cobbs was referring to something specific. Josh seemed to catch her drift, but shrugged as if to say he didn't know.

The service ended with a prayer of benediction by Avis, followed by announcements facilitated by Nick—at which time Pastor Cobbs again bounded onto the low platform urging the congregation to give a special handclap for the new interim pastoral team. "You'll be hearing from both our sister and our brother in the pulpit this next month, so cancel all your vacation plans and be here to give them your support." More laughter and a hearty round of applause greeted his announcement— though Edesa suspected Avis was wishing the floor would open and swallow her about then.

As the congregation began to mingle and head for the coffee table, Edesa caught her husband. "Josh, could you pick up Gracie from the nursery and keep her for ten minutes or so? I need to talk to Kathryn Davies."

Josh frowned. "I guess, though I need to catch Justin Barnes and talk to him about what's happening at youth group tonight. But . . . never mind. I'll figure out something." He turned to go.

"Ask Precious then!" she called after him. Typical Josh *"Don't want to but I'll do it anyway"* Baxter. She had no doubt he'd "figure out something," but she felt a little guilty since they both had people they wanted to talk to.

She found Kathryn pouring iced tea at the coffee table. *"Hola, Kat.* I'll take one of those." She smiled her thanks. "Uh, do you need to stay here, or could we find a quiet corner to talk?"

"No, no, I was just keeping busy. I don't have to stay— Oh! I brought something for you." Kat disappeared through the swinging doors that led to the church kitchen, offices, and classrooms and reappeared carrying two plastic grocery bags, so full they were starting to split. "I brought you some vegetables from the fruit market down on Clark. For the House of Hope. There's even some cheese in there, though you might want to freeze it. It's past its sell date."

Edesa hesitated. *From the market or its Dumpster?* But she

took the bags. "Uhhh, sure. *Gracias* . . . or would you like to give them to Miss Estelle for Manna House?"

Kat flinched. "No, I'd rather you take them." The girl flushed under her slight tan. "To tell you the truth, Edesa, I don't think Estelle likes me."

"Oh, Kat! That's not true. Here . . . come sit down." Edesa set aside the bags and pulled two chairs together. "In fact, she said something really interesting when I talked to her on Friday."

Kat twirled a loose strand of dark-brown hair around a finger. "Like what?"

"Well, let me back up. Remember I told you that I teach a Bible study at Manna House on Friday mornings? When I got home from the shopping trip with Estelle's cooking class on Thursday, I still didn't know what I was going to teach. And then Josh made a joke, said I should teach on Jesus feeding the five thousand. 'Talk about making a little food stretch a long way,' he said, or something like that."

Kat chuckled.

"Anyway, I did just that! Because it showed how Jesus was concerned about people's physical needs as well as their spiritual needs. We ended up having a really lively discussion. Made me wish you could've been there."

"Sounds neat. Wish I could've too."

"Anyway, afterward I was talking to Estelle about the Bible study and about our shopping trip the previous day, and she said something really interesting. She said you have a really good heart"—no need to mention that Estelle said it wasn't connected to her brain—"and what you really want to do is feed people."

Kathryn seemed to flush again, adding a rosy glow to her striking blue eyes and dark hair. "She said that? Well, yeah, I'm concerned about people eating healthy food, but . . . what did she mean I want to feed people?"

Edesa leaned closer, elbows on her knees. "I think what she meant is, you've been Dumpster diving and talking about a nutrition class because you care about people and food. But it's hit and miss—especially the Dumpster diving. Even the nutrition class idea is talking *about* food, not providing food itself."

Kat looked puzzled.

"I think what Estelle meant is . . . she believes you have a heart to *feed* hungry people—like Jesus fed the five thousand."

Now Kat rolled her eyes. "Oh, please. I can't work miracles."

Edesa smiled. "Don't you see? Jesus saw the people were hungry—and He did something about it. I think Estelle was saying you would do better to shift your primary focus from *food* to *hungry people*. There are hungry people in this city, right here in the Rogers Park neighborhood. How do we feed them?"

Kat just stared at Edesa for a long moment. "I—I think I get what she means. But . . . how?"

Edesa leaned back in her chair. "Good question! But remember what Beverly said last Thursday, that what they need is access to more food pantries? Well, I did a little research and found a few food pantries here in Rogers Park." She dug out the list she'd made from her purse. "You might check these out, see if they could use another volunteer. It would be an experience of getting food to hungry people on a regular basis."

The girl took the list and studied it. Finally she nodded. "Thanks. I'll check these out." Then she gave Edesa a funny look. "Estelle really said that about me?"

Edesa laughed. "Yes, she did. You need to give that woman another chance. I think you two have more in common than you think. Well . . ." She started to get up. "I better rescue Josh, who's been riding herd on Gracie—"

"Wait." Kat held up a hand. "Uh, do you have another minute? I need to ask you a question."

"*Sí*, of course." Edesa sat.

Kat lowered her voice, as if not wanting anyone else to hear. "Why do you have to be baptized to become a member at SouledOut? I mean, does being baptized as a baby count?"

Edesa felt as if they'd just done a U-turn at high speed. She hadn't seen *this* coming. What was the girl really asking?

They talked awhile longer, and only later—after Josh interrupted to say his parents had invited them last-minute to come over for Sunday lunch . . . after catching Gabby in time to give her car keys back and switching Gracie's car seat to the Baxters' minivan . . . when she was relaxing in her in-laws' backyard as chicken sizzled on the grill—only then did Edesa remember that she'd left the two bags of Dumpster food sitting in the church.

She gulped. Hopefully they wouldn't smell too bad by the time someone found them and threw them out.

Chapter 12

Kat carried her whole wheat sandwich with avocado and alfalfa sprouts out onto the back porch of their apartment and sat cross-legged in a plastic lawn chair to eat her lunch. A warm breeze raked its fingers through her tousled hair. *Mmm. Nice.*

Brygitta joined her a few minutes later, tossing a bag of potato chips onto the small wrought-iron porch table. "Nice breeze out here," she said, pulling up another lawn chair. "Wish we had some of those pretty flower boxes, though." Brygitta pointed at the lush ivy vines in the boxes hanging from the back porch railings of the apartment building across the alley.

Kat took a bite of her sandwich. "Where'd you say Nick went?"

"To some hospital with Pastor Cobbs to visit the father of one of the members, don't remember who. Guess that's part of what he has to do for his internship. A little bit of everything."

"Oh." Kat wished Nick were here so she could bounce Edesa Baxter's food pantry idea off both of them. She hardly knew what to think. But for the moment, she was enjoying the peace and quiet. The Douglasses and Rochelle had driven Conny to the South Side so the little boy could spend the afternoon with his daddy—which, come to think of it, brought up another thing they should talk about. What in the world were they going to do if Rochelle *didn't* bring up the subject of HIV-related precautions? So far their new housemate hadn't said anything, even though Bree got home from her shift last night by nine thirty and they were all home.

"Did Nick say anything to you about becoming members at SouledOut?" Bree broke into her thoughts.

"What? Oh. Yeah, he did. Told me he's going to become a member next Sunday and asked if we—you and me—wanted to become members too."

"So what do you think?"

Kat shrugged. "Well, he showed me this paper with the membership commitment or covenant or whatever they call it, and it said something about being baptized."

"Yeah, that's usually . . . oh." Bree's eyes widened. "You've never been baptized? Not even as an infant?"

Kat snorted. "Well, if I was, I don't remember it." She laughed self-consciously.

"You should ask your folks. Maybe that counts."

"I wish. But even if I was, I'm not sure it meant anything. My parents didn't exactly raise me in the Christian faith." Kat made a face. "They only went to church when it was dictated by what their social circle or business associates did."

Brygitta's brown eyes were wide with concern. "But you *did* become a Christian at the Midwest Music Fest a few years ago. If they baptized you as an infant, maybe it was like a prophecy or a spiritual seal or something, even if your parents didn't know what they were doing."

Kat shrugged. "Maybe."

"Do you want to become a member at SouledOut?"

"Well, yeah. Sure. I think. I mean, it's the church I've chosen to be at, isn't it? What about you?"

Brygitta frowned. "I don't know. I hadn't really thought about it till Nick brought it up. I mean, I'm here for the summer, and I like it well enough. But then I'll be going back to CCU to finish my last semester and . . ." She bit a fingernail. "Don't know if I want to commute back and forth to church every weekend. Come to think of it, Nick has another semester too. Is he going to commute?"

Kat stopped in mid-chew. She hadn't really thought about what was going to happen in the fall. She knew in her head that both Bree and Nick had another semester to finish up their graduate work, but it hadn't really sunk in that both of them would be going back to CCU while she . . . what? "Uh, I guess he'll have to. He needs a six-month internship to get his M-Div." But would he live here and commute to school? Or live on campus and commute back to Rogers Park?

Did it matter?

Well, yeah.

Brygitta eyed Kat curiously. "What are you going to do this fall? We have to give up the apartment when the Candys come back."

Good question. What *was* she going to do this fall? Get a teaching job, hopefully. She'd sent in an application to the Chicago Public Schools. But she'd read somewhere that CPS might close some schools because of the economy. Which meant a whole lot of teachers out of work. Who was going to hire *her*?

Kat shook off the slight panic in her throat with a toss of her head. "Well, if I can't find a *real* job, can I take over your shifts at the coffee shop when you go back to school? I'd at least be working full-time then."

Brygitta laughed and reached for another handful of potato chips. "Be my guest. I can just hear your parents now . . . 'Our daughter? Oh, you mean Kathryn. Yes, yes, we sent our daughter to graduate school to become—ta-da—a *barista!*'"

Kat snatched the potato chip bag. "Hey. The world needs baristas too."

❊

Two thirty. Nick wasn't back yet. Brygitta had gotten a long-distance call from her parents or grandmother or somebody, or maybe the whole clan. Kat could hear a clamor of voices even though the phone wasn't on Speaker. Was that Polish they were speaking? Whatever. Bree was going to be awhile. Maybe she'd go for a run along the lake by herself. She had some thinking to do.

Scattered clouds dotted the sky, and the weather report said a twenty-percent chance of rain later that evening. But in mid-afternoon the temperature was a pleasant midseventies and the breeze coming off the lake held steady as Kat ran north on the jogging path. She felt a little silly running with her backpack, but she'd dumped out her usual stuff and stuck in the list of food pantries Edesa had given her, the membership papers Nick had left on the desk in the study, her Bible, her cell phone, and a bottle of water. She'd find a bench or somewhere she could watch the lake and try to sort out the jumbled thoughts in her head.

Half an hour later Kat parked herself under a tree and fished out the list of food pantries. One was at a community center, another at a church . . . Edesa had strongly suggested she volunteer at one of these food pantries. But didn't Edesa know she was volunteering five mornings a week at Mrs. Douglass's STEP program? She already had to juggle her shifts at the coffee shop to do that, which differed from day to day. So far, she'd been able to trade shifts with Brygitta when she got assigned to any mornings.

But she was curious about that Bible story Edesa mentioned, about Jesus feeding the five thousand. She kind of knew the story but hadn't read it recently. In fact, she hadn't been reading the Bible very much *period* since moving into the city that summer. Especially when she had to be at the elementary school every weekday morning at nine sharp. Just getting showered, dressed, fed, and out the door on time left no time for "devotions," as Bree called it. Kat supposed she could read the Bible just before bed but so far hadn't developed the habit.

So where was this story? She'd written down the reference somewhere . . . *Aha. Matthew 14:13.* Unscrewing the cap on her water bottle, she sipped half the bottle as she read the chapter once, then read it again. Anytime she'd heard anyone talk about this story, they'd focused on Jesus' miracle. Which, she had to admit, was something else. *Twelve baskets of leftovers?* All from five little loaves of bread and two fish? But this time what Jesus said *before* He did the miracle caught her eye. The disciples had wanted to send the people away—go someplace else—to get food, but Jesus said they didn't need to go away. *"You give them something to eat."*

Kat leaned back against the tree, watching the sunlight play on the tips of the gentle waves coming into shore. Was that what Estelle meant by what she'd said? The way Edesa told it, it was almost as if she'd said, "Kat, *you* give them something to eat."

Kat, you give them something to eat . . .

A strange feeling bubbled in the pit of her stomach. Snatching up the paper with the list of food pantries again—no, that was the membership thingy, couldn't deal with that now—oh, there it was. She grabbed her cell phone and punched in the number for the church one, the Rock of Ages Food Pantry somewhere in the area . . .

But all she got was a voice mail with several options. Duh, of course, it was Sunday afternoon. She listened impatiently through the list—Sunday morning service times, weekly Bible study, number for the church office, extensions for the pastor, youth pastor—and then: *"If you're calling about the food pantry, the pantry is open every Wednesday, four to eight p.m., and we're located at . . ."*

Scrambling to her feet, Kat stuffed things into the backpack and started off at a trot, back the way she had come. She would visit the food pantry this Wednesday if she could work things out at the coffee shop. But that Bible story made her curious about something else. Maybe Nick was home by now. If so, she needed to ask him something. He oughta know this Bible stuff.

❁

Nick was in the kitchen making himself a towering sandwich that threatened to topple over before he got the top slice of bread on.

Kat dropped her backpack on a chair. "Good grief, Nick. Didn't you get any lunch?" Bits of tuna fish, coleslaw, pickle, mayo, mustard, tomato, and cheese littered the kitchen table.

"Nuh-uh," he grunted, taking a big bite. Chewing and swallowing as if desperate, he tried to answer with his mouth still half full. "Couldn't believe how many people Pastor Cobbs knows in that hospital. We had to visit them all. I think the man only eats two meals a day. Somehow I missed that on the job description of being a pastor. Think it's too late to go into construction?"

Kat snickered. "Well, given that sandwich you just built, I'd say forget it." She plopped down in a chair at the table. "When you're done feeding your face, I need some help." She told him about reading the story of Jesus feeding the five thousand and what she was curious about.

He lifted an eyebrow. "You want to find *all* the passages in the Bible that talk about Jesus and food? You mean where the Bible talks about feeding the poor?"

"Well, yeah. But other stuff too. I'd just kind of like to know what the Bible says about food."

He took another huge bite and chewed thoughtfully. "Well, okay. The Bible has a lot to say about food—but not sure you want to go into all the Old Testament regulations. Some Jewish people keep kosher, but most Christians don't feel those rules apply anymore. The Bible also uses food metaphorically—you want some of those passages too?"

"Sure." Then she made a face. "To be honest, I've been kind of lax about studying the Bible. I'd like to, you know, dig in a little."

Nick finished his sandwich, swept the table crumbs into the trash, and stuck the mayo and mustard back in the fridge.

"Come on. I've got an online concordance. We can get you started now if you'd like."

"Where's Bree?"

"Dunno. Apartment was quiet when I got home."

Kat peeked into their bedroom. Brygitta was sacked out on the bed, the fan in the window drowning out any noise from the rest of the apartment. "Out cold," she told Nick. "Family phone call must've worn her out."

Soon the two of them were hunched over Nick's computer in the study, hunting up words in his concordance. Kat had a fairly long list of Scripture references when they heard thumps coming up the stairs and then the front door burst open.

"Mister Nick! I'm home!"

Kat rolled her eyes at Nick as Conny barreled into the study. "Guess we're done here," she murmured.

"Hey, give us a minute, buddy," Nick said, rumpling Conny's hair. "Miss Kat and I are doing something. Almost done. Go on."

"Awww . . ."

Kat saw Rochelle come in the front door and head for the kitchen. Her turn to fix supper. "Go on, Conny," she urged. "Go help your mom." She watched till Conny was out of earshot and then shut the study doors and lowered her voice. "In case you haven't noticed, Rochelle hasn't brought up the subject of you-know-what. If she isn't going to do it, then I'm—"

"Kat, open the doors."

"What?"

"We shouldn't be in my bedroom with the doors closed. It doesn't look right."

Kat gaped at him. "What are you talking about? I just want to say something to you in private. Good grief, Nick."

"I know." He looked chagrined. "But somebody at church questioned whether it's appropriate for a single guy to share an apartment with three women. I don't want to do anything that makes people talk—"

A knock on the doors made both of them jump. Kat pulled open one of the doors.

Rochelle.

"Uh, am I interrupting something?"

Nick jumped up and opened the other door wide. "No, no, it's fine. We didn't mean to have the doors closed. Kat asked me to look up something on the Internet for her."

Kat frowned. What in the world was Nick getting so defensive for? She noticed Rochelle was wearing a soft, melon-colored skirt and contrasting lime top that brought out the glow in her honey-brown skin. No doubt about it, the girl was a looker, even more so now that she was off the street and getting some new clothes. She was suddenly conscious of her own rumpled running shorts and sweaty T-shirt. And her hair must be a mess after running in the wind at the lake.

Rochelle cleared her throat. "Anyway, I was wondering if you guys are going to be home this evening—later, I mean. Like, after Conny is in bed. There's, um, something I'd like to talk about with the three of you."

Kat didn't dare look at Nick. "Uh . . . sure. I don't have any plans."

"Me either," Nick said.

"Great. Is Bree—?"

"Napping. But it's time for her to wake up or she'll be up all night. I'll tell her."

Rochelle nodded. "Okay. Thanks. Uh, guess I better get

supper on. Catfish okay? And greens. Mom cooked up a batch and gave us some." She turned and headed back to the kitchen.

As she disappeared, Nick cleared his throat.

Kat backhanded his shoulder. "Don't say it."

Chapter 13

The pounding of his feet seemed to mark time with the blood pounding in his ears as Nick ran hard along the jogging path the next morning. The sun had been up for an hour already, but widespread clouds hid its face, turning the choppy waters of Lake Michigan to a dull blue-gray. Disappointing. Being witness to the sunrise over the lake had been one of the highlights of his morning runs—which had to be even earlier now that he had to be at work by eight thirty.

He passed joggers and early morning dog walkers, feeling a kinship with others beginning their day along the lake. That was the beautiful thing about Chicago—a profusion of parks and trees and forest preserves scattered all over the metro area, giving city dwellers room to move and play and breathe. Not to mention Lake Michigan stretching as far as the eye could see both north and south, then fading into a horizon blending sky and water, like a freshwater ocean.

Thank You, God . . .

Sporadic thought-prayers huffed along with his labored

breathing. *Thank You for my job with Software Symphony . . . Wow, God, still can't believe I'm doing my internship at SouledOut . . . thanks for working all that out . . . and that Rochelle brought up the sticky subject of precautions last night . . .*

That was a relief. He hoped the honest discussion had put Kat's worries to rest.

But his spurts of thanksgivings were also mixed with troublesome thoughts. That interaction with Kat about the closed doors was awkward. He wished it hadn't happened. But after Pastor Cobbs told him somebody had brought up his living situation as "inappropriate" for a pastoral intern, he felt a little jumpy. The pastor said he wasn't asking him to move out—not for the present, anyway—but thought he ought to be aware that at least one person had questions, maybe others. And he'd asked Nick not to be offended if he checked in with him from time to time about it. Nick had said of course. No problem.

But . . . who was that person? What did that busybody know, anyway? He and Kat, Bree, and Livie had always been just good buddies, practically like siblings, for the past three years. Livie had gone back home for now, of course, but Rochelle was a single mom with a kid, and—good grief—her parents lived right upstairs! Even CCU had coed dorms these days—well, guys on one floor, girls on another. As far as sharing the apartment, let anyone who had questions come visit at any time. They had nothing to hide, nothing to be ashamed of.

Which was true. All true.

Except . . . something had changed. His feelings toward Kat definitely didn't feel "just" brother-sister lately. In fact, he'd been distracted by her nearness yesterday as she'd leaned over his shoulder in the study watching him navigate the online concordance, her loose hair brushing his cheek, the smell of her—like sunshine and fresh air and water—filling his senses. He'd been wanting to tell her, felt as if he'd burst if he didn't. He needed to know if she cared about him in that way—or if she could. Explore what that might mean for the future. Their future.

But if he did, if their relationship changed, how would that affect their living arrangement this summer? Girlfriend-boyfriend in the same apartment? Maybe it wouldn't be appropriate.

A groan escaped from somewhere deep inside, and he ran off the path and slowed to a stop, bending over, hands on his knees, trying to catch his breath.

Oh, God . . .

But a glance at his watch pulled him upright again. Time to get back or he'd never make it to work on time.

✳

Kat was already in the kitchen—her night to cook—when Nick got home from work that evening. Her thick, wavy hair had been pulled back into an excuse for a ponytail, wisps falling out in damp tendrils around her face.

"Need any help?" he asked, snitching a cherry tomato from the pile of vegetables on the counter.

"Sure, if you like to chop. I need those onions and other stuff cut up for a stir-fry." She handed him a knife.

"Okay. Give me five minutes to change my clothes. Bree's at . . . ?"

"Evening shift. She relieved me at five."

"Rochelle and Conny?"

Kat shrugged. "I think I heard Conny upstairs at the Douglasses'. Didn't Rochelle say something last night about job hunting today? Mrs. D might be babysitting."

"Right, she did. Okay, give me five."

He was back in two. A few precious minutes alone with Kat before Conny figured out somebody was home and thundered down the stairs. Nick picked up the knife and reached for an onion.

"Did you wash your hands?"

"What?"

"You know, the list of precautions. 'Always wash hands before handling food.' Should do it anyway, HIV or no HIV."

Nick grunted, went to the sink, and scrubbed his hands with soap.

"Use a paper towel to dry your hands."

Nick raised his eyebrows. "Thought you had a thing against using paper towels. Uses up too many trees."

She had the grace to blush. "Yeah, I know. But I read somewhere that dishcloths and hand towels are some of the germiest things in the house. Guess we gotta compromise somewhere."

Nick grinned and used a paper towel to dry his hands before resuming onion-peeling operations. "So, you feel better now that Rochelle brought up the subject of precautions?"

"Uh-huh. You were right, *Pastor Nicky.*" Kat flicked him with a pot holder before taking the lid off a pot of boiling water and measuring two cups of rice into it. "If we'd brought it up, she probably would've felt like we were judging her or finding fault or something. But for her to bring it up, well, it seems okay to talk about it whenever we need to." She stirred the rice, put the cover back on, and turned the heat down on the stove. "Makes me mad, though—"

Nick stopped slicing the onion, hearing her voice soften even though she used the word *mad*.

"—that a sweet girl like Rochelle has to struggle with HIV because that jerk husband of hers fooled around with sluts and whores behind her back."

"Whoa. Sluts and whores? Pretty strong language. We don't know the story."

"So? Wouldn't have happened if he'd been faithful to her. Like the *Bible* says." Kat banged a big frying pan onto the stovetop.

"Yeah, well . . ." Nick sliced the onion. Why was he defending the jerk husband? Worse, why was he making Kat upset? "You're right. Whatever happened in their marriage, it's not fair." He decided not to add that "jerk husband" must be paying for his sins since he had to have HIV issues too.

They worked in silence for the next few minutes, Nick chopping his way through the pile of mushrooms, red pepper, a yellow summer squash, and a funny long eggplant while Kat heated sesame oil in the fry pan and sautéed some sliced ginger and garlic. "Smells wonderful," he ventured—but was interrupted by the laugh-track ringtone on his cell phone, muffled in his pocket.

Caller ID said Rochelle Johnson. "Hey, Rochelle," he said, catching Kat's eye and pointing at the phone. "What's up?"

He listened for a few moments. "No problem. Thanks for letting us know." He closed the phone. "Rochelle said she's just now leaving downtown and the El is running very slow. Said to go ahead and start supper without her, but wanted to know if we could take care of Conny till she gets here, which I'm glad to do . . . Oh, wait." Nick glanced at the calendar hanging on the kitchen wall. "This is *Monday*."

"All day." Kat tossed him a mischievous grin.

"I totally forgot that Pastor Cobbs set up a regular meeting with me and Mrs. D on Monday evenings! Oh, Kat, I'm sorry. I didn't mean to volunteer you . . ."

She waved a dismissive hand. "Don't worry about it. I'm perfectly capable of entertaining a six-year-old for an hour or so. But we better get this stir-fry going. Don't want to send you off to the lions before you've got something in your stomach."

"I think it's the lions that need to be fed so they don't eat me," he teased. But he felt relieved. That could have been a mess-up, volunteering to take care of Conny and then skipping out to a meeting. Good thing he remembered, though. Not a good start to his internship if he forgot his first Monday night meeting.

But as Kat whisked the steaming hot rice and the fragrant vegetables to the table—the girl really did know how to cook— he regretted having to rush off. There were several things he wanted to talk to her about, like . . .

"I'm pretty sure Pastor Cobbs will ask me if I'm good with the membership covenant he gave me so we can do the membership thing next Sunday. Uh . . . did you get a chance to read the stuff I showed you? What do you think about becoming a member next week too?"

Kat set four plates on the table but shook her head. "It says you've got to be baptized. I sent my folks an e-mail to ask if they baptized me as an infant, but even if they did, I'm not sure it would count, since I basically grew up pagan until . . . well, you know. You were there. Hey, grab the silverware, will you?"

The Midwest Music Fest. He had, indeed, been there. That

was the first time he'd laid eyes on Kathryn Davies at the Crista University booth, where Kat had been telling Brygitta how she'd prayed to become a Christian at the concert the night before. He'd been struck then by her unusual beauty—all that dark brunette, wavy hair and bright-blue eyes. A fun contrast to Brygitta's "cute" features and short, pixie-like haircut. And spirit! Kat had decided then and there to transfer to the Chicago school, bailing on a medical school track at Arizona State she said she didn't want, and pursuing a teaching degree at CCU, even though her parents had gone ballistic.

Nick had admired her spunk and let's-just-do-it spirit from the get-go.

But he'd never thought about encouraging her to get baptized after her decision to become a Christian. *Huh*. And he thought he was pastor material?

"Hey, I'm sure we can talk about that with Pastor Cobbs and Mrs. D—"

She cut him off. "I know. But not right now. You better go upstairs and grab Conny so we can eat. Besides, there's something else I need to ask you that's more immediate—but go! Shoo! Before the food gets cold."

Nick let her practically push him toward the door. "Okay, okay, I'm going. Just tell me what you want to ask so I'm not quaking in my shoes all evening." Which wasn't far from the truth. What did she want to ask him that was more immediate than Sunday?

Chapter 14

Appreciate the ride, Mrs. . . . uh, Sister Avis." Nick grinned apologetically. "Sorry. My folks taught me to call adults by Mr. and Mrs., and it's hard to give it up."

Avis Douglass chuckled. "You and Josh Baxter. He still calls me Mrs. Douglass—when he doesn't forget and call me Mrs. Johnson. That's how he knew me when our families first met and he was still in high school." Her voice softened a bit as she drove up Clark Street toward the Howard Street shopping center. "My first husband, Conrad Johnson, died of pancreatic cancer. Peter Douglass is my second husband, though I'm sure you've figured that out. We got married at Uptown Community Church before it became part of SouledOut."

"So your grandson is named after your first husband?" Nick felt a bit awkward at Mrs. D sharing all this personal information—but honored too, as if she were talking to a peer.

"Yes. Conny never knew his biological granddaddy, though. As far as he's concerned, Peter's his grandpa—which he is. Conny needs all the positive male role models he can get since . . . well, you know, the situation with his father, Dexter." The woman glanced sideways at Nick. "Conny's pretty crazy about you too. Do you feel like you've grown another appendage?" She chuckled.

"Pretty much." He laughed too, and then cleared his throat. "By the way, I want to thank you for advising us to wait for Rochelle to bring up the whole thing about precautions. She talked to the rest of us last night . . . it was good. Just the right thing."

"You three all right with Rochelle living with you?"

Nick hesitated for just the briefest of seconds. "Yeah, I think so. I mean, it's just something none of us have had to deal with before, so it seems a bit challenging. But when it comes right down to it, not such a big deal. Unless—"

"Unless she cuts herself and you have to deal with blood, right?"

How'd she know what he was thinking? But she was right on. "Yeah."

"You don't have to do this, you know. We . . . well, Peter and I could work on another solution for her living situation. Things are in a better place between us than when she disappeared last February."

He didn't answer for a few moments. It did complicate things having Rochelle and Conny in the apartment mix. But . . .

"Thanks. Nice to know there could be another option. But as I see it, God had a hand in bringing Rochelle to us. I mean, Kat finding her while Dumpster diving, of all things, when she'd been missing for several months was nothing short of a miracle! And then Livie moving out, making room in our apartment just when Rochelle and Conny needed a place to come off the street . . . well, had to be more than just coincidence." He smiled sheepishly. "Don't you think God brought all this together?"

"Now that's what I'm talking about! Hallelujah!" Avis smacked the steering wheel with her hand. Laughter was in her voice. "You, young man, are beginning to sound like me. Watch out, SouledOut!"

Nick felt warmed by her affirmation. But he realized they were only a few blocks from the shopping center and he wanted to ask her something. "Uh, Sister Avis, I noticed that the membership covenant Pastor Cobbs gave me talks about being baptized as a requisite to becoming a member. Can you say more about that?"

Avis glanced at him thoughtfully. "We practice 'believer's baptism'—that is, someone old enough to make a genuine decision to follow Jesus. Not really tied to age. Depends on the person's understanding. Sometimes a young person, sometimes an adult."

"And membership at SouledOut?"

Avis didn't answer immediately, concentrating on pulling into the parking lot of the Howard Street shopping center and finding a parking space near the church. She shut off the motor and turned to him. "The covenant emphasizes baptism first, because the most important thing is becoming a member of the family of God—the body of Christ. Not just a member of a particular church."

"But getting baptized doesn't make you a Christian. It's the heart commitment to Jesus, the decision to accept His gift of forgiveness and salvation."

She smiled. "You're right. But as you know, in the New Testament, as soon as someone believed, they were baptized.

And Jesus told His disciples to make more disciples and baptize them. So . . . baptism is being obedient."

Nick fiddled with the door handle. "What if someone has been a Christian for a while but didn't get baptized . . . or maybe they were baptized as an infant. What is SouledOut's position on that?"

"As an infant? Were you—?"

"No, no. I was baptized as a teenager. Fourteen. Just wondering is all."

"Infant baptism. Hmm. I certainly have friends who were baptized as infants in their denomination who have a vibrant faith. But not everyone. For some it was a meaningless ritual. So it might depend on the person . . . but as for someone who became a Christian but hasn't been baptized yet, I'd say to them—let's do it! What are we waiting for?"

Nick was tempted to laugh. That sounded like Kat. *"Let's do it! What are we waiting for?"* "Thanks, Sister Avis." Ha! He got it right that time. "Oh, one more question . . . if someone wanted to get baptized at SouledOut, how would they go about it? I mean, how long a process is it? Could they do it right away?"

A slightly knowing smile touched Avis's lips. "Well, the pastors usually meet with the person to talk about the meaning of baptism and to be sure that the person is making—or has made—a genuine faith declaration in Jesus. We usually wait until there are two or three people who want to get baptized and then schedule a baptism at the lake. It's always a very joyful experience."

Wait? Nick's heart sank a little as they got out of the car and headed for the doors of SouledOut. He wished he knew what

Kat really thought about becoming a member this Sunday—and getting baptized. Then he could bring it up tonight in the meeting with Pastor Cobbs and see if that was possible. But . . . no. He needed to talk to Kat first.

❀

Two hours later Nick opened the passenger side door of Mrs. Douglass's Camry and sank into the front seat. "Wow," he said, buckling his seat belt as she started the car and pulled out of the parking space. "That . . . was quite a meeting. I mean, I really appreciated the prayer time before we even talked about anything. Most meetings I've been in at various churches 'open' with a prayer, but nothing like that."

The three of them—well, Pastor Cobbs and Sister Avis, mostly—had just worshipped God for a good ten or fifteen minutes, no requests, before asking God for guidance and wisdom as they pastored the church in the coming months. The experience had filled him with awe, as if they indeed had been ushered into God's throne room. They'd made him feel so included in the prayers, part of the team, even though he'd been too choked up to speak into the prayers.

"How are you feeling about the sermon themes for the summer?"

"The sayings of Jesus surrounding His death and resurrection? Awesome. Pastor's sermon yesterday about Jesus' prayer for unity among the disciples was a great kickoff."

"And your first assignment?"

Pastor Cobbs had given him Jesus' interaction with Peter on the beach after the resurrection. Nick nodded. "I'm excited.

Can't wait to really dig into the text." He gave her a sheepish glance. "Okay, scared spitless too."

She laughed. "You are going to do just fine."

They said good-bye on the second-floor landing of the three-flat, and Nick used his key to let himself into the apartment as she continued on up the stairs to the third floor. It had been a good meeting, and he was starting to get a feel of what might be expected of him as an intern—though Pastor Cobbs had warned him that Robert Burns's famous quote about the "best-laid schemes o' mice an' men" was doubly true for pastors. One never knew who or what would come walking through the church door on any given day, sending orderly plans into a tailspin.

But he felt drained, even if it was only nine twenty. The day had started early with his run along the lake, and hitting the sack early would feel good.

"Oh, yay, you're back!" Kat finished a text she was sending on her cell phone and scrambled off the couch. "There's something I want to talk to you—oh." She must've seen the look on his face because she stopped short. "Rough meeting?"

He dropped into the padded armchair. "No . . . meeting was great. Just tired. Was thinking about hitting the sack."

"Oh." Kat's features fell. "I was hoping . . . well, this is kinda important, but . . . guess it could wait. Except I just got my new schedule for July and I have to work the evening shift tomorrow." Her face brightened. "What if I fix you a mango smoothie? We've got a ripe one. Would that perk you up for ten minutes?"

Tempting. "Make that mango-pineapple, and I'll give you fifteen."

"Done!" Kat headed for the kitchen. "Oh, I hear Bree. Good.

That's three. Tell Rochelle, will you? Just don't wake Conny. I'll make smoothies for all of us."

Brygitta came in the door and was cajoled with the same smoothie offer. So it wasn't just him and Kat? Even though Nick didn't know what this was about, he'd assumed . . . what? Maybe hoped—hoped for more time to talk, just the two of them. But five minutes later Kat brought four tall glasses brimming with creamy-gold liquid into the living room and passed them out.

"Mm, good." Rochelle, curled up on one end of the couch in a big, roomy sleep shirt, sucked on the straw in her smoothie. "And no, didn't have any luck job hunting today, so don't ask. What's up with you, Kat?"

Kat set her own smoothie on the coffee table and leaned forward, arms resting on her knees. "I want to ask you guys a favor . . . Come visit a food pantry with me."

That's what this was about? Nick felt a brief stab of disappointment.

"What in the world for?" Bree's face was a comical mix of puzzlement and *here we go again.* "What's a food pantry— upscale Dumpster diving?" She rolled her eyes.

Rochelle gave Bree a dark look. "Don't make fun. A lot of poor people depend on the food pantries. But . . ." She eyed Kat. "If this is about me and Conny eating your food without paying, just say so, okay? I *am* trying to get a job so I can contribute to the food expenses." Frowning, she stirred her smoothie with the straw so hard it bent.

"No, no, no. This has nothing to do with you or our food budget or anything. See . . ." And Kat went on to explain how she'd wanted to talk to Edesa Baxter about teaching a nutrition class together, but so far all they'd done was go on a fake shopping trip with Estelle Bentley's cooking class at Manna House, which she'd found embarrassing. "But on Sunday Edesa suggested visiting one of the food pantries in the area, maybe even volunteering. She said food pantries were a surer way of getting food to people who need it than, uh . . ." Kat floundered.

"Than Dumpster diving?" Bree was enjoying this. "Well, finally, someone has talked some sense into you."

Nick listened. Why was it so important to talk to all of them about this? Usually if Kat got a bright idea, she'd just do it and then announce it to the rest of them. And . . . what did her quest to study what the Bible said about Jesus and food have to do with this?

"So, do you want our blessing or something?" Bree shrugged, slurping her smoothie. "I say, fine, go for it. Sounds like right up your alley."

Kat took a deep breath. "Actually, I want you guys to come with me. There's one at Rock of Ages Church not too far from here." She still hadn't touched her smoothie. "I mean, it would be really helpful to talk it over with someone, and you three are my current family, probably know me better than anyone. The Rock of Ages food pantry is open on Wednesdays, four to eight. I work the afternoon shift at the coffee shop that day, but I get off at five. So does Nick. And you work morning shift that day, Bree. And Rochelle doesn't have a job yet. So maybe we could all—"

"Slow down, girl." Rochelle's forehead puckered into a frown. "I've seen my fill of food pantries the last few months, and I'm trying to get my act together so I don't *need* to go there. So maybe count me out."

Kat nodded slowly. "Okay. I can understand that. But if you

change your mind, your perspective would be— Oh, sorry." Kat's cell phone sitting on the coffee table pinged with a text message. She looked at it, then shut it off. "What about you, Nick? Bree?"

"Hmm. I'll think about it." Bree yawned.

But Nick nodded. "I'll go with you, if you can wait till I get home from work. Except I'm supposed to cook supper Wednesday night."

"I'll trade with you for Thursday," Rochelle piped up. "I'll make something in the Crock-Pot so you all can eat whenever."

Kat gave Nick a happy smile. "Thanks, Nick." She stood up. "Okay, my fifteen minutes are up. See, I keep my promises."

Rochelle gave Kat a hug on the way to her bedroom. "Thanks for understanding."

Bree gave her a hug too. "Sorry I sounded snippy. I know this is important to you. It's just . . . hard to keep up with you sometimes." The two girls hugged a few moments longer, then Bree headed for the bathroom.

Nick waited until it was just the two of them in the living room. "Kat? I wanted to ask you something too—about becoming members on Sunday. I'd like—"

"Can't." Kat shrugged. "Haven't been baptized. Not even the baby thing. I texted my parents and asked. Here's my mom's reply." She picked up her cell, found the text message, and showed it to him.

It read: *No. You aren't getting involved in some cult, are you?*

Chapter 15

A crack of thunder rattled the windows of The Common Cup and startled Kat just as she was putting the lid on a mocha decaf for a woman in a rumpled business suit. Some of the hot liquid spilled, wetting the dollar bills the woman had laid on the counter. "Oh! I'm sorry." Kat grabbed a damp cloth and dabbed at the dollar bills. "I'll make you a new mocha."

"Never mind," the woman said, drumming her fingers. "I don't have time . . . Here, I'll put the lid on. Keep the change." Snapping on the lid and grabbing the tall cup, the woman marched quickly out the door, casting an anxious eye at the darkening sky.

Kat made a face at Billy the Kid, her nickname for the other barista on her shift, a twenty-year-old with fake blond stand-up hair, a lopsided grin, and flirty eyes. "Win some, lose some, I guess."

He picked up the bills from the counter and opened the register. "I'd say you won this one. She put down a dollar too much. Lucky you."

Kat snatched the extra dollar and put it in the tip jar shared with all the staff and glanced at the wall clock. Four thirty! Why did it have to threaten rain just as she was about to get off work? She'd been planning to dash home, meet Nick, and walk to the food pantry. But if it was going to rain . . .

It did rain. Buckets. At five o'clock Kat whipped off her apron and pulled out her cell. She hit a speed dial number and the phone rang once . . . twice . . . "Nick? Thank goodness I caught you. I'm going to go straight to the Rock of Ages Church to save time. Are you still coming? . . . No, I don't want to wait till next week! The rain will probably let up soon, usually does . . . Okay. See you."

But her relief person was late. "Sorry. The rain . . ." The girl brushed past Kat, hustled into the back room to dump her stuff, and then came out again to take up her place at the counter. "Who's next?" she chirped.

Well, at least the hard rain had rolled on and it was only a drizzle now. The air was warm and muggy. Popping up the small umbrella she kept in her backpack, Kat walked quickly, dodging puddles, squinting through the drizzle at street signs, from time to time stepping into a doorway to check the Google map of the neighborhood she'd printed out.

She'd called the church yesterday and actually talked to the woman who oversaw the food pantry, a Beatrice Wilson, sounded African American. When Kat said she'd like to visit the pantry to find out what they do—she'd introduced herself as a member of SouledOut Community Church to make the visit sound more official—the woman had asked if she could come by earlier, before the pantry opened at four, but had reluctantly acquiesced when Kat said she didn't get off work until five. "Don't know how much time I'll have to talk," she'd said. "Sometimes we get real busy."

Kat felt a little guilty saying she was a member of SouledOut—though a week ago the word to her simply meant "my church." Once she'd decided to attend SouledOut regularly, she thought of herself as a member—a new member, sure, but *there*. Now it seemed so complicated, having to get baptized and everything.

Well, she couldn't think about that now because . . . here she was.

Kat tipped her umbrella back and gazed at the brick edifice on the corner of two residential streets. Rock of Ages wasn't a large church and looked a bit worse for wear. Could use a paint job around the stained-glass windows. A sign on the front doors—also in need of paint—said "Food Pantry Wed 4–8 Side Door" with a large arrow pointing around the corner.

She looked up and down both streets, but no sign of Nick. Well, she wasn't going to wait in the rain. She followed a Hispanic woman with two little girls through the side door—and found herself squeezing into a crowd of people packed into a small vestibule.

"Number thirty-two!" a burly man standing at an inner doorway called out.

The crowd jostled as a woman with a thick black braid down her back and wearing an Indian tunic and trousers threaded her way through the crowd and disappeared through the doorway. Kat noticed that the Hispanic mother she'd followed was signing in at a table just inside the door and getting a number. She sidled up to the table as the woman left and spoke to the white-haired white lady on the other side. "Is Beatrice Wilson here?"

The woman nodded. "Back in the pantry, helping people.

Are you a volunteer? We're shorthanded today. I think someone forgot to send out the new July schedule."

For a nanosecond, Kat considered saying, "Yes." That'd be one way to get a feel for the food pantry, by jumping in! But she didn't have a clue what to do. She shook her head. "Sorry. If you get a chance, just tell Mrs. Wilson that Kathryn Davies from SouledOut Community Church is here."

"I can't leave the table in case someone else comes in. Tell that gentleman by the door. Maybe he can get word to her."

Kat felt somewhat daunted by the number of bodies between the table and the burly man at the inner door. When he called out, "Thirty-three!" she decided to wait until Nick arrived. Maybe the crowd would have thinned by then.

"Is it always this crowded?" she asked the white-haired lady.

"Oh, we often serve a hundred or more families on Wednesday—though on good weather days, most of them wait outside. But the rain today brought them in . . . Oh, hello, Mrs. Montoya." The woman greeted a newcomer. "So glad to see you again."

Kat turned from the table—and found herself face-to-face with Nick grinning at her. And Rochelle. And Bree.

"What? I thought only Nick was coming! And . . ." Kat looked them up and down. "Hey, no fair. You guys are *dry*."

Nick laughed. "We hitched a ride with Peter Douglass. He left work the same time I did and gave me a lift. Rochelle and Bree were waiting for me in the foyer, but it was still raining so Mr. D said he'd drop us off on his way to some business appointment . . . Uh, maybe we should get out of the way here."

The four of them squeezed around the crush of damp bodies until they were standing against the wall of the vestibule.

Kat gave Rochelle and Bree quizzical looks. "So what made you two change your minds?"

Rochelle shrugged. "Like you said. Whatever's pulling your chain about food pantries, you might need my perspective. And like Nick said, Peter has a business appointment this evening, so Mom was happy to have Conny for company."

"I just came along for the ride," Brygitta confessed. "Didn't particularly want to eat Rochelle's Crock-Pot supper by myself."

Kat grinned. "Whatever. Glad you're here. Though I'm not sure we're going to get a chance to talk to Mrs. Wilson—"

"You folks from SouledOut Community?" The man Kat had noticed calling numbers loomed up beside them, two hundred fifty pounds at least, his long hair pulled back into a ponytail that trailed down his back. They nodded. "We're pretty short-handed here today. Sister Beatrice wants to know if you could give us a hand for an hour or so. If one of you will take over at the registration table, Miss Sylvia can take the rest of you back into the pantry and tell you what to do."

Kat couldn't believe it. "Sure! Right, guys?" She raised her eyebrows hopefully at her housemates, who all looked at one another and shrugged.

Leaving Brygitta at the registration table—"Just come back and check on me," she hissed at Kat nervously—the other three followed the white-haired lady through the inner door and into a large room filled with shelves and tables. Canned goods and nonperishable items were stacked on shelves along two walls. Another wall contained folded clothing marked by size and type—*Infant 0–18 mos . . . Children's Tops . . . Women's Sweaters Lg . . . Men's Sport Shirts Misc*—and a rack with hanging clothes. Two large freezer chests sat along a third wall, and in the middle were tables with baskets of bread and baked goods, fresh fruit, and vegetables. Kat's eyes widened. *Whoa.*

Several people were "shopping" the various shelves and tables with paper shopping bags, assisted by two African American women, one middle-aged, the other younger and enough of a look-alike to be her daughter.

"Sister Beatrice, these are the young people from that other church."

The woman turned. She seemed a motherly sort, plump and a bit frazzled. "Oh, thank you, Sylvia. Would you finish assisting Miss Dharuna?" She looked from one to the other of the newcomers. "Four of you? I was just expecting Miss Davies. Which one—?"

Kat extended her hand. "I'm Kathryn Davies, Mrs. Wilson. These are my housemates, who decided to come." Kat introduced each by name. "I hope we won't be in your way."

"Well, as I said on the phone, we're awfully busy during open hours on Wednesday, but if you'd be willing to help out, we could bring more people through a bit faster. Some of our volunteers didn't show today."

Kat nodded eagerly. "Just tell us what to do."

Mrs. Wilson gave them a quick rundown. Each person coming through the food pantry was assisted by a volunteer who stayed with them as they "shopped" because supplies were limited and they wanted enough to go around. Each person or family was allowed to take a certain number of items—posted—from the nonperishable section, frozen foods and meats, and from the tables of fresh produce and baked goods. Same with clothing and shoes. Once done shopping, they should be escorted out another door.

"They're allowed three shopping bags total—two for food, one for clothing. Oh, I want you to meet my grandbaby, Stacy. Stacy, honey, can you show these young people where the bags are?"

Stacy was no "baby" but an older teenager, maybe sixteen or seventeen. Half a dozen questions popped into Kat's mind as the girl acknowledged them with a shy smile and showed them the paper shopping bags to pass out, as well as plastic bags for frozen food. But Beatrice Wilson was already at the door speaking to the man on the other side. A moment later Kat heard him call out, "Numbers thirty-four, thirty-five, and thirty-six!"

As the people holding the numbers came in, Mrs. Wilson assigned each of them to Kat and her friends. Kat tried not to look aghast at the skinny white woman she'd been assigned to. The woman—Mrs. Wilson called her Lady Lolla, of all things!—was maybe in her fifties and dressed in a long, slinky, tight-fitting white dress that was probably an evening gown in its earlier life, complete with glittery earrings and necklace (costume jewelry, surely), bright-red lipstick and blush, all beneath brassy red hair. But Kat swallowed her shock, handed the woman her first bag, and ushered her to the wall of nonperishables.

Lady Lolla shook her head. "I don't need no more beans. It's just me an' Ike, ya know. Would like some of those bagels, though. And are them oranges? Got any frozen fish?"

They did indeed have packages of frozen fish in the freezers. As it turned out, Lady Lolla only took one bag full of groceries, thanked Kat sweetly, and announced, "I used to be a model, you know. For Marshall Field, back in the day."

"That's nice," Kat murmured.

As soon as Lady Lolla was out the exit door, Kat alerted the man near the vestibule—whose name turned out to be Tony— and another family was ushered in with two children in tow. Tony introduced them as the Hidalgo family, and they filled up two bags with boxes of cereal, pasta, canned vegetables, canned fruit, two loaves of bread, a bag of apples, frozen pot pies, frozen vegetables . . . as Kat tried to keep track of the number of items they were allowed to take. The preschool children—two little girls with straight black hair and large black eyes—were then outfitted with tops, shorts, shoes, and pajamas before the parents said, *"Gracias, gracias,"* and made their way out.

It was that way for the next two hours. Kat's "customers" were a more diverse crowd than she'd expected, from obviously homeless characters to neatly dressed mothers and grandmothers, many Hispanic, but blacks, whites, Middle Eastern, and Asian too. Her heart gave a pang at the elderly customers, a few well over eighty. Didn't they have family members to care for them?

Anyone who wasn't inside the food pantry room at eight o'clock had to be turned away, and Kat realized why they'd chosen Tony for the job of gatekeeper. One slightly inebriated man—at least he sounded that way from the yelling in the vestibule—got fairly abusive. But then . . . all was quiet.

When the last customer had been ushered out, Beatrice Wilson sat down heavily on a chair and fanned herself. "My, my, my, you children were a godsend. Why was it you came again? You want to volunteer?"

Kat saw her friends look at one another. "Uh, not exactly," she said hurriedly. "Mostly we just came to learn what a food pantry is all about." She saw Rochelle and Bree edge toward the exit door. Couldn't blame them. Her own stomach was pinching with hunger. "I know you're tired, Mrs. Wilson, but can I ask just one question? How can you give all this stuff away free? The used clothing, yes. But . . . fresh bread? Bananas and apples and carrots? Where does it come from?"

Mrs. Wilson sighed. "Donations, mostly. People in the church and neighborhood provide most of the nonperishables. But some of the stores in the area will give day-old bread, or vegetables and fruit they have to clear out for new stock if we come pick it up. All the frozen foods, too, come from stores. We have drivers who volunteer to pick stuff up, people to stock it, volunteers to help customers—like you did today."

Nick leaned in. "Is that the way most food pantries function?"

"Oh my, no. It's the way most start out. But a church or organization can buy whole boxes of food from the Chicago Food Depository for just pennies a pound. Our church has applied and is setting up a food pantry budget now."

"MeMaw?" The girl Stacy touched Mrs. Wilson on the shoulder. "We should lock up and get home now. You've been on your feet a long time."

Beatrice Wilson got heavily to her feet. "What would I do without you, child? Anyway, Miss Davies, I thank you an' your friends for pitchin' in today. Not sure what happened to our usual volunteers. But God surely sent you."

❋

Kat barely heard Bree and Rochelle chatter and complain good-naturedly as the foursome walked home. At least the rain had stopped, though the evening was thick with humidity. Nick walked alongside her silently. But finally he said, "Penny for your thoughts?"

She gave him a tired smile. "I'm feeling kind of overwhelmed by how many people came to that food pantry. I mean, it's Rogers Park! Not a ritzy neighborhood, but you don't see boarded-up buildings and vacant lots like the west side of Chicago, not the obvious poverty. Is there that much hunger here too?"

Nick shrugged. "I guess so. Some of those people waited two hours to get a couple bags of groceries. Must really need them."

"Same thing at the food pantries I used," Rochelle piped up from behind them. "Seemed like more and more people came every week. Not enough food pantries to go around. What they need is more churches opening food pantries all over the city."

Which was exactly what Kat was thinking.

Chapter 16

~~~~~~~~~~~~~~~~~~

Nick barely saw Kat the next day, just "Hi" and "Bye" the next morning after he came in from his run before she flew out the door to do her volunteer thing at Bethune Elementary. Rochelle and Conny were all excited that her parents were taking them to see the Chicago fireworks that evening—always on the night before the Fourth—and when Nick got home from work, Kat was already at The Common Cup for an evening shift.

But she'd been on his mind all day. In spite of how tired they'd been when they got home from the food pantry last evening, Kat had seemed animated. All during their late supper of Rochelle's black-eyed peas and rice in the Crock-Pot—surprisingly delicious spooned over corn bread—she had talked about nothing else. She'd asked about the various people each of them had helped. The Cuban woman who spoke no English. The old man who'd shuffled into the food pantry in his stocking feet and filled up his clothing bag with nothing but shoes. The

Muslim woman so shrouded in her head scarf that only her eyes showed. The cute Latino kids who got so excited about a Barbie shirt or Batman sneakers.

They'd shared stories. Laughed about the mistakes they'd made. "I tried out my high school Spanish on one woman who came in," Brygitta had confessed, "trying to ask her to write her name on the sign-in sheet—you know, *'Escribe su nombre en el papel'*—and she looked horrified. I think I asked her to, uh, *'Excreta su nombre'*—"

Kat had screeched, "You didn't!" and they'd all fallen out laughing in spite of themselves.

"What? What?" Conny had asked, flying to the table. He'd already eaten supper with Grammy Avis and had been playing nearby in the living room. But they'd forgotten about his big ears. Rochelle had whisked him off to get him in his pj's, after which he'd begged Nick to read him a story before she tucked him in bed . . . and by the time he was done, Kat and Brygitta had disappeared into their bedroom.

And now it was already Thursday night, and his membership at SouledOut was coming up on Sunday. He wasn't satisfied with his last conversation with Kat about membership and the fact that she hadn't been baptized.

With Rochelle and Conny gone to see the fireworks and Kat at work, Nick had fixed an easy Chinese chicken salad for himself and Bree and they'd eaten it out on the back porch. When he asked whether she'd thought about becoming a member on Sunday, Bree said she wasn't sure she'd still be coming to SouledOut once school started again, so probably not. Disappointing, but made sense.

But that still left Kat.

Bree disappeared after supper to catch up on e-mails, but Nick sat down at the kitchen table with the Membership Covenant he'd be making on Sunday. He wasn't sure why he wanted his friends to join him in the commitment to this church he was making—Kat especially. But his pastoral internship committed him for the next six months at least. It'd be nice to have his closest friends there for support.

He read through the covenant. "On profession of faith in our Lord and Savior Jesus Christ, having been baptized in the name of the Father, Son, and Holy Spirit, I joyfully enter into this covenant with my brothers and sisters of SouledOut Community Church . . ."

There it was, that baptism thing. But if Kat really wanted to become a member, surely they could do something about that before Sunday.

He really liked the covenant. "To walk together in Christian love . . . to participate in its worship and ministries . . . to contribute financially through tithes and offerings . . ." A lot of the basics. But also some other commitments he didn't usually see in church memberships. "To maintain regular Bible reading and prayer . . . to be just in all dealings with others . . . to aid my brothers and sisters in sickness or distress . . . to reconcile differences and seek for unity and avoid division . . ."

Oh, Lord, make me worthy—

The front door opened. "I'm home!" Kat stuck her head into the kitchen. "Oh, hey, Nick. Where is everybody?"

Nick's heart skipped a beat or two. Kat's hair was down, all waves and curls around her face, instead of bunched on the back of her head with a clip. Her blue eyes never failed to stand out even more, framed by all that dark hair. She wore the barest of makeup, but her cheeks were pink from the walk home from the coffee shop.

He found his voice. "Well, Rochelle and Conny went to see the fireworks with the Douglasses, Bree is somewhere chatting on the Internet, and I saw Nick somewhere around here—"

"Goose. I meant besides you." Kat laughed and flopped into another chair at the kitchen table. "Any leftovers from supper? I'm famished!"

Nick hopped up and whisked a covered plate out of the refrigerator and got a fork. "Set aside just for you, mademoiselle. Chinese chicken salad. Still good, I think."

"Looks fabulous." Kat dived in. "Mmm." As she chewed the chilled chicken, lettuce, mandarin orange sections, and almond slivers, she pointed her fork at the papers in front of him. "What're you doing?"

"Reading through the Membership Covenant for SouledOut. Did you get a chance to read through it?"

She sighed. "Not really. Kind of got hung up on the first section that assumes you've been baptized."

"Mind if I read it to you while you eat? I'm trying to absorb it all. Reading it aloud would be good for me too."

Kat shrugged and forked another mouthful of salad. "Sure. Go ahead."

He read through it. The personal faith commitments. The commitments to the rest of the body of Christ. The commitments to serve others.

She nodded slowly. "It's great. I like that one about 'courtesy in our speech.'"

He took a slow breath and blew it out. "So . . . if we could do something about getting you baptized, would you—"

"Nick! There's, like, only two days before Sunday. There's no time! Yeah, sure, I might want to become a member at SouledOut at some point, but I need more time to think through this whole baptism thing. I don't even know how they do it! Maybe you have to take a class or something. Do you know?"

Nick hesitated, remembering what Avis Douglass had said about the pastors meeting with the person and usually waiting until there were two or three people who wanted to be baptized and doing it in the lake. "Well, yeah, but . . ."

Kat laid a hand on his arm. He felt her touch all the way up his arm and down to his feet. "You're sweet to want me to become a member the same Sunday you do, Nick. But I need more time to find out what it's all about. But you . . . go for it. I'm cheering."

She got up from the table and put her empty plate into the dishwasher. "The salad was yummy. Hey—tomorrow's the Fourth. Do you have the day off? The STEP program is on holiday, but Bree and I are both scheduled for morning shift at the coffee shop, which means I oughta get to bed. But maybe we could do something later? At least you and me and Bree since we didn't get to see the Chicago fireworks tonight. Maybe they do something up in Evanston."

Nick nodded, swallowing the lump of disappointment in his throat. "Yeah. We should do something." He watched her go, flitting out of the kitchen like a leaf on the wind. He realized more clearly why he'd been pushing her. The membership covenant said things about faith and church that meant a great deal to him. And he wished they were making those same commitments together, a foundation they could build on for wherever their relationship might take them in the future.

But she was right. Of course she should take time to understand the process for baptism at SouledOut, not be pushed to take shortcuts just for him.

Just for him . . .

But he wished she would. Just for him. Wished she wanted to, just for him.

Chapter 17

The morning shift at The Common Cup that Friday was longer because of the holiday hours and because more customers had time to kick back and hang out with their friends. By the time Kat and Bree got home, Nick had rounded up some bicycles from the Douglasses and the family on the first floor—one of which even had a kid seat for Conny—and asked if they wanted to bike up to Evanston to hear a band concert and see the fireworks.

"Bikes! Sounds fun. But I thought . . ." Kat had assumed she and Bree and Nick would go to the fireworks tonight, just the three of them. Hadn't Rochelle and Conny gone downtown to Chicago last night with Mr. and Mrs. D? It'd been awhile since the three of them had spent much time together, now that they were all working and had such crazy schedules. Not that she really minded Rochelle and Conny going along if Rochelle kept her little boy entertained. But the way Conny hung on Nick, he was liable to be distracted the whole time.

Nick seemed to read her mind. "How could I say no?" he murmured to her.

Kat shrugged and dragged Bree to the kitchen to see what they could put together for a picnic. Why fight it? It'd still be fun.

With everybody pitching in, they soon had a picnic of tuna sandwiches, carrot sticks, celery boats with peanut butter (Conny's idea), grapes, home-popped popcorn, tortilla chips, a jar of salsa, and hunks of cheese to nibble on. Rochelle looked at the food on the table and made a face. "Doesn't seem like a Fourth of July picnic without grilled chicken and potato salad."

A quick retort sprang to the tip of Kat's tongue. *You were home all morning while Bree and I were working. Why didn't you make some?*—but she swallowed it. What had the Membership Covenant said about "courtesy in speech"? "There's still Saturday," she said instead.

"Sure." Rochelle shrugged. "We could grill on the back porch."

Kat was glad she'd caught her tongue. Like Bree said, Rochelle was trying. She busied herself distributing the food between the four of them, using a couple of backpacks and grocery sacks to hang from the handlebars.

Nick rode the bike with Conny on the back, and Kat worried that none of them had helmets. But they kept to the side streets until they hit Calvary Cemetery, which divided Chicago from Evanston along the lakefront. The only way around was busy Sheridan Road, but they rode on the sidewalk until they got past the huge cemetery. After that, they were able to pick up a bike path for most of the way running the length of the parks along the lake up to Northwestern University.

Once Kat got used to using the gears on her slightly ancient bike, she enjoyed the ride. It was a nearly perfect day, midseventies. Clouds scuttled about, but no hint of rain. They rode single file, dodging joggers and walkers who seemed to ignore the cinder footpath and insisted on cluttering the bicycle paths, sometimes two or three abreast. Rochelle rode close behind Nick, probably to keep an eye on Conny, who was having the time of his life, holding out his arms and screeching, "Wheeee!" or "I'm flying!" to people they passed. Kat chuckled. He really was a sweet kid.

The lakeside parks were full of picnickers—and, Kat had to admit, the pungent smell of chicken and hamburgers sizzling on a dozen grills made her mouth water. But she couldn't help but remember the faces of some of the people who'd come to the food pantry the other night—like Lady Lolla and the old man who'd showed up in his stocking feet. How many of them were able to celebrate the Fourth with a picnic in the park? How many of them were still hungry?

Kat's mind was so distracted she almost ran into Rochelle and Nick, who'd stopped their bikes at the edge of a man-made lagoon with a little island in the middle. Nick turned around as Bree caught up and he pointed to the far end. "That's where the band will be playing. They're setting up now. Where do you guys want to picnic?"

"I'm hungry!" Conny announced.

"Me too." Nick laughed, lifting him out of the kid seat. "That was some bike hike. But *you*, young man, got a free ride while I did all the work."

Bike hike was right. Kat's legs felt wobbly as she locked up her bike with the others to a park sign and unloaded the food.

Bree had snatched a few towels from the apartment to serve as blankets. "At least they're dark-colored and won't show any grass stains—I hope," she said, eyeing Kat guiltily. Kat made a face back at her. It was sometimes hard to remember they were just subletting the Candys' apartment and using a lot of their stuff.

The concert band from one of the neighboring suburbs struck up some great tunes, both classical and popular, and the music backdrop made the tuna sandwiches, nibble food, and sodas taste just right for a picnic. Kat leaned back on her elbows, soaking in the holiday atmosphere as Joplin and Mozart and Motown filled the air. Amazing that so many different kinds of people had all descended on the parks, just having a good time. Maybe heaven was a little bit like this . . .

Funny. Kat had rarely thought about heaven before Pastor Clark died . . . how many weeks ago? She quickly pushed the thought away. His death and all the talk about seeing him again in heaven had made her think about her parents in a new way. Would they be in heaven? A heaven they didn't believe in?

"I gotta go to the ba'froom!" Conny announced. Reluctantly Rochelle started to get up, but Conny said loudly, "I want Nick to take me to the boys' ba'froom. They got those pee potties!"

A few heads turned in their direction and smiled. Rochelle seemed flustered, but Nick scrambled to his feet, laughing. "No problem. Come on, Conny." The two ambled off, hand in hand, to the brick beach house at the other end of the lagoon.

Rochelle watched them go. "Nick would make a good dad," she murmured.

Kat caught Bree shooting her a look. *"Don't even go there,"* she mouthed back.

✳

The Evanston fireworks had been spectacular. It was especially fun to see Conny's delight as red and blue rockets streaked skyward and exploded with ear-splitting booms or snap-crackle-and-pop, and sparkling stars rained down like celestial willow trees. The little boy sat high on Nick's shoulders as they'd moved with the crowd closer to the beach where the trees didn't obscure the view, creating an undulating wall of people "oohing" and "aahing" together as if a Leviathan monster had emerged from the lake.

And then it was over in a frenzy of exploding colors.

The trek home in the dark by bicycle turned out to be a madhouse as the hordes of people moved out of the parks. The streets were full of cars moving bumper to bumper, horns honking as people threaded in and out with their folding chairs and food coolers. But they finally made it back to the three-flat with no major mishaps and one sleepy boy who'd fallen asleep against Nick's back.

Everyone said they were going to sleep in . . . but for some reason Kat woke up early, felt wide awake, and got up. She padded quietly to the kitchen, made a pot of coffee, and took a steaming cup out onto the back porch along with her backpack. The sky—what she could see of it—was brilliant blue without a cloud anywhere, the early morning sun flashing golden in the windows on the top floors of the buildings around her.

What a spectacular day! And because she'd worked a long holiday shift on the Fourth, she had the rest of the weekend free. She sipped her coffee, feet up on another porch chair, enjoying the slight breeze kissing her face and reliving the fun evening they'd had biking to the Evanston fireworks.

But her mind tripped over Rochelle's comment when Nick had trundled Conny off to the "ba'frooms." *"Nick would make a good dad."* Had she been just talking in general? Sure, seeing how Nick related to Conny in such an easygoing way had given Kat a new appreciation for him too. At school she'd never had a chance to see him around little kids.

But . . . what if Rochelle meant he'd make a good dad for Conny? If so, it took some nerve to just come out and say it—like she had designs on him or something.

Kat squirmed. Was something more going on with Rochelle and Nick than met the eye? Yeah, he'd always been a tease and sometimes a flirt, but he was definitely more than that . . . In fact, he'd always been the glue that held their little foursome together back at CCU, mostly by knowing when to be funny and when to be serious and say the right thing. Part of it was that pastor thing he had going. As a new Christian, she appreciated knowing Nick knew the Scriptures and could give her a straight word from the Bible.

But come to think of it, he seemed a lot more serious lately—not so goofy and laid back. She kind of missed that side of Nick—but she also missed the long talks they used to have. Almost seemed like there was something he was holding back, a part of himself he wasn't sharing with her. Or maybe he was just bent out of shape because he had to do that membership thing alone—not sure what was up with that.

Or did it have something to do with Rochelle and Conny?

Kat didn't like not knowing what was going on with Nick. He was one of her best friends! And lately she'd found herself hoping . . . more than a friend. Hanging around so many seminary students at CCU, she'd told herself she did *not* want to be a pastor's wife. But what if that pastor was Nick? Her face flushed right there on the back porch for even thinking it. He'd never remotely hinted at such a thing. But someday she did want to get married, have kids, raise a family—and what guy did she know better than Nick? In fact, knowing Nick raised the bar pretty high for any other guy to leap over. Even the way he related to Conny had given her another glimpse into the man he was becoming . . .

Help! She had to stop this. Any moment now one of the others would wander out onto the porch and probably read her face like a book. Might even be Nick!

Jumping up, Kat slipped quietly into the kitchen to refill her coffee, then settled down again on the porch. She hadn't done much with the Bible study she'd wanted to do . . . now would be a perfect time. Digging into her backpack, she found her Bible and the list of scriptures Nick had found for her. Starting with the first one, she paged through the Old Testament until she found Isaiah, chapter 55, and began reading. *"Come, all you who are thirsty, come to the waters; and you who have no money, come, buy and eat!"*

Whoa! Kat's eyes widened. Sounded like Isaiah was talking to poor people—people without money—calling them to "come, buy, eat." Just like that food pantry they'd visited. People who had no money could come, "shop," and go home with something to eat. But was that just an image to talk about something else?

She read further and ended up reading the whole chapter. Then she sat there thinking a long time . . . until a childish voice at the screen door said, "Miss Kat? Mommy's still sleeping, but I'm hungry. Can I have some cereal?"

Kat jumped up and grinned at the little boy. "Got any money?"

Conny's forehead puckered in confusion. "No-o."

"Then you've come to the right place, little man. No money gets you a *big* bowl of cereal!"

Chapter 18

Today's the day!" Kat grinned at Nick as she and Brygitta walked on either side of him to church on Sunday morning. The TV weatherman had said the temperature was headed into the eighties, but at the moment it was only a cool sixty degrees, perfect for a walk. Rochelle and Conny had already gone with her parents since Avis was preaching and wanted to go early. "Are you excited or nervous?"

Dressed in nice khaki slacks and a pale blue summer dress shirt, no tie, Nick looked the picture of cool—until he let slip a nervous smile. "Both." He sent a sideways glance at them. "Wish you two were doing it with me."

"Oh, Nick," Bree moaned, "don't start."

"I know, I know. But hey . . . we took the Urban Experience class together, moved to this neighborhood together, and got involved at SouledOut together. Can't blame a guy for wishing we were doing the membership thing together." He said it lightly and grinned, but Kat sensed there was more feeling there than he let on.

She took his arm playfully. "Hey, I'm going to look into that baptism thing, then I'll play catch-up. Deal?"

Nick gave her a smile and nodded, but she left her hand in the crook of his arm as a show of support until they turned into the parking lot of the Howard Street shopping center. Making their way into the "sanctuary" of SouledOut, with its floor-to-ceiling windows looking out into the shopping center, the three of them settled into their usual row toward the back.

Justin Barnes was the worship leader that morning. Kat didn't know the young man very well, just that he also worked with Josh Baxter and the youth group, and she'd heard him share his story at the Memorial Day beach outing, how God had saved him off the streets and turned his life around. He sure acted like he had a lot to be thankful for when he led worship. And today was no different.

"Good morning, church!" Justin boomed. "Let's get on our feet and give God some praise this morning!" The rest of what he said was drowned out by a surround-sound of hallelujahs, amens, and shouts of "Glory!" as the praise team launched into a spirited rendition of "I'm trading my sorrows . . . for the joy of the Lord!"

Trading sorrows . . . shame . . . sickness . . . pain—for joy. As she sang the words, Kat again envisioned some of the faces she'd seen at the food pantry. So many people crammed into that little foyer! Not many looked as if they had the joy of the Lord, though almost everyone had expressed appreciation for the food and clothes they'd received. So many hungry people in just this Chicago neighborhood? And it was only one neighborhood out of hundreds!

Kat was mulling over the food pantry so hard she barely

realized the praise and worship time was over until Pastor Cobbs announced Nick Taylor's membership. "This young man received a vote of confidence from the congregation a week or so ago about doing his pastoral internship here at SouledOut— and praise God, he wants to make his commitment to this church official by becoming a member, even though he is still a seminary student. So, Brother Nick, let's do this thing!"

The congregation laughed and nodded and said "Amen!" as Nick joined the shorter man on the low platform and responded affirmatively to the membership questions. Did he acknowledge Jesus Christ as his Lord and Savior? *Yes.* Did he desire to enter into a covenant with the members here at SouledOut Community Church as part of the family of God? *Yes.*

Kat listened intently. The questions Nick was asked somehow took on a deeper meaning when asked in person rather than just being words on paper. Could she make those commitments? She wasn't regular in her Bible study and prayer. And what did it mean to relate to brothers and sisters in the body of Christ in a spirit of love? To maintain unity by reconciling differences? It all sounded good, but—just like that one about "courtesy in speech"—not so easy to actually live out.

As he finished the questions, the pastor asked the congregation if they could make these same commitments to Nick as their brother in Christ, to which there was a chorus of "We do!" accompanied by the usual happy hallelujahs. But for a moment Kat felt bereft, as if she'd just been left behind. Why hadn't she ever considered baptism before now? It had never occurred to her it would stand in the way of becoming a member. But no one had said anything about baptism when she'd taken her first step of faith, and she'd mostly done church-hopping while going to CCU. SouledOut was the first church she'd ever been serious about.

Nick returned to his seat as Justin got up again to make announcements. Kat gave Nick's arm a quick squeeze and whispered, "You did good. I—" But she stopped before adding she wished she could've been up there with him.

It was what it was.

Pastor Cobbs announced that Sister Avis would be giving the sermon that morning. Kat eyed her through half-closed lids as the pastor prayed for her. She'd always enjoyed the way Mrs. D led worship and was curious to hear her preach. The woman looked calm and dignified in the modest royal-blue suit she was wearing. Her very dignity was a little intimidating. But . . . this was the same woman who'd wrapped Kat in a big embrace outside the coffee shop that day after Kat had witnessed Mrs. D's reunion with her daughter, causing Kat to weep at the distance she felt from her own mother, too busy with her social life in Phoenix to even write or call very often. There were times when Kat wished for another one of those hugs—but Mrs. D had her own daughter and grandson back now.

Get over it, Kat, she told herself. She was getting too emotional today. What was up with that?

But when Mrs. Douglass introduced her text, Kat nearly fell off her chair. "Brothers and sisters, turn in your Bibles to Isaiah 55 . . ."

That was the same chapter she'd just read yesterday morning! The one that had really made her think.

"As you all know," Avis went on, "today is communion Sunday, and we will all share the bread and wine as Christ commanded us, to remember His death until He returns. But sometimes we do so almost automatically, its rich meaning diminished simply because we do it so often. Why did Jesus choose bread and wine for His memorial? What is significant about these common elements? Let's read."

Kat hastily turned her own Bible to Isaiah and read along the words that were now somewhat familiar to her.

"'Come, buy wine and milk without money and without cost,'" Avis Douglass read in her rich voice. "'Why spend money on what is not bread, and your labor on what does not satisfy? Listen, listen to me, and eat what is good, and your soul will delight in the richest of fare . . . I will make an everlasting covenant with you, my faithful love promised to David . . .'"

Kat sat mesmerized as Mrs. Douglass talked about what good news it would be to people who were hungry and thirsty but had no money to be told they could eat and drink without having to pay. Well, yeah! Like Lady Lolla, the scrawny would-be model who looked as if she hadn't had a decent meal in ages. Or the single moms who came with their kids, getting honest-to-goodness food without having to pay for it. Those food pantries really were good news!

She turned her attention back to Mrs. D, who was saying that all of us are spiritually hungry and thirsty, even though we may not always realize it. And through the prophet Isaiah, God was announcing good news! God was calling all of us—people who have nothing as well as people who seem to have "everything"—to come and be part of the "everlasting covenant," the family of God.

There was more from the chapter—but Kat kept thinking about the food pantry. One of the food shoppers from Manna

House, what's-her-name, had said that's what this city really needed, more food pantries.

More food pantries.

And Rochelle had gone a step further, saying she thought more churches ought to start food pantries.

As Mrs. Douglass wrapped up her sermon, she emphasized that God had taken the initiative, sending out His invitation to all who were hungry and thirsty. "And so we come to the Lord's Table today, remembering Jesus who came to offer us that spiritual food and drink, sealed by His sacrifice on the cross."

Taking the initiative, like God did.

Mrs. Douglass stood aside as Pastor Cobbs stood up and called Nick Taylor to come up and join them. "As our newest member and pastoral intern, Nick will be helping to serve communion," the pastor said as the praise team members returned to their instruments and began to play softly. "All believers are welcome to come to the Lord's Table to receive the bread and the wine."

Kat felt a flicker of surprise as Nick left his seat and helped Pastor Cobbs bring the communion table forward. He hadn't mentioned he was going to help serve communion. The older pastor read the familiar passage of Scripture when Jesus shared the Passover bread with His disciples and said, "Take, eat, this is My body. Do this in remembrance of Me . . ." He did the same with the wine. Pastor Cobbs then broke the loaf of bread on the table and gave half to Avis Douglass and the other half to Nick. Lines started to form as people received a small piece of bread from either Mrs. D or Nick, then dipped it in the cup of wine held by Pastor Cobbs before eating it.

Kat followed Bree in the line going toward Nick. As she got

closer, she noticed the cloth covering the communion table—
why hadn't she noticed it before? They'd been at the church a
couple of months, and communion was served the first Sunday
of each month. But somehow she'd missed the table covering. But today her eyes locked on the cloth, which had been
embroidered all around its edge with figures of many races and
nationalities.

She drew in a quick breath . . . so beautifully done. So like
the people she'd seen at the food pantry. All kinds. All ages.
Hungry. Thirsty. Without money to pay—

"Kat?"

Nick was whispering to her. Oh my goodness, she was next.
She held out her hands like a cup and he put the piece of bread
into them, murmuring, "The body of Christ, broken for you,
Kat."

Kat nodded and gave him a little smile. He was in his element, bless him. Then she stepped over to Pastor Cobbs, dipped
her bread, and put it in her mouth.

But all the way back to her seat, her eyes were searching for
Edesa Baxter. She had to talk to her right after the service!

Chapter 19

Edesa felt a gentle squeeze on her hands as Avis Douglass put the torn piece of bread in them. "The body of Christ, broken for you, dear sister Edesa," Avis whispered, giving her a tender smile. Then Avis tore off another small piece of bread and turned to Edesa's husband, who was right behind her. "The body of Christ, broken for you, Josh."

Edesa felt goose bumps on the back of her neck. It never failed to touch her to hear her name mentioned as she received the broken bread representing Christ's broken body. *Broken for me.*

Today it felt even more meaningful receiving the bread from Avis, her Yada Yada sister for the past several years, and now in her new role as an interim pastor. Was that how it felt when Jesus broke the bread in the intimate upper room and passed it to His disciples—His closest friends—after they'd spent three intense years together, eating, praying, walking dusty roads in the desert, swallowed by crowds in the city, sailing through storms on the Sea of Galilee?

Stepping toward Pastor Cobbs who was holding the cup of wine, Edesa dipped her bread and put it in her mouth, eyes closed, as Pastor Cobbs murmured, "The blood of Christ, shed for you, Sister Edesa."

The scripture Avis had read during the sermon echoed inside Edesa's head as she waited for Josh to dip and eat his bread: *"Why spend money on what is not bread, and your labor on what does not satisfy? Listen, listen to me, and eat what is good . . . hear me, that your soul may live."*

Labor. The whole process of making bread to eat—tortillas, to be exact—had been a daily chore where she'd grown up in Honduras. Her mother had mixed the flour with water, lard, baking powder, and a tad of salt, then rolled pieces of the dough into a ball, slapping and patting it into a flat tortilla, which was fried in a hot skillet on the stove. The flat tortillas were then eaten with beans, maybe some meat and vegetables, morning, noon, and night . . . and the next day the process began all over again.

Josh saw that she'd waited for him and took her hand as they returned to their seats. But Edesa's mind was still back on the bread "that does not satisfy." She remembered always feeling a little bit hungry. Sometimes her father had work, sometimes he didn't. A family of six children—two boys and four girls—was a lot to feed.

But somehow her parents had managed to send her to school, then to the U.S. to college. And somehow they'd instilled in her a deep faith in Jesus, the Bread of Life who satisfied the deepest hunger of the spirit.

A wave of homesickness swept over Edesa, thinking about her family back in Honduras. How her mother, Eunice, and papa, Jubal, would love to see Gracie! And meet Josh. They hadn't been able to come for the wedding, it had happened so fast . . . but now that Josh was out of school, maybe—

"Want me to pick up Gracie from the nursery?" Josh's voice cut into her wandering thoughts. She realized communion was over, someone had said the benediction, and people were starting to drift over to the coffee table.

"*Sí. Gracias.* Sorry, I was thinking about something . . ."

But he was already heading for the double doors that led to the back rooms.

Edesa stood up and gathered her things. The aroma of fresh coffee tempted her, but it might perk her up, and a Sunday afternoon nap after she put Gracie down sounded even better.

"Edesa?" Kathryn Davies appeared, breathless. "Do you have a minute?"

Was she going to ask about teaching a nutrition class again? Edesa glanced hopefully toward the doors to the back rooms, but . . . oh well. She smiled graciously. "*Sí*, I have a moment until Josh gets back with Gracie."

Kat pulled up a chair so Edesa sat back down too. Looked like this might take longer than a minute. The young woman pushed back a stray lock of hair. "Thank you for encouraging me to visit one of the food pantries in Rogers Park. I got a chance to visit the one at Rock of Ages—actually, Nick and Brygitta and Rochelle came too."

Surprise. Edesa hadn't actually expected Kat to follow up on her suggestion, at least not so quickly. "That's great! Tell me about it."

Kat laughed. "It was quite an experience." Edesa listened, her smile widening as Kat described how they got roped in as volunteers. "The place was really jammed, even with the rain. Not just the homeless, but whole families, kids . . ." Her voice trailed off and her gaze grew distant as if her mind was chewing on something.

"So . . . what do you think? Sounds like they could use more volunteers."

Kat's attention jerked back to Edesa's face and her blue eyes danced with a sudden excitement. "That's just it. Their pantry is open on Wednesday at four and my shifts at The Common Cup either end at five or start at five, which would make it hard. And really, they were so crowded! They even had to turn some people away. Rochelle said more churches need to start food pantries—the same thing those women from Estelle Bentley's cooking class said. So I've been thinking . . . what if we started a food pantry here at SouledOut? Like on the weekend when it'd be easier to get volunteers."

"Start a—" Edesa nearly choked. "Here? At SouledOut?"

Josh appeared with Gracie. "Mommeeee!" The little girl let go of her daddy's hand and launched herself into Edesa's lap.

"Okay if Gracie stays here with you while I go find Justin?" Without waiting for an answer, Josh headed off toward the milling crowd around the coffee table.

Edesa was glad for the distraction. "Hey, sweetie. Say hi to Miss Kathryn." She nuzzled Gracie's dark, silky hair, trying to collect her thoughts.

Gracie giggled and eyed the other woman mischievously. "Miss *Gato!*"

Kat grinned. "*Meow* yourself, Gracie." But she raised her eyebrows at Edesa as if still asking her question.

Arms wrapped around Gracie, almost for support, Edesa

cleared her throat. "I hardly know what to say. That's a huge idea. Something that would need a lot of prayer for sure."

Kat nodded eagerly. "See, you started me thinking when you talked about Jesus feeding the five thousand. I read that story, oh, maybe five times. The disciples wanted to send the people away, someplace else, to get something to eat. But Jesus said, *you* feed them." Kat's whole face was alive, her startling blue eyes and long lashes framed by the wavy fall of rich brown hair. "And then you told me what Estelle Bentley said, that she thought what I really wanted was to feed hungry people. And . . . and I think that's what God is calling me to do. Feed hungry people!"

Edesa blinked. *Oh, Señor Dios, help us.* Was she responsible for turning Kathryn Davies loose on this idea? That aspect of the biblical story certainly had spoken to her too. But she hadn't meant it as a "word from the Lord" to start a food pantry at SouledOut!

Gracie wiggled, trying to get down. There wasn't time to talk about this now. But Kat seemed so earnest, so sincere, so . . . serious. Standing up in order to hoist Gracie onto her hip, Edesa said, "I don't know, Kat. It's a great idea, but whether that's what we're called to do here at SouledOut is a big question. I . . . I promise I'll pray about it." Was she dodging the issue? "You'd certainly need to talk to Pastor Cobbs. Are you sure you can't work around your work schedule to volunteer at Rock of Ages? Learn more about what it would take?"

Kat stood too, the light in her eyes fading a bit. "Well . . . I'll see what I can do. But you should've seen the crowd packed in there, Edesa! If more churches had food pantries, the burden wouldn't be on just a few. And SouledOut would be a great place, you know, right here on Howard Street near the El—"

"Mommeee! I'm thirsty! Want some lemonade!" Gracie squirmed so hard Edesa had to set her down.

Kat suddenly blushed. "I'm sorry. I'm blathering. But . . . could we talk some other time? I'll do more research and come more prepared." She held out her hand to Gracie. "Want to come with me, sweetie? I'll get you some lemonade. Is that okay?" She eyed Edesa.

Edesa nodded and watched as Gracie grabbed Kat's hand and pulled her toward the coffee table, which usually had something cold to drink too. *Whew.* She blew out a breath and sat down with a *whump.* Her thoughts tumbled. Kat's idea was exciting, but overwhelming too. At least all she'd promised to do was pray about—

"Miss Edesa?"

Startled, Edesa realized Rochelle Johnson had sidled into the row of chairs and sat down beside her.

"Rochelle!" She leaned over and gave Avis's daughter a warm hug. "Please don't 'Miss Edesa' me. Aren't we the same age? It's so good to see you." That was an understatement. Rochelle probably had no idea how fervently the Yada Yada Prayer Group had prayed for her and Conny—and just look at how God had answered their prayers! *Gracias, Jesús.* "Where's that handsome boy of yours?"

Rochelle snorted. "Pretending to be one of the big boys. But do you have a minute?"

Edesa almost laughed. Maybe she should hang out her shingle, right here at this chair. "*Sí.* What's up?"

Rochelle seemed momentarily flustered and glanced about as if making sure no one was nearby. "This might seem silly, but . . . you and Josh. You two have a good marriage—I've seen you together. How do you make it work?"

Edesa tried not to show her surprise. Was Rochelle thinking about trying to get back together with her ex? Dexter, if she remembered right. But hadn't he been abusive? According to Avis, they'd had to get an order of protection—years ago, when Conny was just a baby—and she was sure there'd been a divorce. But what did she know? Maybe the man had wised up, was getting help, wanted to step up to the plate. Or maybe it was a new beau. She wouldn't be surprised. Rochelle was certainly a beautiful young woman—lovely skin, like her mom, though lighter in shade. Large eyes. Sweet face. And all that gorgeous hair!

She smiled at Rochelle. "I don't think I've got a one-minute answer. But *gracias,* that's a nice compliment. I feel grateful to be married to a man who loves God too. That's the first thing. It gives us an important foundation."

Rochelle nodded soberly. "Yes. I realize that now. Oh, Dexter made a show of going to church when we first met, but that's all it was—a show. I'm seeing what a difference a man who loves God and wants to follow Him could make in a relationship. But you and Josh . . . I mean, he's white and you're black. And you're, you know, Spanish or something too. I mean, how does that work out?"

"Oh!" Edesa was taken aback. She knew their interracial marriage, though more common these days, was still unusual enough to make people curious. But why was *Rochelle* asking? "Well, having families who support us has been important. The Baxters have accepted me like a daughter—that goes a long way. As for my parents, they haven't met Josh yet, but they know all about him, and I'm sure they'll like him. Uh, speaking of . . ." She cleared her throat discreetly as Josh headed in their direction.

"Hi, hon. I'm ready to go. Mom and Dad said they'd drive us home. Where's Gracie?"

"Kathryn Davies has her. Can you—?"

Rochelle jumped up. "That's all right. We can talk another time."

"Of course." Edesa stood up too and gave Rochelle another hug. "Call me," she whispered and watched as Avis's daughter hurried away.

"What's going on?" Josh asked as they scanned the crowd looking for Kat and Gracie. "You're suddenly very popular with the young ladies."

"Oh . . . girl stuff." Edesa was too overwhelmed to talk to Josh right now. First Kathryn with her big idea for a food pantry at SouledOut. And then Rochelle, asking how to make an interracial marriage work.

What was *that* about?

Chapter 20

Nick wished his parents could've been in the worship service today. They'd always been supportive of his desire to go to seminary, but he wasn't sure they really believed he'd end up a pastor. They were all too familiar with his shenanigans in high school and what his mother called his "weird sense of humor." But this was the real deal. Not only was he doing an internship at SouledOut Community Church for his master's of divinity, but he'd just made a membership covenant with the same church. Not just his name on a membership list either, but a serious covenant with these people.

He felt as if he'd just leaped out of an airplane. No turning back.

Maybe it was just as well his folks weren't present. Too easy to slip into the "kid" role. But he'd call them and try to share what this meant to him.

"Congratulations, young man." Peter Douglass clapped Nick on the back and shook his hand. "I was busting my buttons this morning as if you were my own son." The businessman-elder's smile widened, stretching the trim mustache above his upper lip. "You've made quite an inroad into our family's life in just a few short months, you know—moving into our building, working at my shop, being on the pastoral team with my wife, and now 'big brother' to our grandson. Maybe I better watch out!" The man laughed heartily but Nick was tongue-tied. To hear it put like that sounded as if he were worming his way into these situations deliberately.

"Nick . . . Nick." Peter Douglass suddenly got serious. "I'm just messing with you. I'm glad God brought you into this church and into our lives. You're young, but I see the hand of God on your life. If I can be there for you in any way, son, just let me know."

Relieved, Nick nodded tentatively as the man glanced around the large room, buzzing with after-service conversations, kids ducking in and out of clusters of people, and the usual crowd around the coffee table. "Well, better collect Rochelle and Conny. I'm going to drive them to the South Side this afternoon."

"Conny's going to visit his dad? How's that working out?" The moment he asked, Nick wished he could take it back. "Sorry, not my business."

Peter smiled wryly. "That's all right. Doing it for Conny's sake—but no way am I going to let Rochelle take Conny by herself. We've decided to take him and pick him up, so Dexter knows we're on his case. Takes a big bite out of our Sunday afternoons, but . . ."

"Well, if you want me to take him sometime, let me know."

Peter lifted an eyebrow. The pause lasted only a second or two but felt longer to Nick. "Hmm, don't think that'd be a good idea. But thanks anyway." The older man slapped Nick again on the arm. "See you tomorrow at work." And he moved off.

Not a good idea? Nick felt confused. He understood why Mr. Douglass didn't want Rochelle to be dealing with her ex by herself. But wouldn't it be helpful to give Mr. and Mrs. D a free Sunday afternoon now and then? He was sure Conny would feel comfortable going with him. He frowned. Did Mr. Douglass think he wasn't man enough to stand up to Dexter?

"Hey." Kat showed up at his elbow. She sounded breathless. "I'm ready to go. You want to walk home?"

More than ready. "Sure. Where's Bree?"

"Has to work this afternoon. She already left. I take over for her at five. The owners are good about not scheduling us for Sunday morning."

Now this was nice. Nick's spirit lifted as they pushed out the double glass doors and headed across the parking lot.

The day was beginning to feel sultry, and Kat seemed pensive as they headed down Clark Street. But he wouldn't mind drawing out this time with Kat longer than the walk home. "You want to stop at one of the Mexican cafés and get a bite to eat? The Douglasses are taking Rochelle and Conny to see his dad, so it's just us for lunch. But I'm on supper tonight."

She shrugged. "Sure."

The tiny café they stopped at was mostly takeout, but it had six small tables if you wanted to eat in. Nick ordered a large burrito with a side of rice and beans, and Kat ordered two cheese enchiladas and a lemonade. "I'll get this." Nick quickly pulled out his wallet to pay at the counter before they sat down.

"Oh. Okay. Thanks." Kat sucked on her lemonade as she took it to the table.

Nick was surprised. He'd expected Kat to protest, to insist on paying for her share. He smiled inwardly. His dad was old-fashioned, had taught him a guy pays for the girl he's interested in. *Well*...

The food came quickly. Should he say a blessing over the food? He didn't want to appear sanctimonious. But Kat seemed oblivious, staring out the window at people passing on the street. Nick breathed a silent *Thank You*, took a bite of his burrito, and then said, "Any chance I can join the conversation going on in your head?"

Kat turned from the window and grinned apologetically. "Sorry . . . oh, didn't know the food was here." She dug in with her fork, took a bite of her enchilada, and then pointed the fork at him. "You know that food pantry we visited?"

"Yeah. Quite an experience. Pass that green hot sauce, will you?"

She absently pushed the skinny bottle his way. "What would you think if we started a food pantry at SouledOut?"

"Started a—!" Nick stared at her. "You're kidding."

"No. I just want to know what you think about the idea."

Nick blew out a breath. Why was he surprised? Kat was often two jumps ahead of anyone else when she latched onto an idea. "I thought you were going to ask what I thought about you volunteering at Rock of Ages. Which would be great."

She made a face. "You and Edesa Baxter. Okay, you're right. I should volunteer. But it's not that easy to fit their hours into my current work schedule. And remember what Rochelle said? *More churches should start food pantries.* Remember how crowded it was at Rock of Ages? If more churches set up food pantries, it would share the burden of feeding the hungry people in this neighborhood . . ."

Nick listened as Kat talked excitedly, waving her fork, about realizing just how much Jesus cared about hungry people. Look at how He fed the five thousand, she said—and that was just counting the men! *"You feed them,"* He told His disciples. "Which made me think. Rather than just let Rock of Ages feed the hungry, maybe *we* should feed them too!"

"Might start by feeding yourself—your food's getting cold," he teased. "But seriously, sounds like a big job. How would you even start?"

Kat shrugged. "I don't know. Maybe we could start by asking for food donations from the congregation, and encourage people to get donations from their workplaces too. Like at Software Symphony, you could set up a box or barrel or something for employees to donate food. Mr. D would support that, don't you think?" She didn't wait for an answer but rattled on about Saturday mornings, how it might be easier to recruit volunteers on the weekend, and once it was up and running, they could find out how to apply to the Chicago Food Depository and apply for free USDA food.

She eyed him breathlessly. "So? What do you think?"

"I think," he said carefully, "you've got a tiger by the tail. Don't you think it'd be smart to volunteer at Rock of Ages for a while and get some experience before getting in over your head?"

"O-*kay*. But after that. What do you think about the *idea* of a pantry at SouledOut?"

"I think," he said, chosing his words carefully, ". . . you should talk to Pastor Cobbs and Sister Avis. They're the pastoral team now. It would definitely need their blessing."

Kat threw up her hands. "And yours! You're on the interim team now too!"

"Yeah," he protested, "but I'm so new to SouledOut, I have no idea how such a thing would fit with the ministry priorities of the church."

Kat's eyes and voice softened. "Nick, if I were to get involved in something like this, it would mean a lot to me to have your support. In fact, I'm not sure I could do it if you thought it was a dumb idea."

Nick laid down his fork, his own burrito only half-eaten. She *needed* his support? Did she have any idea how much that meant to him? Now he was the one who stared out the café window, only vaguely noticing the Sunday afternoon traffic backed up on Clark Street. What *did* he think of her idea?

After a long minute he turned back, reached across the tiny table, and took Kat's slender hand. "Okay. It's a fantastic idea. Not sure *how* you'd pull it off, but I have no doubt you'd figure out a way. We don't take Jesus' commandment to 'Love your neighbor as yourself' seriously enough. Your idea is beautiful. I . . . love your heart, Kat." *And I love you,* he wanted to say. But the words stuck in his throat.

She gripped his hand with both of hers. "Thank you, Nick. That means a lot." Tipping her head, she looked at him earnestly. "You meet with Mrs. D and Pastor Cobbs tomorrow night, don't you? Would you ask if I could come talk to the three of you about this idea?"

"Kat!"

"Okay, okay! I wouldn't have to come tomorrow night. Just ask if I can meet with you all sometime soon."

※

Nick went for a run along the lake that afternoon, even though the temperature had spiked into the high eighties. His mind was running too. Honestly! Trying to keep track of Kat's wild ideas was like playing with quicksilver. In fact, her request for him to bring it up in the weekly pastoral meeting had so thrown him off that he never did say the main thing he'd wanted to say. Well, maybe he'd work up the courage when he got back if she hadn't left for work yet.

Sweat ran down his face and trickled under his armpits as he jogged along the path, hardly noticing the beach volleyball games and Frisbee players, his mind on Kat. The girl had definitely gotten under his skin. He loved looking at her. She didn't have the classic blond looks of an Olivia or the pixie cuteness of Brygitta. Or even the exotic beauty of Rochelle Johnson, with her creamy-brown skin, large dark eyes, and full lips. Kat was certainly pretty with her wavy hair and striking blue eyes. But it was more than that. Her face and personality were so . . . so *alive*. And he felt alive when he was with her.

Why was it so hard to tell her how he felt? Okay, partly because he didn't know how she'd react. Did she only think of him as a buddy? Sometimes he got clues it might be more than that. Even her saying she *needed* his support if she did something like the food pantry made him feel she depended on him to be more than just a buddy.

But if she didn't . . . he didn't want to ruin the close friendship they enjoyed by adding a romantic element that would make her afraid to be close to him. And their living situation made it even more complicated. Right now they were all just housemates and friends. But if a romance got thrown into the mix, the whole delicate balance could get very, very complicated.

Arrgh! Nick pounded out his frustration by increasing his pace. Leaving the jogging path, he zigzagged back through the residential streets, only slowing a few blocks out so he could cool down by the time he arrived back at their three-flat.

Kat was sitting on one of the flat concrete arms bracketing the three wide steps leading into their building, her laptop on her knees. A sprinkler went around and around on the postage-stamp bit of grass off to the side, watering Mrs. D's flowers. "Hey," he said, flopping down on one of the steps below her, panting slightly.

"Hey, yourself. Nice run?" She frowned at the screen, but after a moment tapped a key and closed the lid. "Just e-mailing my parents. Trying to keep in touch more—you know, after what Pastor Clark's brother said at his funeral, how much he regretted that they'd lost touch." She sighed. "It's not that easy talking to my parents, but I'm trying. At least with an e-mail, I get to say my whole spiel before my father can disagree with . . . whatever."

Nick mopped the sweat off his face with his T-shirt. "My folks don't do e-mail. If I don't call at least once a week, they call me." He hesitated but then blundered ahead. "Hope they can meet you someday. They'd like you." He grinned at her. "I'd like to meet your parents too." Was that too obvious?

Kat cut her eyes at him sideways. "Not sure about *that*. Meeting my parents, I mean." She seemed to be studying him as she slid her laptop back into its case. "On second thought, meeting you and Bree and the Douglasses would probably be a smart move. They think I've gone off the deep end and that I'm living with a bunch of religious nuts." She simpered at him. "Might be good to see how *normal* you all are."

It was that "normal" comment. Nick couldn't resist. "Is that so?" Scrambling to his feet, he snatched the laptop case off her lap and set it down, lifted Kat off her precarious seat into his arms, and hustled down the steps.

"Nick!" she screeched, kicking her legs. "What are you doing?"

"I'm hot. Thought I'd cool off!" Grinning, he headed into the sprinkler.

Kat screeched again. "Stop it! Let me down! I've got to go to work in half an hour!" But she was laughing, holding on tight around his neck as the sprinkler *chu-chu-chued* back and forth, getting them both thoroughly wet.

He didn't see Rochelle and the Douglasses until he heard a familiar childish yell. "Nick! Me too! Me too!" Conny appeared on the sidewalk, let go of his mother's hand, and ran straight toward the sprinkler.

Sputtering, Kat slipped out of Nick's arms and escaped . . . replaced by Conny, jumping up and down in front of him. Oh well, he was already wet. He grabbed Conny's hands and hopped around in the sprinkler as the little boy giggled happily.

"Just don't stomp on my flowers!" Avis Douglass called as she and her husband disappeared inside the foyer, shaking their heads.

"You come too, Mommy!" Conny yelled, running back to the sidewalk and grabbing his mother's hand. He dragged Rochelle into the sprinkler with one hand and grabbed Nick's hand with the other. "Dance, Mommy, dance! We're dancing in the rain!" Soon Rochelle was laughing too.

As the three of them paraded around in the sprinkler, Nick glanced over his shoulder in time to see Kat pick up her computer case and disappear inside behind the Douglasses.

Arrgh. Sometimes Conny's timing was off. Way off.

Chapter 21

Kat hadn't counted on having to change out of wet clothes before going to work. Still, she couldn't help grinning as she toweled her hair. It'd been fun—even if they had been acting like a couple of teenagers. She hadn't realized Nick was so strong. He'd picked her up like a rag doll . . . and her face flushed as she remembered the feel of his arms holding her close against his body, her own arms around his neck.

Too bad Conny and Rochelle had shown up right then.

Admit it, Kat, she told herself, pulling on a dry pair of capris and a knit shirt. *The guy's a hunk—even if he does want to be a pastor.* She snorted trying to stifle her laughter. *Pastor Nick the Hunk.* No, no, she couldn't call him that . . . he might take it wrong.

Or maybe she wanted him to take it wrong. Or right.

Enough of this! She had to get to work! Bree would jump all over her if she was late relieving her at the coffee shop.

Zipping down the carpeted front stairs, she met Rochelle, Conny, and Nick coming up, Conny clinging to his mom with one hand and to Nick with the other, looking for all the world like a little family. "We're wet!" Conny giggled.

"And I'm late! It's all your fault, Nick Taylor." Kat playfully slapped him on the arm as she passed. *Pastor Nick the Hunk.*

"Hey! Sorry supper isn't ready!" he called after her as she turned on the landing and kept going. "I'll save you something."

"Okay!" And she was out the door. She wasn't hungry now, but she'd definitely be hungry by the time she got off at nine.

Kat made it to the coffee shop in record time by running every half block. Only three minutes late. "Sorry," she said to Bree as she tied on her apron. "Long story. Ask Nick."

Bree tossed her own apron into the laundry bin. "No problem. But I just remembered it's Livie's birthday this week. We oughta do something."

"Yikes! I forgot. Sure. Let's talk when I get home tonight . . . Coming!" she called, scurrying out of the back room as the bell on the counter dinged. She smiled at the man standing on the other side of the counter with two preteens who were ogling the brownies and oversized cookies in the glass case. Must be dad's night out with the kids. "What's your craving tonight, eh, boys? Have you tried our specialty ice cream?"

❄

When Kat got home that evening, Rochelle and Bree were in the living room watching TV. The rant from the TV sounded like "Madea" . . . had to be a Tyler Perry movie. Kat tossed her backpack on a chair. "Where's Nick? He said he'd save me some supper."

Rochelle was sitting cross-legged on the couch, hugging a

pillow. "Did. There's pasta salad in the fridge." Her eyes never strayed from the TV.

Kat headed for the kitchen, found the pasta salad, and dished up a generous helping of shell pasta, veggies, ham, and cheese all mixed with some kind of vinaigrette. Looked yummy, though she might pick out the ham.

Bree wandered in. "There's some garlic bread too. I'll toast it for you."

"Thanks. I can do it if you want to finish your movie."

"Nah. I've seen it before. Madea gets on my nerves some-times." Bree tipped her head toward the other room and lowered her voice as she put a couple of slices of garlic bread in the toaster oven. "Besides, Rochelle's kinda been in a bum mood since they got back this afternoon."

"Why? Because Conny and Nick pulled her into the sprin-kler? Give me a break."

"Nah, that wasn't it. Some fuss with Dexter, I think. Anyway, she asked Nick if he'd read to Conny before bed. Said her son needed some normal guy-time after his visit with his dad. I think Nick's still reading to Conny."

"Ha. Not sure chasing around in the sprinkler falls under *normal* . . . Uh, is that garlic bread done yet?" Kat was hungrier than she'd realized, and she didn't really want to talk about Conny. "So what should we do for Olivia's birthday? If we're going to send her something, we'd need to get it in the mail tomorrow."

Bree pulled out another kitchen chair. "I've got a better idea. Why don't we invite Livie and her sister, Elin, to come visit next weekend? It's already been several weeks since she went home . . . well, home to their aunt in Madison, I mean. Anyway, it'd be fun."

"That's a great idea, Bree! Except . . . where would they sleep? Rochelle and Conny took her place, you know."

Bree snorted. "Details, details. Make Nick sleep on the couch and give them the study or something."

"I'm sleeping on the couch? What did I do?" Nick's voice behind them made both Kat and Bree jerk around in their chairs as he came into the kitchen. Kat snickered at the puppy-dog look on his face.

"Hey. Private conversation," Bree pouted. "Don't sneak up on us like that."

"It's not a private conversation if you're talking about me." Nick pulled out another chair. "What's up?"

Kat told him Bree's idea about inviting their former house-mate and her younger sister to visit next weekend. "It's Olivia's birthday Thursday."

Nick shrugged. "Sure, I'll sleep on the couch. Great idea." He shifted in his chair and eyed Kat.

She was just about to say, "What?" when Rochelle wandered into the kitchen. "Any pasta salad left? I'm still hungry." The young mom got herself a plate from the cupboard. "Thanks for reading to Conny, Nick. I just tucked him in and he asked if you'd come say prayers with him."

"Oh, uh, sure. I guess." Nick rose somewhat reluctantly. "Be back in a minute."

Rochelle helped herself to some of the pasta salad and joined them at the table. "What's this about Nick sleeping on the couch?"

Kat munched on her garlic bread, letting Bree fill Rochelle in on their idea. What was that look Nick had given her? Like he had something on his mind. Why did it seem like Conny or Rochelle showed up every time she and Nick had something going on? Coincidence, she knew, but still . . . annoying sometimes.

"Olivia's your friend who lived here before Conny and me, right?" Rochelle sighed. "Maybe Conny and I should give up our room. Your friend was here first."

What was with the Eeyore attitude? "Not necessary, Rochelle," Kat said. "It'll be fine . . . Are you okay? Did something happen this afternoon with Dexter?"

Rochelle poked the pasta salad with her fork. "Oh, I dunno. He was acting pretty decent for a while, letting Conny stay with him, taking him to school. But now he's . . . oh, just being a jerk."

Bree leaned forward, frowning. "Is he giving you a hard time about seeing Conny only once a week?"

Rochelle grimaced. "Actually, I don't want to talk about it."

Kat and Bree exchanged glances. *O-kaay.* Kat hopped up, stuck her empty plate in the dishwasher, and filled the teakettle with water. "Tea, anybody? By the way, I'm thinking of volunteering at that food pantry again this week. I have to work the afternoon shift on Wednesday, but if Mrs. Wilson—or Sister Beatrice or whatever they call her—doesn't mind me coming late, does anyone else want to come?"

"Can't." Bree sighed. "I've got the evening shift that day."

Rochelle chewed her pasta thoughtfully. "I might be interested if I can find somebody to watch Conny. I'll ask Mom."

Kat was surprised. She'd thrown out an open invitation, but she hadn't expected Rochelle to volunteer—not after what she'd said about food pantries being too much of a reminder of her months on the street. Kat regretted being annoyed at her earlier. "That'd be great, Rochelle. Let me know."

"So." Rochelle's mood seemed to brighten. "Tell me more about your friend. Let's plan something fun while she's here. You said her sister's still in high school?"

The three of them had their heads together when Nick came back. "Hey, Nick. Is your laptop handy?" Bree asked. "We want to check out what's going on in Chicago next weekend. See if there's some kind of ethnic festival . . . or maybe we could do a picnic at Millennium Park if there's a concert."

"Has anyone called Livie yet to find out if she and Elin want to come?" Nick said.

Bree rolled her eyes. "Details, details. Okay, you get the laptop, I'll call Livie."

Olivia screamed so excitedly when Bree called with their invitation that the rest of them could hear—and the phone wasn't even on Speaker. So Nick was assigned to find a festival or outdoor concert to attend, Bree said she'd work on getting Livie and Elin here, and Kat volunteered to come up with food.

As the kitchen-klatch broke up, Kat hung back and cornered Nick. "You looked like you had something on your mind earlier. Is everything okay?"

Nick seemed flustered. "Oh . . . yeah. It's all right. Maybe another time." He sidled away. "Night."

Kat watched him disappear into the study. Something was *definitely* on his mind.

❀

"Hi, Miss Kat!" Latoya Sims grabbed hold of Kat's arm and hung on as they entered the wide hallway of Bethune Elementary the next morning, which gleamed from the weekend cleaning and smelled strongly of lemon oil. "What we gonna do today?"

"You're early." Kat grinned at the bouncy eight-year-old as she headed for the school office. "Want to help me photocopy our math games for today?"

It was the fourth week of the Summer Tutoring and Enrichment Program, and Kat felt as if she was hitting her stride. She'd had to get up early that morning to prepare her math lesson, and she'd also found some fun crafts and games online that could be made with simple household items—paper plates, paper bags, newspaper, a pizza takeout box, a pair of dice, straws, cotton balls. She was eager to try them this week. Making the games would be as much fun as actually playing them.

Avis Douglass stuck her head out of her inner-office door as Kat was showing Latoya how to put in the number of copies and then press Start on the photocopy machine. "Kathryn? What's your schedule like today? Do you have to rush off to work at noon?"

"No. I've got the evening shift today. Do you need me for something?"

Avis stepped into the outer office and smiled warmly. As usual, she looked the picture of an elementary school principal, wearing a fawn-colored pantsuit, a black shell, and gold-and-black-onyx jewelry, complementing the cinnamon tone of her smooth skin. "No. Just thought we could use a catch-up over lunch. My office?"

"Um, sure." Kat hadn't brought any lunch with her, had planned just to go home and eat leftover pasta salad. But STEP usually had extra bag lunches for the kids who stayed for afternoon sports. In spite of the fact that Mrs. Douglass had been a lot friendlier since Kat had helped reunite her with her daughter, she couldn't help feeling a bit weird being called to the "principal's office."

Three hours later Kat's tutoring students—Yusufu, Kevin, and Latoya—scurried off, carrying their new math game and craft project as Kat scrubbed white glue off the craft table in the schoolroom they'd been assigned. It'd been a fun morning in spite of having to repeat instructions too many times. She'd be able to tell Mrs. Douglass that all three of her students had already become more confident doing long division, and now they were reviewing their times tables. Which meant, she reminded herself with a quick glance at the clock, she'd better grab a sack lunch and skedaddle to the office.

The inner-office door was already open and Avis Douglass beckoned her in. "I should have given you more warning," the older woman said apologetically. "Those sack lunches leave a lot to be desired, I know. Which is why"—she waved at her desk, which held a steaming cup of soup and a homemade sand-wich—"I bring my own from home."

Kat sat in the "visitor" chair. "That's okay. It's got an apple. That'll hold me until I get back to the apartment."

Avis picked up the cup of soup, blew on the hot liquid, and peered at Kat over the rim. "Speaking of the apartment, I wanted to ask how things are working out with Rochelle and Conny. I feel responsible that you ended up taking my family in, and I'm sure living with a six-year-old takes some adjustment."

Kat swallowed. What was she supposed to say? If there *were* problems, did Mrs. D think she was going to just blurt them out? She was Rochelle's mother, for goodness' sake.

Avis seemed to read her mind. "I'm sorry. That's unfair to put you on the spot. I just don't want you to feel you're stuck if things aren't working out. I love my daughter and Conny is the light of my life—and I can never thank you enough for giving them a place to call home, even for these summer months—but I know it must have its challenges. I don't want you to feel like you have to pretend it's all okay."

For some reason, Mrs. Douglass's honesty put Kat at ease. She shrugged. "Okay. It's an adjustment—for them too, I'm sure. But Rochelle has tried hard to fit in and pulls her own weight with cooking and chores. Really, it's fine. Though . . ."

The principal's eyebrows went up. "Though . . . ?"

"Well, Rochelle seemed kind of upset when you guys brought Conny home from spending time with his dad. All she said was Dexter was being a jerk. But . . ." Should she say it? "I remember what you said about her husband being abusive. I just hope . . ." Kat didn't know how to finish what she'd started.

Avis shook her head. "I don't think he's being physically abusive. He knows we'd call the police. But by the way he's acting, I think Dexter liked it better when Rochelle was homeless." Her voice had an edge. "She thought she needed him, which gave him the upper hand . . . and he had Conny, even though Rochelle has legal custody. But now that she has a place to live and we got Conny out of there, he keeps acting like a jerk. Asking questions about where she's living, making accusations. It's nonstop."

"Accusations? Like what? What do you mean?"

Avis hesitated, as if not sure she wanted to explain. "Oh, questioning your motives . . . and why would she let Conny live with white strangers rather than with his own dad. That kind of thing."

"He's got a problem because we're white?" Kat had wondered if her lily-white parents might question her living with racially mixed housemates but never considered how black relatives might feel.

Avis gave a wry smile. "Don't worry about it, Kathryn. I probably said too much. It's his problem."

Kat nodded. Mostly she wished they weren't even trying to let Conny see his dad.

"Mind if I change the subject?" Avis's voice was warm again. "Rochelle was telling us about your visit to the Rock of Ages food pantry last week. Is that something you're interested in, Kathryn?"

Kat nodded. "In fact, I was hoping to talk to you and Pastor Cobbs about it. Nick is going to ask tonight at your meeting when I could come talk to the pastors. But . . ." Before she knew it, Kat was telling Mrs. Douglass the scriptures she'd been reading and what she felt like God was calling her to do: start a food pantry at SouledOut. "Even Estelle Bentley said she thought what I really want to do is feed people. And I think that's true." It had all spilled out so fast Kat had to gasp to catch her breath.

Avis tented her fingers and looked at Kat a long time. Kat began to feel nervous. Maybe she should have waited to tell Mrs. D until a more "official" time. But then the older woman spoke. "Kathryn, can I ask—have you prayed about this? Not just you. But have you asked another sister to pray *with* you about whether this is what God is calling you to do?"

"Well, I asked Edesa Baxter to pray about it and she said she would."

"I see." A small smile tipped the corners of Avis's mouth. "Well, it's an amazing idea, but if I were in your shoes, I would want to be certain whether *God* is calling me to do this. And on my end, I would want to be certain whether God is calling *SouledOut* to partner in this. It's the kind of thing that could overwhelm you *and* the church if we try to do it in our own strength. And it's God who needs to open the doors. So . . . here we are, and I think we should do first things first."

Do? What did she mean?

The principal got up and closed the office door, pulled up the second visitor chair, and held out her hands to Kat. "Let's pray right now, shall we? You and me. We'll pray about whether God wants Kathryn Davies to start a food pantry at SouledOut Community Church, and if so, to open the right doors to make it happen."

Chapter 22

The job at Software Symphony was only supposed to be part-time, but Peter Douglass had been letting Nick work extra hours when he wasn't needed for church responsibilities. "If things keep holding steady by summer's end, I might be able to offer you a salaried job with benefits," he said when Nick came to work on Monday.

He was grateful, Nick told himself, walking home later that day. He needed the work, since his six-month internship at SouledOut only paid him for ten hours a week—though "paid" was a bit of a joke. Even Pastor Cobbs had been somewhat embarrassed at the small honorarium. But working the mail room at a software company wasn't exactly the most exciting work in the world. Not sure he wanted to do it full-time. Nick was hoping by summer's end he might be able to increase his hours at the church, maybe even negotiate for a raise? If so, he'd stick with part-time at Mr. Douglass's company.

Bree was on the computer and Rochelle was in the kitchen when he let himself in the front door. Bree said Kat had already left for her evening shift at The Common Cup. *Figures.* The way things were going, they could miss each other all week.

Like last night—an almost full moon had been peeking in and out of the clouds, and he'd had this crazy idea of meeting Kat when she got off work at nine and walking her home. That in itself would've given her a hint, wouldn't it? If he did that a few times, it wouldn't seem too awkward to tell her his hopes for their relationship.

But that was before Rochelle had asked him to read bedtime stories to Conny, who wanted not one, but two, and then three stories . . . and it was hard to turn the kid down. He'd been through a lot for a six-year-old. And from the little Rochelle had let drop, Conny's Sunday afternoon visit with his dad hadn't gone so hot. Kids picked up on stuff like that, even if it was stuff between the parents. By the time he got done reading, Kat was already back and plotting the coming weekend around Olivia's birthday.

"Mister Niiiick!" Conny came barreling out of the kitchen. "Mommy an' I made lemonade. Want some?"

"You bet." Nick let Conny drag him into the kitchen, where his mom had already poured a tall, frosty glass.

"Hey." Rochelle grinned at him and handed him the glass. "Figured you'd be hot after that long walk home. Supper isn't quite ready. You and my mom have a meeting with Pastor Cobbs tonight, don't you? When do you need to leave?"

"In about an hour. Hey, what's that picture you're drawing, buddy?"

Conny had scrambled back into a chair at the kitchen table and was making dozens of dots and dashes with a blue marker all over two big stick figures and a smaller stick figure, arms and legs splayed. The little boy giggled. "It's you an' me an' Mommy playing in the sprinkler." Satisfied, he put down the blue marker, picked up the drawing, and ran over to the refrigerator, holding it up on the door. "Can I hang it up here?"

"Sure, baby." Rochelle confiscated a magnet from the grocery list and stuck it on Conny's drawing. "That was fun, wasn't it?"

Nick was touched by the drawing, but he wasn't sure he wanted it up there on the refrigerator. It'd be awkward to keep hearing "That's Nick an' me an' Mommy" every time someone asked Conny about it. But what could he do? Every kid wanted to show off their artwork on the fridge. Unless . . .

"Hey, that's pretty good. What else can you draw? Can you draw a dragon? Wait till you see the monster *I* can draw." Downing the last few gulps of lemonade, Nick grabbed a sheet of paper and a purple marker and set to work beside Conny, trying to ignore the gratified looks Rochelle kept sending their direction. A few more pictures on the refrigerator door just might obscure the trio in the sprinkler.

❀

Mrs. Douglass offered to give Nick a ride home after the pastoral team meeting at the church later that evening, but he waved her off. "It's a great night for a walk. Thanks anyway." He could hardly believe it when Pastor ended the meeting at eight thirty. That gave him just enough time to get to the coffee shop and walk Kat home after all. He even had a good excuse.

"You again!" Kat laughed as she came out the door at 9:05. "Watch out, twice is a habit. Now I'll expect it, and if you don't show up, I'll throw a hissy fit. See what you started?"

Nick grinned. He knew she was teasing, but the words *"Now I'll expect it"* played hopefully in his ears.

"Don't really like you girls walking by yourselves this time of night—"

"Uh-huh." He heard the mild mocking in her voice. "So why don't you send someone to walk Bree or me home every night we work the evening shift, eh?"

"—and besides," he said, quickly shifting gears, "you asked me to ask the pastors tonight if you could talk to them about starting a food pantry. Thought you might want to hear about it."

"Nick!" Kat grabbed his arm. "You remembered! I was afraid you'd forget. Tell me! I already mentioned it to Mrs. D, but what did Pastor Cobbs say?"

Nick stopped walking and gaped at her. "You talked to Mrs. D . . . when? Didn't you just ask me yesterday to bring it up tonight? Which, I gotta tell you, Kat, was kind of awkward for me, doing this third-party thing. But I did it because you asked me to. Didn't know you were going to go ahead and do it yourself." *Huh. Women!*

"Hey, come on, Nick, don't get huffy. It wasn't like that. She asked to talk to me after STEP this morning and said Rochelle told her about all of us checking out the food pantry at Rock of Ages last week. She wanted to know what my interest was . . . so it just came out."

Nick walked in silence for a few moments, then shrugged. "Well, okay. Funny that she didn't say anything about it, though, when I brought it up."

"So . . . tell me. What'd they say?" Kat's voice was eager again.

"Well, how does next Monday evening sound? If you don't have to work the evening shift, I mean."

"Really? I can come to your meeting and tell them my idea?" Kat twirled around on the sidewalk like a ballet dancer, then walked backward in little bouncy steps facing him. "So tell me, did they say anything else?"

"Watch it!" Nick reached out, grabbed her arm, and pulled her back to his side. "Only if you don't trip over this curb coming up . . . okay." He guided her across an intersection and they started down the next block. "Mostly they just listened, asked a few questions. I didn't try to speak for you, just told them a little bit about the four of us helping out at Rock of Ages—"

"Oh! Speaking of that," Kat interrupted, "I called Sister Beatrice this afternoon and told her some of us would like to come again this week. Bree can't, has to work, but Rochelle said she'd like to go. How about you?"

Nick shook his head. "Can't. Pastor Cobbs asked me to lead the prayer meeting at SouledOut on Wednesday night. It used to be a Bible study led by Pastor Clark, but it's just been a prayer meeting since he died. Except I'm supposed to prepare a short devotional to start." He gave a short laugh. "Guess it'll be good prep before I give an actual sermon in a couple Sundays."

"Oh. Sorry . . . I mean, I'm glad for you, but sorry I can't be there. But you'll do fine, I'm sure."

Nick was sorry too. "Anyway, Mrs. D did say one thing about the food pantry idea. She said the most important thing was to pray about it first, because something like this needs to be 'bathed in prayer'—those are her words."

Kat laughed. "Exactly the same thing she said to me in her office today! And she did it too, prayed with me right there."

"Yeah, well, same thing. The three of us prayed about this food pantry idea before we went on to the next agenda item."

Nick looked sideways at her face in the glow of the streetlights. "Made me realize I need to ask your forgiveness, Kat."

She looked up at him, puzzled. "Forgiveness? Whatever for?"

He cleared his throat. "Because we sat in that café yesterday and talked for an hour about your food pantry idea, but I didn't say anything about prayer, didn't offer to pray with you about it." Nick sighed. "I don't know, Kat. Sometimes I wonder if I'll ever make a very good pastor. Seems like I forget some of the most basic things."

Kat took his arm again and he pressed her hand close to his side. "Hey," she said softly, "don't be so hard on yourself. It's kind of hard wearing so many hats, don't you think? I was asking you as my friend, not as a pastor."

They walked in silence, hand in arm, as they turned into their block. She'd hit the nail on the head. When he was with Kat, he didn't know what hat to wear—and the hat he wanted to wear didn't belong to him yet.

It must've been her hand tucked into the crook of his arm, her nearness, the fresh smell of her hair that gave Nick the courage to stop before going up the three wide steps leading into the three-flat. "Kat . . . you *do* know you're more than just a friend to me, don't you?" Not waiting for her to answer, he leaned close and brushed her cheek with a gentle kiss.

191

Chapter 23

Kat lay on the bed, eyes wide open in the dark, letting the slow-moving air from the fan in the window caress her skin. Brygitta's steady breathing from the other twin bed was a relief. If Bree knew she was wide awake at midnight, she'd be on her in a minute, wanting to know what was wrong.

Nothing was wrong! A giggle nearly escaped from the well of pleasure bubbling inside. Every now and then she put two of her fingers together and brushed her cheek, trying to remember exactly how Nick's lips had felt when he'd kissed her there. The kiss had taken her by surprise . . . as well as the fact that she'd felt a jolt of electricity all the way down to her knees.

She'd just looked at him, startled. Not knowing what to do or say, she'd backed slowly up the steps to the front door, her hand slipping out from the crook of his arm. He didn't follow, just watched her go, but his eyes seemed to be full of questions. So at the door she'd blown him a kiss with a little smile, said, "Backatcha," and went inside.

Duh. What a stupid thing to say! *Backatcha.*

And as she thought about it, she felt a little confused. *"More than just a friend."* Did that mean, like, *girlfriend*? What if he just meant a special "bud." But what about that kiss on the cheek? Except Rochelle had kissed Nick on the cheek and he'd insisted it didn't mean anything. Was that how he felt about kissing her on the cheek? Just a friendly gesture, nothing more?

Kat kicked off the sheet and flopped over on her side. It sure seemed like it meant something. But maybe she shouldn't assume anything, see what happened in the next few days.

Punching the pillow to find a comfortable spot for her head, Kat tried to relax. She really needed to get some sleep. But it was another hour before she drifted off.

❀

Opening one eye to focus on her bedside clock the next morning, Kat sat bolt upright. *Eight twenty!* She had to be at Bethune Elementary by nine! She must've forgotten to turn on the alarm. Bree's bed was empty and unmade—already gone to work. Nick was nowhere to be seen when she padded through the apartment. He must've left for work too. The front door stood open into the hallway and she could hear Rochelle and Conny's voices upstairs at the Douglasses.

Shunning her usual shower, Kat splashed water on her face, dressed quickly, grabbed a banana, and half ran to the school. Yosufu, Kevin, and Latoya must've picked up on the fact that she wasn't really prepared, because she had to practically sit on them all morning to get them to cooperate. From STEP, she headed straight to the coffee shop—she had the afternoon shift for the next two days—and by the time she got home to cook supper, she was in no mood to dance around Nick, trying to figure out what happened out on the stoop last night. Though he did give her a big grin as he helped himself to seconds of her honey-baked lentils over brown rice. "Great stuff, Kat."

But after supper Nick excused himself, said he had to prepare a "devotional" for the prayer meeting the next evening, then disappeared into the study.

Okay. Pretend it never happened. Wait for him to make the next move. If it was a move in the first place.

Kat scurried home as fast as she could after work on Wednesday afternoon, using her cell phone to ask Rochelle to meet her outside the three-flat to save time since they were already late showing up at the food pantry. As she came out the door, Rochelle handed her a submarine sandwich Bree had made before her evening shift. "Smart girl, giving us a portable supper." Rochelle grinned, unwrapping her own sub as they walked along.

"Who's taking care of Conny? The GPs?" Kat was glad Rochelle hadn't tried to bring Conny along, though it had crossed her mind she might if she didn't find child care. After all, there were other kids running around the food pantry who'd come with their parents.

"No. You know the family on the first floor with the two preschoolers? Believe it or not, they actually invited Conny to go play at the park with them this evening. Kind of amazing, 'cause Mom says she hardly ever sees them. Guess their kids are in day care a lot." Rochelle waved her sub sandwich. "But they seemed pretty excited that there's another kid in the building. And Conny's good with younger kids—he gets to be the bossy 'big kid' for a change."

Kat snickered. Seemed to her Conny was perfectly capable of being the "bossy kid" no matter who he was with. But she said, "That's great." Because it meant she and Rochelle could do this thing together without being distracted by Conny, and she'd have someone to debrief with. In fact . . . was this one of the "doors" Mrs. D had prayed would open if the idea for a food pantry was a God-idea? It was just a little thing—care for Conny—but still.

"Rochelle, remember what you said last week after we were at Rock of Ages, that more churches should set up food pantries? Well, it started me thinking . . ."

As they walked, Kat found herself telling Rochelle what she felt God was asking her to do—to feed hungry people. As they approached the stone church on the corner, where a line straggled out the side door and groups of people clogged the sidewalk, she said, "Your mom said I should pray about it with some other people, to be sure it's God's idea and not just mine. Would you be willing to pray about it with me?"

Rochelle shrugged. "Well . . . sure. I'll pray about it."

She'd meant pray *with* her. But Kat let it go.

The foyer at Rock of Ages wasn't as jammed this week, since the weather was decent and people could wait outside. But Sister Beatrice immediately put them to work alongside two other volunteers, and for the next two and a half hours, Kat hardly had time to think or take a breath. Seemed like for every person who went out the door with a bag of groceries, two more were ready to come into the pantry.

She recognized several people who'd been there the week before—like the Lady Lolla character, dressed today in a short red taffeta sheath with some kind of sheer netting gathered around her pale shoulders like a shawl. Hard to miss. The rail-thin woman ignored the canned goods again and eagerly pounced on the ears of corn on the fresh produce table. "Ike, he do love corn on the cob." She giggled. "Though he can't eat it too good 'cause he's missin' some teeth."

Lady Lolla and Ike . . . What is their story? Kat wondered.

But many faces were new to Kat. A young black woman, cute as a pixie, aided her overweight mother—or aunt or grandmother—whom she called Mimi. Both were dressed neatly, but they each filled a large shopping bag with a variety of food. They certainly didn't look homeless, but obviously "hungry" and "homeless" were not necessarily synonymous.

However, it was the preschooler with little beaded braids all over her head whose eyes grew large at the boxes of macaroni and cheese and the elderly man who slowly filled his bag with trembling hands that got to Kat. *Hungry people.* Young people. Old people. Edesa was right. At that moment, Kat didn't particularly care what kind of food they ate, she just wanted to open a loaf of bread and a couple jars of peanut butter and jelly and make them a sandwich, then and there.

After Tony the Bouncer, as Kat thought of him, shut the doors at eight o'clock, she and Rochelle stayed awhile longer to help straighten shelves and clean up, along with the other two volunteers, an older couple—retirees, Kat supposed—members of Rock of Ages, who spoke with a slight Scandinavian accent. Kat was hoping to talk to Sister Beatrice again, but the motherly manager was bustling around with a sheaf of papers on a clipboard doing an inventory of what needed to be replenished.

So Kat grabbed a dustpan and held it for the pleasant-faced husband who was wielding a broom. "Why did you decide to volunteer at the food pantry?" she asked with a teasing grin. "You could be playing golf."

The man chuckled. "Don't want to miss Jesus."

What? Kat blinked. "Miss . . . Jesus?"

His pink-cheeked wife peered around his shoulder with a patient smile. "The sheep and the goats. Matthew 25." But she took the broom away from him. "Please, Anders. We need to get home before it gets dark." With an apologetic smile, she hustled Anders out the door.

The sheep and the goats? Odd thing to say. But Rochelle seemed anxious to go too, so they waved good-bye to Sister Beatrice and Tony and headed back through the neighborhood streets the way they had come. To Kat's surprise, Rochelle walked two blocks without saying anything, a frown etched between her eyebrows.

"Hey, are you okay?"

Rochelle didn't answer for a few moments. Then, "I guess. Just . . . not sure I should've come."

"Why? I was really glad you were there. I saw you talking to some of the pantry folks. They all seem to like you."

"Oh. Well, thanks." Rochelle gave Kat a half smile. "Feeling kind of guilty, I guess. I was on the street, needed the food pantries just like these people. It was only for four months. Now I've got a roof over my head and plenty of food to eat. But I was talking to Tony, and he said he felt discouraged, because it's the same people every week. Month after month. Nothing ever really changes."

"But it changed for you."

"Did it?" Rochelle looked away for a long moment. "I'm still getting a handout. Not paying for my rent or our food. Makes me feel just like I did showing up at the food pantries. Kind of embarrassed. Second-rate. Like a leech."

"Rochelle! We don't feel that way. And it's just until you get a job."

"Yeah, right. *If* I get a job. If you haven't noticed, nobody's beating a path to my door, wanting to hire someone with HIV. And then what are my choices? Food stamps. Public assistance. Still a handout."

Kat didn't know what to say. It was true in a way. They were supporting Rochelle and Conny. And so far, none of Rochelle's job applications had called her back—

"Don't get me wrong, Kat. I'm real grateful. But . . ." Rochelle glanced at her sideways. "You aren't going to like me saying this, but it makes me wonder if this food pantry idea of yours—starting one at SouledOut—is a good idea."

Oh great. Just what she needed—someone throwing cold water on her idea before it even made it to the light of day. "Not sure I see what your job situation has to do with starting a food pantry," she said, realizing her tone came out terse. "People are still hungry. You said yourself that more churches should start food pantries."

"Yeah, I know." Rochelle shook her head. "It's just . . . I'm realizing that giving away food is just putting a Band-Aid on a much deeper problem. Doesn't really solve anything. Once it's gone, people are hungry again. And every time they get a handout, it kills a little more of their spirit. At least, that's what it did to me."

A half dozen retorts sprang to Kat's mind. *So? Do we just ignore the fact that people are hungry? What are people supposed to do in the meantime, before they get a job or get off the street? Just because*

we can't do everything doesn't mean we shouldn't do something . . .
But she pressed her lips together, afraid that if she said anything
it would come out wrong.

As they turned into their own block, Rochelle said, "Look,
I'm sorry. Maybe the food pantry is a good idea. It was just—I
don't know. Being there tonight brought up all these feelings. I
was just being honest with you."

"Okay." That was all Kat trusted herself to say. She was
almost relieved that the first-floor family was already home
from the park and Conny needed a bath and putting to bed.
Besides, Kat felt a little guilty that she'd shared with Nick and
even opened up to Rochelle about her idea—her "calling," as
she was starting to think of it—before she'd even told Brygitta.
After all, Bree was her best friend. At least *she'd* be encouraging . . . she hoped.

As soon as Bree got home from the coffee shop that night,
Kat steered her out the kitchen door onto the back porch where
she had two glasses of herbal iced tea and a candle flickering,
and she laid it all out once more, from reading how Jesus had
fed the five thousand to her appointment to talk to the pastoral
team next Monday about starting a food pantry at SouledOut.

Brygitta's brown eyes had gone wide. "My goodness, Kat—"

"Don't say it. I know, sounds like just another crazy idea,
but I'm getting enough of that from everyone else, thank you.
This time it's different, Bree. I know I can't do this without
God—or without your support either, for that matter. So all I'm
asking is just pray with me about it."

Brygitta was quiet for what seemed a long minute, and then
she suddenly leaned over and grabbed Kat in a fierce hug. "Oh,
Kat, of course I will. I've been a Christian a lot longer than you

have, but you're the one with the faith to pray about something as big as this." She let go of her hug but took Kat's hands in her own. "Let's do it. Let's pray right now."

But they'd only just started when the back screen door slammed and Nick's voice interrupted. "Is this a girl thing, or can I get in on this prayer meeting too?"

Kat's heart seemed to leap into her throat, but she swallowed it. "Didn't you just come from a prayer meeting? Aren't you prayed out?"

"Nope." He pulled up another porch chair with a grin. "Just prayed up. Whatever. I'm in."

Kat felt his strong clasp as Nick joined hands with her and Bree, and they kick-started the prayers again. She still felt confused about what that kiss on the cheek had meant the other night . . . but right now, she was just glad to have her hand in his.

Chapter 24

A Pavarotti memorial concert? And it's *free*? You're kidding, right?" Kat's mouth dropped when Nick told them what was on the schedule at the Millennium Park pavilion as they cleaned up the kitchen Friday evening. She wasn't an opera buff, but a tribute to the famed tenor was sure to be fantastic.

"Nope, not kidding. There really is a memorial concert this month. Only problem. Wrong weekend. *This* weekend it's Community Music School Night with local talent doing chamber and orchestral music."

"Not—oh!" Kat snapped him with the dish towel she was holding. "You are so mean, Nick Taylor! Local talent? What does *that* mean? Oh, never mind. Whatever. What time are Livie and Elin getting in at the bus station?"

Bree fished out her notes. "They're taking that new Megabus. Supposedly dirt-cheap. The one from Madison is scheduled to get in at . . . hmm, eleven Saturday morning. But it drops off passengers at Union Station, not the bus depot."

Both Kat and Bree had traded shifts at the coffee shop so

they could have Saturday free. Even Rochelle and Conny seemed excited by the plans for the weekend visit. On Saturday morning, while Kat, Bree, and Rochelle packed food for their day in the city, Nick and Conny made "Happy Birthday" and "Welcome, Olivia and Elin" signs to stick up all around the apartment.

Kat supposed it made sense to include Rochelle and Conny for their day in Chicago, since they were doing this as a household, not just the original friends. But having a kid along would certainly change the dynamic. *Oh well,* she told herself, wrapping cold, baked chicken in aluminum foil and stuffing it into her backpack. She'd just enjoy the weekend for what it was.

Loaded with backpacks of food, sunscreen, and water bottles, plus a large tote bag with picnic paraphernalia, the five of them caught the El by midmorning and rode the Red Line downtown. The train was packed with weekend shoppers and teenagers plugged into iPods—not the usual ties and briefcases. Bree and Rochelle found seats on one side and Nick and Kat on the other, while Conny bounced from window to window. Smiling to herself, Kat wondered whether she'd finagled the seat beside Nick, or the other way around. Didn't matter. He chatted easily about the guys he was getting to know at work and asked more about her second volunteer stint at Rock of Ages . . . that is, when Conny wasn't squeezing himself past their knees to look out the window on their side.

"Hey, you." Kat pulled the little boy onto her lap on the third interruption. Might as well give him some attention. "What did the doctor say when his nurse told him there was an invisible man in his waiting room?"

Conny looked at Nick, as if hoping for a clue, then back at Kat. "I don' know."

"He said, 'Tell him I can't see him now. Next!'"

Nick snickered. The little boy looked puzzled for maybe two seconds and then broke into a grin. "I get it! He can't see him 'cause he's invisible!"

"Make that an invisible *boy*," Nick teased, tickling his ribs.

Conny giggled. *"I'm* not invisible!"

"We noticed," Kat and Nick chorused—and broke up laughing just as the El went underground into the subway tunnel.

They all piled off at the Adams/Wabash station, came up onto street level, and caught a bus that took them over the Chicago River to Union Station with five minutes to spare before eleven. But the Megabus was late. Figured. Rochelle took Conny inside the station to use the restroom . . . and they still had to wait another twenty minutes. But when the big blue-and-yellow bus pulled up to the curb on Canal Street, Olivia was the first one off, followed by a younger version of herself—same shoulder-length blond hair and fair skin—smiling shyly.

The next few minutes were filled with laughter, hugs, and introductions right there on the sidewalk. Conny looked soberly from Olivia to Elin and back again, and then said to Olivia, "Is that your daughter?" which cracked everybody up, especially Elin.

The bus driver was unloading bags from the storage area, and Olivia and Elin collected two wheeled suitcases, the carry-on size. Kat poked Nick. "Uh-oh. I forgot they'd have overnight bags. What are we going to do with those?"

"Hopefully we can find some lockers," Nick said.

They decided to walk the seven or eight blocks back to State Street in the Loop, where they were able to catch a free trolley to . . . "Navy Pier?" Olivia said, her eyes dancing. "Yay! I was hoping we'd do something like that. I wanted Elin to see the fun side of Chicago."

"Oh, we're going to show Elin *Chicago,* all right." Bree grinned mysteriously.

Which was why they'd chosen to take Olivia and Elin for a ride on the gigantic Ferris wheel at Navy Pier as their birthday surprise. Sorting themselves into two of the enclosed cars—*with* the suitcases, since they couldn't find any lockers—the lighted wheel took seven minutes to go around just once, giving them a panoramic view of Chicago's glass-and-steel skyline on one side and glittering Lake Michigan, dotted with sailboats and sightseeing boats, on the other. Rochelle, Nick, Conny, and Elin ended up in one car on the wheel, with Olivia, Brygitta, and Kat in the one just behind it. Kat noticed that the car up ahead rocked continuously.

In spite of a light rain early that morning, the day had turned out perfectly—scattered clouds, temps in the mideighties, a light breeze off the lake. They ate their sack lunches at a picnic table, then walked to the far end of the pier gawking at the tour boats, art sculptures, assorted shops and cafés, through a conservatory of tropical greenery and fountains, but decided against the stained glass museum—not with a six-year-old!—and back again. By this time Conny was dragging and Nick carried him piggyback for a while as Rochelle walked alongside.

Crossing Lake Shore Drive to Millennium Park, they cooled off in Crown Fountain, which was a long wading pool with two glass "video towers" at either end featuring changing faces that "spit" water into the shallow pool. Rochelle peeled off Conny's shirt and shoes and let him splash in the pool—but he soon dragged her in too, along with Nick and Elin.

"Cute kid," Olivia said, joining Kat and Bree on one of the stone benches, babysitting the backpacks and suitcases. "How's that working out?"

Kat shrugged. "Pretty good, I think. Rochelle doesn't have a job, so she hasn't been able to help with the rent yet. But she pulls her weight in other ways. Don't you think, Bree?"

Brygitta nodded. "But Conny's got a thing for Nick. Ask *him* how it's going."

"I noticed," Olivia murmured. "He's not the only one."

Kat looked at her sharply. What did Livie mean by that? She wanted to ask, but just then Elin ran up, grabbed her big sister by the hand, and pulled her into the shallow pool. "My sandals!" Olivia screeched.

"They'll dry!" Elin laughed, and the sisters joined Rochelle, Nick, and Conny dodging the long streams of water coming from the changing faces on the two towers at either end.

Bree slathered another layer of sunscreen on her arms. "Elin seems like a neat kid. I'm glad Livie moved home to be with her."

Hadn't Brygitta heard what Olivia said? Wasn't she curious about what their friend meant by *"He's not the only one"*? Kat watched the others cavorting in the shallow water. *He . . . who?* Nick? As in, Nick's not the only one Conny has a thing for? The little guy did seem smitten by Olivia's kid sister, who was chasing him around the splash pool. Maybe that's what she meant.

But the comment kept niggling at her as the water-play ended and they all wandered toward the music pavilion, setting up their picnic on the sloping lawn. *"He's not the only one."* Maybe it was the other way around. Maybe she meant Conny's not the only one who's "got a thing" for Nick. Kat's face flushed as she spread out the sheet they'd brought to use as a picnic blanket. Were her growing feelings for Nick that obvious? Or did she mean—

Kat pushed her thoughts aside. She was making too much of an offhand comment. She'd just ask Livie if she found the right moment . . . or maybe forget the whole thing. Digging into the backpacks, she brought out the chicken, pasta salad, and munchies while Brygitta and Rochelle laid out paper plates, napkins, and small bottles of fruit juice.

"See, Elin," Olivia said, helping herself to the pasta salad, "no worries about spoiled mayo in this heat, because it's seasoned with vinaigrette or something. Hang around Kat long enough, and you learn a few tricks like that." She gave Kat a playful push. "But come on, you guys, I still need to hear what's been happening since I left!"

They talked and laughed and ate until the concert started and the community music schools were introduced to much clapping and cheers. They couldn't see the chamber groups onstage unless they stood up and walked over to the rows of "ticket seats" closer to the stage, but Kat didn't mind. She lay back on the grass, backpack under her head for a pillow, and closed her eyes, letting the rich sounds of strings and horns and reeds fill the evening with lyrical sounds. These local groups weren't bad. Not bad at all.

Conny quickly got bored with the concert and whined about going home, but somehow Rochelle got him to cuddle up with his head in her lap and he soon fell asleep—not even waking when the concert was over and Nick hauled him up over his shoulder and carried him as they walked to the subway station.

"Sweet." Elin grinned as the rest of them walked behind, pulling the suitcases.

The El was crowded with concertgoers heading home, but they all managed to get on the same car, with Rochelle and Nick—still carrying Conny—finding seats toward the front, and Kat and the others scattered here and there. But as the car gradually emptied at various stops, Kat, Brygitta, Olivia, and Elin managed to get double seats close together.

"Thanks, guys." Olivia sighed, twisting in the seat ahead of Kat and Bree. "Couldn't ask for a better birthday. I've really missed all of you—and I wanted Elin to meet you so much."

Elin grinned playfully. "That's all Livie talks about—the Four Musketeers! I think she was jealous, though, when she heard you found someone else to move in so quickly after she left."

Olivia's cheeks colored. "Okay, so I was, a little. But it's been fun to meet Rochelle and Conny. She's really sweet. God worked it all out, didn't He?" She glanced toward the front of the car. "You didn't tell me she was so pretty, though! She could be a model, don't you think? And Conny—he seems like a super kid."

Kat saw Elin's eyes follow her sister's glance. "Those two." The teenager tipped her head in Nick and Rochelle's direction with a sly smile. "Are they, you know, an item?"

Kat stared at the girl, her mouth suddenly going dry.

"Nah," Bree said quickly. "Nothing like that. Why?"

"I don't know. They look cute together. I think she likes him. And Conny sure adores Nick. Every kid needs a father to look up to—I oughta know, right, Livie?" Elin sighed. "Wish our mom would choose someone like Nick—except older. Nick would make a good dad for Conny, don't you think?"

Kat was flabbergasted. The girl needed to shut up. But she noticed that Olivia's face wore a tiny smile.

Kat hunkered down in her seat and closed her eyes, as if dozing the rest of the way home. Back at the apartment they got Olivia and Elin settled in the study on the futon and made up a bed on the couch for Nick, while Rochelle disappeared into the far bedroom with the still-groggy Conny. Kat had imagined they'd talk that night until the wee hours, but they all went to bed.

The apartment gradually quieted until only the fan disturbed the silence. But Kat was wide awake, staring into the darkness. She heard Bree's bedsprings squeak. "Kat?" It sounded as if Bree had risen up on one elbow. "You don't think Elin's right, do you? That Rochelle is sweet on Nick? I mean, she just appreciates Nick taking an interest in Conny, don't you think?"

Kat didn't answer. Slowing her breathing, she pretended to be asleep.

But . . . was *that* what Olivia meant when she'd said, *"He's not the only one"*?

Chapter 25

D on't want to miss Jesus."

Kat opened her eyes with a start. Thin streams of daylight peeked into the bedroom through the Venetian blinds. It must be morning . . . but where did *that* thought come from?

Oh right. That's what that older man said the other night when she'd asked why he volunteered at the food pantry. Funny. She still didn't know what he meant.

Well, she was awake now. Might be nice to get up and have a little quiet time before the hurly-burly of everyone getting up and out the door to church. They had another whole day with Olivia and Elin, which would be fun, since it was a lot cheaper for the sisters to leave early Monday morning than Sunday evening. But this might be the only time she'd have all weekend to read her Bible and pray by herself—a habit that wasn't quite a habit yet, and she was still working her way through the list of scriptures Nick had helped her find about food.

Clad in a pair of leggings and an oversize T-shirt, Kat tiptoed through the living room, past the long lump on the couch that was Nick, still sacked out, and into the kitchen. She quietly made a pot of coffee, then eased out the kitchen door onto the back porch of the apartment with a steaming cup in one hand and her Bible and the list of scriptures in the other.

Sparrows chirped and flitted in the trees that somehow managed to survive in the tiny backyards along the alley, and blue sky peeked between scattered clouds above the rooftops. The early morning coolness after a muggy night felt like a kiss. What a morning! And the fragrant coffee was perfect. Mm, this was nice, very nice.

"Don't want to miss Jesus."

The man's strange comment pricked her mind again. And his wife had jumped in as if explaining what he meant. Something about sheep and goats in chapter 25 of Matthew.

Why not look it up? Kat put down her coffee cup and opened her Bible to the New Testament. She found the gospel of Matthew and skimmed through chapter 25 until she came to a heading that said "The sheep and the goats." Hmm. Seemed to be talking about the end times and who would be going into heaven. The King—obviously Jesus—was inviting "the righteous" to receive their reward. She read silently.

"For I was hungry and you gave me something to eat, I was thirsty and you gave me something to drink, I was a stranger and you invited me in, I needed clothes and you clothed me, I was sick and you looked after me, I was in prison and you came to visit me." Then the righteous will answer him, "Lord, when did we see you hungry and feed you, or thirsty and give you something to drink? When did we see you a stranger and invite you in, or needing clothes and clothe you? When did we see you sick or in prison and go to visit you?" The King will reply, "I tell you the truth, whatever you did for one of the least of these . . . you did for me."

Hey, this scripture talked about giving the hungry something to eat, as well as a lot of other things, like taking care of the sick and visiting people in prison. Was Matthew 25 on her list? Yes, there it was. But there was more to the story. Another group—the goats—was sent to "eternal punishment" because they *didn't* feed the hungry and all that. And King Jesus said, "Whatever you did not do for one of the least of these, you did not do for me."

Whoa. That was deep.

Kat stared at nothing in particular, mulling it over. *The least of these.* Obviously talking about ordinary folks who don't seem important, the poor, the homeless—people like that. So what did the man at Rock of Ages mean when he said, "Don't want to miss Jesus"? He worked at the food pantry, helping to feed hungry people, because . . . he might miss doing it for Jesus?

Kat sipped on her coffee. Why did she want to feed hungry people? She was still getting used to thinking about the *people* who were hungry, not just about "food issues." But it hadn't occurred to her that by feeding hungry people, she'd be doing it for Jesus.

Or that *not* doing it was neglecting Jesus.

Whew. She needed to think about this a lot more. Kat was almost glad when she heard noises in the apartment—voices yelling, "I'm next!" for the shower, no doubt, and Conny's feet running back and forth. *Yikes.* Speaking of hungry people, there were seven of them for breakfast this morning! She should make cheese and veggie omelets or something—something special. And—double yikes! Today was Second Sunday Potluck after worship, and they hadn't even thought about what to take. She'd better get rolling!

❄

At Brygitta's urging, Kat gave up the idea of making something for the potluck, deciding instead to pick up a watermelon on the way to church. The Douglasses gave Rochelle and Conny a ride to church, and Kat realized that if Rochelle and her folks took Conny to see his daddy after the potluck, it would just be the ol' Four Musketeers—plus Livie's sister—for the rest of the afternoon, a relief in a way. Might temper Elin's "matchmaking," which had gotten pretty darn uncomfortable.

Olivia seemed excited to be back at SouledOut after nearly a month, and people greeted her and her sister warmly. Elin's eyes were wide, taking it all in. "Never been to a church in a mall," she stage-whispered to Kat. "But I like those banners. Who made them?"

Three colorful new banners hung at the front of the big room behind the low platform. On closer inspection, it was apparent that some of the Sunday school classes and the youth group had made the banners with simple felt figures, symbols, and words. The banner in the middle said, "It's a new commandment! Love one another." The banner on one side showed a Jesus figure in a white robe washing somebody's feet. On the other side, a little boy held out what looked like a basket with bread and fish in it, giving it to Jesus—the white robe again.

"Do you think Jesus really wore a white robe all the time?" Kat murmured to Elin.

The teenager giggled. "Probably not. They didn't have washing machines back then." She tipped her head to the side, studying the banners. "Interesting. The kids gave Jesus a brown face and dark hair . . . Were they being realistic, you think? Making Him more Middle Eastern? Or making Him like themselves?"

"I think we all do that," Nick butted in, coming up behind them. "Make Jesus like ourselves, I mean . . . Hey, we better find seats. Service is ready to start."

As it turned out, the banners were part of Pastor Cobbs's message that morning. The sermons were still focusing on things Jesus said just before and just after His death and resurrection, even though Good Friday and Easter were long past. "Today our text is from John's gospel, chapter 13," the pastor said, once the praise team had put their instruments away and everyone had settled down.

After reading the biblical story, Pastor Cobbs said, "The disciples were shocked by what Jesus did. Washing their dirty feet! He wasn't just making Himself 'one of them,' like a buddy or friend. No, washing feet was what servants and slaves did in a culture where people wore sandals and walked on dirt roads most of the year. Peter was too embarrassed to let Jesus do it. His big ol' feet were probably cracked and grimy, with dirt under his toenails. Maybe stinky too. 'No way!' he said. Until Jesus said that if he didn't let his feet be washed, he couldn't be part of this New Way. So of course, Peter being Peter, now he wanted Jesus to give him a whole bath! It was always all or nothing."

Kat laughed along with everyone else but suspected she wasn't the only one who squirmed a little. *All or nothing.* Yeah, that sounded familiar.

Pastor Cobbs chuckled as he looked at his Bible. "I like this next part. Jesus said, okay, now, do you guys understand what I just did? Uh-huh. Sometimes I feel like saying that here after I give one of my sermons. 'Hey, people! Do you understand what I just said? Did you get it?' 'Cause sometimes I wonder . . ." The pastor mopped his perspiring face with a small hand towel as people snickered. "Okay, I'm getting off topic. *Jesus* said, you call Me Teacher. You call Me Master. And I just washed your feet! I'm setting you an example. I want you to serve one another just like that."

"That's right, Pastor!"

"Say it now!"

Several voices chimed in from around the congregation. Kat wondered what Elin was thinking. No one ever talked to the pastor during a sermon in other church services she'd attended since becoming a Christian. But she was getting used to it at SouledOut. Why not let the pastor know you got the point?

As Pastor Cobbs wrapped up his sermon, he focused on several verses later in the same chapter. "As this special supper came to the end, Jesus told His disciples He was giving them a new commandment. To love one another. Why was it new? Because He was showing them what *God's* kind of love looked like. Not the kind of love the world practiced—I'll be nice to you if you're nice to me, the ol' scratch my back, I'll scratch yours. Or I'll love you as long as you don't mess up. No. *God's* kind of love means serving each other. Doing the dirty work. Sacrificing your own plans. Sacrificing *yourself.* Being hurt and not hurting back. Forgiving when you've been done wrong— *that* kind of 'love one another.'"

By this time, several people were on their feet, including Avis Douglass and her husband. Some people were crying. Over the hubbub, Kat heard Avis cry out, "Jesus! Help us be more like You!"

Kat cast an eye at Olivia and Elin. Pastor Cobbs's sermon today was a little more emotional than usual. She hoped Livie's sister wasn't too turned off. Because the man could really preach. And make Scripture sound as if it'd been written just yesterday. For today.

As the service closed, Nick leaned close to Kat's ear. "And I'm supposed to preach next week. How am I supposed to follow *that?*" Kat gave him a reassuring squeeze on the arm—but frankly, in his shoes she'd be nervous too.

As tables were set up and food brought out for the potluck, Bree and Olivia cut up the watermelon and arranged it on one of the church platters. Kat looked for Edesa, hoping to ask if her Honduran friend had any helpful thoughts about the food pantry idea, especially with her master's degree in public health. But Edesa, her mother-in-law, Jodi, and Avis Douglass were all huddled together in a corner of the room talking earnestly about something, and then she saw them holding hands and praying together.

Wonder what that's about?

She did manage to catch Edesa after the meal long enough to tell her she was going to meet with the pastoral team Monday night, but that was all. "I'm sorry, *mi amiga,*" Edesa said, trying to clean spaghetti out of Gracie's dark locks. "I do want to hear what God has been saying to you this week about the food pantry. Can you call me during the week? Maybe after your meeting tomorrow night? I will be praying— Gracie! Come back here!"

Kat felt a bit disgruntled as Edesa ran after her escapee. *Arrrgh*. It wasn't as easy as Mrs. D made it seem to get people to pray with her.

But the afternoon with Olivia and Elin turned out to be a lot of fun, and for a few hours at least Kat put cappuccinos and tutoring lesson plans and hungry people out of her mind as the five of them played a pickup version of Ultimate Frisbee out on the sand at Pratt Beach, adding total strangers to their teams as the game got wilder and funnier. After nose-diving into the sand a few times too many, they cooled down by walking along the long concrete "bench-wall" running between park and beach, looking at the different sections painted by various community groups, families, churches, and individuals. "Gets painted all over again every spring," a fat man informed them helpfully as he came by walking a yappy little dog.

By the time the Douglasses brought Rochelle and Conny home, they'd ordered two deep-dish pizzas from Giordano's and rented *Secondhand Lions*. But it was rated PG, so movie time had to wait until Conny went to bed—and he begged "Mister Nick" to read to him, which put off the movie even longer. Kat noticed that Olivia and Elin exchanged sly glances.

"Sorry." Rochelle grimaced as "big guy" and "little guy" disappeared. "Seems like he especially wants Nick to read to him after spending the afternoon with his dad."

"Yeah, I can understand that," Elin snorted. "That's how I feel about my Uncle Ben after visiting my mom and that loser she's dating. Feel like I need to hang around somebody male who feels *safe*, just to get my head back on straight."

Rochelle gave her a high five. "You got it, girl."

The movie went till eleven, accompanied by copious amounts of popcorn, soft drinks, and bellyaching laughter at the antics of the two old codgers played by Michael Caine and Robert Duvall. But then it was time for last-minute hugs and good-byes, because when Kat woke up the next morning, Livie and Elin were already gone, escorted by Nick on the El to be sure they caught the six o'clock Megabus.

Chapter 26

Monday was one of those days—busy from start to finish, as well as warm and sticky. Kat got permission from Mrs. Douglass to take her three STEP students to the neighborhood library on Clark Street to get library cards and check out books. She insisted that they keep the books at the school to begin with, until they had an understanding with the parents about when books had to be returned. But she had fun reading *Charlotte's Web* to them, encouraging the kids to read short passages along the way.

Then she had to hustle to The Common Cup for the afternoon shift and never did get a chance to eat lunch. By the time Kat arrived back at the apartment at five thirty, she was hot, tired, and seriously hungry, and ate two helpings of Nick's college-guy-version of shepherd's pie, even if it did have too much hamburger in it.

Kat freshened up with a shower after supper, hoping she and Nick could walk to SouledOut for the pastoral team meeting, but he said Avis Douglass had already offered to drive them and it was hard to turn down an air-conditioned ride after the hot, muggy day. Mrs. D seemed preoccupied about something, though, and didn't talk much on the way, though she did say she'd been praying about Kat's idea all week and was looking forward to their conversation that evening.

Kat was nervous as they gathered in Pastor Cobbs's office. She should've jotted some notes about what she wanted to say! But after welcoming them with a big smile and his sideways "church hug," Pastor Cobbs asked Sister Avis to lead them in some worship. Worship? Kat thought they would just open with prayer and get on with it. But Mrs. D opened her big Bible and read from Psalm 13. "'How long, O Lord? Will you forget me forever? . . .'" Her voice wavered a bit as she read on. "'How long must I wrestle with my thoughts and every day have sorrow in my heart? . . . Look on me and answer, O Lord my God.'"

A strange psalm. Sounded like complaining, not worship. Kat glanced sideways at Nick, but he had his elbows on his knees, chin propped on his fists, listening intently as Mrs. D came to the end of the psalm. "'But I trust in your unfailing love! My heart rejoices in your salvation! I will sing to the Lord, for he has been good to me.'" Avis closed her Bible and squeezed her eyes shut. "Oh yes, Lord," she said, almost as if the rest of them weren't in the room. "I trust Your unfailing love! Because You are a good God, and You have been so good to me. Thank You, Jesus! Thank You!"

Kat was surprised to see a few tears trickle down her cheeks. Was something wrong? Did Mrs. D have sorrow in her heart, like the psalm said? Kat thought everything was hunky-dory now that Rochelle and Conny had been found and were in a safe place.

Avis started to sing, "O come, let us adore Him . . ." Pastor Cobbs joined in, and then Nick. Wasn't that a Christmas carol? But Avis didn't sing the verses, just the chorus several times, changing the words to "For You alone are worthy" and "We give You all the glory." Eventually Kat joined in, closing her eyes and singing the familiar refrain, letting all the busyness of the day and the past weekend fade into the background, just focusing on God, who was worthy of her praise.

And suddenly she realized . . . *This is worship. I'm worshipping.* Kat's throat caught on the last refrain and she simply listened as the other three sang sedately, almost as if walking down an aisle toward the throne: "O come, let us adore Him . . ."

Yes, Lord, her heart whispered, *I want to trust Your unfailing love.*

She almost jumped and her eyes flew open when Pastor Cobbs clapped his hands once. "Well! Let's talk about this food pantry idea of yours, Sister Kathryn. Why don't you start at the beginning, tell us why you feel this is something God is calling you to do, and why you think SouledOut is the place to do it."

Nick smiled encouragement, so Kat took a deep breath and began—how she'd been encouraged to think less about "food issues" per se and more about people who were hungry. How Edesa Baxter had encouraged her to volunteer at a food pantry, which she had, but came away feeling that more churches needed to be feeding the hungry, and why not start at SouledOut, which already had a heart to minister to all sorts of people? And how she was learning the Bible was full of stories about God's concern for the poor and hungry. "Why, in Matthew 25, He told people that if we don't feed the hungry and visit people in prison and stuff like that, it's really Jesus we're neglecting!"

Both Nick and Avis Douglass smiled broadly at Kat, as if surprised. She flushed. Guess they weren't used to hearing her use scripture like that. But it felt good to base her passion on something solid other than just her own fly-by-night idea.

Kat paused, wondering if she should stop . . . but something nudged her spirit to put it all out there. Was she willing to put it *all* on the table? Taking another deep breath, she blew it out and spoke again. "Um, when I told Mrs. Douglass—uh, Sister Avis—about my idea last week, she encouraged me to pray about it, to ask God if this was *His* idea, not just mine. I have been praying, and I continue to feel that God is calling me to feed hungry people, but I guess the only way I'll really know that is if other people affirm the idea too. You know, where two or three agree—" Kat stopped.

She looked at each of the faces watching her, listening to her. Pastor Cobbs, his face kind and attentive. Avis Douglass, the woman who'd wrapped her in a motherly hug that day Rochelle had been "found," in a way her own mother had never done. And Nick, pastoral intern, her friend and—dare she think it?—soul mate.

Yes, these three needed to agree that God was calling *her.* But surely it had to be more than just two or three people agreeing *she* should do this. No way could she do this alone! If this food pantry was truly God's idea, God would need to call *others* to its mission as well. But who?

※

Kat walked home in the still-bright evening of midsummer, though the sun had disappeared behind the city buildings. Nick had slipped out of the office with her when her part of the meeting was over and said if she wanted to wait till they were done, he'd walk her home or they could ride with Mrs. Douglass. But he didn't know how long the rest of the meeting would be and let it go when she said she'd like to get home. It'd been a long day.

As much as she would've liked to walk home with Nick, Kat was glad to have a little time to herself to think about what had just happened. She'd blurted out her thoughts, that God would need to call others to help with a food pantry too, wondering all the while if that would kill the idea right there. But for some reason, Pastor Cobbs's smile just got wider. Had he really said, "I believe this idea *is* of God, and I believe God is calling you. How the rest of it fits together, I don't know yet. But God sometimes just shows us one step at a time."

Avis Douglass had nodded in agreement. "Have you given any thought to a start date?"

Start? Kat had nearly fallen off her chair. They were actually asking when it could *start*? "Well, right now I'm volunteering mornings at STEP and working at the coffee shop about twenty hours a week. And we'll need time to figure out logistics, locate food sources, get volunteers—stuff like that. So . . ."

Pastor Cobbs and Avis Douglass had put their heads together, pulling out a calendar, pointing, whispering . . . and then had turned back to her. "STEP is over at the end of this month," Avis said. "That would free up more of your time in August."

Pastor Cobbs had rubbed his chin thoughtfully. "So September might be a good time to start. Although it wouldn't hurt to do a trial run, see what bugs need to be worked out, see what interest there is. What would you think of doing a trial run in August, starting, say, the first weekend?"

The first weekend in *August*?! Kat had hardly been able to believe her ears. And besides, her heart had been beating so loudly, it felt as if blood was rushing up to her head, through her ear canals, and then free-falling all the way to her feet.

They'd prayed together, asking for God's blessing on this idea for a food pantry, asking God to open doors, to give favor, and to put this vision in the hearts of others if it was truly from the Holy Spirit. And then they'd prayed for Kat, asking God to draw her close to Him as she walked forward in this call.

Now, turning onto the residential street that led to their three-flat, Kat realized she didn't feel like going up to the apartment just yet. The evening was still warm, but a light breeze was coming off the lake, lazily making its way through the narrow streets of Rogers Park. Settling down on one of the concrete arms buttressing either side of the wide steps, she put her back to the brick wall and closed her eyes, listening to the cicadas drumming up a racket in the trees.

But as she replayed the meeting again and again, Kat couldn't stop the tears of surprise and joy that spilled over. After so many years of having her parents fuss at her about "getting distracted" with silly ideas, it was hard to believe that three people she respected so much had actually affirmed the idea for a food pantry at SouledOut. Even more amazing, they'd not only affirmed the food pantry but had affirmed *her*.

How long she sat there, she wasn't sure, but after a long while she heard the front door of the three-flat open. "Who . . . oh, Kat. It's you." Rochelle's voice. "I came down to get the mail and saw someone sitting out here. Didn't know the meeting was over. Where's Nick?"

Kat looked up, realizing the light had faded and the street

was full of deepening shadows. "Not back yet. Meeting wasn't over. I walked home."

"Oh. Well, when he gets here, will you tell him . . . Oh, there they are." Avis Douglass's Camry drove past slowly, no doubt looking for a parking space. "I gotta run back up, Conny's supposed to be getting on his jammies, but will you ask Nick if he'd come up as soon as he can? Conny's been begging to see him before he goes to sleep."

Kat grunted. The door wheezed shut and she heard Rochelle's footsteps fading up the stairs. Seemed like Rochelle and Conny expected Nick to be at their beck and call no matter what. Should she tell him or not?

Several minutes went by before Avis and Nick came walking back up the street and turned into their walk. As Avis came up the steps, she reached out and lightly touched the top of Kat's head before disappearing inside. The touch seemed to flow down Kat's entire body. Like a blessing. As if she was saying, *"I care."*

Kat brushed a new set of tears away with the back of her hand . . . and was surprised to see that Nick had sat down on the end of the concrete arm and was looking at her. Kat sniffed, fished for a tissue, and blew her nose. "How was the rest of the meeting?"

Nick shrugged. "Okay. Mostly scheduling decisions. A few pastoral situations. And some personal stuff, which I can't . . . you know."

"Yeah, sure." Kat blew her nose again. "Rochelle said to ask you to come right up. Conny wants to see you before bed."

Nick didn't move.

"Uh . . . Conny?" Kat gestured toward the door with her thumb.

"He can wait." Nick was quiet another long moment. Then . . . "I was proud of you tonight. You've given this food pantry a lot of thought and prayer, and you obviously impressed Pastor Cobbs and Sister Avis."

Kat grimaced. "Maybe not enough, though. I mean, first weekend in *August*? If I let myself think about what all it's going to take, I may panic."

She saw him grin in the glow of the porch light that had winked on. "Well, yeah, there's that." He laughed. "But you've thought about the most important things. *Why* you want to do it. Why it *needs* to be done. Why *God* wants it done."

Kat nodded, not quite knowing what to say.

To her surprise, Nick reached out and gently tucked a flyaway lock of frizzy hair behind her ear. "To be honest, Kat, I don't know if I'm 'called' in the same way you feel called to this, but I want you to know I'll support you any way I can. Help out. Be an errand boy. Do whatever to help make it happen. Okay?"

"Oh, Nick." Scrambling forward, she gave him a grateful hug. "That means so much." She felt his arms go around her and he held her close . . . for a long moment. And she didn't pull away.

Chapter 27

Hands on her hips, Edesa Baxter stared at the two full laundry baskets sitting by the back door of the apartment. There were times when living on the third floor of the House of Hope suited her just fine. No running feet overhead from kids living in the other apartments. No percussive thumps coming through the ceiling from speakers sitting on the floor. No loud voices and footsteps going up the stairwell past their apartment, except for Cordelia Soto and her kids living across the hall, also on the third floor. And she loved sitting on the window seat that hugged the bay windows in the front room, feeling like a bird hidden among the leaves of the trees planted along the parkway below.

Sí, there were a lot of things she liked about their third-floor apartment.

But laundry day wasn't one of them. Not when the two washing machines for general use were clear down in the basement. And especially not when one of the dryers had recently died, and the other one took twice as long to dry clothes as it should.

Why hadn't she asked Josh to take the laundry down before he headed out on his round of errands that morning? She didn't know when he'd get back. Vandals had stolen the recycling bins the city provided for their building, and he was haggling with the Department of Sanitation about providing replacements. Plus he had half a dozen other stops for the House of Hope—she couldn't remember what all he'd said. Just that he'd had to borrow Gabby Fairbanks's car because of all the running around.

"Mommeeee. Want more apple juice!" Two-year-old Gracie tugged on Edesa's skirt, holding up her sippy cup.

Absently Edesa got out the bottle of juice and filled Gracie's cup without asking, "What do you say, *niña*?" as she usually did. How was she going to manage Gracie *and* two laundry baskets going down three flights? It wasn't like she could just wait another day. Each of the six apartments in the House of Hope had been assigned a laundry day, and Wednesday was her day. And she'd really like to get the laundry done and folded before tonight when they had their weekly "household meeting" with everybody.

Besides, it was her birthday. Twenty-seven years old today. Not a "milestone" birthday, but still . . . she wished they'd canceled the household meeting and gotten a babysitter so she and Josh could do something special, maybe go out to dinner? It seemed like a long time since they'd had a night out.

Twenty-seven. Somehow that sounded a lot older than twenty-six, and made the three-year difference between her and Josh seem even wider. Here she was, almost thirty, and he'd still be in his twenties—

No, no, don't go there, she told herself. It was *God* who'd brought them together and she loved Josh, loved the Baxter family she'd married into, loved the child they'd adopted. And maybe someday Gracie would have a brother or sister.

Except . . . more kids, even more laundry! Edesa rolled her eyes heavenward. *Make that "someday," Señor.*

Well, she couldn't just stand there. "Come on, *niña*. Let's see who's home. Maybe somebody can watch you while I get the laundry started." Edesa took Gracie by the hand, went out into the stairwell, and knocked at the door across the hall. No answer. Not surprising. Cordelia—a sweet Latina mom with two youngsters—took her kids to Little Village two or three days a week to play with their cousins while she did housecleaning jobs. It was fun having another mom on the same floor who spoke Spanish, even though she and Cordelia came from different countries.

No one was home in 2A or 2B either. Where was everybody? Some of the moms had jobs, but usually somebody was home. Gracie plopped down on the second-floor landing. "I'm tired. Don't wanna walk."

Edesa picked her up and continued on down to the first floor. No point in knocking at 1B. Gabby was at work and both her teen boys were in summer camp programs this month. Edesa shook her head. Those two boys couldn't be more different. P.J. was into sports and was the spitting image of his dark-haired dad, while Paul, a budding musician, had inherited his mom's "Orphan Annie" curly hair.

She knocked on 1A. Her last chance. If Tanya or Precious or Sabrina weren't home, she'd just have to—

The door opened. "Hey, Miss Edesa." Sabrina, Precious McGill's eighteen-year-old, wearing her year-old toddler on her hip, stood in the doorway looking bored. Edesa didn't blame her. It was hard being a teenager with a baby, missing out on summer's fun. "Mama's not here if you're looking for her."

"Actually, I have a favor to ask. Could you watch Gracie for fifteen minutes while I get my laundry into the washing machines?" She'd worry about getting it dry later.

Sabrina shrugged. "Sure." The pretty black teenager held out a hand to Gracie. "Want a hot dog, sweetie? I was just gonna feed Timmy some lunch." She rolled her eyes at Edesa. *"Now* maybe he'll let me set him down. Been clingy all mornin', ain't ya, you Lil' Turkey."

Edesa tried not to wince—not her choice for Gracie's lunch—but she thanked Sabrina profusely before running back upstairs. Beggars couldn't be choosy, as the Americans liked to say.

But she had no sooner lugged both baskets down the outside back stairs and unlocked the basement door when her cell phone rang. Edesa snatched her phone out of her pocket. Caller ID said Kathryn Davies. *"Buenos días,* Sister Kathryn! *Cómo estás?"*

She heard laughter on the other end. "That's what I need, Edesa. Someone to make me use my Spanish. Uh . . . *tienes tiempo para hablar?"*

Did she have time to talk? "Uh, well, sure, for a few minutes . . . Wait just a moment." She tapped the Speaker button and set the phone down on top of the dryer that wasn't working. Hopefully that was one of the errands Josh was doing today, getting parts to fix it. "Okay. What's up?"

"Well, you said to call and tell you about my meeting with the pastoral team Monday night. Sorry I didn't call yesterday. I'm trying to make up work time I took off over the weekend when Olivia and her sister were here. In fact, I'm on my way to work right now—just left the school—but didn't want to wait too long before I told you what's happening."

Edesa stuffed assorted underwear, dish towels, and socks into the first washer as Kathryn talked breathlessly. Then she sorted wash-and-wear into the second washing machine—both of which had seen better days, but at least they still worked. *Gracias, Jesús.*

But as her caller went on, Edesa stopped sorting clothes to listen more carefully. She'd never heard Kat Davies talk like this—about realizing that starting a food pantry had to be God's idea or it would flop, and realizing she couldn't do it alone, that others would need to feel called as well. "So I'm wondering if you would pray for that specifically, Sister Edesa, that God would call others to catch the vision for a food pantry at SouledOut. I can tell people about it, yeah, me and my big mouth are good at that." Edesa heard Kat give a self-deprecating laugh. "I might be able to twist a few arms or drag people into it. But that's not the same thing as being called by God. I—" The girl's voice seemed to catch.

"Oh, Kathryn, *sí,* I will be so glad to pray with you about this. When did you say the pastors suggested you start?"

Kat's voice on the speaker sounded almost like a whisper. "September. But Pastor Cobbs suggested doing a trial run in August—right after I'm done volunteering with the STEP program the end of July."

"Oh." Edesa almost laughed. "What's that—less than three weeks away? We certainly do need to pray! Only God can pull this off! Let's pray right now." Turning on both washing machines and with the phone to her ear, Edesa slowly walked back up the outside stairs to her apartment, praying every step of the way.

"Oh, thank you, Sister Edesa. I appreciate it so much—Oh, hey, I'm here at the coffee shop. Gotta go. But if you don't mind, I'll call back in a day or two. I have a feeling I'm going to need a lot of prayer."

Edesa kept thinking about the phone call as she picked up Gracie, promising Sabrina she'd return the favor by keeping Timmy soon, read a Winnie the Pooh story to Gracie before putting her down for her nap, and then fixed a quesadilla for her own lunch. Funny how Kat's phone call was affecting her. The enthusiastic girl had come to her first with her idea, and seemed to consider her a major prayer partner in this project. But did God mean for her to be a major *player* in this project as well?

Licking the melted cheese off her fingers, Edesa realized something had shifted. For weeks now, she had felt God nudging her to gently challenge Kat to a deeper walk with God, to come alongside and help channel her enthusiastic ideas into "reasonable service." But right now, Kat's call was challenging *her*.

"*Señor,*" she breathed, head in her hands over her empty plate, "if You are calling me to get involved in this food pantry idea, please make it clear."

It was only when she finally rose from the small kitchen table and filled the sink with soapy water to wash up the breakfast and lunch dishes that she realized she'd never added detergent to the two loads of dirty clothes.

Chapter 28

Frustrated, Edesa threw the dish scrubber into the sink. She had no choice. Checking to make sure Gracie was asleep, she ran down the back stairs to the basement, stopped the washers, measured detergent into both machines, and ran back upstairs. Heart pounding from the exertion, Edesa listened . . . no sound from Gracie's bedroom. She peeked in. All was well.

So why was she suddenly crying?

Her knees suddenly feeling wobbly, Edesa made it into her bedroom, turned on the fan, and sank down on the double bed. She still had a lot to do—dishes weren't done, laundry would need drying, she needed to prepare for the Friday Bible study at Manna House, make supper, and pick up the apartment for the household meeting that night. But if she could shut her eyes for just a little while, until the laundry needed switching or Gracie woke up, whichever came first . . .

But it was the phone that rattled her out of a deep sleep. Two rings, three . . . four . . . five . . . before she picked it up in the kitchen.

"Edesa?" Josh on the line. "Thought you and Gracie might be out. Just wanted to tell you these errands are taking longer than I thought. Might not be home till supper. Will you be okay?"

Not till supper. She sighed. "Sure. We'll manage."

"Is everything all right? You don't sound too good."

Get a grip, Edesa. "I'm fine. Just fell asleep when Gracie went down for her nap. Still groggy. But, Josh, I wish . . ."

"Yeah? Wish what, sweetheart?"

"I wish we could skip the household meeting tonight and go out, just you and me. Since it's my birthday."

"Aw, honey, I know. But Bertie just moved in a few weeks ago, and you know Gabby wants to get started off on the right foot, with everyone in the building present when she reviews the house rules and stuff. I'm sorry. But we'll do something to celebrate your birthday this weekend, okay?"

"Okay . . . *Te amo.*"

"Love you more. See you in a couple hours."

Hanging up the phone, Edesa took a deep breath and glanced at the wall clock. She'd slept for almost an hour and did feel better. Josh was right. It wouldn't be good to skip the household meeting. After all, he was the property manager and she was volunteer staff for the House of Hope. What did it matter if they celebrated her birthday today or two days from now? That would give her a few more days to pray about Kat's phone call, and then she could talk about it with Josh. Right now, she needed to finish the dishes and get started on that Bible study she had to teach on Friday before Gracie woke up.

When the phone rang again shortly after four, Gracie was up and Edesa hoped it was Josh saying he was on his way home, but the caller ID said Gabrielle Fairbanks. "Hi, Edesa! It's Gabby . . . I just got home from picking up the boys. For some reason our hot water is off. I'm down here in the basement but can't see what's wrong. Hopefully it's just the pilot light on the water heater. Can you ask Josh to look at it? Did you have hot water when you did your laundry today?"

"I don't know. I didn't stay to check. I usually do the wash-and-wear in cold water anyway." Edesa cradled the phone between ear and shoulder so she could pry open a small container of red play dough for Gracie, who was busily smashing blue kiddie clay into flat pancakes. "But, uh, Gabby, could you do me a favor and put my white load into the dryer—be sure it's the one that's working. I'm up here alone with Gracie."

"Oh, sure. Hang on a moment . . ."

Edesa heard the banging of washing machine lids, and then Gabby came back on the line. "Um, Edesa? Not sure what happened, but the powdered soap is still sitting on top of the clothes, though the clothes look wet. Did you stop the machines and then add the soap? Maybe you forgot to start them again . . . Edesa? Edesa, are you crying? It's not a big deal. I'll start them now . . . Okay, okay, you hold on. I'm coming up."

❉

Edesa felt better after a good cry on Gabby's shoulder. "Don't mind me," she finally said, blowing her nose. "I'm fine, really. Just one of those days. Probably my monthly's a little off. Stupid of me to feel sorry for myself just because it's my birthday. I'm acting like a ten-year-old."

She kissed the top of Gracie's head, who'd crawled into her

lap when she saw her mother crying and had patted her cheek, crooning, "Be happy, Mommy, be happy."

Gabby snorted. "Hey, you've got nothing on me. *I* win the feel-sorry-for-myself award on neglected birthdays. Remember the year Philip kicked me out? I was sure no one would remember my birthday, and I ended up getting Chinese takeout, renting a couple movies, and barging in on Precious and Tanya for a blubber-fest." The curly redhead started to laugh. "Later it turned out to be one of my most amazing birthdays ever." She poked Edesa with an elbow. "Who knows? Maybe for you too."

The front door of the apartment opened and they heard Josh holler, "I'm home! Where are my girls? I've got *Pastelitos de Carne* to go!"

"See?" Gabby jumped up from the kitchen table. "Now you don't have to cook on your birthday. But I do, so I'd better run. See you at seven?" She hesitated and gave Edesa a funny look. "Sure you're all right?"

"*Sí, sí!* Go, go. But you can tell Josh about the hot water heater on your way out." No way did she want to be the one to tell her husband he still had work to do after he'd been out all day.

But as it turned out, it was just the pilot light that'd gone out, and by the time the residents of the House of Hope began to arrive—minus the kids, who were all watching *Doctor Doolittle* in Gabby's apartment under the supervision of Sabrina and P.J.—she and Josh had feasted on the deep-fried pastries filled with meat, rice, and vegetables, bathed and put Gracie to bed, and even had a few moments to cuddle on the couch in the living room. "Don't worry, sweetheart," Josh had whispered into her ear, "I haven't forgotten your birthday."

Neither had the others. Precious from 1A was the last to arrive, holding a birthday cake ablaze with lit candles out in front of her as if afraid her hair would catch fire. "Make a wish quick, girl, and blow out them candles, or we gonna be eating wax with our frosting!" Chagrined at her earlier "poor me" tears, Edesa laughed with delight, breathed a silent prayer for God to bless everyone under the House of Hope roof, and blew—though it took three breaths to blow out all twenty-seven candles.

Eating the rich double-fudge chocolate cake turned out to be the "spoonful of sugar making the medicine go down" as Gabby (housemother) and Josh (building guru) tackled items on the agenda—particularly the announcement that the washers and dryers in the basement would be temporarily out of commission until he got them repaired. Until then, residents would need to use the local Laundromat. Next, a review of the House Rules for the newest residents, including a reminder that Quiet Hours for loud music and noise in the stairwell were nine o'clock on weeknights and eleven o'clock on weekends. And last but not least, a request to use the temporary cardboard boxes in the basement for recyclables until the city delivered the replacement bins.

"Anything else?" Gabby asked as the time edged toward eight o'clock. She grinned at Josh. "I think you have something, right?"

Josh—the only male in the gaggle of females crowded into the Baxter living room—scrambled to his feet. "I do. *Señora*"— he bowed dramatically and held out his hand to Edesa—"right this way."

Laughing, Edesa took his hand. "What?" Her confusion— or maybe sheer curiosity—grew as he led her out the apartment door and started down the stairs, followed by all the House of

Hope residents, most of whom were as curious and excited as Edesa. On the first floor, Gabby opened her apartment door and called to the kids to join them for a surprise.

Which made for a noisy troupe piling out the front door of the House of Hope and spilling onto the sidewalk. By now Edesa could hardly imagine what in the world Josh had up his sleeve, especially when he said, "Close your eyes!" and led her several yards down the sidewalk.

Then they stopped. Edesa felt everyone crowding around and heard a few gasps. "Okay, you can look," Josh said, putting his arm around her shoulders.

Edesa opened her eyes. Parked in front of her was a navy blue minivan with a huge red bow on top. Her eyes widened. "Josh! You bought . . . a car? How can we—"

His arm gave her a big squeeze. "I distinctly remember both of us agreeing a few weeks ago that we *definitely* needed to get a car," he murmured. "And don't worry. It's secondhand, a 2003 Chevy Venture. It's in terrific shape, and I got it for a very good price—even less than we agreed we could spend. Just sorry it took me all day."

All day. She leaned into him. "Oh, Josh. I'm sorry . . ."

"For what, sweetheart?" He handed her a car key. "Go on, look inside."

By now, Gabby, Precious, and the other residents were clapping, *oohing,* and *aahing,* and once the minivan was unlocked, the kids scrambled in and out. Edesa was thrilled to see that they could carry at least seven passengers in the three rows of seats, with room in the back for . . . hauling food for the food pantry?

Where did that thought come from?

"See?" Gabby whispered to her as Josh finally relocked the

car and removed the big red bow to make it less attractive to car thieves. "Didn't I say you just might get an awesome birthday after all?"

❋

Why was she so tired? Josh, bless him, had gone up and down the stairs after the house meeting Wednesday evening, running their clothes through the sort-of-working dryer before he took it apart the next day, so she couldn't blame running up and down stairs. And she did manage to finish planning her Bible study during Gracie's nap on Thursday, so she wasn't really feeling anxious when she went to bed last night. But she still felt as if she was dragging when Josh, driving the "new" minivan, dropped her off at Manna House at ten Friday morning to give her time to set up for the Bible study at ten thirty.

Sweet of Josh to keep Gracie till she was done teaching. She waved good-bye to them at the door, then headed for the kitchen on the lower level. Coffee . . . she needed a good strong cup of Estelle's coffee to pick her up. But on second thought, she made a cup of peppermint tea instead. Maybe she was fighting a touch of the summer flu. Her mama had sworn by peppermint tea for whatever ailed you.

After a brief hug for Estelle in the kitchen and poking her head into Gabby's office to say, *"Hola!"* Edesa hurried back to Shepherd's Fold on the first floor—and was surprised to run into Avis Douglass's daughter. "Rochelle! And Conny! Hey there, little guy." She gave them both warm hugs. "What are you two doing here?"

Rochelle was certainly looking better in the few weeks since she'd come off the streets and started living with the Crista University students. Though still slender, her face had filled out, her honey-toned skin seemed more golden, and her dark eyes were bright. She must be managing the HIV with proper meds and good food, which was encouraging.

"Oh, we're on a mission for Kat." Rochelle grinned at Edesa. "She asked if I'd check out places to get flyers printed for the new food pantry at SouledOut—you heard that the pastors gave the go-ahead, didn't you? One of the copy shops is nearby so I decided to drop in, thought you might be here. Are you still teaching your Bible study on Friday mornings?"

Edesa felt pleased that Rochelle—who'd been an occasional guest at the shelter—would remember the Bible study. "*Sí*. In fact, I'm getting ready to start now. Can you stay? I'm teaching on a special prayer the apostle Paul prayed for people he cared about—"

Rochelle shrugged. "Sure. And . . . I'd like to talk to you afterward, if you have time. Uh, is Gracie here? Maybe Conny could play . . ."

Edesa shook her head. "But we can get him some books or drawing supplies to keep him busy." Conny, however, had already made a beeline for a plastic bin of Legos someone had left in a corner of the big room.

The next five minutes were busy as they dragged the assorted couches and chairs into a semicircle, and right at ten thirty, eight or nine women straggled in—a pretty good turn-out for a pleasant summer day. Edesa had long since given up evaluating the success of the Bible study on how many of the residents turned out. *If only one woman is touched by something in the Word, that's enough,* she often told herself.

Her Scripture passage was from Paul's letter to the Colossians, chapter 1, where the apostle prayed for the tiny church. Passing out the shelter Bibles—some in Spanish—Edesa asked various women to read his prayer requests for this group of people: that they'd understand the will of God . . . that their lives would be pleasing to God . . . that they'd prosper in the work God had given them to do . . . that they'd draw on the strength of God to persevere when things got tough . . . and finally, that they'd give thanks for their inheritance in the kingdom of God.

As usual, the women—many struggling just to hold body and soul together—had a lot of tough questions.

"How we s'posed ta know what the heck the will of God is?"

"Don't think losin' my apartment was the will of God!"

"Did you say *prosper* in the work we s'posed to do? *Humph.* Gotta get me a job first."

But some said they could sure use some strength from God when things got tough, and a few admitted some of their choices probably didn't please God, so they could use prayer for better ones next time.

"No easy answers," Edesa said to Rochelle ruefully as they pushed the couches and chairs back into place an hour later. "But it's good. The women always challenge *me* and make me wrestle with the Scriptures too." She flopped down on one of the threadbare couches they'd just arranged back into one of several "conversation groups" around the room. "Whew! Teaching wears me out. But you wanted to talk? We usually stay for lunch, but I think we still have half an hour . . . Oh, there's Josh and Gracie! Hi, honey! Give us a few minutes, okay?"

With a wave toward the couch, Josh headed for the corner with Gracie and squatted down beside Conny, who was still engrossed in building a complicated Lego structure. Rochelle curled up on the other end of the couch but seemed distracted as she watched what was going on across the room, where Josh seemed to be asking Conny questions about what he was building and pointing out things to Gracie. Finally she murmured, "He's really good with Gracie, isn't he? Josh, I mean. Even though she's adopted."

Edesa smiled. "Yes, he is. From day one, he's loved her like his own." *She is his own,* she felt like adding.

"Yeah, I can tell." There was a long pause. Then . . . "Nick Taylor is good with Conny too."

A prickly feeling crawled up Edesa's spine. "Rochelle, what's going on? Are you and Nick . . . ?" She stopped, not sure what to say.

Rochelle's cheeks flushed. "I . . . don't know. He's really taken a shine to Conny and seems to respect me as a mom. I never wanted to be a single mom, but, well, things didn't work out with Dexter. In fact"—she rolled her eyes—"he's been making things real difficult. But when I see Nick with Conny, I think, that's the kind of man I'd like to be married to, the kind of man Conny could look up to. Except, well . . . he's white." She eyed Edesa nervously. "Like Josh."

Edesa chuckled. "*Sí*, like Mr. Pale Face over there. Believe me, girl, mixed marriages have their challenges. We have been very fortunate."

"Yeah. You guys seem to be making it work." Rochelle studied her nails for a moment. "To be honest, I'd like Conny to be raised by a decent black man, someone like my dad or my stepdad. Black boys still have it tough, developing a positive identity and defying the stereotypes. But that was before I met Nick, and . . . well, he's a really great guy. And I'm thinking, maybe it would be okay. Him and me and Conny."

Seeing the serious expression on Rochelle's face, Edesa reached out and took the girl's hand. "Rochelle, I agree. Nick Taylor is a really nice guy. But tell me this. Has *Nick* ever said anything to you, that he's interested in you that way?"

Avis's daughter laughed nervously. "I don't know! I mean, not exactly. But he treats me really nice—a *lot* nicer than Dexter ever treated me. I feel . . . respected. And sometimes I catch him looking at me, you know, like he finds me attractive."

Laughter and childish giggles came from the Lego corner as Edesa fervently prayed about what to say. But before she could say anything, they heard the familiar banging on a pot from below announcing that lunch was ready. Several of the residents sitting around the room moseyed toward the stairwell. Out of the corner of her eye, Edesa saw Josh pick up Gracie and head toward them.

But Rochelle seemed oblivious. She leaned forward, her eyes intense. "Edesa, do you think it's all right for the woman to, you know, let the man know she's interested? I mean, I know a lot of girls who do, but they always seem so . . . brazen about it. Throwing themselves at guys. I don't want to do that, but I'd like Nick to know I'm interested in him. That I like him. A lot."

Josh had come up behind the couch where they were sitting, and out of the corner of her eye, Edesa saw his eyes widen slightly. He'd overheard.

"Oh, Rochelle. I—"

"Mommy! Mommy!" Conny launched himself between them, grabbing his mother's hand. "Didn't you hear the signal?

Everybody's going downstairs. Can we stay an' eat? Please? Gracie gets to. I wanna stay too."

Rochelle allowed herself to be dragged off the couch. "Okay, okay. I'll ask Miss Estelle if she has enough. We didn't sign up for lunch." Casting an apologetic smile over her shoulder at Edesa, the mother and son headed for the stairwell leading to the dining room below.

Edesa followed along behind with Josh and Gracie. But she touched Josh's arm and held him back until Rochelle and Conny were out of earshot. "Josh," she hissed, "you need to talk to Nick . . . soon."

Chapter 29

ck. It was starting to rain.

Nick had left the apartment early Saturday morning, needing a good run to wake up his brain so he could really concentrate on the final prep for his first sermon at SouledOut tomorrow. He'd been mulling over his assigned passage for a couple of weeks—Jesus' last words to Peter after the resurrection—and had made a lot of notes, but he definitely needed to carve out a significant hunk of time today to pull it all together.

He groaned. Why had he agreed to rustle up a large bin—or two or three—to collect nonperishable food at SouledOut? By tomorrow! When was he going to do that? But he'd promised Kat he'd help and Sunday was the big day when the food pantry was going to get announced at church. Somehow . . .

Nick cast an anxious eye at the sky. He hadn't even had time to process the news Sister Avis had shared in the pastoral team meeting last Monday night after Kat left, or what its implications might be. But he couldn't think about that today. After tomorrow.

He'd been hoping a good run would help clear his mind so he could sort things out. But he'd no sooner made it to the jogging path along Lake Michigan than he felt the first big drops. The clouds overhead hung dark and heavy. He'd better head back before the skies really opened up.

By the time Nick got back to the three-flat, his heart was pumping and it was hard to tell if he was damp from sweat or the drizzle in the air. Taking the outside back stairs two at a time and coming into the kitchen, he saw his newest housemate frying up a batch of grated potatoes.

"Morning, Rochelle." He was suddenly hungry, but he should probably shower first. Heading through the kitchen, he was distracted by a sheet of paper lying on the kitchen table. He picked it up. "Rochelle! Did you design this flyer?"

The young woman at the stove turned and eyed him shyly from under her mane of thick black hair. "You like it?"

"Yes, I like it. Great design." He had no idea Rochelle had such artistic talent. "But, more important . . ." Nick craned his neck and glanced into the dining–living room area. "Does Kat like it?"

Rochelle grinned. "She does. This is just the first one asking people to donate canned goods and stuff for the food pantry. I designed a few more announcing the food pantry itself—you know, to post in store windows and places like that—but I wasn't sure what its name is going to be. Would you like to see them?"

"Sure." Nick pulled out a chair at the table. The shower could wait. "Those fried potatoes or whatever you're making sure smell good. Any chance a hungry jogger could have some of those with breakfast? I'll set the table, grovel, do anything."

Rochelle turned the gas flame under the frying pan down low, scurried out of the room, and was back in thirty seconds with a large manila envelope. "Here. And yes, you can set the table. Everybody's here except Kat—she had to be at the coffee shop by six. And Conny's still asleep—uh-oh, spoke too soon. Hey there, young man!" She smiled at the sleepy boy who'd just wandered in, dressed only in a Spider-Man pajama top and his underpants. "Want some breakfast?"

Rubbing his eyes, Conny crawled up into Nick's lap. With one arm wrapped around the little boy, Nick opened the large envelope, pulled out three brightly colored flyers, and laid them on the table. "See those, buddy? Your mommy made them. Isn't she great?"

"I *know*." Conny yawned. "We went to Grampa Peter's shop yesterday and she drawed them on his computer. I saw you in the mail room, but Mommy said we couldn't bother you."

"Really? You wouldn't have bothered me. Then I could've introduced you to my working buddies. They've heard all about you." Nick studied the three flyers again and then held one up. "I like this one best so far." It had photos of all different kinds of food running around the edge of the page like a colorful ribbon.

"I can read those words." Conny pointed. "It says 'Food Pantry.'"

"Hey, that's good. What else?"

The boy giggled. "You read it."

"Okay. It says 'Come to the Table on Saturdays, 10 to 12.' And it's got the address of SouledOut Community Church." Nick looked up. "So that time's been decided?"

Rochelle shrugged as she dished up the hash browns, melted

some butter in the same pan, and poured in some beaten eggs. "Don't know for sure. Like I said, they're just rough drafts. Are you going to set the table or not?"

"Right, right, right." Nick quickly put the flyers back into the envelope and pushed Conny off his lap. "You can help put the silverware around, okay, buddy?"

By the time he got the plates on and the orange juice poured, Rochelle was dishing up the scrambled eggs. So far no sign of Brygitta. But if Kat had the early shift, Bree probably didn't have to work till the afternoon or evening. "So we'll let her sleep," he said, rubbing his hands gleefully. "All the more for the rest of us, right, buddy? You want to say the blessing?"

Conny considered. "Okay." He folded his hands and scrunched his eyes shut. "Thank You, God, for the food and for my mommy an' for Grammy Avis and Grampa Peter an' Mister Nick an' Miss Bree an' Miss Kat. Amen."

"And your daddy," Rochelle prompted.

"I already said amen. Can I have some eggs?"

Rochelle eyed Nick, and he shook his head slightly. He respected Rochelle's efforts to keep Conny connected to his dad, but that might be pushing it.

"So what's next with the flyers?" Nick took a bite of the fried potatoes. "Mm, these are great."

"Well . . ." Rochelle dished up her own plate. "Kat asked if I could make copies of the first flyer today so she can pass them out at church tomorrow. She wants people to pass them out to their neighbors and take them to their work. I don't mind except"—she tipped her head toward the window—"weather guy said it's going to rain all day. Don't really want to take Conny out in the rain. But maybe I can ask my stepdad if we can make copies over at Software Symphony—especially if he's going to work today and we can get a ride."

Software Symphony. "That's it!" Nick grinned. "Kat asked me to come up with a big bin or something to collect foodstuff from SouledOut members. I just remembered . . . we have a couple big trash cans in the mail room—heavy-duty plastic things—we might be able to do without. I'll ask Mr. D if we can borrow them for a few weeks. They're not too pretty, but—"

"Maybe you could decorate them. I know somebody who'd love to help, right, big boy?" Rochelle reached over and knuckled the top of Conny's head.

"Yeah! Can I help decorate 'em, Mister Nick?" Conny bounced up and down in his chair.

Wait. Finding the bins was one thing. Decorating was another. He really needed to work on his sermon. "Uh . . . I'm preaching tomorrow and I still need a good chunk of time to prepare. Maybe Bree can—"

"Maybe Bree can what?" A sleepy Brygitta wandered into the kitchen wearing a loose robe over her T-shirt and shorts, her dark-brown pixie cut tousled, her face bare of any makeup. "Any of that food left for me?"

Rochelle pushed the remaining potatoes and eggs her way as Bree picked up a glass of orange juice and eyed Nick over the rim. "So what are you volunteering me for?"

Nick told her about the bins to collect food. "Gonna try to borrow some from Mr. D's shop—but they're pretty ugly. Rochelle suggested we decorate them, and I was just wondering if you—"

"Can't." Bree shook her head. "I've got to go to work this afternoon." She sighed and spooned what was left of the food onto a plate. "I'm getting pretty tired of this work schedule. It's all over the map. Hard to plan *anything.*"

Rochelle got up from the table abruptly and stuck her empty dishes in the sink. "At least you've got a job," she muttered and stalked out of the kitchen. "Forget it."

Bree stared after her as their housemate disappeared into the other room, then turned back to Nick. "Gosh, I didn't mean anything."

Nick didn't say anything. Even he was a bit taken aback by Rochelle's sudden change in attitude. What was that about? Come to think of it, though, she'd been doing a lot more around the apartment—like making breakfast for everybody this morning—maybe to make up for not having a job. Were they taking her for granted? Probably. Rochelle was dealing with a lot—parenting a six-year-old as a single mom, dealing with a disgruntled ex, managing HIV with all its implications, job-hunting for weeks and coming up zero . . . which, frankly, was hard to understand. Look at the talent evident in those flyers she'd designed—

"Take care of the flock."

Peter Douglass's words suddenly echoed in Nick's ears. That's what Rochelle's stepfather had said to him when she and Conny first moved into their apartment. Seemed awfully similar to the Scripture passage he was supposed to teach on tomorrow. *"Do you love me? Feed my sheep,"* Jesus had said to Peter, the disciple who'd turned chicken and denied even knowing Jesus.

Huh. What did "Take care of the flock" and "Feed my sheep" mean on a Saturday when he was feeling pressure to prepare for his sermon, find bins for the food pantry collection, decorate said bins with an eager-beaver kid who craved his attention, and juggle the expectations of his housemates? One of whom was the girl he—

"Nick? Earth to Nick . . . your cell phone is ringing." Bree poked him before clearing her dishes and disappearing out of the kitchen. "I'll clean up the kitchen. But I want to get my laundry started."

Digging the phone out of the fanny pack he wore while running, Nick glanced at the caller ID. Josh Baxter? "Hey, Josh. What's up?"

"Hi, Nick. Say, was wondering if we could get together sometime today? Thought both of us could use some guy time. I'm surrounded here at the House of Hope with estrogen and thought maybe you could use some rescuing, too, from your all-female household. Well, except for Conny, but you know what I mean."

Nick snorted. "Definitely know what you mean! Man, wish I could. But I'm preaching tomorrow at SouledOut and I've still got to pull it together. My first time, you know. Trying not to fall flat on my face. And I've got some other stuff I promised Kat I'd do today too, related to launching this food pantry. But, hey, any chance I could take a rain check? Tomorrow afternoon or evening maybe? I'd really like that."

"So you can't get together today? Well . . . okay. We could try for tomorrow. Let me check what Edesa's got going on. We can talk at church in the morning, okay?"

Nick hung up reluctantly. What he wouldn't give to just chuck the whole business for the day—sermon, food pantry, Conny, Kat—and just hang out with Josh. How long since he'd done just that, hang out with the guys?

But as he showered and dressed, then called up his sermon notes on his computer, the words kept chasing themselves around in his mind.

"Take care of the flock."

"Feed my sheep."

Arrgh. Figuring out how to *do* that was just as hard— harder—than figuring out how to preach it. But what kind of pastor would he be if he didn't live what he preached?

At the other end of the apartment, Nick heard Rochelle running the vacuum cleaner in the bedroom she shared with Conny. Closing his computer, he passed Conny watching cartoons in the living room, headed down the hallway, and knocked on the open door. "Hey!" He noticed Rochelle had wrapped a bandanna around her thick hair, probably to keep it out of her face while she did housework. Somehow the girl managed to look great no matter what she wore.

He waited until she turned off the machine. "Did you talk to your stepdad? Are you going over to the shop to make copies?"

She shrugged. "Yeah. He's going to work in about half an hour, so guess Conny and I'll go with him. It's still raining."

"Tell you what. I'll go with you guys, check out the bins, and see what Conny and I can come up with to decorate them while you're making the copies. If we do that this morning, I think I'll still have time to do my sermon prep this afternoon. Sound okay?"

Her face lit up with a smile. "Thanks! Conny will really like that. Me too. It'll be fun." Rochelle pulled off the bandanna and shook out her hair with a playful toss. "It's a date."

Chapter 30

Where was everybody?

Kat checked her cell phone again just to be sure she hadn't missed a text message or voice mail, but . . . still nothing. Not that Nick was obligated to tell her he'd gone out, but it was kind of strange that the apartment was totally empty. Brygitta, of course, had shown up at The Common Cup for her shift just as Kat was ready to leave, but where were Rochelle and Conny? It wasn't exactly a rule, but her apartment mates were usually pretty good about leaving a note on the fridge.

Her finger itched over the speed dial . . . *Nope.* She wasn't going to call Nick and whine, *Where are you?* It had been a strange week anyway since that long hug last Monday night—not to mention his kiss on her cheek before that. Neither one of them had said anything about either incident since—though they'd hardly had any time alone all week, with her working a couple evenings, Nick at prayer meeting on Wednesday, she and Rochelle volunteering again at the Rock of Ages food pantry, and all four of them going out to a movie last night while the Douglasses babysat Conny. TGIF and all that.

But she'd asked him last night to help her find some kind of bin to set up at the church tomorrow for donations to the food pantry. She'd been hoping they could go out together that afternoon once she got home from work, maybe ask at the Dominick's near SouledOut for a big box or something. They could decorate it together—that'd be fun.

If he got back from who-knows-where.

Digging out a package of flour tortillas and cheese, Kat fried herself a large quesadilla for lunch and was just chopping up some green onions and lettuce to go with the salsa on top when she heard laughter and loud thumps coming up the front stairwell. A few moments later the front door flew open and Conny, Rochelle, and Nick stumbled in, laughing as they wrestled a large plastic trash can into the living room.

Kat came to the door of the kitchen, knife in her hand. "What in the world?"

"Hi, Miss Kat!" Conny yelled. "We got your food bin!"

Kat gave it a once-over. Pretty beat up. "Uhhh, I see. What does the other bin look like?"

Conny screwed up his face. "Huh?"

Rochelle laughed. "What does the—ohhh, funny." She bent down and whispered in the little boy's ear.

"A joke?" He still looked puzzled. "I thought she was talking 'bout the other bin we left at Grampa's shop."

Nick grinned at Kat. "Mr. D graciously donated two trash cans for contributions to the food pantry, but as you can see, they need a little, er, help. Conny and I tried to decorate one with a big sheet of butcher paper we found in a storage room, but by the time we got it taped on, it sorta looked like a trash can with the trash on the *outside*—"

Rochelle snickered and rolled her eyes in agreement.

"—so Rochelle got the bright idea to leave that one there for donations from Software Symphony employees and bring the other one back here to spruce up for the church."

"Right." Rochelle absently redid the rubber band holding back her thick hair at the nape of her neck. "I think my mom has a stash of those disposable plastic tablecloths in bright colors— the kind you get for a party—and if she's willing to part with them, we could wrap this can in one or two of those."

"And cut out pictures of food from magazines and paste them all over it!" Conny yelled. "Mommy said I could do that part."

Nick nodded, still grinning. "Let Rochelle make a sign for it—she did a bang-up job on your flyer. Hey . . . show Kat the copies you made."

Kat took the stack Rochelle handed her. "This is great, Rochelle. Thanks for doing that. Uh . . . sounds like you three had a good time at the shop." She tried to ignore a twinge of envy. After all, they'd just been doing stuff she'd asked them to do for the food pantry—though *she'd* meant Nick helping *her* come up with a usable receptacle for donations. But Nick had spent the morning having fun with Rochelle and Conny while she'd been on her feet serving up an endless parade of iced coffee and chai tea to go.

Get a grip, Kat. Just a misunderstanding. And since he'd already found a bin to use, maybe she and Nick could do something else—if the stupid rain let up.

"Anybody for quesadillas?" she asked brightly. "I've got the makings out."

"Sure! Just let me run upstairs and check out my mom's stash of disposable table covers." Rochelle was already halfway out the door. "They've already been used, so I don't think she'll mind. I'll grab some food magazines too. And the food ads from the newspaper. Come on, Conny, you can help carry the magazines."

Nick followed Kat into the kitchen as footsteps scurried upstairs. "If you don't mind, Kat, I'm going to duck out on decorating that trash can. I really need to work on my sermon for tomorrow, and I just spent most of the morning tracking down the bins you asked me to find . . . Here, want me to chop up some of those green onions? Quesadillas sound great." He chuckled again. "Believe me, trying to keep up with Conny can work up an appetite!"

She handed him the knife. But disappointment pressed Kat's lips into a thin line as she busied herself grating more cheese. *That sermon.* So much for hanging out with Nick today and figuring out just what was going on between them. If anything.

❋

Kat helped Rochelle and Conny decorate the trash can with bright-yellow plastic table covers, and sure enough, the sign Rochelle made practically looked professional.

Food Pantry Donations
Nonperishable Foods Only

The "professional look," however, quickly dissipated amid the magazine pictures of pizza, milk gallons, canned goods, and bags of flour Conny cut out and wanted to paste all around the bin. Kat tried to help him know the difference between perishable—food that had to be refrigerated—and nonperishable, but she finally gave up. The glossy pictures in the food magazines were so much more appealing than the ads for flour and canned corn from the newspaper.

The Douglasses took the bin to SouledOut the next morning in the trunk of Avis's Toyota, propped wide open, and when Nick, Kat, and Bree arrived it was standing near the double doors where people had to pass it as they came in. Kat saw more than one person stop, stare, turn to someone else, and say, "What food pantry?"

They should've waited to set it out till *after* the announcement at the end of today's service. Well, too late now.

"I have to sit up front with Pastor Cobbs," Nick whispered to Kat as she and Bree settled into their usual seats toward the back. "Keep praying for me."

Kat gave him an encouraging smile. "Break a leg."

Had she been praying for Nick? Or had she been so consumed with ideas for launching the food pantry that she hadn't given him the prayer support he'd wanted? She shut her eyes as the praise team tuned their instruments. Hopefully, prayers worked retroactively. *Lord, be with Nick in a special way as he gives his first sermon here at SouledOut.* He'd certainly spent enough time preparing yesterday—all afternoon and most of the evening too. She shook off that thought and added, *Prepare our hearts to receive Your Word.* She'd heard Mrs. D pray that way for Pastor Cobbs before he preached. How often had she prayed that *she'd* be ready to hear from God through the Sunday sermon? Not often . . . uh, maybe never.

As the praise team sounded the notes of the first worship song, Kat breathed silently, *Prepare* my *heart to receive Your Word this morning, Lord.*

Avis Douglass was the worship leader that morning, and before Nick got up to preach, she read the sermon text from the gospel of John, chapter 21. "If you have your Bibles, follow along as I read verses 19 through 26."

After reading the conversation between Jesus and Peter, Mrs. D prayed for Nick and sat down. He looked a bit nervous standing up there behind the skinny wooden pulpit, but to Kat's surprise, once he opened his mouth and plunged in, he seemed to relax, even get excited about the story. "To fully appreciate this amazing conversation, we need some background."

Kat smiled. Gosh, he looked good this morning. He was tan from his runs along the lake, his eyes were alive, and he talked with a smile, as if he was truly enjoying himself. She listened as he gave the background. This was the third time Jesus had appeared to His disciples since the resurrection. They'd been fishing all night—nothing. Then Jesus showed up, told them to throw their nets on the other side of the boat, and they pulled in 153 fish! "Isn't that a bit odd for the gospel writer to mention?" Nick said. "An exact number of fish? Obviously, Jesus cared about His disciples *as* fishermen. He knew they needed a good haul." And then, he said, Jesus took some of the fish and made breakfast for them—an ordinary activity that became sacred: eating together.

Eating together. Kat leaned forward, listening intently.

"And then comes this amazing conversation. Don't forget, Peter had *denied* Jesus three different times the night of his arrest and trial. So it seems significant that Jesus asked Peter three times if he loved Him—as if giving this once cocky, now devastated disciple a chance to redeem himself. Because Jesus is all about forgiveness and redemption."

Nick went on, spending time exploring each of Jesus' commands—or were they invitations?—to Peter: "'If you love me, feed my lambs.' Lambs . . . that might refer to the little ones in our care or out on the street, or it might mean those who are young in the faith, who need careful tending. And the second time. 'Take care of my sheep.' Notice that? 'Take care of . . .'"

Nick looked around the room as if making eye contact with everyone who was listening. "That's pretty broad. What if Jesus said to *you*, 'Take care of My people.' What does it mean to take care of each other in this church?"

Now people around the room started to respond.

"Well?"

"That's right, brother. Say it."

"Come on now."

And finally, Nick said, Jesus told Peter to "Feed my sheep." "We know Jesus valued making sure people's physical needs were met—after all, He'd not only healed hundreds of people, but He'd just made breakfast for these hungry fishermen. But Jesus had also made it clear during His ministry that 'Life is more than food and the body more than clothes.' You can look that up in Luke 12 or Mark 6."

Pages rustled around the room as people did just that while Nick continued. "Jesus was telling this crusty old disciple to take care of God's people—body, soul, and spirit. We not only need bread—and we all know we need food every day to stay alive—but we need spiritual food too. Every day. Feeding on God's Word. Taking it in. And giving it out to those around us."

Kat stared in wonder at Nick standing up there on the short platform. His teaching had gone really deep—at least deep for her. She'd read that story in the Gospels before but had never stopped to think about all the implications. For herself. For her relationship to others.

She was so busy pondering the various things Nick brought out in his sermon, even after he sat down, that she almost didn't hear Pastor Cobbs call her name. "Sister Kathryn Davies has a special announcement."

Brygitta practically pushed her out of her chair, and a moment later Kat found herself at the mike, nervously telling about the food pantry they were going to "try out" here at SouledOut on Saturday mornings during the month of August to test the possibility of setting up a more ongoing food pantry for the hungry in the Rogers Park area. "Rochelle Johnson and Brygitta Walczak have a stack of flyers you can pass on to your friends and coworkers at your jobs to collect food for the pantry, and we have a big bin back there to collect nonperishables. We're going to start with canned goods first, which are obviously easier to collect and store, but eventually we hope to find sources for perishable items like vegetables, fruit, dairy, meat, and fish—food like that."

Hands started to shoot up and a few voices called out questions, but Pastor Cobbs stepped up and took the mike. "I'm sure there are a lot of questions. Feel free to speak to any of the pastors or elders or Sister Kathryn here after the service. At some point, we'll have a congregational meeting to evaluate what we've learned and decide how—or whether—to move ahead. Let's pray."

Kat escaped to the back of the room near the bin during

Pastor Cobbs's prayer. Sure enough, people crowded around with a lot of questions, some just saying what a great idea, but many took flyers. "Psst, we're going to need more." Rochelle held out empty hands and grinned. "They're all gone."

Kat sank down into a nearby chair. The roller coaster was in gear now. No turning back. She felt both excited and terrified. *Oh, God, I have no idea what I'm doing!*

"Kathryn? Do you have a minute?"

Kat looked up into the beaming smile of Edesa Baxter. "Sure. Please! Sit." She pulled up another chair. As usual, Edesa's nutmeg skin seemed to glow, almost as bright as the yellow cloth wrap she wore, holding back the tiny twists all over her head.

"Whew, it's warm." Edesa fanned herself with a paper bulletin. "I have been praying about what you said on the phone last week about more people needing to feel called. I'm not exactly sure what God is saying yet—but I do have an idea. Would you be able to come to our Yada Yada Prayer Group meeting this evening and present your idea for the food pantry? Rochelle and Brygitta too, if they'd like to come. It'd be great if you could tell them more of your personal journey like you told me, which I realize you didn't have time to do this morning. But I think the Yada Yada sisters would be very interested, and some might be able to help."

Kat turned to Rochelle, who was still standing beside her. "What do you think? You usually take Conny to see his dad on Sunday afternoon."

Calling Brygitta over, the four women put their heads together. Rochelle said she'd like to go and thought she could get back before five since her mom was part of Yada Yada and would want to be back in time too. Brygitta said sure, she wasn't scheduled to work that Sunday. She'd like to go.

"I'll ask Nick if he'll take care of Conny," Rochelle said. "The meeting is five o'clock till eight, right? Uh, speaking of Conny, I have no idea where he is. I better go find him." She hustled off, and Kat saw her head through the swinging doors that led to the back Sunday school rooms.

"Excuse us, ladies." Josh Baxter seemed to show up out of nowhere with Nick in tow. "Sorry to butt in, but . . . Edesa? Nick and I would like to get together this afternoon, say around three. I know we're going over to my folks for lunch, but we should be done by then, right?"

"Sí. But you'd need to be home by five—no, four thirty. I'm going to Yada Yada tonight, and these girls are coming tonight too, so Kat can share about the food pantry. I need you to put Gracie to bed."

The two men looked at each other. "Ahh, that's kind of tight—"

"Just a heads-up," Bree said. "Rochelle was going to ask if Nick would look after Conny this evening, too, after they get back from seeing his dad." She eyed Nick mischievously. "Maybe you two can hang out together with Conny and Gracie. Works for us, right, girlfriends?" She laughed.

"Not exactly what we had in mind," Josh said. He wasn't laughing. "Edesa, can we talk?"

Uh-oh. Kat watched Josh and Edesa move off and whisper intensely for a few minutes. What was going on? She looked at Nick and raised her eyebrows. He just shrugged, as if to say he didn't know either.

"That was a great sermon," Kat offered, trying to fill in the awkward silence. "I was proud of you, Nick. Gave me a lot to think about."

"Ditto," Bree put in. "A lot of food for thought."

Nick chuckled. "Was that a pun?—Oh, hey, Josh and Edesa."

Josh and Edesa rejoined them. "Okay, didn't think it'd be this complicated, but we've got a plan," Josh said.

Kat half listened, her own mind drifting to Edesa's invitation to go to the prayer group they called Yada Yada that evening. Would they be meeting again at the Douglasses', like they had the night she snuck the earrings Rochelle had taken from her mom back into Mrs. D's bedroom? That'd be convenient, right upstairs. And not till five. If Josh and Nick *weren't* getting together this afternoon, maybe she and Nick could—

But it sounded like the guys were going to hang out for a couple of hours that afternoon after all, then pick her up, along with Bree, Rochelle, and Conny, drive over to Josh's folks', drop them off at Leslie Stuart's apartment, which was on the second floor of Jodi and Denny's two-flat, where Yada Yada was meeting, pick up Gracie, and then—

"—Nick and I'll do something with the kids while you guys are at Yada Yada. Sound okay?"

Kat felt her hopes deflate. So much for any one-on-one time with Nick. And then the weekend would be over. Again.

Chapter 31

Nick ducked, whirled, and lobbed the basketball straight into the basket.

"Man!" Josh Baxter threw out his arms. "Why didn't you tell me you could shoot three-pointers? I would've suggested tennis . . . or lacrosse or something. Or do you play those too?"

Nick grabbed the basketball as it rolled across the outdoor court and held it against his hip, breathing heavily. "Nope. Don't really play basketball anymore either. Not since my first two undergrad years at CCU. Kinda rusty now."

Josh snorted and flopped down on a bench. "Uh-huh. Would hate to play against you if you *weren't* rusty." He pulled out two water bottles from his backpack and threw one to Nick. "Here."

Dropping the ball, Nick caught the bottle of water and chugged down half of it before wiping his mouth with the back of his hand and capping the bottle again. "Thanks." He eased himself onto the bench beside Josh, one foot on the ball, and took in the large open space around them. "Nice park. I like that about Chicago. Lots of parks scattered around the city. Especially along the lakefront."

"Yeah. Usually the courts are full of kids playing pickup games. We were lucky to find this one empty."

Nick closed his eyes, tipped his head back, and stretched his arms along the back of the bench, enjoying the feel of the sun on his skin, even though he was still sweating from their one-on-one. He hadn't realized how much he missed hanging out with the guys and just shooting some hoops or shooting the breeze. Kat and Bree and Livie were great friends, and they'd gotten pretty tight during the Urban Experience class. And he didn't regret their decision to spend the summer in the city. Still . . .

He opened his eyes and turned to Josh. "Thanks for asking me to hang out. I needed this."

"Yeah. Me too." Josh laughed. "Didn't think it'd take a professional scheduler to make it happen, but it's not like it was when I was single."

Nick snorted. "Huh. I'm single and it's still complicated. Even more complicated now with a six-year-old in the house."

"Mm. Hope you don't mind adding Conny and Gracie to our guy time. At least we got a couple hours to ourselves first."

"Nah, it's okay. Conny's a neat kid. And he seems to need some guy time himself whenever he comes back from visiting his dad. Not sure why, but . . ." Nick shrugged. "Makes me feel good I can be there for him, even if he isn't my own kid." Nick suddenly leaned forward, forearms on his knees, and looked sideways at Josh. "How was it for you, adopting a kid who isn't yours biologically? If I'm getting too personal, just tell me."

Josh leaned forward too, adopting the same stance, forearms on his knees. "No, it's fine. Gracie was so little, still an infant when she came into our lives. I'm really the only daddy she's ever known, so I guess it's easier. Only thing . . . wish Edesa and I could've had a few years just us before starting a family. Wasn't easy, being an 'instant parent.'" He gave a wry grin. "Maybe you know Edesa's three years older than I am . . . We got married while I was still in college. Sometimes I feel like I had to grow up too fast. Don't have much time to"—he gestured between the two of them—"you know, just hang out with friends."

"Are you sorry?"

"Nope. I'm crazy about Edesa. It just happened faster than we thought it would. I mean, Gracie dropped into our lives even *before* we got married."

"Yeah." Nick was quiet for a long minute. Then he cleared his throat. "Been thinking about that myself. Feeling like maybe it's time—though I'd rather wait a few years before starting a family."

"So . . . have you said anything to her?"

"Not exactly. Actually, not really. I mean, it's complicated."

"Of course it's complicated. But you like her a lot?"

Nick grinned self-consciously. "Is it that obvious?"

Josh slapped his knee and chuckled. "Well, it's obvious that she likes *you*."

Nick's heart did a skip. "You're kidding. You know this?"

"Know this? She told Edesa straight-out."

Now he swallowed. "She . . . told Edesa? Straight-out? I mean, she said—"

Josh was laughing hard now. "Asked Edesa what she thought of the girl telling the guy that she's interested. One reason I wanted to get together with you today. Just to figure out where *you* are."

Nick could hardly believe his ears. "Man. I've felt so confused. That girl has really gotten under my skin, invaded my dreams. She's all I think about. But . . . every time I think I've worked up the courage to tell her how I feel, I turn into a mumbling idiot. And to be honest, I really wasn't sure how she felt."

"Just tell her, man!"

Nick shook his head. "Yeah, but . . . I'm worried how that would change things in the apartment. I mean, we're all just apartment mates now, but factor in a romance . . . I don't know."

"Hm. Good point. And you haven't known each other very long. I mean, it's pretty fast, don't you think? You might want to take it slow."

Nick frowned. "What do you mean? We've been friends for three years. Long enough for me to know her pretty well, know I've fallen in love with her. I just haven't been sure if she—"

"Wait. Wait, wait, *wait*." Josh threw up his hands. "Are we talking about Rochelle Johnson?"

Nick gaped at him. "*Rochelle!* What? Why would you say that? No! I'm talking about Kat!" He stopped, realizing Josh was staring at him. A horrible feeling crawled up his chest. "Oh, man. You said . . . you mean . . . ?"

Josh nodded slowly. "Uh-huh."

Nick groaned and buried his face in his hands. "I don't believe this." Josh had said it was obvious "she" liked him. All the time meaning . . . Rochelle. Not Kat. For a moment he'd been ecstatic, thinking Kat really did like him that way. Did that mean he was back at square one with Kat? Not really knowing how she felt?

Even worse, if what Josh said was true, that *Rochelle* was talking about him to other people, had feelings for him . . . Nick groaned again. "Uhhhhh. Houston, we've got a problem.'"

He heard Josh laugh and lifted his head. "Sorry." Josh immediately looked sheepish. "I know it's not funny. In fact, you're in trouble, my brother. But . . ."

Nick waited. "But what?" He threw out his hands. "Look, I need some help here, *brother!*"

"Okay, okay. You gotta tell her."

"Tell . . . ?"

"Tell Rochelle."

"Oh, *right.* Just say, 'Oh, by the way, Rochelle, heard you've got a thing for me. Sorry, not interested.'"

"Then you gotta tell Kat. Tell Kat how you feel about *her.* And Rochelle will get the message."

Nick buried his head in his hands again. If only he'd told Kat how he felt about her before now. Why had he waited? Why hadn't he kissed her on the mouth that night on the steps, like he'd wanted to, instead of on the cheek? He'd told her he was proud of how she'd presented the food pantry at the pastoral team meeting . . . hadn't exactly seemed the time to kiss her *that* way. But why not? That was his trouble. He thought too much about stuff. Worried about how it would change things in the apartment. Worried about what people at SouledOut would think. He was trying to please everybody—or not rock the boat.

Coward. That's what he was. And now look at the mess he was in.

"Hey, man." Josh broke into his misery. "Hate to say this, but it's four thirty already. We're supposed to drop the girls off at Yada Yada and pick up the kids there . . . You gonna be all right?"

❃

According to plan, Josh and Nick dropped off Kat and Bree at the Baxters' two-flat and picked up Conny and Gracie. As Conny scrambled into the minivan, Rochelle muttered, "We shouldn't have told Conny you guys were taking care of them tonight. He kept wanting to come home early, which didn't go over too well with you-know-who."

Great, Nick thought. Just one more person who was going to be mad at him.

But once Gracie was buckled into her car seat with "big boy" Conny buckled in beside her, Josh said, "Hey, I've got an idea. Let's go ride the merry-go-round down at Lincoln Park Zoo. Might only have an hour before it closes, but . . . what do you kids say?"

"Yaaay!" Conny yelled. Gracie laughed and clapped her hands too, though Josh said he doubted she knew what it was.

Nick was glad to have something to do, and glad it wasn't just him and Conny trying to kill two or three hours. They found street parking—"The zoo's free," Josh muttered, "but they get your money for the parking lot"—and walked through the zoo to the large carousel.

Josh tried to wave him away at the ticket booth as Nick pulled out his wallet, but Nick insisted on paying for Conny. "You've got Gracie, I've got Conny—even-steven."

Josh gave him a strange look, but for the next few minutes they were busy helping the kids climb onto their chosen "zoo friend." Gracie wanted to ride the big ostrich, but Conny made a beeline for the tiger. "I can get on by myself! You don't have to help me!" So Nick dropped back to where Josh was strapping Gracie onto the big bird and hopped onto the baboon next to them.

The music started and the carousel jerked forward, accompanied by childish squeals as the animals went up and down, up and down. Josh, standing with one hand on Gracie's leg to steady the little girl, leaned toward Nick. "That's something we oughta talk about—you and Conny," he said, talking loudly over the music and general noise. "He obviously likes you a lot—and vice versa. But I'm thinking that's been giving Rochelle ideas— about you and her, I mean. Maybe you need to set up some boundaries."

Nick just stared at Josh. But his mind whirled in circles like the carousel the rest of the evening. What was he supposed to do—just ignore the kid? Good grief, he thought it was a good thing to give Conny some guy attention, surrounded as he was in a house full of females. Of course, his grandfather lived in the apartment upstairs. Maybe they'd spend more time together if Nick weren't so available. And if his relationship with Conny was giving Rochelle ideas . . .

But he had to admit he'd grown really fond of Conny. Liked spending time with him. He felt like a big brother or an honorary uncle. His relationship with Conny had given him ideas too—about wanting a family, wanting kids.

But his kids and Kat's. Someday.

Oh, God, he groaned again silently as Conny and Gracie chattered all the way home about what they liked best about their short visit to the zoo. *What am I supposed to do?*

"Looks like we beat the girls home," Josh noted, pulling into a parking space in front of the three-flat. "Don't see any lights in your windows. Mind if we just drop you and Conny off? It's already eight o'clock, past Gracie's bedtime. I'll go pick up Edesa and we can mosey on home."

"No problem." Nick slid the side door of the minivan open so Conny could scramble out. He leaned into the car and held out his hand to Josh. "Thanks for the afternoon, man." He gave a rueful laugh. "Just . . . pray for me."

"You got it, brother." Josh gripped his hand and grinned. "Just do it. Tell your girl how you feel. It'll all work out."

Yeah, yeah, it'll all work out. Nick wasn't so sure. But he tried to put it aside as he took Conny's hand, hustled him up the steps, and pushed open the front door. "Hey, kiddo, what say you see how fast you can get into your jammies and then we'll have some ice cr—"

A fist slammed into Nick's face from the dark interior of the foyer. Pain shot through his nose into his brain. "So *you're* the guy stealin' my kid!" The angry hiss took shape . . . a man. The shadowy figure swung again—this time a slug to his gut. Nick staggered backward, back onto the flat stoop at the top of the steps, gasping for breath. "That's all I hear—Nick this! Nick that!" the man shouted. "Well, *back off,* creep! He's *my* kid."

"Daddy!" Conny screamed. "Daddy, *stop!*"

Chapter 32

For some reason, Kat felt a tad shy sitting among the lively group of Yada Yada sisters in Leslie Stuart's apartment. An odd feeling for an extrovert—she was usually the one who broke the ice in any group with her easy chatter. But she felt as tongue-tied as Brygitta, who sat wide-eyed across the living room, taking in the room decorated in gorgeous shades of melon and lime. All around them a hodgepodge of women—an assortment that would rival Forrest Gump's "box of choc'lates"—babbled in comfortable familiarity in spite of ages spanning Gen-Y to Baby Boomers, wearing everything from plus-sizes to skinny size 4, and hair done in meticulous "extensions," to a few she'd have to label frowsy.

At least she knew several of the women in this group—Avis Douglass and Edesa, of course, but also Estelle Bentley, Jodi Baxter, Florida Hickman, and Stu, their hostess, who attended SouledOut Community Church. But as she was introduced to others, Kat tried hard to peg their names to their faces: Adele, an imposing black woman, who wore her salt-and-pepper hair in a

short "natural," which seemed a bit odd for someone who oper-
ated her own beauty shop. A blond girl they called Yo-Yo, who
looked rather boyish in her short, spiky hair and cargo shorts.
And somebody said Ruth—a somewhat rumpled middle-aged
woman who talked like a Yiddish grandmother—had five-year-
old *twins*! A round-faced, motherly woman, Delores Enriques,
showed up late wearing the smock of a pediatric nurse, and a
couple others showed up whose names she'd have to get again.

After fifteen or twenty minutes of chitchat and iced tea, Stu
rounded up the women who'd spread out into the dining room
and kitchen and herded them into the melon-and-lime living
room. "Sisters! Avis says let's get started so our guests can have
some time to share too."

Kat gulped. That meant her.

But just as she'd done at the pastoral team meeting, Mrs. D
first read a psalm and then led the women in a slow, simple
worship song. Once again Kat felt her spirit relax as her mind
focused on the words being sung.

Jesus is Lord . . . again and again.

How we love You . . .

Hallelujah . . .

So different from some of the bouncy contemporary songs
they often sang in chapel at CCU—"what God has done for
me"—which was all right in one sense. She *was* thankful for
what God had done for her. But this simple chorus just worshipped Jesus. Loving God for Himself.

It felt like such a holy moment. Kat had to blink away a few
tears as the beautiful voices of the dozen or so women filled the
room, finally drifted into a hum, and then silence, broken only
by a few whispers here and there.

"We love You, Lord."

"Gracias, Señor, for Your Son,"

"You're an awesome God!"

"Well." Avis Douglass's voice finally broke into the hush. "We're so happy to have two of the Crista students join us tonight, as well as my daughter, Rochelle . . ."

Several people interrupted with clapping and whooping.

"All right, Ro*chelle!*"

"Talk about an answer to prayer!"

"Thank You, *Jesus!*"

Rochelle ducked her head as if looking for a hole to crawl into, and everyone laughed. Even her mother was beaming. "Sorry, honey. But these sisters have prayed for you and Conny—and me—many times, and it's hard to keep quiet when we see the answer to our prayers sitting right here in the same room." More laughter and clapping.

"But we need to move on." Avis cleared her throat. "Some of you already know about the announcement that was made at SouledOut this morning. Our sister here, Kathryn Davies, has felt God nudging her to start a food pantry—but it's been quite a journey for her. Edesa wanted to give her a chance to share some of that journey with our Yada Yada Prayer Group and see what God might be saying to some of the rest of us. Kathryn?"

Kat felt her cheeks flush. She'd made a list that afternoon of some practical ways people could support setting up a food pantry, but it was obvious she was being asked to share the background, her personal journey leading to this calling. But where in the world to start?

Bree must've found her tongue, because she blurted out,

"Tell them how you first became a Christian, Kat—you know, at the music fest. That's where all this started."

Which was true, Kat admitted to the others. She'd been so blown away by meeting all those gung-ho, funky Christians, who talked about eliminating poverty and confronting racism and guarding God's creation by "living green," that she'd jumped into the Christian faith with both feet. People who believed in God *and* were socially responsible—who reached out to others *because* they believed in God—seemed to meet a deep need in her spirit she had never quite identified before.

"Maybe it was the fact that I'd been a pre-med major before I transferred to CCU, but I especially got interested in food issues—growing food responsibly, eating healthy, avoiding wasting so much food—that kind of thing. I changed my major to education, decided I wanted to become an elementary teacher, but I have to admit I got pretty passionate about educating people about all those food issues too. Even when I came to SouledOut—"

"You can say that again, girl!" Florida Hickman snorted. "Never forget you walkin' in the church door with all that half-gone food you'd hauled outta a Dumpster! Lord, have mercy!" Several people laughed and wagged their heads.

Kat's cheeks burned. She'd really thought church people would be happy with her "save the earth" Dumpster diving. But apparently not. "Anyway, um, Estelle Bentley said something to Edesa once, that what I really cared about was hungry *people*, I just didn't know it yet . . ."

Again she was interrupted by comments.

"Uh-huh, sounds right."

"Listen to Estelle, girl."

Kat blinked. She wasn't used to such interactive sharing—kind of like people at SouledOut talking to the preacher right during the sermon. But out of the corner of her eye, she saw Estelle Bentley give her a smile and an encouraging nod, so Kat went on.

"That started me thinking about food in a new way, thinking about the people who needed food, not just 'food issues.' I even started digging into the Bible to see what Scripture has to say about food and feeding the hungry."

"A good place to start, that is," Ruth, the aging mother of twins, declared. Heads nodded and some of the women leaned forward, as if eager to hear more.

As she glanced around the room, Kat realized how God had not only been using the Scriptures but so many different people to nudge her along on this journey, some of whom were in this very room: Estelle's comment . . . Edesa suggesting she volunteer at a food pantry to get some practical experience . . . Rochelle giving her opinion that more churches ought to be running food pantries . . . the man at Rock of Ages who said he volunteered at the food pantry because he didn't want to miss Jesus . . . the pastoral team at SouledOut—including Avis Douglass—not only supporting the idea but affirming her heart for this ministry, as untried and untested as she was . . . and Bree, her friend and roommate, who, in spite of her own misgivings about the idea, was willing to pray with her about what God wanted her to do. "Even Pastor Nick's sermon this morning"—she felt her face flush, calling him that—"about Jesus telling Peter to 'take care of my lambs' and to 'feed my sheep' fits in here somewhere, just haven't figured how yet!"

As she mentioned each of these people, Kat almost choked up. "Everywhere I turn, it seems God is nudging me on, even though, I confess, the closer I get to the food pantry becoming a reality, the less I know what I'm doing. And I used to think I knew a lot!"

That got a laugh around the room. *"Now* maybe you ready," Florida chuckled.

Avis had her Bible open. "I'd like to encourage you to take this verse to heart, found in Proverbs 16, verse 3: 'Commit your actions to the Lord and your plans will succeed.'" She closed her Bible. "So why don't we pray with our sister about—"

"Now hold on a darn minute, Sister Avis . . . sorry for inter-rupting," the spiky-haired girl said. "We ain't talked yet 'bout what God is sayin' to the rest of us 'bout this. SouledOut ain't my church, but this pantry thing gonna happen on Saturday mornin's, right? I mean, I'd like to help an' maybe some of the other sisters would too." She looked around the room. "Anybody else?"

In amazement, Kathryn saw more than half the hands in the room go up. Including Rochelle . . . and Bree. "Probably can't do it every Saturday," Stu said, raising her hand, "but if you get enough volunteers, maybe there can be a rotation."

"And all of us can start collecting food, right?" Yo-Yo went on. "I like doin' this practical Jesus-stuff, since I ain't as spiritual an' heavenly minded as some of the rest of you all."

"Oh, Yo-Yo," someone protested, but others just chuckled.

Bree dug a little notebook out of her bag and passed it around, suggesting that people who were interested in helping write down their names, telephone numbers, and e-mail "—so we can start making a schedule." Kat looked at her friend in amazement. *So "we" can start making a schedule?* Bree caught her eye and smiled, as if to say, *I'm in too, girlfriend.*

"So whatchu gonna call this food pantry thing?" Yo-Yo said. "Gotta have some kinda name—Hey, I know! This gonna happen at SouledOut, right? An' looks like the *sisters* gonna be helpin' to make it happen big-time. What about 'the SouledOut Sisters Food Pantry'?" She grinned at Kat. "Kinda catchy, don'tcha think?"

Kat grinned back. It was catchy. She liked it. Except . . . "Uh, we don't want the guys to think they aren't welcome to help. In fact, we're going to need some men to volunteer." She was thinking of Nick. And lugging bulky boxes of food. Hauling tables. Setting up. Taking down. Heavy stuff.

Yo-Yo shrugged. "I dunno. I saw a tavern called Three Sisters Tavern, an' it didn't stop the men from gettin' drunk there."

Now the whole room cracked up. Even Avis had to wipe away a few tears of laughter . . . but finally they sobered up and all the Yada Yada sisters locked hands with each other and their guests and prayed up a storm for the SouledOut Sisters Food Pantry.

A name that looked like it was going to stick.

Chapter 33

The Yada Yada meeting went on for another hour, but there were times Kat felt like she was eavesdropping on a private conversation — especially when Mrs. D reminded everyone that things shared at Yada Yada were confidential and not to be shared outside the group without the person's permission. She said that just before she said she had something to share that still wasn't public knowledge.

Kat remembered the little huddle of Avis, Jodi, and Edesa talking seriously after church a week ago and the feeling she'd had that "something was going on." And Mrs. D had seemed preoccupied lately more than usual. She cast a quick glance at Rochelle—did Avis's daughter know what this was about? But Rochelle, who was sitting cross-legged on the floor, leaning against a corner of the flowered couch, had her head down, picking at something on her jeans.

"Some of you know about the threatened school closings and that Bethune Elementary has been on the 'possible' list. Well, unfortunately, that has moved from 'possible' to 'likely'—"

"No!" Several of the women reacted in shock.

"Where those kids gonna go?"

"School s'posed to start in just six, seven weeks!"

And "Oh my goodness. This affects Jodi too."

Avis held up her hand but nodded. "Yes, if Bethune closes, Jodi will be out of a job too. But let me explain. I said 'likely' because it's on the short list of school closings, but a group of parents, teachers, and lawyers are petitioning the school board for an emergency hearing to protest."

The room started to buzz with frustrated comments and Mrs. Douglass had to raise her voice to be heard. "Sisters, let me finish. I appreciate your concern, but there's more." She waited for the room to quiet. "I really need some prayer for wisdom, because Nonyameko and Mark have written to Peter and me *again*, asking if we'd consider coming to Durbin for two weeks this summer to see the work they're doing with the Women's AIDS initiative in KwaZulu-Natal. And—"

Again the room buzzed, and Kat figured out from various comments flying about that there'd been an earlier invitation to come for six months to a year, which the Douglasses had turned down. But now, some thought, why not? It was only two weeks. Go for it! Wouldn't it be great to see Nony again? But what about her interim pastoral role at SouledOut? And the school board hearing . . .

Kat's head was spinning. What did these school closings mean for her application to teach school in the Chicago school district? She still hadn't gotten an interview. And if the Douglasses went to South Africa for a couple of weeks, how would that affect *Nick's* job at the church? Did he even know? Oh, right. He'd said Mrs. D had shared some confidential stuff at the last pastoral meeting after she'd left. Probably this news.

She saw Bree trying to catch her eye, tipping her head toward Rochelle. Oh dear. Rochelle was now hugging her knees, staring at the floor. Hopefully she and Bree could talk to Rochelle when they got home, give her some support for whatever she was feeling about all this.

Avis had to quiet the room again in order to go on. "That's why Peter and I need your prayers," she said. "Pastor Cobbs isn't worried about me taking two weeks from pastoral duties, but obviously there are implications to a trip like this. And how it fits with my job terminating at Bethune." She shook her head with a rueful smile. "Well, God knows."

The women prayed fervently, sometimes two or three praying at the same time . . . and then there were more sharings. Both of Ruth's twins had chicken pox. One of Stu's clients had tried to commit suicide. Delores was having trouble with an overbearing supervisor at the county hospital. Yo-Yo's brother was still in Iraq. And so they prayed again.

Just when Kat thought they were prayed out and it was probably time to go, Stu brought out a flaming birthday cake to surprise Edesa, who'd had a birthday earlier that week. The group had chipped in on a little miniature fountain that you plugged in to hear the water splash and gurgle over several layers of stones as a reminder to Edesa that her name meant "Abundance of Water," which seemed to delight the pretty Honduran woman to no end.

Kat felt a pang. *Do I even know what my name means?*

But the festivities did end when Edesa got a call on her cell that Josh and Gracie were on the way over to pick her up, so Rochelle, Brygitta, and Kat followed Avis to her car for a ride home. Rochelle sat up front with her mother, but they were all pretty quiet. Kat wondered how much she'd known before tonight about what Mrs. D had shared. Surely her mother would've told her own daughter before dropping those bombs in a group?

Turning into their street, Avis slowed to look for a parking space, but as they passed the three-flat, Rochelle suddenly screamed, *"Mom! Stop! Stop the car!"*

Avis slammed on the brakes, but even before the car was fully stopped, Rochelle was out of the car. *What—?!* Kat fumbled with the rear door latch even as she heard Avis say, "Oh, Lord, no—where's my phone."

Bree was right behind Kat as she scrambled out of the car, and then they heard it: Conny yelling, "No! I won't go! Stop it! Let me go!"

Heart pounding, Kat ran for the three-flat on Rochelle's heels. She saw a man coming down the steps, holding Conny by the hand, but Conny was struggling and yelling. And beyond them, on the top step—that looked like Nick! Why was he all bent over? Was he hurt? Who was the guy holding Conny's arm?

Rochelle was yelling too. "Dexter! Let go of Conny right this minute! Where do you think you're going? And what have you done to Nick?! If you've hurt him, I'll—"

Kat darted around the three of them and up the steps. "Nick! Nick! Are you all right?" . . . just as the front door opened and Peter Douglass's big voice boomed, "What's going on—Dexter! What are you doing here?! Get your hands off Conny!" He ran down the steps. Conny must have taken advantage of the confusion and pulled his arm away, because a moment later Kat saw him leap into his grandfather's arms.

Nick was trying to get to his feet, and that's when Kat saw

the blood running down his face from his nose. "Oh, Nick! Are you okay?" she cried. Bree appeared beside her, and they both helped him to stand. Kat's heart was pounding. Just how hurt was he?

She glanced back to the walk. Rochelle was hitting the other man's chest with her fists, getting in his face. "What's going on, Dexter? What are you even *doing* here? Conny baby, are you all right?"

"Yes, Mommy! But he hurted Mister Nick!" Conny pointed up to where Nick was leaning against the brick wall of the building.

"I called the police." Avis had come up just then, joining her husband and Rochelle, and the three of them stood like a wall between Dexter and the street. But at a nod from Peter, she took Conny from his arms and hustled up the steps. "Come on, baby, let's go upstairs. It's all right. Everything's going to be all right." She cast a worried look in Nick's direction but disappeared into the foyer with the little boy.

For a moment Dexter's eyes seemed to dart fearfully from Peter's angry face up to the group on the steps. And for the first time Kat had a good look at Conny's father. Rochelle had called him a "ladies' man"—no wonder. The guy was drop-dead good-looking, like Denzel Washington or somebody.

But then he drew himself up, a sneer on his pretty features. "Go ahead. Call the cops. *I'm* Conny's father. I have a right to see my son, and that creep there was interfering."

"What?!" Rochelle sputtered. "Nick was babysitting Conny so I could go to a meeting, you jerk!"

Nick moaned and said, "I gotta sit." Kat and Bree helped him sit down on the closest concrete arm bordering the steps, where he fished out a handkerchief and pressed it against his bloody nose. Kat sat beside him, not knowing what to do. Did he need an ambulance? He still seemed to be trying to get his breath.

But Dexter wasn't cowed. "So that's the great Mister Nick," he sneered. "That's all I hear. *Mister Nick* this, *Mister Nick* that. Didn't know you had a thing for white dudes, Rochelle."

"It's none of your business, Dexter."

"Oh yeah? It *is* my business. You and Conny living with this cracker and a bunch of white chicks too? Court just might give me custody if they knew how you're slutting around."

"Shut your mouth!" Peter snapped. "You have no cause to talk to Rochelle like that."

"Humph. He's called me worse, Dad. And it's still none of your business, Dexter. I can be with anybody I want. We got a divorce, remember?"

Kat was startled by her words. *"I can be with anybody I want."* Did she mean Nick? What was she implying? Had she been telling Dexter that—

But at the same moment she heard a siren in the distance, coming closer. The others heard it too, and heads turned. Dexter took advantage of the distraction to push past Rochelle and head for the sidewalk.

"You wait!" Peter grabbed him. "We're not done here. This man is injured—"

"Let him go," Nick spoke, breathing heavily. "It's . . . it's all right, Mr. D. We . . . I don't need the police."

Dexter turned and snorted. "Aw. Ain't that sweet." But then he jabbed a finger at Rochelle. "Frankly, sweetheart, I don't care who you shack up with. But my son's coming back to live with *me.* As for *you,* 'Mister Nicky-boy'"—he turned the finger on Nick—"you butt out of my son's life, or this little chat we just had ain't the last of it."

With an ugly laugh, Dexter broke into a run and disappeared, just thirty seconds before the police car, blue lights flashing, turned the corner into their street.

Shaking with the intensity of the last few minutes, Kat slipped an arm around Nick. "Come on," she urged. "You're hurt—let's get you upstairs." Nick nodded, rose, and with Bree on the other side of him, they took a few steps toward the door.

"Wait." Peter Douglass held up a hand. "Nick, I'm asking you, please, make a police report. It'll help us get an order of protection against Dexter."

"Yes!" Rochelle ran up the steps to stop him. "He was trying to take Conny! Please, Nick."

The police car doors slammed. "You the folks called the police?"

Chapter 34

Laying his head back on the arm of the overstuffed couch, Nick took the ice pack Kat handed him and held it to his face. *Uhhhh.* He didn't know what hurt worse, his nose or his gut. Couldn't remember the last time he'd been in a fist-fight—maybe back in fifth grade, when somebody called him a "Sunday school sissy." And that time he'd landed the first punch—much to his parents' disappointment. "It's one thing to defend yourself, Nicholas," his father had said. "But violence is never the best way to deal with a problem. Better to suffer an insult than fight back. Look at Jesus."

He couldn't agree more—now—but he wished he'd had more warning Dexter was itching for a fight. At least he could've defended himself, held his own. But he hadn't seen it coming, got sucker punched before he even knew what hit him.

But what was worse, he hadn't protected Conny. If the girls hadn't arrived just then—and Mr. D, who heard Conny scream-ing—Dexter would have made off with him . . . under his watch! He groaned. *Oh, God, Oh, God . . .*

"Oh, Nick. I still think we should go to the ER and get you checked out."

Kat's voice. He half opened his eyes and saw her hovering twelve inches over his face, worry lines between her blue eyes. Her dark hair fell in long wavy tresses on either side of her face, almost tickling his chin. Once the police had left with his statement and he'd gingerly navigated the stairs to the second floor, she had gently washed the blood off his face with a cool washcloth, pulled off his gym shoes, and made him lie down on the couch while Bree prepared an ice pack. Now he had a crazy urge to pull her down and kiss her—but even the slightest movement sent stabs of fire through his gut. Scratch that.

"I agree with Kat," said Bree. Nick slid his eyes sideways and through half-open lids saw Brygitta sitting cross-legged on the floor a few feet away, as if she was keeping vigil. "You ought to see a doctor, Nick. You might have a broken nose or a ruptured spleen or something."

"Look, I'm okay," he wheezed. "Don't think they do anything for a broken nose anyway. Ever see a nose cast?" He gave a snort at his own joke, but the pain in his diaphragm cut that off quick.

"You're stubborn as a mule, you know that, Nick?" Kat pulled back and stood up. "I'm going for some Tylenol, and you're going to take it."

Nick closed his eyes again, letting the cold of the ice pack numb the pain in his face. Once the police were gone, Rochelle had run up to the third floor to see about Conny. Just as well. He wasn't ready to talk to Rochelle . . . What was he going to say? He'd let her down, failed to protect her kid—on top of all that other stuff Josh Baxter had laid on him.

But a few moments later he heard the front door of the apartment open and footsteps crossing the room. "Hey, Nick. How you doin'?" Rochelle's voice was gentler now than her Mama Bear explosion outside.

Nick winced inwardly. Couldn't avoid it. He had to say something. He struggled to sit up. "Hi, Rochelle. I'll be all right . . . but how's Conny? I know the poor kid was scared. I—"

"He's fine. Worried about you. Mom is putting him to bed upstairs, though, otherwise he'd be all over you."

"And then you *would* need to go to the hospital." Bree giggled.

Worried about me. Great. That was going to make it even harder to straighten things out, to set those boundaries like Josh said. And Dexter—the man had the completely wrong idea! But, good grief, Rochelle's comments didn't help any. *"I can be with anybody I want"*? Huh! She'd basically let Dexter think he and Rochelle *were* "shacking up"! *Oh God, can this situation get any worse?*

Kat appeared with two pain pills and a glass of water. "Oh, hi, Rochelle. Patient needs to take his meds." She took the ice pack and handed the glass and pills to Nick. Grateful for the interruption, he swallowed—one, two, three—and traded the glass for the ice pack again. He wanted badly to lie down again, but he still had something he needed to say.

"Rochelle, I'm so sorry. You left Conny in my care and I . . . I let you down. Dexter might've taken him—thank God you guys showed up right then! But I'm—"

"What are you talking about, Nick?" Kat cut him off. "He attacked you! It's not your fault."

Oh, Kat, don't—

"Yeah. And Conny was raising such a ruckus, *somebody* would've noticed and called the police," Bree added.

"I know, but—" Nick wasn't sure if the pain he felt was from the beating he got or his failure to protect that little boy. "But I was responsible for him. Don't know if I could forgive myself if something had happened to Conny."

Rochelle reached out and patted his free hand. "I know. I don't blame you, Nick. And he *didn't* take Conny—Mom and Dad said that was God looking out for my boy."

Nick nearly broke out in a sweat at her touch. *No, no, no . . . not in front of Kat.* He pulled his hand away. "You're right. We should be thanking God for protecting Conny."

A knock at the door, followed by Peter Douglass poking his head in, saved the day. "How's the patient? Oh, there you are, Nick." Rochelle's stepdad joined the others circling the couch, making Nick feel like Exhibit A. "Just wanted to tell you to feel free to take the day off tomorrow." He chuckled. "Don't be surprised if you end up with quite a shiner from that punch in the face."

Yeah, no kidding. Nick's eyes already felt puffy. Staying home tomorrow would be nice . . . *Wait.* Kat and Bree would be gone, which would mean he'd be there alone with Rochelle and Conny. Perfect opportunity to speak to her, but he wasn't ready for The Talk yet. He hadn't even had time to process Josh's revelation that Rochelle was interested in him "that way." And maybe he needed to talk to Kat first.

"Uh, thanks, Mr. Douglass. I'll let you know tomorrow, see how I feel."

❁

Nick didn't sleep very well that night. *Dexter's crude comments . . . Rochelle's flip retorts . . . Josh's revelation . . . the feel of Kat's body against his as they'd hugged that night . . . the spring-fresh smell of her skin when he'd kissed her cheek . . . Dexter's sucker punch to his gut . . . the police asking question after question about what happened . . .* Disparate images and discordant voices ricocheted against each other in his mind like rough stones in a rock tumbler.

Not to mention the body aches.

He got up early and made his way to the bathroom. The bruises around his eyes had already set in. He could almost hear the good-natured taunts of the other guys in the mail room. *"So! Taylor. What's the other guy look like?"*

Yeah. He'd love to stay home today. Lock himself away in the study and come out in a week.

But in the wee hours of the night, he'd decided what he needed to do.

As soon as he heard stirring in the apartment overhead, he called Peter Douglass's phone. "Mr. Douglass? . . . Uh-huh, yeah, I feel a bit better this morning. I'd like to come in today . . . I know I don't have to, but actually, I need to talk to you, and would rather do it at the shop . . . Would appreciate a ride, though . . . Yeah, yeah, thanks. I'll be ready."

He made coffee, which earned him a scolding from Kat when she breezed into the kitchen. "Nick! What are you doing up? You should still be in bed taking it easy." She'd pulled her hair back into that careless clip she often wore when she was just going to work or tutoring students at STEP, and her face was clear of any makeup—but she still looked striking. He was so busy staring at her he almost forgot to answer.

"Oh, uh . . ." He took a slug of coffee to wake up his brain.

"Didn't sleep that well. Decided I might as well get up. Moving a bit slow, so I need some extra time to get ready. Mr. Douglass is picking me up around eight—"

"You're going to work?" Kat's blue eyes flashed. "Good grief, Nick. Mr. D gave you the day off!"

Nick grinned, in spite of the bruises. "Well, I might, if you'd take the day off too." His face sobered. "Actually—" He stopped. He'd started to say, *"Actually, I want to talk with you"*—but that sounded so routine, so stiff, as if he wanted to talk over schedules or the chore list. That's not what you say to a girl if you're planning to tell her you're in love with her.

Kat rolled her eyes. "Yeah, right. I'm not the one who looks like he got hit by a truck. Really, Nick." She eyed him a moment. "Okay, I know that stubborn look. At least you're going to eat a decent breakfast. How about a banana-mango-strawberry smoothie? Ought to go down easy."

Fortified by the smoothie, a few more pain pills, and a shower, Nick was ready to go when Peter Douglass knocked on the back door. But when Nick opened the door, Conny was standing there too, holding on to his grandfather's hand. "He wanted to make sure you're all right," Peter said.

Nick knuckled the top of Conny's head. "Sure, I'm all right, buddy. Don't you worry. Everything's going to be okay."

Conny let go of his grandfather's hand and hugged Nick around the knees. "I hate my dad! He was mean to you!"

Nick was startled by the little boy's vehemence. He squatted down with difficulty. "No, no, buddy. Don't say that. Your dad . . . believe it or not, your dad loves you. He was just kinda jealous that I get to spend more time with you than he does."

"Don't care." Conny sniffed. "He shouldn't have hit you."

Nick gave a little laugh. "Well, I agree with you there." A crack of thunder in the distance rumbled their way. "Hey, your grandpa and I gotta go to work before it starts to rain. See you tonight, okay?" He held open the screen door. "Why don't you go inside and see your mom, wake her up." So far Rochelle hadn't shown her face that morning. Was probably taking advantage of Conny staying upstairs last night to sleep in.

Another crack of thunder hustled them down the back steps to the car, which Peter kept in the detached garage behind the three-flat. "He sure likes you," Peter said as he drove out of the garage and headed down the alley.

"Yeah. I like him too." Nick sighed. That's part of what he needed to talk to his boss about.

Peter didn't press. But as they came through the door that said "Software Symphony, Inc.—Harmonizing All Your Software Needs," he said, "Come on into my office. No need to scare the troops in the mail room." He chuckled as he led the way into the tastefully appointed office and motioned to a comfortable, padded chair. "Okay, what's this about? Church? Work?"

Nick shook his head. "To tell the truth, I've been thinking about what Dexter said last night—"

Mr. Douglass snorted. "Forget that. You're just one more victim of his malicious mouth. Don't take it personally."

"Yeah, well, it was kind of personal." Nick made a face. "But I'm serious. I really need to talk about this. He's assuming there's something going on between Rochelle and me, and to tell you the truth, I can see what it looks like from his point of view. If Conny's always talking about me and the stuff we do together, and Dexter knows he and his mom are staying in the same apartment where I live, what's he supposed to think? I mean, sometimes I've wondered what other people at the church think. Never thought about it when the four of us first sublet the apartment from the Candys. I mean, we were just friends. We're all adults and felt like we could handle being housemates, especially since there were three females and just one me. But to be honest, I've been a little surprised Pastor Cobbs or the elders haven't got on our case—you know, 'appearances' and all that."

Peter nodded. "Well, have to admit we've had to handle a question or two from some of the members, especially when your name came up as a pastoral intern. But . . . we pretty much defended you, for the same reasons you mentioned, plus the fact that Avis and I live right upstairs and some of our own family members now live in the apartment—kind of like a multigenerational household. I think we'd know if there was anything questionable going on."

"Yeah, well, thanks for the vote of confidence. But it's not quite that simple." Taking a deep breath—as deep as his sore gut allowed—Nick told his boss about the man-to-man talk he'd had with Josh on Saturday. He felt his face going red as he recounted what Josh had said about Rochelle talking to Edesa about her feelings for him. "And Josh thinks my relationship with Conny is a big part of what's giving Rochelle these, uh, romantic notions about me. Which is why I wanted to talk to you, Mr. Douglass. I really need some advice about what to do."

Peter Douglass had leaned back in his high-backed chair and frowned slightly as Nick talked. "I see." He rubbed his chin soberly. "Have you given any encouragement to Rochelle to think you, uh, might be interested in her?"

Nick flung out his hands. "Not that I know of! Unless inadvertently, the way I relate to Conny . . . I don't know. I just thought of myself as a 'big brother' or 'bachelor uncle' or something. But she's obviously been thinking of me more as a 'daddy figure' to Conny." He leaned forward. "I really don't know what to do, because I care about your grandson, Mr. Douglass, and as you said, he seems to really like me. I don't want to hurt him or make him feel rejected. And"—he might as well put it all on the table—"there's more."

Peter's eyebrows raised.

"It's Kat. I . . . I do have feelings for Kat. I've never actually told her how I feel, which is pretty dumb, I know, but . . . well, that's when I began to get more sensitive to the fact that our living situation might be a problem. It's one thing to be housemates in mixed company, like brothers and sisters—but to date one of my housemates would change the whole dynamic. I've— What?"

A slow smile had spread over Peter Douglass's face. "So. I was right."

"Right?"

He nodded. "I saw this coming. You aren't as subtle as you think, young man. I've known for a while you had special feelings for that young lady."

"Oh man." Nick shook his head. "Huh. If you can see it, why can't Kat? She . . . I don't know, Mr. Douglass. I wish I knew how she feels about *me*. I mean, we're good buddies and all that. But what I feel for her definitely is *not* a buddy. And something's gotta pop soon because, frankly, I'm going nuts!" Nick sighed. "Actually, I have given her some hints lately about how I feel. But just when I think she's gotten the hint, then . . .

I don't know. She pulls away. Or we pass like ships in the night for days on end because of our schedules."

Mr. Douglass chuckled. "She's probably just as confused as you are, Nick. Don't make her guess. Tell her how you feel, straight-out. Don't beat around the bush."

"Don't you think I want to? But it feels so complicated while we're all sharing the same apartment—me and Kat and Bree, and now Rochelle and Conny. And this . . . this thing with Rochelle, knowing how *she* feels, complicates it even more!" Nick slumped back in his chair. "I really don't know what to do."

Peter was quiet for several long moments. Then he leaned forward, clasping his hands and resting his forearms on the desk. "Tell you what. I think Avis and I have decided to do this thing in South Africa. We plan to take a couple weeks in August to visit our friends Nonyameko and Mark Sisulu-Smith as soon as the STEP program is over. Why don't you stay in our apartment, house-sit for us? That would give you some space. And you still have a semester to finish at the seminary in September, right? Maybe we can let you stay on with us until you go back to CCU."

"Really? Mr. Douglass! That would be great." Nick could hardly believe it. He could romance Kat and no one would question whether it was inappropriate. Except . . . "But did you say August? That's still a couple weeks away." He shook his head. "I gotta do something about this, uh, misunderstanding Rochelle has. Everybody heard what Dexter said—and she didn't help any, telling him she could be with anybody she liked. I mean, how was he supposed to take that? The rest of you standing around heard that too—including Kat."

"I see your point." Peter pursed his lips thoughtfully. "All right. I'll need to talk to Avis about this first, but . . . maybe you could move upstairs with us this week, before we leave. I think we could manage that. And would it help if I talk to Rochelle? Put her straight?"

Nick was so tempted to jump on the offer. Let Mr. D do the dirty work! It was one thing to tell a girl he was in love with her . . . quite another to face telling a girl he wasn't interested— a young woman he cared about and didn't want to hurt.

He sighed. "Don't I wish. But I think she needs to hear it from me."

"Good point." Peter Douglass stood up. "Now I've got work to do. As for you—I want you out of here by noon. Go home and take a nap. That's a direct order from the boss."

Chapter 35

Nick was already gone by the time Kat got out of the shower. Why was he being so stubborn? He was in no shape to go to work! Now she was going to worry about him all morning. They should have insisted that he see a doctor.

She heard Conny chatting up a storm in Rochelle's bedroom—Mrs. D must've sent him home when she left for the summer program at Bethune. Which meant the principal was probably already there. *Hmm.* If she hurried, Kat might be able to catch her before the kids arrived. She wanted to talk to Mrs. Douglass about her chances for a job with Chicago Public Schools—which didn't look too good if they were closing schools and putting teachers out of work. Still, she wanted to ask if Mrs. D would be willing to write her a recommendation.

"How's Nick?" Bree mumbled from her bed as Kat gathered her backpack, keys, and water bottle.

"He looks awful, didn't sleep much last night, but of course he's gone to work." Kat paused at the bedroom door. "You don't sound too good either. You okay?"

"Don't know . . . feel like I've got a cold coming on." Bree rolled over. *"Uhhh . . .* think I'll sleep a little longer. Don't have to go to work until one."

"Okay. I'll try to check in on you after I'm done tutoring." Kat hesitated, not really wanting to offer, but . . . "Guess if you're really not feeling good, I could cover for you. I'm scheduled for the evening shift."

Bree waved her away. "Don't worry about it. That'd make a really long day for you. I just need a little more sleep . . . turn that fan on high, will ya? Helps drown out you-know-who."

On the way out, Kat filled her travel cup with the last of the coffee Nick had brewed, then scurried down the front stairs. Uh-oh. Was that thunder? She'd better hurry.

The sky was dark toward the south of the city but lighter overhead. Maybe the thunderstorm would pass by the bottom of the lake and miss them entirely. Kat arrived at Bethune Elementary still dry with ten minutes to spare before she was due in her classroom. She knocked at the inner door in the school office that said Avis Douglass, Principal.

"Oh, hi, Kathryn. Come in." Mrs. Douglass smiled at her. "How's the patient?"

Kat dropped into a chair. "Being stubborn. Went to work with your husband even though Mr. Douglass gave him the day off." She bit her lip to keep from pouring out her frustration with Nick. "Men. Don't understand them."

Avis Douglass chuckled. "Me either, and I've been married to two of them. They make terrible patients—either moaning helplessly with the slightest fever or getting all macho and ignoring the fact they're about to keel over."

Kat couldn't help but laugh. "Yeah, well . . . don't know why Nick insisted on going to work, but he wouldn't listen to me."

Mrs. Douglass pursed her lips a moment. "You really care about Nick, don't you?"

Kat was startled. Where did *that* come from? "Well, uh, sure . . . We're good friends . . . He's a great guy . . ." She felt as if she were tripping over her words.

"I mean, care about him in a special way."

Kat felt heat flooding into her face. Nick's words that night he'd walked her home from work, which she'd repeated over and over to herself many a night, echoed in her ears. *"Kat . . . you do know you are more than just a friend to me, don't you?"* And then his lips had brushed her cheek with that gentle kiss.

She couldn't deny it. Her feelings for Nick—was it love?—had been growing stronger by the day. But she didn't know what to say. She felt confused by what happened last night—Dexter all furious because he thought Nick and Rochelle were "shacking up." Well, she knew *that* wasn't happening—but Kat wasn't so sure there weren't some sparks there. When Livie and her sister were visiting, they got a big kick out of pairing up Rochelle and Nick as a cute couple. Even Rochelle's taunts last night in response to Dexter's accusations, saying, *"I can be with anybody I want to,"* had practically implied there *was* something going on with Nick.

Looking down at her lap, Kat tried to regain her composure. As much as she'd love to pour out all her confusion to someone, she couldn't—not to Rochelle's *mother.*

"I'm sorry, Kathryn. I didn't mean to put you on the spot. But if you ever want to talk about it . . . well." Avis cleared her throat. "So. You came in to see me about something?"

"Um, yes. I wanted to ask if you'd write a recommendation for me. I applied to Chicago Public Schools for a teaching job this fall, but . . . well, it's not very likely, given the school closings and everything. Still, until they actually say no, I want to give it my best shot."

"Of course. I'll be glad to. You've done a good job this summer with the tutoring program. But you're right—it's a long shot. We all may be looking for jobs come August. But you never can tell what God might do! Lord, we're going to trust You for just the right job for Kathryn this fall . . ."

With a start, Kat realized Avis had moved right into a prayer for her. She bowed her head, but the short prayer was already at "Amen." She looked up.

Avis gave her an encouraging smile and then looked at her watch. "Oh . . . it's almost nine." She stood up. "We better get this morning's program on the road. Can you go out to the playground and call the kids inside?"

❋

The morning went relatively well, in spite of Kat's mental distractions. But once her charges had made a dash for the lunchroom, she grabbed her backpack and hustled out the door. She'd promised Brygitta she'd check on her. So far so good. Bree hadn't called to ask her to sub for her—hopefully the extra sleep had revived her and she was already getting ready for work.

Kat let herself into the apartment. All seemed quiet. Ah, a note from Bree on the table. *Gone to work but feeling kinda lousy. Nick came home. Said he needed a nap.*

Nick was home? Nothing about Rochelle and Conny, but they were obviously not there. Too quiet. Kat tiptoed over to the study and peeked in. Nick was sacked out on the foldout futon, dead asleep. Well, good. Either he'd wised up or . . . no, she was not going to presume he was feeling worse. Had she even prayed for him since Dexter beat him up? Like those Yada Yada sisters had prayed last night for all the concerns they'd shared?

Kat sank onto the living room couch, grabbed a cushion, and hugged it while a few tears crept down her cheeks. *Oh, Lord, please help Nick get better. It's so hard seeing him hurt like this. Protect him from any serious internal injury. And . . . and I feel so confused about what I'm feeling for him. Even more confused about what he's feeling. Or what's going on with Nick and Rochelle—if anything. Please, God, just make it clear.*

She reached for a tissue and blew her nose. Well, that was probably a stupid prayer, but at least she'd prayed. Those women at Yada Yada seemed to just tell God whatever was on their hearts, even if it didn't sound "churchy." So . . . that's what was on her heart right now. And now it was in God's lap.

She felt better already.

Okay, she had until five o'clock to get to work. Maybe she'd walk up to the Dominick's food store in the Howard Street shopping center by SouledOut and talk to them about donating some dated perishables to the new food pantry—vegetables, day-old bread, stuff like that—that they were just going to toss. Wouldn't hurt to ask.

❈

Kat left the big grocery store, trying not to show her frustration until she was out of sight. What was so complicated about her request? How about a simple yes or no? No, SouledOut wasn't an outlet for the Chicago Food Depository—not yet, anyway.

No, they weren't receiving USDA foods—yet. But they had to start somewhere, didn't they? And most of the store's dated food was going to get thrown out into those compactors anyway. If they hadn't put in those compactors, she could've fished it out of their Dumpsters. What would it hurt to just let the SouledOut Sisters Food Pantry have it? Good grief! It wasn't like the food pantry was going to compete with them or lure customers away.

Okay, Lord, sorry. Getting upset wasn't going to accomplish anything. What was that verse in Proverbs Mrs. D had read at Yada Yada? *"Commit your actions to the Lord, and your plans will succeed."* Might as well start committing stuff to the Lord—stuff like this— because there were probably going to be a lot of frustrations and hurdles to jump over if the food pantry was going to be a reality. She could only do so much. God was going to have to do the rest.

Kat was only a few sentences into her silent prayer as she strode down Clark Street when her cell phone rang. "Bree? What's up? . . . Uh-oh. Sorry to hear that . . . Yeah, I can come in an hour early. Can you hang on that long? I need to go home first, but I could be there by four . . . Okay. Bye."

She glanced at her watch. If she hustled, she had time to go home first, maybe even fix a sandwich, before heading over to The Common Cup. Besides, she wanted to check on Nick and make sure he was doing okay—for her own peace of mind, if nothing else.

Conny was sitting cross-legged in front of the TV watching some kids' program on PBS when Kat let herself into the apartment. Strange for the middle of a summer afternoon. Kat glanced at the study doors . . . not closed, so she guessed Nick wasn't sleeping anymore. "Hey, Conny, have you seen Nick?"

No answer. Totally engrossed in the TV. She waved a hand in front of his face. "Earth to Conny . . . where's Mister Nick?"

"Oh, hi, Miss Kat. Uh, he's talking to my mom. They told me not to bother them." Eyes glued once more to the TV.

What? Nick and Rochelle were talking privately? A flicker of jealousy sent Kat to the study, but a quick glance inside the half-open doors showed no one inside. And she'd be able to hear them if they were in the kitchen. What did that leave—the bedrooms? Heart thumping, she walked quietly down the hall, past the bedroom she shared with Bree, past the bathroom, to the bedroom at the end of the hall. The door was closed. Kat stood still and listened . . . but she heard no voices inside.

She was tempted to open the door but couldn't bring herself to do it. What was she thinking? This was crazy. They're not in there. She should just go make herself a sandwich and get over to the coffee shop and relieve Bree. Heading back toward the kitchen, she reminded herself to breathe. *You're acting like a thirteen-year-old, Kat Davies.*

But as she passed through the dining nook and entered the kitchen, she stopped dead in her tracks. The door to the porch was closed, but she could see the back of Nick's head through the large window in the top half, as though he was sitting down in one of the plastic chairs. Beyond him, Rochelle was standing up, gesturing about something. And then Rochelle laughed.

For a nanosecond Kat was tempted to bounce out onto the porch with a cheerful, "Hey, can I join the party?" just to break up this little tête-à-tête—but she knew she couldn't pull it off. She was too close to saying something she'd probably regret—or too close to tears, which would be even worse.

Turning on her heel, Kat grabbed her backpack and headed out the front door, slamming it shut behind her.

Chapter 36

W as this what it'd feel like to stand on the edge of the Grand Canyon, as if any moment the ground beneath his feet would crumble and he'd fall headlong into the abyss below? Now that he'd worked up the courage to ask Rochelle if they could talk, Nick was afraid to open his mouth. What he said in the next few minutes might blow up everything right in his face.

God, I really need Your wisdom. Help me say the right thing in the right way. I don't want to hurt Rochelle and Conny—but I gotta do this thing!

Why didn't Rochelle sit down? She'd been going on for two minutes apologizing for Dexter, she never thought Conny's dad would go that far, she was so sorry he'd been hurt, and was he sure he was okay?

And then she suddenly laughed, a tinkling laugh full of merriment that crinkled her dark eyes at the corners. "I'm sorry, Nick," she gasped. "It's not funny—but you do look like a raccoon with those two black eyes." Rochelle put a slender hand to her mouth, trying to stifle her giggles.

Oh brother. What he wouldn't give to just join in the joke, reassure her he was going to be fine, it wasn't her fault, and talk about something else. Anything else.

The slamming of a door inside the apartment made him jump. Had somebody just come in? *Oh no, couldn't be worse timing—especially if it's Kat.* "Hang on just a minute, Rochelle. I'll be right back."

Nick slipped inside the apartment and looked around. Nobody in the living room except Conny, glued to the TV. "Hey, buddy, did someone just come in? Conny! I'm talking to you!"

Conny glanced his way for half a second. "Miss Kat just went out."

Kat had been here? How long? Had she seen him and Rochelle talking on the porch? *Oh, God, this isn't happening.*

"Was she here very long?" He tried to keep his voice low, but he spoke sharply. "Conny! Look at me!"

Conny shrugged. "I dunno. Not very long." He eyed Nick warily, as if weighing the tone of his voice.

Nick sighed. He shouldn't take it out on the boy. "Okay. I won't bother you anymore." He walked slowly back out onto the porch, closing the kitchen door behind him. "Sorry. Just heard something and wanted to check on Conny, make sure everything was okay."

Rochelle had claimed another plastic chair on the other side of the square table between them. She gave him a warm smile. "Thanks. I appreciate you looking out for Conny. Means a lot to me."

There it was. He couldn't avoid it now. Nick drew in a deep breath and let it out. "Actually, that's what I wanted to talk to you about, Rochelle. About Conny."

Rochelle tipped her head slightly, her thick, wavy hair falling to the side as she looked at him, puzzled. "About Conny?"

"Well, actually, about what happened last night. I—"

"Nick! Please. Believe me when I say it wasn't your fault! You didn't do anything wrong. Even if Dexter had absconded with Conny—which he didn't, thank God."

Nick put up both his hands. "I know. I appreciate that. But I've been thinking seriously about what Dexter said, and—" He saw her about to open her mouth to protest. "Please, Rochelle, let me finish." There was nothing to do but plunge ahead. "I . . . I think my living here in the apartment with you and Conny is causing confusion—not just for Dexter, but for Conny too." *And you,* he should add. But he wasn't quite ready to address that yet. He'd already decided not to say he knew she'd talked to Edesa about her feelings for him. Hopefully he could let her off the hook without embarrassing her. "So I wanted to let you know that I'm going to house-sit for your folks when they go to South Africa in a couple weeks—maybe even move out sooner, but I'm not sure about that just yet."

"Move out!" Rochelle's eyes flashed—but he couldn't say whether it was from anger or disappointment. "But . . . what about Conny? Just like that, walk out of his life?"

"Rochelle. I'm only moving up one floor. I can still do things with him from time to time."

"Oh sure. 'From time to time,'" she mimicked. "But you've been putting him to bed, you're the one he wants to go see first thing in the morning because you're *there.* Why would you do that to him? He . . . he needs you, Nick. You're like family."

For some reason, Nick felt a sense of calm fill his spirit and he grew bolder. "That's just the problem, Rochelle. I didn't see it before, but no wonder Dexter got bent out of shape. I'm not Conny's daddy, and I'm not your live-in boyfriend. And I can't— I shouldn't—be here for him every minute. It's confusing for Conny—and for you too."

She snorted. "Well, that's just great. Because after that circus last night, I'm getting a court order to keep Dexter away. So now Conny won't have *any* man he can count on in his life." She got up abruptly and walked over to the porch railing overlooking the tiny backyard, garage, and alley, her back to him. Her arms were folded across her chest and she seemed to be breathing heavily.

Nick was tempted to protest. Yes, he'd be there for Conny! She could count on him! But he held his tongue. There was time to work out what his relationship with Conny should be, but—like Josh Baxter had said—he first had to establish what it wasn't.

After several long minutes, Rochelle turned slowly back to him. "You said it was confusing for me too. What did you mean?"

This was where the rubber met the road. He needed to choose his words carefully. "Just what you said. You and Conny see me like family. And there's nothing wrong with that, if you see me as a big brother or 'Uncle Nick' or something like that. But Dexter obviously thinks it's more than that—I think 'shacking up' was the term he used. And maybe he's not the only one. What about the people at church, or the kids in the youth group . . . what do they think?"

"Oh, so suddenly you're worried about what people *think*? You got all goody-goody because you're a pastor now?"

Nick winced at that. But Rochelle threw out her arms in

disgust. "And . . . and why do you keep quoting Dexter? Why are you paying *any* attention to what he says? The man's crazy. If I never see him again, it'll be too soon. And I don't care if Conny ever does either."

Nick pointed to his battered face with a wry grin. "Personally, I don't want to see the man again either." The grin faded and he searched for the right words. "But the reality is, there's been a huge misunderstanding, and . . . he *is* Conny's dad. And Conny may want—may need—to have his father in his life when all this settles down. But me living here in the same apartment, that's one thing I can change to help keep things clear—for Dexter, for Conny, for you, for anyone else who might have questions. I'm *not* living with you. And I'm never going to be Conny's daddy."

Rochelle's face suddenly looked pained and her voice softened. "Why not? Is that so out of the question, Nick? I mean, I know you care for Conny, and he adores you. And . . . I like you a lot too, Nick. And I think you like me. We get along great. Is it so inconceivable that it could grow into something else?"

Nick swallowed. No need to tell Rochelle he knew what she'd said to Edesa. She'd just told him herself. He shook his head. "It's not going to happen, Rochelle. I'm sorry."

She drew herself up again. "Why?" She shot the words at him. "Is it because I'm black? Funny how all you enlightened white folks get when it comes right down to it. Or . . . or, I know. It's because I'm HIV positive. That's it, isn't it? You can't be with me because I might infect *you*, right?"

He shook his head. How could he tell Rochelle he'd never thought about either of those things in relation to her because, well, he wasn't thinking about her as a potential partner at all.

Hadn't weighed "reasons" for *or* against. "Rochelle, believe me, that's not it. It's because"—there was no way around it—"there's someone else."

Her eyes widened and for a moment she seemed speechless. "Someone else? Who?"

Nick looked away. How could he tell Rochelle when he still hadn't spoken to Kat herself? Maybe he'd done this all wrong. Maybe he should have talked to Kat first, then Rochelle. *Oh, God, did I bungle this whole thing?*

Rochelle suddenly pushed herself away from the railing. "You know what? Forget it. Maybe Conny and I are the ones who should move out. We moved in here last, upset the nice little nest you and your college buddies had carved out for yourselves. Don't know where we'll go, since my folks seem willing to have *you* move in with them, but not us. Figure that one out. But—"

"Rochelle, don't. Please. Actually, even if you and Conny weren't living here, I would need to move out. For the same reason. It's . . . confusing things here."

Rochelle just stared at him. And then her eyes widened and she sank down into the chair across from him again. "Well, spit in my eye . . . it's Kat, isn't it? You're in love with *Kat*." She sucked in a deep breath and blew it out again—and then started to laugh, a mirthless sound. "Criminy. I should've known."

Chapter 37

Nick sat at the kitchen table, staring at the scrambled eggs he'd fixed for himself. Bree had come home from work early, said she was feeling rotten with a cold and didn't feel like cooking supper even though it was her turn. Would he trade with her for tomorrow? He'd said sure, but awhile later Rochelle had come out of her bedroom where she'd holed up after their talk and said she and Conny were going "out," and they'd get supper on their own.

No one to cook for but himself. Was this how it was going to be living upstairs at the Douglasses' while they were gone? He wasn't sure he was going to like it.

Now his eggs were getting cold. Had he done the right thing? In one way he felt immensely relieved. It felt good—right—to be honest. But he knew Rochelle was hurt. Or angry. Something. And that didn't feel good. Because he did like Rochelle. She was really a great girl, and he wanted to stay friends. And Conny . . . couldn't deny he had a special place in his heart for the little guy. Somehow he had to make sure Conny didn't fall through the cracks while he sorted out his love life.

Huh. "Love life." Not like he had one. But . . . a slow smile spread across his face. That was something else he was going to change. Tonight, if he could help it.

Yes. He'd talk to Kat tonight. Which meant he should let Avis Douglass know he'd like a ride to the pastoral meeting tonight.

❋

Pastor Cobbs was a bit taken aback when Nick walked into the office at SouledOut with Avis Douglass. "Good heavens, man! What happened to you?"

Nick tried to keep it simple. He had no problem telling the pastor that Rochelle's ex had gotten jealous about his relationship with Conny and had gotten physical. Or that he'd talked it over with Peter Douglass and they'd agreed it might be smart for Nick to move out of the apartment, just to keep things clear from any misunderstandings. House-sitting for the Douglasses while they took this mission trip to South Africa would provide a temporary reprieve until he figured out something more long-term.

But for Rochelle's sake he said nothing about her talk with Edesa. No need to let the whole world know she had a crush on him. Especially since Avis hadn't mentioned anything about it when she'd told him on the way over that Peter had called and asked about him staying in their apartment. "Of course I said yes. And it's all right if you move in earlier, Nick—this week if you'd like," she'd said as they pulled into the shopping center parking lot. "Will you still take your meals with the girls downstairs? How do you want to work it all out?"

He hadn't thought that far—or what to do about paying his share of the rent either, though they only had a month to go before the Candys returned.

"Very wise, young man," Pastor Cobbs said as they settled into their chairs in his office. "I've been willing to go to bat for you over your living situation because I've trusted that it's all been on the up and up. But given the possibility for misunderstanding—as is apparent from what happened with Rochelle's ex—moving out seems like the right thing to do. Why don't we take some time to pray about a more long-term solution?"

Nick appreciated the prayer, suddenly realizing how grateful he was for the spiritual mentors God had brought into his life this summer—the Douglasses, for sure, and Pastor Cobbs . . . even a spiritual brother in Josh Baxter who'd cared enough to talk to him straight. Well, that's after they got it straight *who* they were talking about. Nick stifled a chuckle as Pastor Cobbs said, "Amen."

Most of the meeting was spent talking about how to cover pastoral duties and responsibilities while Sister Avis was out of the country. At least Nick didn't have to preach again until mid-August, and hopefully by then his face would be back to normal. They also spent time praying for some special needs in the congregation, including the tense situation with Avis's grandson and his daddy.

But as they left the building, Nick said, "Thanks for the ride here, Sister Avis. But I can walk home. Actually . . ." He grinned self-consciously. "I want to stop by The Common Cup when Kat gets off work and walk her home."

A small smile flickered at the corners of Avis's mouth. "All right, if you're sure you're okay. At least let me drive you that far and drop you off. I can tell you're still sore from that punch to your stomach."

Which was true. Nick didn't protest but asked her to let him out half a block from the coffee shop . . . though it made him feel like a teenager asking "Mom" to let him out a block away from school. But he grinned and waved her off, slipping on his sunglasses to hide the bruises, even though twilight was falling.

He only had to wait outside The Common Cup five minutes before Kat pushed out the door, her curls damp against her face and long wavy strands escaping from the clip that held most of it off her neck. "Hey," he said, falling into step. "Mind if I walk you home?"

Startled, Kat stopped in the middle of the sidewalk. "What are you doing here?"

"Uh, like I said. Wanted to walk you home." He kept his tone light. "Mind if we walk over to the lake? It's only a few blocks out of our way."

She hesitated but fell into step, hanging back slightly. "You should be home, getting an early night." Her tone was distant, guarded. "What'd you do, go to your pastor meeting tonight? If you won't go to a doctor, you could *at least* cancel a meeting until your body heals."

Nick almost smiled. Classic Kat. Came out sparring. Except this time it worried him. Had she heard any of his conversation with Rochelle? Couldn't have been much, but still . . . if she only heard snatches, she might have gotten the wrong idea. But maybe he should just be up front about it. In fact, it might provide a good segue.

"I had a talk with Rochelle this afternoon." He paused for

two seconds but got no response. "And I wanted to tell you the same thing I told her—that I think me living in the apartment with Conny is causing misunderstandings. With Dexter for sure. That's one reason I went to work today, to talk to Mr. D about it—him being Conny's grandfather and all that. And he had a good idea, I think. Suggested I house-sit for them when they go to South Africa. It's only one floor up, but at least I wouldn't be living in the same apartment with Conny and Rochelle. Actually, the Douglasses said I could move up there sooner, even this week. I wanted to ask what you think."

They'd reached Sheridan Road, which they had to cross to get to the park along the lake, but had to stop for a red light and "Don't Walk" signal. She looked up at him, an anxious frown on her face. "Move out?" Her tone had changed, no longer distant.

Green light. "Come on, we can go." Nick took her arm and felt like shouting when she didn't pull away. He had to admit his sore gut had outlasted his last round of pain pills. Bed would feel good. But not yet. Not until—

"Why don't Conny and Rochelle just move upstairs? That makes more sense to me. Why make you move out? The Douglasses are her parents, after all."

He didn't answer until they'd reached the end of the block, which dead-ended at the park along the lake. The sun had set an hour ago and the cloudy sky had hastened the twilight, but at least the air was cooler here by the lake.

"Gotta sit for a minute." Which was true. He was hurting now. "That bench okay?"

They sat. Kat reached over, took off his sunglasses, and handed them to him. "You don't have to hide behind these. It's just me." She was frowning. "Okay, I hear what you're saying.

But I don't understand why it has to be you who moves out. Why not Conny and Rochelle?"

Nick cleared his throat. "Because that's not the only reason I need to move out." He turned his body, trying not to wince, so he could face her. "It's you, Kat."

"Me!" Her mouth dropped open. "What are you talking about?"

He allowed a lopsided grin. "I'm talking about the fact that sharing an apartment with you and Bree and Olivia—and now Rochelle and Conny—and trying to keep it all aboveboard and not make any waves with the church, avoiding any appearance of evil and all that, has kept me from saying something I've been wanting to say for a long time."

Kat's eyes were wide, questioning, their usual bright blue darkened in the shadows growing by the minute, even as a quarter moon peeked through a break in the clouds, tipping the small waves out on the lake with tiny pearls of light.

Nick reached out a hand, tucked a flyaway strand of hair behind her ear, and then stroked her cheek. "I love you, Kathryn Davies," he said softly. "And I'm going nuts not being able to tell you because . . . it just wouldn't be appropriate to court you while sharing that apartment as housemates. So the sooner I get out, the better."

Kat didn't answer—but she didn't look away either. He thought his heart might pop right out of his shirt, it was beating so hard. Taking a chance, he leaned closer, his eyes searching hers. "I love you, Kat," he whispered, breathing in the apple-fresh scent of her hair, and touched her lips softly with his.

A car honked in the distance.

The moon disappeared behind another cloud.

Waves lapped gently a hundred feet away along the shore.

And then . . . she was kissing him back, her hands holding his face, her mouth hungry. "Oh, Nick . . . oh, Nick," she finally whispered in his ear, her arms going around him. "I love you too. So much."

He didn't care that his nose hurt from their kisses or that his gut was screaming to unbend. Kat was in his arms, and as far as Nick was concerned, they could sit that way on this bench all night.

Chapter 38

Kat could barely concentrate the next day as she followed the STEP schedule with her three tutoring students. Latoya hollered in time to stop her from pouring orange juice into the little cereal boxes she'd just opened for their "breakfast snack." Story time went well, though. She had started reading *The Lion, the Witch, and the Wardrobe* a few days earlier, which had Kevin, Yusufu, and Latoya begging her not to stop. Then came the real work of the day, helping the kids do story problems using the math they'd been reviewing all summer, but her mind kept drifting to Nick's words whispered in her ear last night.

"I love you, Kat."

She was grateful when it was time for supervised games out on the playground, followed by the drama option, with another volunteer doing theater games in the gym.

As soon as she could escape, Kat hustled over to Morse Avenue to work a double shift at the coffee shop, covering for Bree who was still sick. Made for a long day, but just as well. It kept her away from the house, and Nick had suggested they say nothing about this new step in their relationship until after he moved upstairs. It was going to be hard enough helping Conny understand the change in living arrangements without adding complications.

But by Wednesday, she thought she was going to burst. Nick was moving his stuff up to the Douglasses' tonight—supposedly he'd had a chance to talk to Conny the night before. But with Bree sick, the cooking schedule was all messed up. Was it her turn to cook tonight? She couldn't remember—but it must not be, because she smelled something good when she got home at five thirty.

She wandered into the kitchen. Rochelle was at the stove and Conny was playing with some action figures at the kitchen table. "Hey, Rochelle, smells yummy. What's for supper? Need any help?"

"Nope." Rochelle didn't even turn around. "I'll call people when it's ready."

Kat just stared at her back. What was *her* problem? Maybe Nick's talk with Conny hadn't gone so well. But if Rochelle wanted to be left alone, fine, she'd leave her alone.

But she was dying to talk to *somebody*. Bree could keep their little secret, couldn't she? But when she peeked in the bedroom door, her roomie was asleep and a humidifier was running, making the room feel muggy. Ugh. Maybe she'd sleep on the couch tonight.

The front door opened and Nick came in wearing the sunglasses that helped hide his black eyes and carrying a few empty boxes. Kat's pulse quickened, but she wasn't sure if it was because he looked yummy enough to eat, or because those boxes meant he really was moving out—or at least up. She made a face at him. "Guess you really are moving out. Need any help packing?"

"Sure—oh, hey! There's my buddy." Conny had appeared in the kitchen doorway. "Come here, little guy—give Uncle Nick a hug."

Uncle Nick? That was a new one. But maybe they'd decided that's what Conny should call him. Probably a good idea.

Conny inched slowly into the dining nook, scowling at the boxes—and then suddenly he ran toward Nick. Kat thought it was his usual jump-on-Mister-Nick hug, but instead, the little boy kicked the closest box and sent it flying, then he ran out of the room and down the hall, slamming the door to the bedroom he shared with his mother.

Kat and Nick eyed each other. She grimaced. "Somebody's not happy."

Rochelle appeared in the doorway, wooden spoon in hand. "What was that?"

Nick pointed at the boxes. "I think it sunk in that I'm moving out."

"Humph. What'd you expect?" Rochelle disappeared back into the kitchen.

Nick sank down onto the couch with a sigh. "Do you think I oughta go talk to him again?" he asked Kat.

Kat sat beside him. "Maybe . . . but wait just a little. I think I'd be as matter-of-fact as possible. Maybe ask him to help you. Might help him understand it's just upstairs."

Nick gave her a grateful smile. "I'd like to kiss you right now," he whispered.

"I dare you," she whispered back.

Kat almost thought he was going to do it, but instead he just winked—or tried to with his puffy eyes—and squeezed her hand before getting up off the couch and heading for the study. "Better get started," he said aloud. "At least Pastor Cobbs took pity on me and didn't give me any responsibilities for prayer meeting tonight. Said I could stay home. If you want to do something, you could pack my books in one of those boxes."

Arrrgh. Why did he have to be so *principled?* But she knew he was right. Not *here.* Not *now.* But if it'd hurry things along, she'd help him pack and push him out the door.

❋

Supper felt a little strained. Conny had come to the table pouty, and . . . was Kat imagining it or did Rochelle keep darting furtive looks at her? But passing around the bowls of shredded cheese, crushed tortilla chips, and black olives to sprinkle on top of the hearty taco soup Rochelle had made filled the silence for the first several minutes, and even Bree—her nose red and her voice hoarse—rolled her eyes with pleasure after the first spoonful.

Nick finally broke the awkward silence. "Uh, say, Conny, I've been thinking about leaving my guitar down here. Don't think your grandma and grandpa would appreciate me practicing up there. Would you take care of it for me?"

Conny's eyes lit up. "Yeah! I'll take real good care of it, Mister Nick."

Hmm, Kat thought. *Uncle Nick* might take awhile.

Silence descended on the table again, broken only by, "Please pass the cheese," or "Do we have another bag of tortilla chips?"

But once Conny had been excused from the table to go play with his action figures, Nick cleared his throat. "As long as we're all still at the table, can we talk about my move upstairs? I'd still like to do my share of the cooking and eat suppers here if that's all right with everyone."

"Sure." Bree sniffled. Kat nodded gratefully. Rochelle just shrugged and toyed with her food.

But Nick went on. "And since the Douglasses aren't charging me any rent—they said I'm doing them a favor house-sitting for those couple of weeks—I want to still pay my share of the rent here for August. That's the last month of our sublet, and then . . . well, we'll all be transitioning come September."

Did Nick just toss her a secret glance? Kat felt her cheeks get hot. Surely he didn't mean they had to keep how they felt about each other hush-hush until then!

"Sounds good to me." Bree sighed and waved her pack of tissues. "Now, if you all will excuse me, I think I'll go hibernate again before I infect the whole lot of you with this yucky cold." Pushing back her chair, Bree shuffled off toward the bedroom.

Rochelle broke the silence that fell on the table in Bree's wake. "Very noble of you." Her voice had stiffened. "Makes me feel even more like a heel, though, since I'm basically mooching off the rest of you. Rent . . . food . . . and you wouldn't have to be moving out if Conny and I weren't here. Seems like I oughta be the one who—"

"Rochelle. Don't."

Kat was surprised at Nick's interruption. She'd said the same thing to Nick herself—that maybe it should be Rochelle and Conny who moved out. Why not, if the idea came from her?

"Like I already told you, Rochelle, even if you and Conny didn't live here, I need to move out. Because"—to Kat's astonishment, Nick reached for her hand, took a deep breath, and smiled at her—"because I told Kat the other night that I intend to court her, and to do that honestly, I shouldn't be rooming here."

For a few moments Kat was speechless. There. It was out! To Rochelle, no less! She was glad and mad at the same time. Nick should have warned her! Or said something before Bree left! She kept her eyes on his face, half-afraid to look at Rochelle, knowing she was blushing.

But when she did glance at her, she saw that Rochelle—so tough on one hand, so vulnerable on the other—was staring at her lap, her thick black hair falling over her tawny face, as if struggling to keep her composure. What the young woman was thinking or feeling, Kat wasn't sure. Did she need some reassurance that they wanted her to stay? Should she say something?

"Rochelle, I—"

But Rochelle stood up abruptly. "Don't bother. I *get* it." She took her dishes into the kitchen and then walked back through the dining nook and living room, disappearing into the hallway.

❋

Rochelle didn't reappear for the rest of the evening, though Nick did coax Conny to help him and Kat move his stuff upstairs, which seemed to have the desired effect—especially when Nick promised to let Conny "practice" on the guitar when they were done.

But later Kat did pounce on Bree, who was propped up in

bed reading, and said her roomie better listen up, cold or no cold. Bree screeched when Kat told her about Nick showing up after work Monday night and walking her to the lake, and the "other" reason why he was moving out.

"I knew it! I knew it!" Bree gasped with laughter—and ended up in a coughing fit. "I bet I knew it before either you *or* Nick! Ha! I knew you two were going to end up together the first time he laid eyes on you at the music fest. He never looked at *me* the way he looked at you that day. It's about time you two figured it out."

Kat felt so relieved to pour out all the tangled-up thoughts and feelings and questions she'd been having the past few weeks—ever since Nick had become a member of SouledOut and she hadn't. Feeling God calling her to "feed people" but not understanding exactly what that meant . . . her mixed-up feelings about Rochelle and Conny . . . not knowing what she was going to be doing for a job when summer ended . . . where Nick fit into all of this . . . and now, where *she* fit into Nick's life.

She and Bree talked a long time before finally shutting off the light on the nightstand between them—and then Kat turned it on again. "What?" Bree moaned. "We've got to get some sleep or I'll never get over this cold."

"Sorry," Kat said, pulling a notebook out of her backpack and finding a blank page. "Just something I gotta do." She wrote for several minutes, tore out the page and folded it, then tiptoed out of the room and slipped the note under Rochelle's bedroom door.

Chapter 39

The door buzzer rang in apartment 3A of the House of Hope, and Edesa Baxter pushed the button on the call box that let the door open three floors below. "Gracie! It's your friend Conny and his mommy. Let's go watch them come up, okay?"

Squealing, little Gracie ran for the door, jiggling the knob until her mother opened it, then she took up her position at the top of the stairs, peering through the railings until she saw Conny's dark head coming up the last flight. "Conny! Conny!" She giggled, sticking her arm through the railing to wave.

The six-year-old grinned up at her and waved back, then ran ahead of his mother to reach the top of the stairs. "Hi, Miss Edesa! Hey, Gracie."

Edesa smiled as she greeted him. That boy was as good-looking as they come. No surprise, since Rochelle looked like a model for *Ebony* magazine. And she'd never met Rochelle's ex, but she'd heard he was "real fine" in the looks department too. *Hope Conny's not a heartbreaker like his daddy, though.* Her own heart felt a pang thinking about all Rochelle had been through with that man—not the least of which was the brouhaha last Sunday.

The two children disappeared into the apartment as Rochelle trudged up the last flight. "Don't know how you do it, Edesa," she puffed. "I'm winded and I'm not even thirty yet."

Edesa laughed. "Me either, *mi amiga.* Josh says living on the third floor will either kill us or keep us young." She led the way inside. "I'm so glad you called. Gracie loves to play with other kids—though I'm surprised Conny is so patient playing with *her,* given the difference in their ages. Do you want some tea?"

"Sure." Rochelle peeked into Gracie's bedroom as they walked down the long hall toward the kitchen. "Hmm. Those big Lego blocks may have something to do with Conny's willingness to play with Gracie. I need to get some of those . . . they're ageless," she murmured.

Edesa turned on the teakettle and then looked a bit sheepish. "I have a quick favor to ask you. Will you watch the kids while I run down to the basement and switch the laundry? At least Josh took the baskets downstairs for me before he left for Manna House. He's over there doing some painting today. He left me the car so I can take you back to the El."

"Sure. Go . . . go."

Edesa scurried down the outside back stairs to the basement. Whatever Josh had done when he tinkered with the washers and dryers, they certainly were working a lot better now. She fished a load of whites out of the first washer and stuffed it into the closest dryer. Heavy towels and jeans went into the second dryer. Then she reloaded the two washers—wash-and-wear in one, sheets and pillowcases in the other. At this rate she'd have the laundry done before Rochelle left. If she didn't forget to turn on the machines like last week. So . . . *estúpido.*

But she didn't scurry on the way back up. *Uhh.* At the rate climbing these stairs was wearing her out, Edesa might regret they lived on the third floor. Not sure what she could do about it, though. No way did she want to trade their cheerful apartment, tastefully painted in *"hacienda* colors"—combinations of rusty orange, green, sunny yellow, and blue—for Tanya's red and black bedroom in the apartment she shared with Precious, even if it was on the first floor.

Rochelle had made the tea by the time she got back to the third floor. "Mm, thanks." Edesa sank into a chair at the small kitchen table. But after a few grateful sips, she looked carefully at her guest. "Are you all right, Rochelle? Do you want to talk about what happened Sunday night? All I know is what Nick told Josh on the phone—and you know how guys are. Just gave me the bare bones—"

"Nick called Josh?" Rochelle cut in sharply. "What did he say?"

"Just that Conny's daddy showed up mad as a wet cat, and he slugged Nick a couple times. And tried to take Conny with him. But you and your mom got back just in time from Yada Yada—*hallelujah!*" Edesa waved a hand in the air as if she were in church. "Oh, he said Nick was going to house-sit for your parents when they went to South Africa to, uh, ease any misunderstanding Dexter has about your living arrangement."

Rochelle squirmed. "Anything else?"

Edesa took a long sip of tea. Even before Nick's phone call on Monday, Josh had told her about his "guy talk" with Nick Sunday afternoon—and how Nick had said it was Kat Davies he was interested in. That was news! Especially after Rochelle had taken Edesa into her confidence about her feelings for Nick. A sticky situation for sure. But Edesa didn't know how much Rochelle knew, so she needed to tread carefully here.

"I'm sure there's more to the story—and I want to know how *you're* doing, Rochelle."

Rochelle shrugged. "Been better. Everything kinda blew up after I talked to you last week."

"Did you talk to Nick about how you felt about him?" *Go gently,* Edesa told herself.

"Not exactly. Well, kind of. After that thing happened with Dexter—criminy, you should see Nick. He's got two black eyes, makes him look like a raccoon. That slimeball slugged him real good. But I guess he's okay. He says he is, anyway." She wagged her head. "Anyway, after that mess with Dexter, the next day Nick says he wants to talk to me, tells me he thinks he should move out. Too confusing for Conny—and me, he says. Dexter said some pretty nasty things about . . . about us, me and Nick. And I guess Nick doesn't want people to talk—though as far as I know, Dexter's the only one whose mind is so warped, that's the first thing *he* thinks. After all, we're divorced, and . . . good grief, Kat and Bree live in the apartment too."

Rochelle drummed her fingers on the table, and Edesa noticed she hadn't drunk any of her tea. "Anyway, Nick made it pretty clear he wasn't Conny's daddy and he didn't want Dexter or anyone else thinking he's my live-in boyfriend either. So, yeah, I got brave and asked him if the idea of us having a rela-tionship—him and me—was so inconceivable. Because Conny's crazy about him, and I told him I liked him a lot and I thought he liked me. But that's when he told me"—Rochelle suddenly had to grab a tissue from the box on the table—"told me there was someone else."

Edesa waited while Rochelle blew her nose. "Someone else?"

"Yeah. He said even if Conny and I didn't live in the apartment, he'd need to move out. That's when I guessed who he's got the hots for. Kat Davies. *Kat!* And he didn't deny it. So I was sure."

Edesa laid a hand on Rochelle's arm across the table. "I'm sorry, Rochelle." She hesitated to say more. She was sorry for Rochelle's disappointment, not that Nick had his heart set on Kat . . . though she'd been a bit surprised when she'd first heard it from Josh. Those two always seemed more like brother and sister, and Kat was, well, rather impulsive and spirited compared to Nick's thoughtful, laid-back persona. But Nick and Kat as a couple wasn't any stranger than Josh and Edesa had been a few years back. Maybe less so. At least Nick and Kat were the same age and had spent several years together at the same school, whereas Josh was three years younger than she was, and they had to deal with a multicultural, double-language, mixed-race household to boot.

But they had the main thing going for them: both she and Josh loved God and loved each other like crazy. *Gracias, Jesús!*

The phone rang. "Excuse me a minute, Rochelle." Edesa headed for the kitchen phone. "*Hola?* . . . Oh, Gabby! . . . He needs what? . . . Turpentine? Well, I guess I could bring it when I take Rochelle to the El. Is he in a hurry to get it? . . . All right. Just a moment . . ." Edesa covered the receiver. "Rochelle, can you and Conny stay for lunch?" When Rochelle nodded, she turned back to the phone. "Tell Josh I'll bring it after lunch . . . All right."

Edesa came back to the table. "Josh needs me to bring him a can of turpentine from the basement. Probably to clean his paintbrushes. Hope I can find it."

But Rochelle's mind was somewhere else. "I asked Nick straight-out if it was because I'm black, which he denied, of course. Then I thought . . . maybe it's because I'm HIV positive. And of course he denied that too. *That's* when he told me there was someone else." She rolled her eyes. "And just to rub it in, last night at supper he said straight-out he's planning to *court* Kat once he moves out. In front of both me and her. Made me wish I could just disappear. So I did. Walked out." She snorted. "Ha. He's going to *court* her. How d'ya like that for a fancy-smancy, white-guy word."

But suddenly Rochelle's eyes filled again and she had to grab another tissue. "But, Edesa, I really thought he might be the one. What if . . . what if I never find a guy like him?"

Oh, Jesús, give me wisdom. "Rochelle, let me ask you something. If it weren't for Conny—I mean, if you were single, not a mom—would you be in love with Nick Taylor?"

"But I am a mom! I've got to think about Conny first. I want a guy who's crazy about Conny and vice versa . . . that's important."

"I know . . . but if Conny weren't in the picture. What then?"

"I . . . I don't know. Why are you asking me that?"

"Because it wouldn't be enough to love Nick just because he'd make a good dad. You'd need to love him just for himself, because marriage lasts a lot longer than raising kids. The kids grow up, leave home, and then what?" She reached out to touch Rochelle again. "Rochelle, how long have you known Nick?"

The young woman had the grace to blush. "Well, uh, about five weeks."

"That's not very long. Do you really *know* Nick the person? His hopes? His dreams? He wants to be a pastor, you know. Do *you* want to be a pastor's wife?"

Rochelle just stared at her. "I . . . I haven't really thought about that. I have to admit it wouldn't be my first choice." Her eyes dropped to her mug, which she toyed with, turning it back and forth with her fingers. Then her shoulders began to shake with silent laughter. "Criminy. Me, a pastor's wife. That's a good one."

Picking up Rochelle's mug, Edesa put it in the microwave to reheat, giving the girl some space to think about what she'd just said. But when the microwave dinged, she set the mug down in front of her and said, "There's something else you need to think about. And that's Kat . . . If Nick is going to 'court' her, as he said, can you live with that? Living together in the apartment, I mean."

Rochelle looked away. Then she reached into her back jeans pocket and pulled out a folded note. "Found this under my door this morning . . ." She slid it toward Edesa.

Edesa picked up the sheet of small notebook paper and unfolded it. *"Dear Rochelle,"* the note said. *"I know that Nick moving out is difficult for you, maybe confusing. You said maybe you and Conny should be the ones to move out instead. But I want to ask you to stay. First of all for Conny's sake. Nick really cares about your son—we all do—and he wants to continue being there for him. He wants to be 'Uncle Nick,' and I think that can happen, even if he's staying upstairs. But second of all, I still believe it was God who brought you and Conny here. I think you know that too. And we all agreed you didn't need to pay room and board until you got a job. That hasn't changed. The fact that you haven't found a job isn't your fault! You've filled out dozens of applications and sent out a zillion résumés. God's been taking care of all our needs, and He'll give you the right job. Just wanted you to know I hope you'll stay.*" It was signed, *"Love, Kat."*

Edesa looked up. "That's . . . quite a note. What do you think?"

Rochelle shrugged. "She didn't say anything about her and Nick. Me having to watch them get all lovey-dovey."

"Maybe she doesn't know how you feel about him—"

A screech from the bedroom brought them both to their feet, and then Gracie flew into the kitchen. "Mommeee! Conny won't give me the yellow one an' I *need* it!"

Conny was right on her heels. "But I had it first! If she takes it, it'll ruin my space station!"

"They're *my* Legos!"

Edesa grabbed Gracie and settled the two-year-old on her hip. "Uh, I think it's time for lunch! How about a picnic on the back porch, *sí?*"

❀

The picnic on the back porch had been a good idea, though Rochelle seemed lost in her thoughts much of the time. And then it was time to go. Conny scrambled into the third seat of the minivan while Edesa strapped Gracie into her car seat in the middle row. "I want Conny to sit with *me*," Gracie pouted.

"I know, *niña*. Another time." Maybe it was a good thing Conny was in the far back, because there was something she'd wanted to ask Rochelle.

She waited until they were on the way, then spoke in a lowered voice. "Rochelle, about the HIV . . . is Conny okay?"

Rochelle glanced furtively into the far backseat. "Yes, thank God! We had him tested after I found out I was infected. I think it happened after he was born, because the doctors said the baby was clean." She was silent a long moment. "But, Edesa . . . in spite of what Nick said, I realize any man who finds out I'm HIV may run the other way. I think I have it under control, and the meds are getting better all the time . . . and I've met some couples where one partner has HIV and they seem to be managing—you know, safe sex and all that. But . . . what if I never meet a guy who's willing to marry me? What if you-know-who"—she jerked a thumb toward the backseat—"never has a real dad? I mean"—her voice trembled—"what if I develop AIDS and . . . and die? What would happen to Conny?"

Edesa cast a quick look at her passenger as the Sheridan El station loomed half a block ahead. Pulling into a parking space, she turned off the motor and faced Rochelle. "*Mi amiga,* listen to me. I'm not going to pretend I know what it's like to be in your shoes. And I understand your desire for family. But worrying about what might happen only robs you of the blessings you do have, right now. You said it yourself—Conny's clean! That's a gift. And he does have family who cares about him—your mom and Peter, to start with. And—"

"Yeah. But they're going to South Africa. What if they decide to stay?"

Edesa smiled. "One day at a time, Rochelle. Don't borrow worries from tomorrow. One thing I know for sure, God knows you inside out, better than you know yourself. If you doubt that, read Psalm 139. We call it the 'Yada Psalm,' because it talks about how intimately God knows us. You're an incredible woman as well as a great mom. You may be surprised what

God has in store for you, the ways He wants to use you to bless others—if you just trust Him with *what is,* rather than worrying about *what isn't.*"

An El train rattled into the station up ahead. Conny's honey-brown face popped up between the two of them. "Mo-om! We just missed the El. Are you and Miss Edesa gonna talk forever?"

Rochelle fished for another tissue, blew her nose again, and gave Edesa a quick hug. "Thanks, Edesa." She opened the door. "Okay, kiddo. Let's go."

Edesa watched as mother and son disappeared into the station before starting the engine. *Oh, Dios, wrap your arms around Rochelle. Let her know how much You love her.*

A few minutes later she pulled up beside Manna House. "Okay, Gracie, let's go see Daddy. He needs his turpentine." Locking the car, she took Gracie's hand and hustled up the steps, rang the doorbell, and was buzzed in. *"Hola,* Angela." She stopped at the receptionist's cubby. "Do you know where my husband is painting?"

"I think down in the rec room. But Miss Gabby told me to tell you to stop by her office first." The Korean girl leaned out the window of her cubby. "Hey there, Gracie. Do you want to help me answer the phone?"

Edesa was about to protest, but Gracie darted into the door at the back of the cubby and crawled up on Angela Kwon's lap. *Oh well, it was her idea, not mine.*

Heading for the lower level, she waved greetings to several of the residents hanging out in Shepherd's Fold. Downstairs, lunch was over and two of the residents were wiping tables and sweeping the floor. Edesa knocked on Gabby Fairbanks's door—the once-upon-a-time broom closet turned into a tiny office.

"Edesa! You're here!" Gabby jumped up from her desk and gave her a hug. "Just a minute . . ." She stepped outside her office and beckoned to someone. A moment later Estelle Bentley squeezed into the office too and pulled the door shut behind her.

Edesa looked from one to the other—Gabby with her head full of red curls and Estelle wearing hers bunched up into that food servers' net cap. "What's going on?" She held up the bag with the can of turpentine. "You said Josh needs this."

"Well, uh, he probably does." Estelle waved dismissively. "I'm sure he can use it to, you know, clean his brushes or something. We just needed to get you here because . . ." She gestured impatiently at Gabby, as if telling her to pick up the conversation.

Gabby nodded, but the corners of her mouth turned up in a tiny smile. "We've been worried about you, Edesa. Complaining about being tired and all that. So we got you something and want you to use it." She picked up a slender package from her desk and handed it to her.

Edesa's eyes widened when she saw what it was. "Oh . . . oh . . . do you think—?"

Estelle stepped away from the door and opened it. "Well, go, girl, and find out!"

Chapter 40

On one hand, Kat thought, things didn't seem that different with Nick living upstairs at the Douglasses'. He still showed up for supper the next night—her turn to cook. Still helped with the dishes and hung around playing with Conny afterward. Still teased Bree about sounding like she was talking in a barrel with that cold of hers.

On the other hand, Kat's whole world had changed. Nick loved her. He'd told Rochelle he wanted to court her—which sounded kind of old-fashioned, but she knew what it meant. Courting wasn't hey-I-like-you-wanna-go-out-on-a-date? It was testing-the-waters-because-I-think-I-want-to-marry-you.

Should she tell her parents she had a serious relationship? Yes, she owed them that much . . . but not yet. She didn't want anything to clip her wings, because right now she felt as if she could fly.

But earth rushed up to meet her on Friday, when Kat realized the first day of the food pantry test run at SouledOut was only one week away—and they had no food. Not one can, not one loaf of bread, not one head of lettuce. In fact, no one out in the neighborhood who might need it even knew there *was* a food pantry starting up at SouledOut Community Church the first Saturday in August! Her head had been so far in the clouds, she hadn't even gone to the Rock of Ages food pantry this past week to let the staff and volunteers know they could refer people there on Saturdays in August.

What had she been thinking?!

Bree had gone back to work at the coffee shop Friday morning and even said she'd take her turn cooking Friday evening. Rochelle hadn't said anything about the note Kat had slipped under her door the other night—hadn't said much of anything, frankly. Kat kind of dreaded supper. Were things going to stay as tense as they'd been the past two nights?

But just as Bree hollered hoarsely that supper was ready, a cell phone rang. Rochelle dug out her cell from the back pocket of her jeans and wandered away from the table. "Hi, Rochelle here . . . Who's this? . . . Edesa? . . . Wait, wait, my Spanish isn't that good. Speak English . . ."

"Can we *eat*?" Conny complained, propping an elbow on the table and kicking the rungs of his chair.

But the next moment Rochelle screeched. "What?! You're *pregnant*? Edesa! That's fantastic!" They all turned, bug-eyed, to look at her and saw Rochelle hopping up and down. *"Edesa's pregnant!"* she mouthed at them and then turned back to the phone. "Why didn't you tell me when I was there yesterday? . . . When? . . . They did *what*?"

Kat grinned at Nick and Bree, whose mouths had dropped. Edesa and Josh Baxter were expecting a baby? That was so cool! Edesa had said Gracie would turn three in August—that was good spacing, wasn't it? She wondered if they'd been trying or if this was a surprise. None of her business, of course.

Rochelle bounced back to the table. "Couldn't believe she didn't say anything yesterday. Conny and I were there, having lunch at her house! But she said she didn't know—not until Gabby Fairbanks and Estelle Bentley tricked her into coming over to Manna House and gave her one of those, uh—" She stopped and eyed Conny, who was busy helping himself to Bree's chicken and rice. Out of his line of vision she made motions with her fingers to describe what Kat could only assume was a home pregnancy "stick" that you peed on. "And it was positive!"

"You mean *they* suspected before she did?" Bree blinked her watery eyes.

Rochelle shrugged. "Well, she's never been pregnant before. She and Josh adopted Gracie, you know."

Nick laughed aloud. "Well, that makes my day! I'm gonna call Josh and put my name on the list for a cigar."

"Oh, right," Kat sputtered. "A cigar-smoking pastoral intern."

"Uhh . . ." Rochelle looked a bit sheepish. "Edesa didn't tell me not to tell you guys, but maybe we should let them tell other people. She might want to tell her Yada Yada sisters—like my mom—herself." She glanced at Conny. "On the other hand, since you-know-who knows, might not be secret long."

Conny rolled his eyes. "My name is *not* 'You-Know-Who.' It's Conrad Johnson the Second—after Mommy's daddy." Which got another laugh.

The tension of the past few nights seemed to have disappeared with the big news. Kat decided to say she was feeling slightly panicked about getting ready to launch the food pantry next weekend, and she asked if anyone could help her post flyers the next day.

Rochelle's eyes widened. "Ohmigosh, I wanted to put the name on the flyers before printing them out—you know, the name we came up with at Yada Yada last Sunday! I gotta ask my dad if he'll let me print them out at Software Symphony tonight!" And she was gone, out the apartment door and running upstairs.

"Wait for me, Mommy! I wanna go to Grampa's work too!" Conny jumped out of his chair and flew after her.

Kat looked at Nick and Bree. "Um, I think that's a 'Thank You, Jesus' moment."

Nick grinned. "Absolutely."

"But . . . I still need some serious prayer about this food pantry. We need food, we need volunteers, we need—"

Bree jumped up. "Volunteers? Hold on, let me get my notebook." She was back in half a minute. "I made a list of the Yada Yada women who volunteered, remember? Phone numbers and everything. I'm sure we're covered for the first Saturday." She flipped pages in her notebook and studied her list. "Yep, yep, not to worry. In fact, you let me worry about making up the volunteer list. Just send anybody to me who wants to help. I'll remind them and everything."

"Oh, Bree, thank you." Kat gave her roomie a hug. But the panic still lingered. "Please, we need to pray about getting enough food to give away. I have no idea how the food collections are going. And I tried to talk to the manager at the big Dominick's in the shopping center to give us any perishables they'd otherwise throw away, but he just hemmed and hawed and told me he'd have to 'check it out' with—"

Rochelle and Conny breezed back into the apartment. "All set." She dangled two sets of keys. "I've got Mom's car if one of you is willing to drive me. I let my license expire."

"I'll take you," Nick said. "But Kat's asking for prayer about pulling this whole thing together between now and next Saturday, so let's do that first. You want to pray with us, Conny?" Nick held out his hands, one to her, one to Conny, and the others joined hands around the table. Kat felt a little weird, Nick holding hands with her on one side, Conny and Rochelle on the other. But his prayer was spot on, that they'd each do what they could do and trust God to bring it all together. "Because we don't want to forget, Jesus, that this food pantry belongs to You. Touch the hearts of people to donate food, and touch the hearts of the people who need it to come. And we look forward to seeing what You're going to do—"

"Amen!" Conny hollered. "Is there any dessert?"

"In fact, there is," Bree simpered. "I was so glad to be feeling better, I bought us two quarts of the coffee shop's fresh strawberry ice cream after my shift. Who wants some?"

No one turned her down . . . and then Nick, Rochelle, and Conny got up to go finish the flyer job at Software Symphony. Kat watched as they went out the door, and for a moment her eyes locked with Rochelle . . . and then they were gone. *Arrgh.* Okay. She was grateful for the support of her housemates, she really was, but she still wrestled with uncomfortable feelings as she loaded the dishwasher—in spite of the note she'd written the other night. There went Nick with Rochelle and Conny like a little family. Had things really changed?

She felt Bree's arms wrap around her from behind. "Hey, you," Bree murmured in her ear, "you've got to trust him, starting now. After all, didn't he tell Rochelle to her face that he's courting *you?*"

"I know," Kat mumbled. "It's just—Rochelle's so doggone gorgeous, how can any guy keep from being attracted to her? And I know he's really attached to Conny. He might have good intentions, but when they're together like that—what if he has second thoughts?"

Bree turned her around and shook a finger in her face. "Now you listen to me, Kat Davies. I've known Nick Taylor longer than you have, and if that guy says he loves *you,* I'd be willing to back it up with a thousand-mile warranty. And that piece of advice will only cost you a promise that you'll let me be your maid of honor."

Kat's mouth dropped. "Whoa! Don't get ahead of me, girl. We haven't . . . we're not . . ." She began to laugh and held out her little finger. "Okay. Your warranty, my pinkie promise." She hooked pinky fingers with Bree, just like she'd done in grade school when she'd promised not to tell the latest whispered secret.

"All riiiight!" giggled Bree, and still holding Kat's pinkie, dragged her over to the refrigerator. "I think we need that second quart of ice cream to seal the deal." By this time they were laughing so hard they both collapsed into chairs at the little kitchen table as they dug into the strawberry ice cream.

"Hey." Nick's voice startled them both. "You two going to leave any of that for me?"

"What are *you* doing back here?" Bree hugged the quart of ice cream possessively. "You forget something? No way you've been to Software Symphony and back already."

"Nope. Rochelle suddenly said she'd changed her mind.

Said she and Conny were going to walk and sent me back." Nick shrugged. "Go figure."

Kat and Bree looked at each other. Kat took the carton of ice cream from her roomie and pushed it toward Nick with a grin. "Knock yourself out."

❋

Kat had to work the early shift at The Common Cup Saturday morning, but she used the occasion to get permission to tape one of the flyers announcing the food pantry in the front window. "Oh, by the way," the manager said, "that wastebasket you put by the door for food donations has been filled up several times this past week, so we emptied it into that big box back in the storeroom. Wouldn't mind if you got it out of there, though."

"Oh!" Kat scurried into the back room. She'd peeked into the wastebasket by the door several times this past week and was disappointed to see how few canned goods had been donated. But the manager had been emptying it into something else? She found the big cardboard box, left over from a shipment of large paper hot cups and lids, and peeked in. Yikes! It was almost full of cans and boxes—canned fruit, canned vegetables, SpaghettiOs, cold cereal, cake mixes, canned sausages, tuna fish . . .

Kat couldn't help grinning. Nick and Rochelle had shown up last night with a trunk full of similar donations from the big bin at Software Symphony. They'd decided to ask Rochelle's mom if they could leave the stuff in the trunk and cart it over to SouledOut sometime this weekend. Now she had to figure out how to get *this* stuff over to the church—but the two donation bins together was at least a start.

Another "Thank You, Jesus" moment.

When Kat got home from work, Nick and Bree and Rochelle were sprawled in the living room, air conditioner on high speed, looking as if they'd just plowed the back forty. That, or they were really hooked on the Smurfs DVD Conny was watching. She told them the good news about the box full of donated food at the coffee shop, and Bree waved the last few flyers. They'd been out in the neighborhood all morning, posting flyers along Howard Street, Morse Avenue, Clark Street, Touhy, Lunt, a couple of El stations, and even in the windows of stores in the shopping center close to the church.

Kat got a sudden lump in her throat. "Wow. Can't thank you guys enough. I was planning on doing that this afternoon—but maybe I'll go bat my eyelashes at the store manager at Dominick's and see if he's ready to cough up some produce and perishables next week." She was hoping to get a rise out of Nick with her flirty joke. Maybe he'd even offer to come with her to protect her honor, ha-ha.

"I've got a better idea." Rochelle waved a hand from one of the beanbag chairs. "If you can wait till my mom picks up Conny around two, I'll go with you, okay? She wants to spend some special time with him today—feeling guilty about leaving the country, if you ask me."

Okaay. Kat didn't know what Rochelle's "better idea" was, but at this point she wasn't going to turn down any offers to help. As for Nick, she ought to know better than to play flirty games. If she wanted him to come with her, she should've just asked.

Nick, collapsed like a marathon runner on the couch, raised his sunglasses slightly and peered out. "Uhhh, okay . . . if you guys are going to hit up the store, I'll figure out a way to pick up the stuff from the coffee shop and get it to the church. But as long as you're at the grocery store, can you pick up some stuff I need for supper? We're going to celebrate." He grinned at Kat before hiding once again behind the sunglasses.

Celebrate? What was he talking about? But picking up some groceries and wheeling the grocery cart up to the manager wasn't a bad idea . . . Here they were, loyal customers, asking a favor from her "favorite grocery store," which would be no skin off their nose.

The manager wasn't impressed. "Sorry, ladies, I'm kind of busy. Haven't had time to talk to the head office yet. Why don't you try—"

"Excuse me." Rochelle shouldered her way in front of Kat and her cart. "Mr."—she peered at his name tag—"Mr. Hernández. It's not going to look too good when one of your customers writes to the Chicago *Sun Times* to tell them that perfectly good food from a major grocery store chain is going to waste when it could be used to feed hungry families in the Rogers Park neighborhood, simply because a certain store manager—the *Sun Times* likes details, names are good—is too busy to consider this very simple request. Chicago has a long history of using boycotts to express their displeasure with businesses that ignore the needs of the people."

It was all Kat could do to keep her face straight. Consumer pressure. Why didn't she think of that?

"On the other hand"—Rochelle shrugged with a *why not* gesture—"it could be very good public relations for this store if SouledOut Community Church, located right here in the shopping center, was able to list this store as one of the primary donors to its new food pantry. Don't you think? As you can see"—she waved a hand between herself and Kat—"we represent a very diverse community—white, black, and yes, Latino too. Mm-hmm. Yes, very good public relations, Mr. Hernández."

Kat pressed her lips together to keep from laughing. The store manager looked extremely uncomfortable. "Well . . . I will need something official," he said. "On church letterhead and signed by a . . . one of your trustees or something. And a notarized waiver that any problems resulting from donated food will not be used to bring any kind of legal repercussions against this store."

Rochelle looked at Kat. "Sounds reasonable to me. What do you think, Ms. Davies?"

Kat nodded. "Absolutely. We'll bring a letter and a waiver early next week." She extended her hand and shook his. "Thank you *so* much, Mr. Hernández. Your community spirit will not go unnoticed. Oh—the food pantry opens next weekend. What day should we pick up the donated food?"

They took their cart through the self-checkout line, since they didn't have that many groceries. Kat felt giddy with success but managed to act nonchalant until they exited the store—and then she couldn't help laughing with excitement. "Rochelle! You were priceless! You oughta be a . . . a union organizer or a foreign diplomat or something. He was putty in your hands."

Rochelle grinned. "Yeah. My dad—my real dad—used to say I could talk him into anything and make him think it was his idea." Her eyes got a distant look and she fell quiet. Then, "I miss him. Might not have married Dexter if he'd been around. I was needing somebody, something. But he died from pancreatic cancer, you know."

No, Kat didn't know. There weren't exactly framed photos

sitting around the Douglasses' apartment of the first "Mr. Avis." Probably in an album.

Rochelle shrugged. "Peter's all right. I'm happy for my mom . . . We're getting along all right now. It was just hard, you know, losing my dad."

Kat didn't know what to say. Rochelle had never opened up to her like this before.

"And, by the way, wanted to say I got your note the other night. Thanks."

That was all she said. But it was enough for Kat.

❀

Nick cooked up a fabulous batch of lemon-pepper shrimp pasta for their Saturday supper. Even took off his sunglasses, in spite of the raccoon-like mask around his eyes, though the bruises were now starting to fade. Conny was still out with his grandma, so it was just the four adults around the table.

"So what's the celebration?" Bree asked. "Gee, candles and everything."

"If this is about the food pantry," Kat put in, "maybe we should wait until next weekend—*after* we survive the launch of the test run. *If* we survive."

Nick grinned. "Nope. We're celebrating the prayers God's already been answering. Kat, you were all stressed out last night about not having any food for the food pantry—and now look. Donations from Software Symphony, from The Common Cup, and by the time people come to worship tomorrow at SouledOut, I bet that bin will be full too. Celebrating now is faith that God's going to provide all we need."

Kat's ears perked. Did he just say, *"All 'we' need"*?

"And don't forget the donations our friend, Mr. Hernández, says he'll give," Rochelle added with a smirk.

"All riiiight!"

"A toast!"

"Thank You, Jesus, for what You're going to do!"

They all clinked their glasses of lemonade and ice water, then let Nick dish up the heavenly pasta and garlic bread.

But for Kat, the celebration spilled over into the evening when Nick murmured, "Wanna go for a walk? Nice night out there."

She almost felt delirious with joy as they walked hand in hand to the lake, not feeling any special need to talk, just enjoying the slight breeze coming off the water and the playful sounds of people throwing Frisbees in the park and dog-walkers tossing balls for their pooches. They found the same bench along the jogging path facing the lake—forever "their" bench—and as they sat, Kat leaned against him, Nick's arm around her pulling her close.

She finally broke their comfortable silence. "Nick, I can't thank you enough for all the support you've been giving to the food pantry. I don't take it for granted. I mean, I know you've got work and all your pastoral responsibilities. I don't want you to feel obligated to, you know, add the food pantry too."

He didn't respond for a long moment. Then he murmured into her hair, "I disagree. Because if I want to be courting Kat Davies, then what concerns her concerns me too. So maybe this food pantry has to be *our* project. Don't you think?"

Chapter 41

Nick was right. By the time Kat got to SouledOut the next morning, people had already brought boxes and shopping bags full of canned goods and nonperishables and were dumping them into the donation bin. By the time worship was over, Kat saw that the bin for the food pantry was nearly full—both from regular SouledOut members and from stuff collected by the sisters in the Yada Yada Prayer Group.

Which was great! Except—where were they were going to store all this stuff until next Saturday?

True to her word, Bree went around with her notebook after the service, asking people if they'd like to sign up as a volunteer for the food pantry. A whole crowd of teenagers was signing up.

Yikes. What if they had *too* many volunteers?

Kat and Nick counted the long tables that usually came out for the Second Sunday Potluck and talked about how to set up the pantry. A separate table for different kinds of food? A table for fruits and vegetables, a table for canned meats and main dishes, a table for condiments and miscellaneous, a table for desserts and sweets, and a couple of tables for whatever the grocery store donated. Bread and baked goods? Dairy products? Fresh fruits and vegetables? Well, semi-fresh at least. They wouldn't know until Thursday, which was when Mr. Hernández said they could come to the back of the store and pick up some boxes of stuff pulled off the shelves to make room for new deliveries.

When they reported to Pastor Cobbs after the service, he said he'd have a letter ready for them by the time Nick got to the pastoral meeting Monday night. "But if you could get the waiver notarized, Nick, I'd appreciate it—wait, that won't work." The pastor scratched his nubby salt-and-pepper hair. "I suppose it's my signature that needs to be notarized. Hmm, I think one of our trustees is a notary—I'll ask him to do it."

Kat felt a little guilty about the extra work for the pastor and promised they'd make sure everything was cleaned up after the food pantry and set up for Sunday morning.

The last week in July seemed to crawl like a tortoise trekking across the Mohave Desert—but also whirled by so fast, Kat could hardly believe it when Friday, August first, arrived. It was the last day of the Summer Tutoring and Enrichment Program at Bethune Elementary. Yusufu Balozi came dressed in a shirt and tie and presented her with a gift—a small wood carving of a mother with three children. A little sticker on the bottom said Made in Uganda. Yusufu grinned wide and pointed at the woman. "That is you, Miss Kat! And Kevin and Latoya and me!"

Kat turned the carving this way and that. She was touched . . . even though the carving was of a native woman with a baby at a bared breast and tightly coiled hair, and the other two children clung to her skirt.

Latoya decided she wanted to give Kat a gift too and pulled a hair rubber with a little red bead off one of her braids and wound it around a clump of Kat's hair. "Don't ever take it off, Miz Kat," the little girl said solemnly.

"Thank you, Latoya." Kat gave her a squeeze. "It's a very sweet gift and will remind me of you." Which was true, though she definitely wasn't going to make a pinky promise never to take it off.

Kevin decided to make her a card with the art supplies. The outside of the folded piece of paper said "I LIKE MATH" in bubble letters, and the inside said "GOODBYE from KEVIN." It was decorated with pluses, minuses, and division signs. Well, if Kevin liked math, Kat could chalk up her six weeks of tutoring at STEP as a huge success.

After a short assembly in the gym, which included any parents who showed up, where each of the kids received a certificate of completion, the last morning was spent as a "field day" out on the playground, with three-legged races, tug-of-war, and a marshmallow-and-spoon relay, followed by grilled hot dogs, potato chips, and ice cream bars. Not a veggie to be seen. Kat sighed. She thought by now Mrs. Douglass would've made *some* effort to include some healthier choices.

Kat had to excuse herself before the hoopla was over, as she'd agreed to a double shift at the coffee shop today in order to take Saturday off. But Mrs. Douglass called to her before she got out the gate. "Just a minute, Kathryn! I have something for you." Kat waited as Bethune's principal, dressed for the day in white athletic pants with turquoise piping down the leg and a white and turquoise T-shirt, met her at the playground gate.

"Here." Avis handed her an envelope. "I thought you might

like to have a copy of the recommendation I mailed to the school board. And"—she also handed Kat a package, shirt-box size, tied with red, white, and blue ribbons—"just a little appreciation gift for the fine work you did this summer. I think you're going to make a fine teacher." With that, Mrs. Douglass gave her a quick hug and trotted back to the throng of children clamoring for seconds on ice cream bars.

Kat was stunned. She hadn't expected to see a copy of the recommendation, much less a gift from Mrs. D. She was tempted to open them both then and there, but decided to at least wait until she got to work. Arriving at the coffee shop a few minutes early, Kat stowed her backpack and found a corner in the back room where she could open the letter and the package. Her eyes teared up as she read the letter. *"I highly recommend this candidate . . ."*

She sure was chalking up a lot of "Thank You, Jesus!" moments.

Slipping the ribbon off the box, Kat pulled out a canvas tote bag. On the side it said, *"Teachers write on the hearts of their students, things the world will never erase."* Now she did have to fish for a tissue and blow her nose. "Oh, Jesus, please make me worthy of being a teacher," she whispered.

"Hey, Kat!" One of the other baristas—the guy she called Billy the Kid—poked his head into the back room. "Is that food pantry thing you're collecting for starting tomorrow? If so, we've got a whole bag of day-old bagels you could take with you, 'cause they ain't gonna sell here. Still good in my not-so-humble opinion."

Grinning, Kat tied on her apron and headed out into the main room. One more "Thank You, Jesus" moment.

✤

Kat, Nick, Bree, Rochelle, and Conny were at SouledOut Saturday morning by eight o'clock to set up tables and organize the donated food. Even with the air-conditioning on, Kat was sweating from sheer nervousness. Would they get everything set up in time for the doors to open at ten? Would they have enough food? What if no one showed up and they were stuck with all this stuff?

Nick had asked Josh *"Gonna be a new daddy"* Baxter if he had a few hours on Thursday to help him pick up the promised boxes of food at Dominick's in the church van. "A lot easier than making a dozen trips carrying those boxes across the parking lot," Nick had told Kat later that night. "We definitely needed the van—we loaded at least six big boxes. We stored as much of it as we could in the refrigerators and freezers in the kitchen. But you'll have to decide what's usable."

The whole Baxter clan showed up early on Saturday morning as well, including Josh's home-from-college sister, Amanda. This generated a lot of squeals as Kat, Bree, and Rochelle hugged Edesa and Josh, the new parents-to-be, and congratulated Jodie and Denny, the grinning grandparents-to-be. "Hey! What about me?" Amanda pouted. "Doesn't the auntie get any recognition? After all, I'm the designated Chief Babysitter." Which earned her a round of hugs and congratulations too.

Then it was down to business.

Conny was given the "job" of entertaining Gracie in the nursery, and while Nick, Josh, and Denny set up tables, the women surveyed the piles of food stacked everywhere in the kitchen. Kat pulled open the doors of the two steel refrigerators—and gasped. "Ohmigosh, look at this." Plastic containers of already-prepared potato salad, shrimp-and-pasta salad, and other ready-to-eat deli food filled one whole shelf.

"Hmm. I don't know about those." Jodi Baxter frowned. "I'd toss them if I were you, waiver or no waiver. What else did they send?"

Bree flipped her notebook to a clean page and they took inventory: ten loaves of bakery bread, still good. Carrots, broccoli, green beans, cabbages, and turnips—just a tad on the wilted side—still okay. Plastic containers of strawberries and blueberries, probably salvageable. Sweet rolls and coffee cakes, probably okay if not too stale. Dented cans, dated yogurts and puddings . . .

Several SouledOut teenagers showed up at nine, along with Yo-Yo Spencer and Leslie Stuart from Yada Yada. All of them were put to work hauling the donated food out of the kitchen and sorting foods by tables.

"Bags! We need plastic grocery bags!" Kat felt a momentary panic. She'd totally forgotten about people needing bags to take stuff home in.

"Don't worry." Jodie Baxter poked her head into one of the lower cupboards in the kitchen and pulled out a box. "We've got a lot of those stuffed in here."

"And some people bring their own," Rochelle reminded her. "Remember the folks who came to Rock of Ages? Most of them brought their own bags. But look—we've got more to worry about than bags. We need to decide how many people to let in at a time, how much food each family is allowed to take, stuff like that. Why don't we get everybody together and decide how we're going to do this?"

Kat was a little taken aback by Rochelle jumping in and taking charge—though she couldn't fault her suggestions. Josh and Nick were assigned to man the doors, like Tony did at Rock of Ages. Bree with her handy notebook volunteered to sign people in—name, address, zip code—to get an idea of how many local people had found them. All the other volunteers would either accompany each customer one-on-one as they went from table to table, explaining how much they could take from each category, or were assigned to a table to help keep it neat and explain "what this is."

As the hands of the wall clock nudged ten, Kat glanced outside. "Oh, Nick, look." At least twenty people were lined up outside SouledOut's front door. "Do you think we ought to pray or something before we unlock the doors?"

"Great idea." Calling all the volunteers to join hands in a circle, Nick asked Denny Baxter, as one of SouledOut's elders, to ask for God's blessing and protection on this first food pantry. As he was praying, Kat peeked through half-closed lids at the circle of volunteers, young and old, hoping she would remember every face so she could thank them all personally . . . and her eye caught a movement at the double doors leading into the back rooms. Pastor Cobbs poked his head into the room, seemed to take in the tables piled with food and the prayer circle, and a smile spread over his face before he withdrew and let the doors quietly shut again.

It felt like a blessing.

Whatever it was, it was the lull before the storm. As the circle broke up and people took their places, Nick and Josh unlocked the doors and let in the first four people—a middle-aged Hispanic couple and two rather disheveled white men, one of whom had tattoos on every inch of visible skin. While the couple was being signed in, the other two headed straight for the tables.

"Uh, sirs?" Kat put on her friendliest smile. "We're glad you're here. But you need to sign in first."

"Oh. Okay." One of the men shuffled back to Brygitta's table by the door.

But Tattoo Guy glared at her. "Why?" His tone was belligerent.

Kat swallowed. Good question. Did she have an answer?

Rochelle inserted herself between them. "Because that's the way we're doing it here. You need to sign in or leave."

"Oh, tough lady, eh?" The man reached around them and grabbed an apple from the table, but before they could say anything, he turned and went back to the sign-in table, munching on the apple.

"Okay. Forget the apple," Rochelle muttered to Kat. "But assign Denny Baxter to walk him through, not one of the teens. I'll take the other guy." And she scurried off with a couple of plastic bags.

Kat stood there, momentarily frozen. Why did she have these conflicted feelings? Grateful that Rochelle had stepped in and told Tattoo Guy what's what—and annoyed at the same time. And what was wrong with her? If she was going to do this thing, she needed to develop more of a backbone.

Most of the people who came through were cooperative, though one guy let a "lady friend" into the line ahead of others who'd been waiting an hour. Several people complained, and Nick had to go out and tell her she needed to go to the end of the line.

Just as she'd seen at the Rock of Ages food pantry, about half the people seemed to be working-class men and women or single moms on welfare, some with children tagging along, who just needed help with the groceries. The rest, Kat guessed, were living in single-room-only "hotels," a number with apparent mental problems, and a few who seemed genuinely homeless, their carts and bags parked outside the church.

She had to grin when who should turn up but Lady Lolla, dressed for the occasion in a full-skirted, peach-colored taffeta dress with a six-inch trim of feathers around the hem, which fell to midcalf. Kat greeted her warmly and took her around to the tables herself. "How's, uh, Ike?" she ventured, hoping she'd remembered the name of Lolla's "significant other."

"Oh, not so good . . . stomach bothers him, you know. You got any cans of chicken noodle soup? That goes down easy."

Kat searched the table of canned goods. No chicken noodle soup. Just dented cans of tomato and fat cans of beef stew. "Just a minute," she said, then slipped into the kitchen. She'd seen some cans of stuff left over from potlucks and youth group suppers in one of the cupboards, but she didn't turn up any chicken noodle soup.

She had to return to Lady Lolla empty-handed. "But tell you what," she said. "If you come back next Saturday, I'll be sure to have some chicken noodle soup for you. How many cans do you need?" Even if she had to buy them herself.

Sending Lady Lolla out the door with two loaves of bread, some canned fruit, and some of the fresh vegetables, Kat noticed that Edesa had taken one of the young women aside—a black girl who didn't look more than eighteen, who had one baby in a front carrier and a toddler by the hand—and was praying with her. Seated in a couple of chairs, the girl was crying, and Edesa had an arm around her.

Kat watched furtively. How did Edesa know the girl needed prayer? Or know she'd be willing to let Edesa pray with her, right there with people milling about?

She glanced toward the front doors. Nick was outside, talking to some of the people still waiting, though the line had thinned. Something he'd said when he'd preached his inaugural SouledOut sermon two weeks ago about "Feed My sheep" resurrected itself in her mind: *"Life is more than food and the body more than clothes . . ."* He was quoting Jesus about that too, she was pretty sure.

And there it was, right in front of her. People were hungry, true. That was obvious by the number of people who'd shown up today—at least thirty. But this girl—and probably most of them, if they'd admit it—was hungry for more than food. Hungry to know someone cared. Someone who'd listen. Hungry for love. Hungry for forgiveness or encouragement or . . . hope. Hungry for . . . well, hungry for Jesus, even if they didn't know it.

Kat suddenly found it hard to catch her breath. God had been calling her to feed people. But maybe giving them food was the easy part.

Was she ready to *really* feed them?

She might have to actually get to know these "food pantry people" as people God loved.

To know all of them by name.

Chapter 42

In spite of all the food they'd collected, they ran out of most items before noon, causing grumbles with the people who came last. The "sweets and desserts" and bread tables were completely bare, and most of the canned goods were gone, leaving only dented cans of specialty foods like asparagus, artichoke hearts, pickled beets, and diced pimentos. The perishables from Dominick's had been well picked over, and even Kat agreed they needed to toss what was left.

As they cleaned up, Kat pulled Nick aside. "What do you think of asking the volunteers to stay a few extra minutes to give feedback? This is a test run, you know, and any suggestions for next time would be helpful."

"Good idea." Nick grinned. "Rochelle was just saying the same thing."

Rochelle was just saying the same thing.

Kat tried to ignore the flash of irritation, like an annoying gremlin sticking its claws in her psyche. But she'd better do it or Rochelle might do it for her. She raised her voice. "Anybody who can stay to debrief for five or ten minutes, I'd appreciate it. We need your input."

A couple of the teens had split already, Stu had to leave for an appointment with a client, and Edesa excused herself to put Gracie down for a nap and lie down herself at her in-laws' house nearby. But once the tables were put away and chairs set up for Sunday, Kat was glad to see that the rest gathered at the back of the room.

Comments ranged from "I thought it went great!" to "Some people took more than they were supposed to." Some had questions: "What if two people from the same family come—do they both get to load up a bag?" and "Shouldn't a family with six kids get more than a single person? I felt funny saying they could only take one loaf of bread."

Kat squirmed when one of the teen girls reported a woman who cussed and made crude remarks. "I told her this was a church, and she shouldn't take God's name in vain, but all she said was—uh, never mind." A few people chuckled.

There were suggestions: "We're going to need more food," Denny Baxter noted. "I mean, more than we had today. Word's going to get around and more people will show up."

"Maybe we should set up a fund and just buy stuff."

"Could we make up a list of the foods people want most?" Yo-Yo asked. "I mean, look at what we've got left over. Even I don't like pickled beets." More laughter.

Brcc was taking notes furiously. Kat caught a high sign from Nick that maybe that was enough debriefing for now.

"Okay, thanks a lot, everybody. We obviously don't have all the answers today, but we're learning as we go along. Please pass the word that we need more food donations! Not just for next week, but all month long."

"People are going to get tired of that before long," Rochelle said, half under her breath. "We need to do something more sustainable."

Yeah, thanks a lot, Rochelle. This *was* their first day, after all! Kat covered her frustration by asking "Pastor Nick" to close in prayer. And once again they joined hands in a circle. But while he was praying, Kat was praying her own prayer. *God, I know I'm over my head here, and I'm grateful for everyone who turned out to help today—and I admit, Rochelle's been a big help too. But why does it feel like she's trying to take over? This is my project, and—*

"Amen," Nick said and squeezed her hand. Kat felt a little guilty. She hadn't really paid any attention to his prayer, though she was sure it was appropriate. And in spite of a few moments of frustration that morning, she felt excited. At least thirty people had shown up today! And most of them had gone home with a big bag of food.

Okay, now she was ready to call her parents. Should she tell them about Nick or the food pantry? Both might be a little much, but . . . oh, heck, why not!

❋

To Kat's delight, Pastor Cobbs called her to the front during the announcements the next morning and handed her the mike. "Give us a report on how things went with the first food pantry, Kathryn. From what I could see, it was a big success."

Kat could barely control her excitement. It felt good to be acknowledged by the pastor. "First, let's see the hands of everyone from SouledOut who volunteered yesterday . . . yes, I see your hand, Gracie. And you too, Conny." Everyone laughed. "I just want to thank all of you who donated food or have signed up to help out on Saturday morning this month at the SouledOut Sisters Food Pantry—and you can blame the Yada Yada Prayer Group for the name." More laughter. "But we couldn't have done it without several brothers too—Peter Douglass, Denny Baxter, Josh Baxter, Pastor Nick, some of the teen boys . . . thanks." She told how many people had been served—thirty-two by Bree's count of the sign-ins—and said they still needed a lot of prayer *and* a lot more food donations. "There's a sheet at the back with a list of the most popular items, and the ones starred have the most nutritional value. Some treats are okay, but please avoid unusual items."

"Uh, miss?" A hand was waving in the air. "Define unusual."

Kat was startled to see the black girl Edesa had been praying with yesterday waving the sheet of paper. She stood up. "Hi, y'all. My name's Diane Pickering. I came to the food pantry yesterday. Uh, Miss Edesa invited me to come this morning. An' I picked this up before service, and I noticed you don't have okra or black-eyed peas, stuff like that on the list. Stuff a lot of black folks like."

Kat was taken off guard. *Okra?* Did people actually eat that stuff? She felt her face get hot. Why couldn't people ask stuff like that privately instead of embarrassing her in front of everybody? "Well, uh . . ."

Pastor Cobbs bounded to her side and took the mike. "Like we said, church, this is a trial run." He put his arm around Kat, who looked down at her shoes. "Your suggestion is a good one, young lady"—this to the new girl—"and I'm sure Kathryn and the others will take your suggestion to heart. But let's give thanks to our Lord and Savior for the people, like this young lady, who came to the food pantry yesterday and—"

Heads turning and a rustling throughout the congregation made Kat look up. The front doors opened and she was startled to see Lady Lolla and a skinny white man using a cane come in. Lolla was dressed as outlandishly as ever, wearing a dingy sleeveless sheath that might have been white or cream once upon a time and ended above her knees, revealing her bony shoulders and knees. Long ropes of cheap Mardi Gras beads dangled around her neck. "'Scuse us," Lady Lolla said, guiding the man—was that Ike?—to a seat near the back. She grinned at the people around her. "'Mornin' . . . 'mornin'.'"

Even Pastor Cobbs seemed a bit taken aback, but he quickly recovered. "Thank you, Kathryn." He was dismissing her, and Kat gratefully hurried back to her seat next to Brygitta. "Our message this morning will be brought by Sister Avis. We also want to pray with her and Elder Peter, who will be leaving tomorrow for two weeks in South Africa . . . Sister Avis? Elder?"

Kat tried to listen as the Douglasses briefly explained the purpose of their trip, to learn more about the work former SouledOut members Nonyameko and Mark Sisulu-Smith were doing with at-risk women in KwaZulu-Natal, setting up small businesses so these women didn't have to sell their bodies just to survive. Any other time, Kat would have joined the group of people who gathered around the Douglasses at the front to pray for their upcoming trip, but she still felt too embarrassed at the way her food pantry report had been co-opted by that mouthy girl.

But after the prayer, as Avis Douglass opened her Bible and

noted the text—the Last Supper with Jesus and His disciples from the gospel of John, chapter 13—Kat fell under the spell of the rich cadence of her voice telling the familiar story. "Notice," Avis said, "that Jesus shared the symbols of the sacrifice He was about to make—the broken bread and the cup of wine—not with a group of holy disciples who had their act together, but with a group of imperfect followers He knew would run away when the temple police arrested Him. Peter—of all people!—after Jesus had washed his feet like a servant, denied that he even knew Jesus that same night. And Judas . . . Jesus even shared the broken bread and wine with the man who betrayed Him. Who sold Him out for thirty pieces of silver."

The room was so quiet, no one seemed to be breathing. Unusual for SouledOut, Kat thought. Where was Avis going with this?

"Jesus shared this Last Supper—what we now call communion or the Lord's Table—with these imperfect, sinful, doubting, backstabbing so-called followers, using the very symbols we will share together this morning to remember the broken body and spilled blood of our Savior. Are we any different? All of us come to the Table imperfect, broken, guilty of denying our Savior, doubting . . . and yet Jesus offers His gift of love and forgiveness to each and every one of us. He died for you. He died for me. None of us deserves it. It was simply an act of God's mercy and grace."

Avis closed her Bible. "Let's remember that as we take communion together this morning." She sat down.

The room seemed deathly quiet. Then Pastor Cobbs and Nick brought the table forward that contained the loaf of bread and a common cup. Kat stared at the embroidered cloth covering the table, with the colorful figures of children around the world. *"Red and yellow, black and white, they are precious in His sight . . ."* She'd never sung that little song as a kid—didn't go to Sunday school that often—but she'd heard it a few times since her own decision to follow Jesus at that music fest several years ago. *Precious in His sight . . .*

People started to go forward to receive the bread and wine. She was startled to see Lady Lolla and "Ike" sashay down the aisle too. Really? Oh brother, what a pair.

Precious in His sight . . .

The girl who'd put her on the spot joined the line moving slowly forward. Her too?

Precious in His sight . . .

Rochelle was heading for Nick, who was breaking bits from the loaf of bread for each comer. Why did she feel so threatened by Rochelle? Was she afraid Avis's beautiful daughter was going to steal Nick—even though Nick had openly declared his love for her? Was she afraid Rochelle was going to take over the pantry—*her* baby, *her* project? *She* wanted the credit for it.

Kat moaned. *Oh, God, I'm such a jerk sinner. Do I really care about feeding people? Getting hungry people fed? And feeding them real spiritual food too—like Edesa did when she loved on that girl and prayed with her yesterday? Or am I just one self-centered white girl who wants to steal some of Your glory?*

The tears were coming hard and fast now. She felt Bree slip an arm around her. "Kat? Kat?" her friend whispered. "What's wrong? Are you okay?"

Kat nodded, snuffled, blew her nose, and mopped her face. She got out of her seat and joined the line, Bree hovering behind her. When she got to where Nick was breaking off bits of bread, he looked at her with concern—she was probably a blotchy mess—but all he did was put a piece of bread in her cupped hands and murmur, "The body of Christ, broken for you, Kat."

Broken for me . . . because I'm a sinner and need His forgiveness.

Kat stepped over to where Pastor Cobbs was holding the cup and dipped her bread into the dark liquid. "The blood of Christ, spilled for you, Kathryn," the pastor said, smiling at her.

She placed the bread, soaked in wine, into her mouth . . . and felt herself being fed.

Chapter 43

The plan was for Nick to drive the Douglasses to the airport early the next morning, with Rochelle and Conny riding along to see them off. Kat and Bree padded out to the back porch to wave good-bye, but when Kat saw all of them piling into Mrs. D's Toyota, she felt a flicker of familiar irritation. The girl needed to get her driver's license renewed! Or Nick would keep getting dragged into these "family moments" with Rochelle and Conny—

No. She couldn't keep going there. "Pinch me, Bree," she muttered under her breath while smiling and waving at the party below.

"What?"

"Just pinch me. Whenever I ask you to. I'm trying to exorcise a nasty little gremlin."

Bree looked at the car pulling away and back to Kat. "Uh-huh. I get it. Okay." And she pinched Kat's arm—hard.

"Ow!"

"Next time it'll be harder!" Bree threatened, banging the screen door on her way back into the kitchen.

Kat followed—but she felt a kind of emptiness, knowing the Douglasses were going to be gone for the next two weeks. Their presence upstairs had been a kind of anchor to this whole crazy idea of spending the summer in the city . . . and now they were gone. She poured herself a cup of coffee and went back out onto the porch. Not only that, but the STEP program was over. No more volunteer mornings over at Bethune Elementary, acting like a teacher.

But if she felt this way, how must Rochelle feel? Her mom and stepdad were flying thousands of miles away to another continent, scouting a program to help women who were victims of the scourge of HIV and AIDS—

HIV and AIDS . . . Rochelle had HIV, though with her anti-retroviral meds, she seemed as healthy as the next person right now, and most of the time Kat didn't think about it at all. But was Rochelle's condition part of the reason Mrs. D was on this journey to the other side of the world?

She should be praying more. Praying for the Douglasses' trip, praying for Rochelle's health . . . *Hmm.* Maybe praying for Rochelle would be better than a pinch from Bree to nip the green-eyed gremlin in the bud.

More effective, no doubt.

Certainly less painful. Her arm was still sore from Bree's pinch.

Thunder rumbled in the distance. Uh-oh. An early thunderstorm. But at least she didn't have to scurry through the rain to Bethune this morning. *Okay, Jesus, here's what I'm thinking. On the mornings I don't have to work the early shift at the coffee shop, I'm going to spend more time praying this month. Okay with You?*

A lightning flash lit up the sky in the distance.

Kat chuckled. "Okay, okay! It's a deal." God could take a joke, right?

But seriously, she should get her notebook and start making a prayer list: Rochelle. The Douglasses. A job this fall—hopefully teaching. The food pantry. Not just the food pantry, but the people who came. Lady Lolla and Ike and the girl named Diane for starters. Next week she'd learn more names so she could pray for people by name—

Wait. Bree had written down everybody's name when they signed in! Even Tattoo Guy. She could pray for everybody by name who came this past weekend, even if she couldn't put all the names with faces yet. She was going to need some help there.

Her eyes widened. That's it! That's what they should do. It would help all the volunteers get to know people by name—and vice versa.

Name tags!

❀

What was it about time that felt like a paradox? The two weeks that the Douglasses were gone seemed to creep by, dragging them all into the dog days of summer. Mid-August was hot and sultry, with frequent thundershowers, leaving the sidewalks and streets steaming in the heat. Sometimes Kat just collapsed in the living room of their apartment, worn out from the heat. One thing she had to say for growing up in Phoenix: at least the heat was dry—not this steam bath.

At the same time, Kat felt like she didn't have enough time to do all that needed to be done to keep the food pantry up and running for five Saturdays. Between her shifts at the coffee shop and sending out more résumés—to preschools, private schools, special ed programs, activity centers, park programs, English as a second language programs, and responding to ads for tutors—she had to deal with Friday Panic every week, sure that the whole food pantry idea would crash and burn before the end of the month.

At least she remembered to buy four cans of chicken noodle soup for Lady Lolla to take home to Ike.

But she had to admit . . . if Rochelle wasn't putting in so much time contacting potential food donors, printing out more flyers, and brainstorming ideas to make things more efficient, things wouldn't be going as smoothly as they were.

Not that everything was going smoothly.

It was still touch-and-go about getting a balance of foods to offer. "We need to sign up with the Chicago Food Depository!" Rochelle kept insisting. "Ask people to donate money instead of food, and we can place an order for what we need from the Depository—for pennies!"

Kat threw up her hands. "But we're still on trial at SouledOut! We can't do anything that official until the church agrees that this is a go."

"Humph. Wouldn't hurt to apply. Takes awhile anyway."

And not everyone liked the idea of name tags. She had to cajole the teen volunteers to wear them. It wasn't cool, they whined. It was babyish. "But it helps the people we serve be able to call you by name. It's more personal." But even when they took a name tag, they slapped it somewhere "cool"—and unnoticeable—on their arm or jeans. *Arrgh.*

And some of the patrons were suspicious. "Who wants

to know?" Usually the same ones who didn't want to sign in either.

But the bumpy ride even carried over to Sunday. "This is a church?" some of the people asked as they came in the doors on Saturday and saw the banners along one wall. "Can anybody come?" And some of them came—a shy young Latino couple with two children, two harmless men with mental disabilities, and even a few of the dedicated homeless, dragging their carts inside. Some of them liked it and came back the next Sunday too—including Lady Lolla in her floozy dresses, sometimes accompanied by Ike, who sat in his chair nodding off with an occasional snore.

Which didn't sit well with a few of the SouledOut members. Nick came back to the three-flat from a Monday night pastoral meeting with Pastor Cobbs saying some people were complaining, though he wouldn't say who. "They're saying some of these marginal people might frighten the children." Nick made a face. "I doubt that it's the *children* who mind."

Kat was curled up beside Nick on the couch. They were alone, but only because Rochelle was putting Conny to bed and Bree had discreetly disappeared into the bedroom. She frowned. "We're not going to tell people not to come, are we? I know some of them are a bit strange, but—"

"No, no. Of course they're welcome—though Pastor Cobbs liked my suggestion. We could assign some of the members to be a 'Sunday Buddy' for anyone who might be 'marginal' or acting inappropriately. You know, just to sit with them, explain what's going on, remind them to be quiet if necessary—that kind of thing."

"Great idea," Kat murmured, somewhat distracted by Nick's

arm casually lying across her shoulders. "We could ask some of the pantry volunteers to do that—they're already getting to know our 'customers.' Though . . ." Now it was Kat who made a face. "A few of those folks could use a bath. It might be hard to sit next to them for two hours."

"Yeah, well, I have the opposite problem sitting next to you, Kitty Kat." Nick chuckled and drew her a bit closer, nuzzling her hair. "Two hours isn't long enough. Mm . . . what's that apple stuff you use on your hair?"

❀

Kat couldn't help worrying about Nick, alone in the Douglasses' apartment. He'd basically decided they shouldn't be up there alone together—"It's not that I don't trust *you*, Kat," he'd said awkwardly, "but I'm not sure I trust myself"—so they spent most of their time hanging out with the others in the sublet, or on long walks along the lake.

But what if Dexter showed up again while Nick was alone and got into the building somehow? Rochelle had gotten the order of protection and so far he hadn't shown up, though she'd gotten several phone calls—which violated the order of protection—but Rochelle had just decided to ignore them. But what if he knew Peter and Avis were gone?

Kat added a squad of guardian angels around the three-flat to her daily prayer list.

At least Nick's black eyes had basically faded by the time he preached again during the Douglasses' absence. And the painful bruising in his midsection from where he'd been punched had subsided, making it possible for Kat and Nick to pick up some

Jamaican jerk chicken after the service and take a long walk to "their" bench along the lakefront for a spontaneous Sunday afternoon picnic, this time without pain.

"That was a good sermon, Nick," she said as they munched the spicy chicken and licked their fingers, watching the fascinating parade of humanity zipping by on in-line skates or racing bikes, or walking in twos or threes, a babble of voices filling the air. "I was proud of you."

He'd preached on the last chapter of the gospel of Matthew, after the resurrection, when Jesus told His disciples, *"All authority in heaven and on earth has been given to me. Therefore go and make disciples of all nations, baptizing them in the name of the Father, and of the Son and of the Holy Spirit."* Nick had stressed that Jesus passed that authority to *us*—"See that word 'Therefore'?" he'd said—so we could share the love of God with "all nations," knowing we were doing so with God's own authority and power.

"All nations. That's everybody," he'd said. "Sister Avis and Elder Peter are sharing the love of God with sisters and brothers in South Africa right now. But that doesn't let us off the hook just because we're not over there. For us, 'all nations' means all the people outside the doors of SouledOut Community Church—the kids hanging out on the corner, the people at your work, the people coming to the food pantry."

Now, sitting on the bench soaking up the sunshine, Kat started to giggle. "I like how you threw the food pantry in there."

"Yeah, well. I told you that what concerns you concerns me, one hundred percent."

Kat was quiet a long time. It was true. It wasn't just that she felt his support. It felt as if he shared her passion for the food pantry, using whatever influence he had as a pastoral intern to help make it a success.

What about her? Were his concerns her concerns in the same way? Nick was called to be a pastor. It might be at SouledOut. Maybe somewhere else. Was she ready to own his life as her life too?

She'd held back from becoming a member of SouledOut earlier that summer. But his sermon had started her thinking. Going out and making disciples and baptizing people had another side to it—the people who were new to faith and needed to be baptized.

Like her.

Kat wiped her greasy fingers with one of the take-out napkins and turned to face him with solemn eyes. She cleared her throat. "Nick? I want to talk to you about something."

❋

Taking out her keys, Kat opened the mailbox for Apt. 2. Empty. Rochelle or Bree must've already gotten the mail. Seemed like she'd hear *something* from all those résumés she'd sent out. Or maybe she'd get a call if one of those places were interested. But so far she hadn't heard a thing. Zero. Zilch.

Okay, God, I'm trying to trust You for a job, but it's only a couple more weeks before school starts . . .

Kat let herself into the stairwell and climbed the stairs to the second floor. She'd had early shift today—seemed like she got scheduled for early shift a lot now that she wasn't tutoring at STEP—and it was her turn to cook supper. Nick had left her a voice mail that he might be late—something about the pastors meeting with the elders at five rather than at seven. Well, that gave her plenty of time to try that African Peanut Soup recipe she'd found in the newspaper. Maybe Avis and Peter Douglass had eaten something like this in South Africa. If it was good, she might try to make it for them when they got back—which was supposed to be early this week sometime.

"Kat? Is that you?" Rochelle came flying out of the kitchen when she came in the front door. She sounded breathless, her eyes wide.

"Hey. Is everything okay?"

"I don't know. Look." Rochelle snatched up a business envelope lying on the dining room table. "It's a certified letter addressed to my mom—from Chicago Public Schools. I heard the door buzzer ring upstairs, but I knew nobody was home and Nick was at work—but I was curious, so I went downstairs. Mailman said he had a certified letter for Avis Douglass. So I told him I was her daughter and he let me sign for it."

Kat stared at the letter. A certified letter. Had to be important. "What are you going to do? Should you call her? What's the time difference there?"

"Mommy! Can I have more milk?" Conny called from the kitchen. Probably having his lunch, though it was already one thirty.

"Just a minute!" Rochelle yelled back. "Uh, time difference . . . eight hours, I think. That means it's"—she scrunched her face—"eight thirty in the evening there."

"That's not late. You should call her, Rochelle. At least tell her she's got a certified letter and does she want you to open it."

"Right. Right . . . you're right. I don't think they leave until tomorrow. Would you get Conny some milk? I'm going to call."

Rochelle pulled out her cell phone. "I'm pretty sure they got international calling in case of emergency."

Kat hurried into the kitchen. "Hey, Superman." She gave Conny a quick hug. "Your mom has to make a phone call. Here, I'll get you some more milk." She wanted to get back into the living room. But even before she'd finished pouring she heard, "Hello, Mom? . . . Yeah, yeah, we're all fine . . . How are you and Dad?"

A table knife. Rochelle needed something to open the letter. Kat scurried back into the living room. Rochelle seemed to be listening, nodding her head and saying, "Uh-huh . . . Uh-huh . . ." Kat twirled her fingers to say, *"Hurry! Tell her!"*

"Uh, Mom? Sorry to break in here, but the reason I'm calling is you got this certified letter from CPS . . . Yeah, yeah, seriously. Should I open it? . . . Okay."

Kat handed her the table knife. Rochelle put the phone on Speaker and slit open the letter. Her eyes scanned the sheet of paper . . . and then she screeched. "Mom! Mom! Listen to this!"

Chapter 44

Nick walked home from his Monday meeting at SouledOut, turning down streets and waiting for traffic at crosswalks as if on autopilot. Meeting with the elders had been different—they'd had to reschedule to late afternoon to accommodate everybody's schedule—but definitely interesting. Peter Douglass, of course, was still out of the country, but Nick knew Denny Baxter somewhat, and it was a pleasure getting to know Debra Meeks a bit more. What a wise lady—kind of like Avis Douglass, though a bit more homespun. David Brown . . . ? Hard for Nick to figure out. The man seemed to bring up more questions than everyone else put together about the proposals the pastor wanted to talk about.

The SouledOut Sisters Food Pantry for one.

The food pantry had run for three Saturdays so far, with an increase in people using the pantry each week—from thirty-two the first Saturday, to forty-nine the next week, and sixty-five this last weekend. There were still two more Saturdays before the end of August, but Pastor Cobbs wanted a joint meeting of pastors and elders to begin talking now about how best to continue.

Everyone seemed to be excited about the food pantry.

Everyone except David. He had concerns. Pantry food was taking up too much space in the refrigerators and counters in the kitchen. Questionable characters were hanging around the church on Saturdays without adequate supervision, inviting theft or damage. Avis Douglass's daughter was handling food—and her with HIV!

Nick had been impressed with Pastor Cobbs's patience. He'd accepted each of David's questions as a valid concern, but didn't seem to think any of them was a major roadblock—just a challenge to be worked out.

And it was Debra Meeks who'd come up with the most amazing idea: hiring Kathryn Davies at ten hours a week to manage the food pantry properly. "To do this right will take at least that much time." Denny Baxter and Pastor Cobbs had both been open to the idea, though it would have to go through the budget committee.

But David Brown had put on the brakes. "We can't go hiring part-time people willy-nilly. We still haven't hired a full-time pastor to replace Pastor Clark! I mean, Nick here is doing a fine job as an intern, but that isn't . . . well, you know, not a long-term solution. And this girl isn't even a member yet!"

Pastor Cobbs had leaned back in his chair and casually stroked his chin. "True. But sometimes we need to respond to what God is doing *now* and get on His time line. Seems to me the pantry is now, the need is now. The train's already out of the station and picking up speed. How can we get on board?"

David Brown had thrown up his hands, as if defeated, but the pastor just said mildly, "It's at least worth exploring." Nick had been given the assignment of running the idea past Kathryn to see if she'd be open to it.

As the three-flat came into view, Nick slowed his pace even

though he knew he was already late for supper. *Would* Kat be open to it? She didn't have a full-time job yet—and if none was forthcoming, maybe her hours at The Common Cup plus ten hours for the pantry could sustain her in the short run.

He smiled to himself. Maybe the short run was all she'd need financially. After all, he'd be graduating in January, and then . . .

Pulling the Douglasses' mail out of the box in the foyer, he quietly took the stairs two at a time to the third floor, dropped the mail in a box for that purpose, and then hustled back down to the second-floor apartment. Something smelled good. Knocking at the door, he opened it—unlocked as usual—and stuck his head in. "Sorry I'm late! Hope you saved some of whatever that is for me."

Kat appeared from nowhere, blue eyes dancing, and pulled him in. "We did wait for you! We're having a celebration!" She turned and yelled, "Nick's here! Come and get it!"

When everyone was at the table, Kat said a brief thank-you prayer and started serving up the soup. Seemed like she and Rochelle couldn't stop grinning. What was going on? Bree shrugged at him as if to say, *"Don't ask me."* But Nick couldn't help salivating as Kat handed him a bowl of the thick, savory soup and a small plate with hot corn bread, slathered with butter and honey. He eyed the golden soup. "What is it?"

"African Peanut Soup. It's got diced sweet red peppers and onions and brown rice . . . and you can add cilantro and peanuts and sour cream if you want."

"Whoa." He took a large spoonful. "Oh, man . . . fantastic." Then he looked around the table. "So what's the celebration?"

"Yeah," Bree pouted. "They wouldn't tell me."

Kat giggled. "We wanted to tell you both. You tell them, Rochelle."

Before Avis's daughter had finished the afternoon's saga, Nick had almost forgotten about his soup. "I can't believe it! The school board actually took Bethune Elementary *off* the closing list because of those extra hearings?"

Kat nodded, the excitement in her face still palpable. "Yep. After Rochelle talked to her mom in South Africa, we called Jodi Baxter—you know she's a third-grade teacher at Bethune, right? She said the two hearings were *packed* with parents and teachers giving testimonies about the superior job Bethune was doing, in spite of overcrowded classrooms. It may have even been a good thing Mrs. D was out of the country, because obviously she wasn't orchestrating this."

Rochelle jumped in. "But according to Sister Jodi, a couple teachers had already panicked about losing their jobs and resigned. She called my mom this afternoon too, to let her know. And—you tell him, Kat."

Nick was enjoying this tag-team tale—but since they were doing all the talking, he decided to tackle more of the African Peanut Soup and corn bread.

"Well, it's not a sure thing, so nobody say anything—not even you, Big Ears." Kat pointed a finger at Conny and he giggled, making chomping noises at her finger as if he were going to bite it off. "But *Jodi* said that Mrs. *Douglass* said to tell *me* that she's going to put in a special request to hire me as a replacement for one of those teachers, especially since I've been working with some of these kids this summer."

Nick's eyes widened.

"Oh, Kat!" Bree clapped her hands to her face. "That would be awesome! I'll feel so much better going back to school if I know you've got a teaching job for this fall."

Nick felt as if his grin could reach ear to ear. "Okay. That's it." He stood up. "I don't care if everybody's watching or what anybody says. I'm gonna do it anyway." He pulled a startled Kat out of her chair, lifted her off her feet in a big hug, and kissed her full on the mouth. "Oh, baby," he whispered in her ear, "this has God written all over it."

"Ewwwww." Conny made a gagging noise behind them. "Mushy stuff."

※

Nick managed to get Kat out the door for a walk to the lake while Rochelle and Bree did dishes. "There's supposed to be a full moon tonight," he said. "Maybe we'll see a moon rise." Any more "mushy stuff," he vowed to himself, was going to be done in private.

But he had something else on his mind. "I've got some news too—though your news changes things quite a bit."

She tugged on his arm she was holding, peering up at him with laughing eyes. "What? Tell me!"

"Well, something came up at the meeting I had today at the church . . ." As they walked the jogging path along the lake, he told her about Debra Meeks's proposal for SouledOut to hire her for ten hours a week, to give the food pantry a chance to really get off the ground in a solid way. "It's a real compliment, Kat. Pastor Cobbs and the elders really appreciate you." He decided he didn't need to repeat David Brown's objections. Not right now, anyway. "I thought, if you don't get a job offer, maybe your hours at the coffee shop and another ten at SouledOut might keep body and soul together for a while. If you're offered a teaching job at Bethune Elementary, it's sort of a moot point, I guess. Still, thought you ought to know."

Kat was quiet a long time. The breeze off the lake blew strands of her loose hair across his face, and they simply walked in silence. Was she disappointed? Trying to decide between a teaching job and the food pantry? She probably needed to think about it. He'd support her, whatever she decided.

"I know who should get the food pantry job."

She spoke in a voice so soft he had to lean close to hear her. "What?"

"I know who should get the food pantry job."

He was a bit taken aback. "What do you mean?"

"I mean, if the church actually comes up with a budget for it, I know who should get the food pantry job. Rochelle."

Nick stopped right in the middle of the jogging path and turned Kat so he could look in her face. "Rochelle? Are you sure?" Oh, David Brown would have a cow over that, for sure.

Kat nodded. "Whether I get the teaching job or not. Because, first of all, she hasn't been able to find any job at all, and this would at least be a first step. Would look great on a résumé. But even more than that, she's good. She's street smart. She's a woman of color—which makes her more accessible to some people, I think. Not just a goody-goody white girl helping out the poor people. And because she's got a vision to take the food pantry out of the seat-of-the-pants operation we've been doing and make it sustainable. She could do it." She seemed to hesitate. "And because . . ."

He waited a long moment, but she seemed lost in thought. Finally he prompted, "Because?"

She took his arm and started them walking again. "Because I think I've been too invested in the food pantry being 'my thing.' It's God's thing. I've been holding on too hard. And it's time to let go."

Chapter 45

The last day of August, Kat stood on the edge of the lake-shore looking out at the horizon, small waves flowing in and tickling her bare feet. Could it be a more beautiful day? The sky arching over Lake Michigan and the Chicago sky-line was so crystalline clear it almost hurt to look at it. A warm breeze off the lake fingered her hair, which she was wearing down and loose around her shoulders. The temperature was heading toward ninety, the weather guy had said. As cold as Lake Michigan could be, even in summer, a dunk in the lake today might feel good.

"Are you ready, Kathryn?" Avis Douglass moved up to her side and took her hand—smooth, dark fingers with painted nails laced with her pale ones. On the other side of her, Nick took her other hand.

Kat turned her head from side to side, smiling at both of them. "As ready as I'll ever be, I guess." Her voice squeaked a little. Okay, so she was nervous.

The three of them moved into the shallows. Not so bad. Chilly, but not painful.

But as the water crept up her calves and reached her knees—
Whoa! The cold water suddenly sent shivers up her back. "Yikes!"

"Ditto that." Avis gripped her hand tighter.

Nick laughed. "I think we've got a ways to go. Hang on,
ladies."

The cold water crept up her thighs, then to her waist. Kat's
teeth started to chatter. To her relief, Avis said, "This is far
enough."

They turned around, Kat still in the middle, now facing
the shore. There on the sand stood most of the congregation
from SouledOut Community Church. Brygitta stood front and
center, her hands clasped in front of her chest, grinning with
delight, her wispy pixie cut standing up in the wind. Rochelle
stood a few feet away beside her stepdad, Conny crouched at
their feet with little Gracie Baxter, poking the wet sand with a
stick. Other comforting faces stood out here and there in the
crowd: Pastor Cobbs with First Lady Rose . . . Edesa Baxter leaning against her husband, Josh, a portrait in black and white . . .
Josh's parents and sister . . . Estelle Bentley, swathed in a purple
caftan and matching headdress, and her husband, Harry . . .
redheaded Gabby Fairbanks and her husband, Philip, holding
hands . . . several of the Yada Yada sisters . . .

Her church family. Come to see her seal her new birth, even
if she had reached toddler stage.

A few faces were missing. David and Mary Brown had
announced that morning during the worship service that "God
is calling us" to one of the big suburban churches west of the
city. Kat thought that was strange, since she was pretty sure the
Browns lived less than a ten-minute drive from SouledOut. Not
that she'd gotten to know them personally or anything, though

Mary Brown had always greeted her nicely. Well, *gushing* might be the word. But Nick had whispered to her, "It's probably for the best." Whatever he meant by that.

Two other faces were missing. Not that she'd really expected them to be there, but miracles could happen, couldn't they? She'd called her parents two weeks ago and told them she was getting baptized and becoming a member of SouledOut Community Church, and did they want to come? It was Labor Day weekend after all, maybe they could take a little vacation to the Windy City. And there was somebody special she wanted them to meet. But her dad had a golf outing to raise money for diabetes research, and her mother didn't want to come alone—

"Kat, you can hold your nose with one hand, but grab my wrist with your other one," Nick was saying. "Then just relax . . . Sister Avis and I will put you under and pull you back up, okay?"

His words were almost drowned out by the sound of the wind and splashing waves. Kat nodded, her teeth still chattering, and felt their hands holding her securely. Closing her eyes and feeling the hot sun on her face, she heard Avis's voice speaking loudly above the wind: "Kathryn Davies, on confession of your faith in Jesus Christ as your Lord and Savior, and in obedience to His commandment to be baptized, we baptize you in the name of the Father, the Son, and the Holy Spirit."

Kat felt herself falling . . . falling . . . but held . . . cold water rushing in over her head and her whole body . . . and then up again, bursting into the sunlight, water streaming down her face.

"Hallelujah!" Avis shouted. "Glory!"

Grinning, Nick put a strong arm around her waist as they

waded through the water back toward shore. And then she heard it, her "family" on the beach, clapping and singing an old gospel spiritual . . .

Tell me, how did you feel when you came out the wilderness
Came out the wilderness, Came out the wilderness
Tell me, how did you feel when you came out the wilderness
Leaning on the Lord!

Towels were wrapped around her, Brygitta and Edesa and Rochelle all gave her hugs, and then Pastor Cobbs was booming, "Gather around, church, and let's pray for our sister, who is also asking to be received as a member here at SouledOut . . ."

As the pastor's words poured blessings over her, Kat felt Nick's arm still around her waist. In one way she was glad she hadn't become a member of the church at the same time Nick had. This had to be her decision, her step of faith, declaring her own desire to follow Jesus. At the same time, she couldn't think of any better way to "own" the life Nick had chosen, to walk alongside him in this journey of faith.

Wherever that journey might lead.

After Pastor Cobbs's "Amen!" people crowded around to congratulate her and give her hugs, but finally the crowd thinned and people headed home. Nick took her hand and pulled her aside. "Let's walk up the beach," he said. Then he looked stricken at the white capris and loose white tunic she'd worn into the water—soaking wet. "Or maybe you need to get out of those wet clothes. We could get you home first."

Kat laughed. "In this heat and wind? They'll be dry in ten minutes. Come on, race you!" And she took off running barefoot in the sand, though it was more like slogging, and he easily caught up with her.

Walking hand in hand in silence, they left the beach and wandered along the path in the lakeside park. "Ah, I know where we're going." She grinned up at him. "Our bench."

"Mm-hmm. Seems appropriate for the occasion."

Appropriate for her baptism? She didn't get the connection, but didn't care either. She was with Nick and that was all that mattered right now . . . though she wondered if he had something on his mind. He seemed a lot quieter than usual.

Someone else was sitting on their bench. "Doesn't matter," Kat said. "We can go sit on the rocks."

"But it does matter," Nick muttered. To Kat's surprise, Nick walked over to the fifty-something woman sitting on the park bench who was eating French fries from a greasy bag, leaned down, and spoke to her. To Kat's greater surprise, the woman chuckled, got up, and walked away. Nick motioned to Kat to come sit down.

"Now I've seen everything!" Kat laughed as she plopped down beside him. "*What* did you say to her?"

"Only that I needed the bench . . . for this." Nick reached for her hand . . . and the next thing she knew, he had slipped something onto her third finger.

Kat stared and stopped breathing. A simple silver ring with a perfect little diamond standing up in the middle, flanked by two small red garnet stones, flashed in the sunlight.

"Will you marry me, Kat Davies?" Nick whispered.

Tears blurred the ring. A lump in her throat made it impossible to speak. But she gave a little gasp and threw her arms around him. With her arms still around him, Nick stood up and swung her around. Then he threw an arm in the air and yelled to no one in particular, *"She said yes!"*

Kat buried her face in his chest with embarrassment. But she heard several passersby clapping and somebody yelled, "Way to go, man!"

Then he pulled her back down onto the bench and pointed to the two red stones on either side of the diamond. "Those garnets—they're the January birthstone. Your birthday's in January—that's one—and I was thinking maybe we could get married that month too, after I graduate—that's two." Though a moment later he looked stricken. "But I guess that's really presumptuous." He searched her eyes. "What do you think?"

Kat felt the grin on her face get wider. "I think it's written in stone."

❋

It was almost midnight when Kat and Nick crept quietly up the stairs of the three-flat. At the door of the second-floor apartment, Nick pulled her close and kissed her, his mouth hungry, urgent—and she pressed her body against his, drinking in the faint, woodsy smell of him, like damp moss in the forest, not wanting to let him go. They stood in the dark wrapped in each other's arms for a long time.

It was all she could do to finally step back and watch him go on up the stairs.

Kat let herself in, closed the door quietly, and leaned her back against it, trying to still her rapidly beating heart. The apartment was quiet. Everyone was asleep. She fought an urge to pull the door open again and run up the stairs after him . . .

No, no, she shouldn't do anything foolish. Both Bree and Nick would be moving back to the CCU campus tomorrow, the Labor Day holiday, for classes that started on Tuesday. Probably a good thing . . . or it might be hard to wait clear till January.

Her own new job as a second-grade teacher at Bethune Elementary would be starting Tuesday as well, and Conny would be starting first grade. She and Rochelle had three more weeks to find a new place to live before the Candys arrived back in town from Costa Rica—*that* was a bit of a panic, but, everyone kept reminding her, God had dropped this place in their lap when they needed a home for the summer, and He would provide for them again.

Too excited to go to bed, Kat made herself some herbal tea and curled up on the couch in the velvet darkness of the living room, reliving the day.

"Do you think your folks will come for the wedding?" Nick had asked, chowing down pizza earlier that evening in a local Giordano's.

Kat had shaken her head. "I don't know. Maybe if you go home with me for Christmas or something, and they get to know you."

Nick had snorted. "If I don't scare them away permanently. I get the feeling they might not like a pastor for a son-in-law." Then he'd looked at her thoughtfully. "I truly hope they do come. But if they don't, I bet Peter Douglass would do the honors and give you away."

Kat giggled. "Would that make Avis the mother of the bride?"

He grinned. "I guess. I think I want to ask Josh Baxter to stand up with me. What about you?"

"Bree for sure . . . um, maybe Rochelle, if that wouldn't be too weird. But Conny could be the ring bearer. And Gracie would be an adorable flower girl."

Bree for sure . . .

Kat jumped off the couch. She'd almost forgotten. This couldn't wait!

Tiptoeing into the bedroom she'd shared with Brygitta all summer, Kat turned on the bedside lamp and shook the lump in the other twin bed. "Bree! Bree! Wake up."

"Wha . . . uhnn . . . what?" Brygitta squinted up at her, her short dark hair splayed against the white pillow. "Kat? What's wrong?"

"Nothing's wrong. Sit up. I've got something to show you."

With a groan, Brygitta rubbed sleep out of her eyes and pushed herself to a semi-upright position. "What?"

Sitting on the bed, Kat held out her left hand, letting the ring sparkle in the lamplight. Then she extended her little finger and hooked it around Bree's.

"Hey," she said softly. "Remember that pinkie promise?"

Reading Group Guide

1. When Josh Baxter marveled at the coincidences that brought Rochelle off the streets, his wife, Edesa, said, "I don't believe in coincidences!" (chapter 3). And Nick Taylor said much the same thing to Rochelle's mother, Avis: "Had to be more than just coincidence . . . Don't you think God brought all this together?" (chapter 14). How do you feel about these statements? What do you think about unusual "coincidences"?

2. Kat Davies struggled with the fact that baptism was a requirement for membership at SouledOut Community Church, even though she'd become a Christian several years earlier. What do you think of Avis Douglass's explanation of why the church covenant emphasized baptism first (chapter 14)? What does baptism mean to you?

3. What do you think Estelle Bentley meant when she acknowledged Kat's concern "about people eating healthy," but said, ". . . what she *really* wants— needs—to do is feed the hungry. Even if she don't know it yet" (chapter 7)? What was the distinction she was making and why was it important?

4. Have you ever worked in a food pantry—or used one? What was the experience like for you?

5. Both Nick and Kat hesitated to let the other one know how they felt about each other, which was frustrating to them (and probably to you as a reader as well)! Did you feel their reasons were silly? Too cautious? Valid? Wise? Why or why not? Have you ever been in a relationship—or wished you were in one—when you hesitated to let the other person know how you felt? Why? Were those reasons valid?

6. When Kat blurted out her idea for starting a food pantry at SouledOut, Avis Douglass asked if she'd prayed about it—and whether she'd asked others to pray with her (chapter 21). Why was this particularly important in Kat's case? What is the real purpose of praying about our good ideas— and asking others to pray *with* us (not just *for* us)?

7. When Kat asked the elderly couple why they volunteered at the Rock of Ages Food Pantry, what do you think the man meant when he said, "Don't want to miss Jesus" (chapter 23—also see chapter 25)? What did this have to do with the parable of the sheep and the goats in Matthew 25 (his wife's explanation)?

8. Throughout this novel, the pastoral team of SouledOut focused on the sayings of Jesus just before and just after His death and resurrection, as

well as related topics. Which one of these teachings spoke the most to you—and why?

a. Chapter 11, Nick—Jesus' prayer for His disciples: "That they may be one as we are one" (John 17:11).

b. Chapter 18, Avis Douglass—on a communion Sunday: "Come, buy wine and milk without money and without cost. Why spend money on what is not bread, and your labor on what does not satisfy? Listen, listen to me, and eat what is good, and your soul will delight in the richest of fare . . . I will make an everlasting covenant with you, my faithful love promised to David" (Isaiah 55:1–3). She related it to Jesus breaking bread at the last supper:

c. Chapter 25, Pastor Cobbs—Jesus washes His disciples' feet: "You also should wash one another's feet" (i.e. serve one another) . . . and "A new command I give you: Love one another" (John 14, 34).

d. Chapter 30, Nick Taylor—Jesus' last words to Peter: "Do you truly love me? . . . Feed my sheep" (John 21:15–17).

9. What do you think Nick meant when he said, "I think we all do that . . . Make Jesus like ourselves" (chapter 25)? In what ways do we do this in our own churches, personal lives, and society? In what ways might this be a good thing? What are the dangers?

10. What was your reaction to the Kat-Nick-Rochelle love triangle throughout the novel? If you were in Rochelle's shoes, would the talk with Edesa in chapter 39 have helped you deal with ending up "odd [wo]man out"? Why or why not?

11. In chapter 41, Kat realizes she "might have to actually get to know these 'food pantry people' as people God loved. To know all of them by name." Why is this significant for Kat? What is the importance of knowing people "by name"? Are there people in your community—or even your church—where this would be a challenge for you?

12. In chapter 44, Kat surprises us—and Nick—by turning down the offer of a paid position running the food pantry . . . "Because I think I've been too invested in the food pantry being 'my thing.' It's God's thing. I've been holding on too hard. And it's time to let go." Why is her statement significant? Is there an area of ministry or work you might be "too invested" in? What would it cost to "let go"? What might be the benefits of letting go—for you? for others?

13. The title of this novel is *Come to the Table*. What layers of meaning does this have for you after reading this novel? How does this invitation relate to how we live out our calling as the body of Christ?

Acknowledgments

How does one acknowledge all who have played an important role in bringing a book to life? And in my case, not just *a* book, but three series, all interconnected, woven together, a fictional world that has come to life: The Yada Yada Prayer Group (7 novels); The Yada Yada House of Hope (4 novels); and SouledOut Sisters (2 novels).

First, I need to acknowledge my **women's Bible study**, going on fifteen years now, which inspired the very first Yada Yada Prayer Group novel. Sisters have come and gone over the years, but essentially we're the same: a group of women who come together every week to study God's Word regardless of what church we go to, challenging one another to grow, praying for each other's heart concerns, and just being there for each other as we take this faith journey together. *Thank you*, my dear sisters, for turning my life upside down and rightside up!

To **Joey Paul, formerly of Integrity Publishers**, who first believed in my story proposal and gave me a chance to write "grown up" fiction—and to **Allen Arnold of Thomas Nelson Fiction**, who took over the series and came up with amazing ways to keep the stories coming in new and fresh ways. And to the talented **Fiction Team at Nelson**, who have shepherded these stories through editing, production, marketing, and promotion with amazing skill: Thanks for all your efforts and encouragements along the way.

To **Chip McGregor**, our first agent, who sat in our living room with Joey Paul, listening to the passion on our hearts as we transitioned from historical fiction for kids to contemporary adult fiction . . . and to **Lee Hough**, our agent with Alive Communications, who has been there for us Jacksons through thick and thin—even when he was on his own journey with brain cancer and chemo, and managed to do so with humor and faith. Lee, when you get tired of agenting, you should write!

To **Breakthrough Urban Ministries** in Chicago—especially to **Arloa Sutter, Director**, and **Beverly Williams, Outreach Coordinator**—who personify God's heart toward the homeless, the poor, the struggling, the addicted, and the hungry, and showed me that each person has a story, a story that isn't over yet because *God cares.*

And to my husband, **Dave**, who is not only my best friend, husband-for-life, lover, and spiritual companion, but a writing partner in the truest sense of the word. Whether we are working on a book together, or writing separate novels, he is there alongside me—brainstorming, reading, editing, giving feedback, encouraging, sometimes pushing me out of my comfort zone, believing in me even when I struggle to believe in myself.

With the apostle Paul, "I thank my God every time I remember [each of] you. In all my prayers for all of you, I always pray with joy because of your partnership in the gospel from the first day until now, being confident of this, that he who began a good work in you will carry it on to completion until the day of Christ Jesus" (Philippians 1:3–6).

Neta Jackson
Evanston, Illinois

About the Author

Neta Jackson's award-winning Yada books have sold over 500,000 copies and are spawning prayer groups across the country. She and her husband, Dave, are also an award-winning writing team, best known for the Trailblazer Books—a forty-volume series of historical fiction about great Christian heroes with 1.7 million in sales—and *Hero Tales: A Family Treasury of True Stories from the Lives of Christian Heroes* (vols. 1–4). They live in the Chicago area, where the Yada stories are set.